KAMIN-TOLAGH

a novel

Edwin Ahearn

BOOK I
BOOK II

Kamin-Tolagh

The tug of history, often very ancient history, is felt throughout these works. A large amount of information about the past is disclosed in the narrative, but for the purposes of these extracts a reader needs to know that long before the land was Arbhal it was Owan, and the Owanil, a gifted, energetic, but often arrogant people conquered and then lost a vast empire on both sides of Arnan, the inland sea.

After some centuries of obscurity, during which their island-based priesthood, the Atarlum, *was essential to the preservation of the Owani culture and language, the Owanil, through a series of opportune events, were able to regain control of their old realm, imposing themselves as an aristocracy on a numerically superior mixed population of Other Races (their own slighting term for all those without a pure Owani pedigree). Their old speech, however (the Owanilú), has become a scholar's language, surviving mainly for ceremonial and religious purposes, and in titles and proper names. Kargul has been the strongest ally for the Atarlum, Preference, and the restoration of exclusive Owani privilege and power. Kamin-Tolagh is the heir of one of the oldest and most powerful of all the Great Families.*

The book begins shortly after the end of the Jinzal War and the investiture of the Rodlakh as Rabsahi. Kamin-Tolagh has won honor and recognition. He is now the trusted Captain of the Household. Yet, there are important confidences that are kept from him. He grows restless and yearns for adventure. The military expedition headed by Shumat, Captain of the Armies, and Kamin Tolagh set out to the Farther West on a mission to destroy the last of the jinzal. What he discovers changes the course of history.

Kamin-Tolagh

I

1.

He knew he was lying beside a smoothly naked woman, who was not his sister. Afternoon was ebbing, and soon he would be hungry, but he fought off full waking, aware he could not have the clarity to recollect more without losing the warm languor he was floating in. Gentle but insistent, the knocking that must have first disturbed his dreaming came again. And again.

Kamin-Tolagh rubbed at his nose with the back of his hand. The woman beside him stirred and murmured a reproach, no words he could puzzle out, but her small hand reached for him. She was hardly more than a girl, and in a while he would remember who she was.

"Captain-*Asai* — " a voice, timidly urgent, his servant. Not his own, one who came with his quarters here at the Residence. Kamin-Tolagh was Captain of the Household, Captain-designate to be exact, but there was not much chance his appointment would be challenged when the Council met. Had he not accomplished great and famous feats of arms, brought his despised House back into favor, won enormous personal popularity? — with all this and a bed to hold any young woman of the Heartland however fleetingly his fancy, why should he feel discontent?

Sitting up abruptly, he called out he was coming; possibly there was urgent Household business. Putting on a dull yellow robe and slippers to match he went to the door. In the outer room a small servant was cringing apologetically.

"It is your lady mother, Captain-*Asai*."

"My lady mother can wait." He ran fingers back through his long hair.

"By your leave, *Asai*, she has been waiting. Petakoi *Asayu* was told you were resting, an hour ago. She now insists — otherwise I would not presume to disturb you, *Asai*."

He reassured the man, who did have a name, it was all right. Amusing, in contrast to the notorious arrogance of his family, to acquire a reputation for unexpected graciousness. "Has my mother been given some refreshment?"

"There is cool wine, *Asai*, Peframi wine."

Kamin-Tolagh nodded, instructed the man to have small food brought, and went out into the sitting-room. It was light enough, but he was not pleased with the ponderous furnishings. The ornate sideboard had probably been here a century, and the big couch was in a massive, obsolete style. No time for changing the room now; there were a couple of deep, highbacked chairs he could keep, given a covering lighter than the present rich brocade, a match for the window hangings, which also must go. There, by tall windows which looked down into the Court of the Ram, Petakoi was standing.

"Yes, mother?"

Displeased by his brisk manner, her mouth turned down as the eyebrows rose. "I do not wish to interrupt your diversions."

"I was finished. For the present."

"You must be more careful." She smoothed her long grey-blue gown as she sat. These are not farm-girls, serving-maids."

"They serve me well enough."

She ignored this. "You have bedded three daughters of the Families in a week."

"Four. Your watchdogs must have nodded. It could have been four times four. They are happy enough to please me. Unmarried heroes are in short supply."

The servant returned. By the time he had set out various dishes on a small table, apologized for the lack of smoked eel, recommended the spiced beef, filled one glass, refilled another with cool yellow wine, and withdrawn, Petakoi had to restate her thesis. "It is foolhardy to treat girls of the Residence Quarter in this way. They will tell you it is bad manners here to be serious about sport, but Kadon Dinul is part of the world. There is envy here, and jealousy, and spite. When fame becomes yesterday's news, you will need the goodwill of the Families if you want to remain a power in Rodlakh's *rabhsayum*."

Kamin-Tolagh waved dismissively. "The Families? The last thing they wanted was the accession of Rodlakh, and what did they do to prevent it? Next to nothing, even at a time when as few as a thousand armed and resolute men could have made all the difference." Seeing his mother was about to remind him of his own failure at that time, when more than a thousand first-line cavalry were his to command, he hurried on past the point. "They are amusing company," airily. "They know good food and agreeable pastimes — "

"And share our beliefs, along with the blood of our race. They are our natural allies."

"That game is finished, mother. I found a better one." Annoying to him she did not see for herself her sacred compact of blood and faith belonged to yesterday. He had done more with a few weeks in alliance with those she called baseborn and usurpers than she in a whole lifetime of plotting to displace them. She had wanted high rank for baKargul; he had achieved it. Their province had bitterly protested forfeiture sixty years ago, of the Kovilanu, their most fertile region, and threatened to fight a new war for it; Kamin-Tolagh had won it back in negotiation.

The sudden smile had no warmth. "I am pleased, of course I am," placatingly, "that you have emerged in triumph, and have your captaincy, and Kargul is whole again. But do not ask me to rejoice over receiving these boons, all long overdue, from the hands that robbed us in the first place. What you call a timely change in alliances, history may see as capitulation."

"What history? The *Mankh'* history? I think not. The *Atarlum* is also going to have to learn to live in the world that is." Decidedly no Deniant, he believed enough of what the *Mankh'* taught to keep from intolerable uncertainty, but it was inexplicable that his mother, who could use faith as a weapon and test of value, a necessary ingredient of all her subterfuges, was still a passionately sincere believer in the One Way. In any event, with the change of Patriarch, her idea of what that Way meant was pathetically out of date.

Her force, nonetheless, remained real. "You must, in the end, be true to your race and your inheritance. Rodlakh and his farm-girl will throw you crumbs from their table, and your mongrel friend the Captain of Armies call you comrade as long as he has a use for your sword. They will use you, but not trust you, use you in more ways than one. *How can you say Kargul has no voice in the realm*, they will say, *do we not have our tame Kamin-Tolagh with a seat in Council?*"

"If I am not trusted, how is it I am going with Shumat to the Farther West?" More emotion than he had intended; his mother had touched very near a sore spot. So soon after the investiture he had begun to see it was not in nature for him to be in the inmost circles of this new *rabhsayum*. The *rabhsai*, Rodlakh, and his Âna, their friend Dolvid who had engineered Rodlakh's accession, in part by bringing Kamin-Tolagh into alliance; Shumat, Captain of Armies, Dolvid's oldest friend; they were all cordial enough, not excepting Âna, who went out of her way to show she had no grudge, and still he was not asked to take part in any of the private gatherings where the realm's future was being forged.

Very deliberately Petakoi forked spiced beef onto a small square of bread, and ate it. Wiping her fingers she said quietly, "You cannot go to the Farther West. This time is too important;

at the start of the reign you must be here at the center, cultivating your circle, consolidating your position. Rodlakh is assembling his Great Council of the Realm; someone has to look out for the rights of Kargul."

"Our tame Kamin-Tolagh?" Seldom that his mother could be caught in such blatant self-contradiction. "If, as you say, I am no better than a token to prove the *rabhsai*'s fairness, better if I am not here to be displayed when this Great Council convenes. You and my father can give Kargul a real voice — loud disagreement, and another fifty years of exclusion."

She controlled annoyance. "This expedition to the edge of the world is for dull soldiers with no greater ambition than soldiering."

This was clearly the reason she was here, not the first time she had tried to dissuade him from his adventure, always with added arguments. "Shumat is going, and I have given my word. Besides, I want to go. Sebhal's renown came from fighting in the West, rediscovering the lost mines of Shâl, but even Sebhal never went right across and beyond Landegh. Fame is power, too."

"Is it? Bolan, like you, won his fame early."

That was pointed with one of her daggerish looks. He had guessed she would bring up Bolan, once most famed captain of the realm, now and abruptly shrunk into discredited insignificance. "Bolan's mistake was the same as yours. He did not know when to leave a losing cause, either. If he had brought the General Cavalry to Rodlakh's side, instead of fighting till they changed sides without him, he could be Captain-General today."

"I thank Great Hrafi," sentaciously, "Some would rather go down fighting for what they believe than win victories for all they despise."

He began to be exasperated. "Is this how you talk behind my back? My victories, our victories were for the realm. Would you rather have *jinzal* besieging Kadon Dinul? What would have stopped them, if Shumat and I had failed? Bolan, you think? My father?"

"Your father commands the cavalry of Kargul."

A laugh. "So his title says."

"They suffered heavy losses in the war."

"Under my father, too."

"He may think it time for others to do the dying. He has the right to refuse squadrons of Kargul for this expedition."

"Not the four squadrons already seconded to the Household; those I command under the *rabhsai*. I was not laughing at our losses. It doesn't matter; I'll go at the head of whatever troops we find; I am a captain of the realm, not merely of Kargul." Amusement returned. "But, mother, command belongs to the victorious: what is going to be said if the one whose bad tactics brought them to defeat at Dônshei denies the cavalry to his son, who led them to victory at Kamsilat and the Gate? Tovakh could not face that." Indeed, he had difficulty in meeting Kamin-Tolagh's eye when there was talk of armies and fights; perhaps he remembered all the years he had been condescending to his son's military aspirations.

"You must not go."

Was she worried about his safety? He had explained before danger would be slight; to deal with the remnant *jinzal*, reliably put at less than one hundred, there would be something like two thousand cavalry. They expected to find some men, also, at Lunu Jinzalladhiyu, but not above a handful of those who had taken part in breeding and training the *jinzal*. Most had been killed and a few captured leading their creatures in battle. "This is no new war, but an extermination."

"Then what glory will there be in it? Far better stay here and cultivate your alliances."

"To be among those who find Lunu Jinzalladhiyu, after fifteen centuries? You would like all that fame to go to Shumat, Dorrmas?"

"Are you so certain it can be found?"

"We have a guide, one of the men who led the *jinzal*."

"You have spoken with him?" with surprising sharpness.

"I have no need to." This was less than satisfactory; that small inner circle about Rodlakh was plainly keeping the prisoners close. "I'll be able to speak with him on the journey. He travelled with the one they called the True *Rabhsai*. Rodlakh, I suppose, does not want people talking about that."

"I wonder why," corrosively.

"I am told the claim is plainly false — " fighting off the uneasiness this subject gave him. "Our guide is called Rhinval, and he looks like an Owani. Like an *atarlai*." He meant the man had the same unconfiding mask of a face often seen among minor servants of the *Mankh'*, but the remark offended his mother with her Island sensibilities.

"There are a dozen families of Ninkufu," crumpling her napkin angrily. "Who intermarried among themselves all through the so-called Night, any of whose sons could pass for *atarlal* of the Island. Wherever found, Owani blood breeds true."

He was amazed. "You could not believe this True *Rabhsai* nonsense."

"Does it matter? The truth of that cannot be known for certain, now. A ruling house whose bloodline goes back in four generations to a tanner is right to be nervous about one who claimed direct descent from Lost Plakhan. About anyone with blood better than his. He'll keep a wary eye on you."

"By giving me command of his Household. By entrusting me with joint-captaincy in this expedition." How many months or years were needed to make her see his friendship with Rodlakh was real?

"You must not go. Your grandfather may die at any time."

"What can I do for him by staying?" All the points his mother made were not enough to explain the vehemence of her opposition, and he wondered whether the real reason was one her pride declined to admit. She and his father had occupied an honored place on the Steps at Rodlakh's investiture, but with all her rant about blood, Kargul's new standing at Kadon Dinul was dependent on his, Kamin-Tolagh's individual eminence, not her ancestry, nor that of his house. Was she afraid with her son absent it would be remembered that except for him Kargul had done everything it could to prevent Rodlakh's accession?

He put a hand on her forearm. "No one is going to do anything to slight our house."

"How could they?" She was withering. "Mongrels, illiterates. I can never see our plowgirl *rabhsayu* without remembering she was your whimpering little weekwife, once, and now at a feast she precedes best blood of the Six Provinces. Rodlakh is madder than his brother, and even more stupid than his father — Lambarr's pathetic lady at least had breeding."

He felt a surge of hot anger, and let it be seen small, as irritation. "That is all finished," standing and walking away. "Finished."

His mother stood, and he decided he did not care whether or not she meant to leave; he was going to go back and wake the girl. She was lively, empty-headed, adoring, and her bright lips reminded him just a little of his absent sister.

Before he could, there was a fresh commotion at the outer door, beyond which a small ante-chamber opened on a corridor. His servant reappeared, but only his back, as he tried to impede entrance of another woman, another not-much-more-than-girl, this one taller, still very pleasing in the Owaniyu way. He knew her; she had a flower name he would recall in a moment. She had been with him here twice last week, and her determination to force her way in was abashed by sight of Petakoi. An abrupt, still moment, servant trying to stammer an apology; "*Asai*, I said you were engaged — "

"How did you get in?" Kamin-Tolagh challenged. He meant, into the New Residence. He could not really blame the servant, who had been told some days ago this girl was to be admitted. *Galedas*, that was the man's name. But the girl, beginning, and remaining, gratifyingly passionate, she had shown signs of clinging, so he had decided he could do without her; he had not imagined she could arrive unexpectedly, without his token to take her past the guards on Pefrai Gate and the Ram's Court entrance.

"I come here to visit my uncle," gradually untangling from the grasp of the servant, and tugging a rumpled sleeve back in place. "I didn't realize, *Asayu* — "

His mother regarded the girl thoughtfully. "You were at a feast — you are Khedinoi, Fornival's niece. His pretty niece, I should say."

"*Asayu*." Grateful to be remembered, the girl made a full deference, deceptively sweet. In reality, she was erratic and moody; at times she had seemed well past halfway to madness — but Kamin-Tolagh had often found girls of her age verging on that state, a muddle of tears and giggles, sentimental sweetness and foul temper, and Heartland Families were very inbred. As his mother said, Khedinoi was niece to Fornival, the realm's leading authority on written law, but she was also more distantly related to, for example, Faëdhal, Master of Tongues, Rhunilat, who supervised running of the Residence, and Linaëyu, wife to Khelagh, largest of all landowners.

Reading her son's displeasure, gratified to have her warnings confirmed, Petakoi was wearing, only for his benefit, a slight ironic smile, as she assured Khedinoi she was no intruder, the business with her son being finished. After proffering a wrist for Kamin-Tolagh to kiss, she abruptly left him alone with the girl.

Who turned on him with instant fervor. "What about my cousin?"

"Who?"

"My cousin, Ondhayu. She is here with you."

Ondhayu, that was the name of the girl in his bed. "You're all cousins, more or less." Did this one expect him to stay away from all the young women of the Heartland she shared blood with, just because she had been in his bed a few times?

"You said I was the only one you wanted."

"When?" If he had said it, it was obviously true at that moment.

"*When?*" she echoed shrilly. Apparently the final insult; on the low table there was a small, sharp knife his mother had used for peeling an apple; Khedinoi swept it up, and lunged at Kamin-Tolagh's throat.

Smiling, he easily stopped and disarmed her. "I have fought *jinzal*," he told her, bent over so they were nose to nose, "armed with swords long as your legs, and with teeth longer than this — " Letting go of her absurdly slender wrist, he flipped up and recaught the little knife, genuinely blithe not to be bored. "You will have to take me from behind, or while I'm sleeping if you want to kill me."

The malevolence in her face was unchanged. "Then I'll kill myself."

Head to one side, he considered that, all at a distance from what was real, borrowing at once from a comedy scene in a puppet-show, and an overwrought chapter from the silliest of romances. "A girl or two killing herself for love — it might help my reputation," he teased. "But don't do it till after the *Rabhsai*'s Games; I shall need a partner for the Vrobani Chase — " a complicated, age-old horseback game, said to derive from the practice, with bachelors of Ancient Vrobhan, of raiding neighboring towns for their brides. Khedinoi loved riding, and was considered one of the best young Residence Quarter horsewomen.

She quickly banished interest that had surged into her eyes. "I never want to be with you again."

"Oh. Then perhaps I shall ask your cousin."

She struck at the bait. "You will lose the game. She is not half the rider I am."

"But pretty," his tone casually assuming Khedinoi's agreement. An interesting thought came to him. "The two of you together could enjoy each other's bodies as well as mine."

As she understood what he meant, it seemed for an instant she would spit at him. He ignored her anger, not as a strategy, but because he was engaged by the real possibility of his offhand proposal, as by its possibilities. He had bedded with two women together as long ago as his seventeenth birthday, at his father's grudging expense, part of his mother's campaign to wean him from attachment to his sister, but they, though gratifyingly memorable, had been *nôd'yanul* plying their craft, not admiring girls with Residence Quarter pretensions and freedom to choose. He launched into a recounting of what she and her cousin would do, with him and with each other for his amusement and theirs, and as he invented the whim warmed into necessity; his suggestions took on an eager, youthful quality, paradoxically innocent.

Khedinoi, interest unwillingly engaged, at last made a specific objection, and Kamin-Tolagh was flooded with happy anticipation; to quibble over details was to endorse the general proposition. Her blunt stipulation as to what would, if she assented, be the final, incongruously conventional act, amused and could almost have touched him.

He caught at her elbow, and she swayed in his direction. "I might enjoy a change," she allowed, not yet fully surrendering. "I am not sure Ondhayu will want to play."

"Let us wake her, and find out."

"*I am awake.*" Ondhayu, sketchily clad in her shift, with its shoulders halfway down her arms, and most of her young breasts exposed, was at the inner doorway. She was bleared with sleep, her lips puffy. Before Kamin-Tolagh could wonder long how much she had overheard, she made three shuffling steps, and took Khedinoi's free hand. "We love games, don't we?" smiling up at her cousin.

So much for my mother's warnings, as the surge of appetite caught him up. He had told her this was a new age of negotiation and felicitous compromise.

2.

Under tranquil blue of a cloudless autumn sky the estuary was scarcely ruffled by breeze from the southeast; the fleet, fourteen vessels of various size, draught and rigging, glided smoothly as if held together inside a vast crystal enclosing invariant space between ship and ship.

"It will not be a quick crossing," Lavsila said.   A strikingly good-looking young man, he exactly echoed Kamin-Tolagh's easy posture, in his lean against the foredeck rail, clad in a shirt of fine linen, breeches of black and gold, and low, soft boots, as if for an afternoon ride. His hair, Kamin-Tolagh would risk money, had been done by a hairdresser no longer ago than yesterday. How did you instruct a hairdresser to turn you out for a harsh expedition to the Farthest West?

Though Kamin-Tolagh had scorned his mother's advice, Lavsila was his ally among and guide to the Families, related to half the Heartland; his father was Ladh-Sivai, a big landowner, and he was a cousin in some degree to Khelagh, richest of all the magnates. Meeting him at the time of the investing, Kamin-Tolagh had been entertained by his often cynical wit. *Being met by him* was closer to truth; Lavsila had the eagerness of the Families to be associated with the Great Families, all the time advertising his indifference to rank or ambition. The man had the reputation of an idler, a dabbler in various skills, but he had volunteered to join the Lunu Jinzalladhiyu expedition, and to manage supplies, and when Shumat opposed that appointment Kamin-Tolagh made Lavsila his personal advisor.

"Why are you not in the flagship with Shumat?" In Lavsila's world, anything not completely understood was sinister.

"General policy," not ready to admit he himself was dissatisfied with how joint-command of this expedition was evolving: while he regarded Shumat as a comrade-in-arms, he remained irritably aware there were secrets Shumat withheld from him. "The highest-ranking officers always take separate ships."

"To lessen opportunities for conspiracy," knowingly.

Kamin-Tolagh displayed boredom. "To improve discipline, and to make sure there is someone left to command if a ship goes down." Lavsila remained unaware of how absurd his constant search for dark purposes had made him; obviously, if he and Shumat had anything to plot about they would have extravagant opportunity riding together in the empty West. "But we shall be too busy conspiring how best to use the mixed forces we have."

"Aren't there fewer than the plan called for? Will these be enough?"

He answered that while they had first wanted two thousand men, Shumat was sure the job could be done with the twelve hundred they would have, when they added two squadrons each of General Cavalry and Kargul waiting at Kamsilat, and the Army of the West provided two hundred mounted bows.

"Bows," disdainfully. "On their little toy horses, no doubt."

"In broken country such as Landegh those toy horses are more surefooted than *pefral*. As for fighting, perhaps you would rather deal with *jinzal* at lance-length than a long bowshot. I would not. I saw what those archers could do at the battle of Kamsilat, and they would be my choice over five hundred additional regular cavalry."

"Well," in mock-astonishment. "If the most famous *péfrapravádai* of Kargul says so. They're tribesmen, no? Little Froghul with legs like barrel-staves?"

"Most are Mixed, now, but their fathers would call themselves Froghul, yes. Shooting from the saddle as they do is learnt young, or never."

The note of admiration had Lavsila quizzical, but he kept his tone derisive. "When you say Mixed, you must mean, mated with the already-Mixed of the Colony? If a half-Gabhaniyu woman of Banakit wants to mingle with a half-ape off Landegh, it is not much loss to anyone."

"You would do better with my mother. She is another one who does not see that talk belongs to the past." He was annoyed Lavsila, a circle-dance warrior of the Heartland, presumed to pass on fighting-qualities of those who had helped defeat the *jinzal* armies.

"Oh, for myself, I don't care whether someone speaks with a *Mankh'* accent or a Frontier slur, so long as he has something to say."

"Then the future Rodlakh *Deghi* promises should be to your liking." In his accession speech the new *rabhsai* had envisioned a realm where merit, not ancestry, was the measure of worth.

"Yes, yes," Lavsila murmured. "We are all orphans now. Who would want it otherwise?" Kamin-Tolagh waited, and the demurrer came. "And yet, Tam, there are thinking men who predict the scale may tip too far on the other side. We can't redress the past by creating a greater injustice, can we?" Lavsila, keeping the tone of reasonable grievance, admitted while the old system of Preference must have barred some talented men of Other Race from holding high office, the majority of them had neither talent nor ambition for seeking advancement, and the score could not be evened by giving posts to unqualified men at the expense of the worthy.

"How is it you Great Families have put up with the House Arbhai-Navu, as it calls itself? Oh, your Kargul, I grant, did its best to nip it in the bud, but they had little or no help from the other provinces. Were they so afraid of Banak's military reputation?"

"The House Arbhai-Navu begins, equally, with Laluvoi."

"Who, you say, was well-liked by the Great Families?"

"She was the Great Families — " astonished a man who could unerringly recite family interrelationships among what were, all said, no better than a handful of puffed-up farmers, could be so forgetful about the important bloodlines. "Her elder brother was father to both Daënakh of Ân and Laënakh of Nîv, and the other married the sister of my grandfather; her uncle, Vindola, was grandfather to Vinilat of Dramal, and father to my grandmother, Faëlu. And when Laluvoi's son, Lambarr, married Saidhan's daughter, the other main strand of descent in the Great Families, the House of Tebadh, also became allied to Arbhai-Navu: Tebadh was descended direct from Plakhat Gabh'Owan."

"Then if your great-uncle, Tobhsila had won his fight with Saidhan," Lavsila tried to regain genealogical respectability, "and then married Laluvoi — "

"I would not be Heir in Kargul," sardonically. "But I would probably have a third cousin who was *rabhsai*."

"You could be *rabhsai* yourself. There is no tanner's blood in your lineage, and everybody knows who won the war for Rodlakh. It may yet happen — " this a conspiratorial suggestion.

Getting no response, Lavsila, after a silence, expanded on his fantasy. "There could be a revolt against Rodlakh. I am told he is planning sweeping measures directed against the Old Blood — confiscatory taxation, new restrictions on religious observances. His marriage is against him, too; any offspring he has will be — "

"If there were an uprising against Rodlakh *Deghi*," heatedly. "My part, as a royal captain, would be to help quell it."

"Yes, yes," Lavsila, soothingly, managing to make it sound as if he was helping maintain a compact of feigned loyalty.

3.

As the royal entourage, riding back from leavetaking, reached the level by the city walls, a small crowd was gathered by the shops there. Amid cheering and shouts, a single clear cry in a man's voice separated itself: *"Do not break the Guilds! — "* and there was the impression the outspoken one had his supporters.

In all the many throngs of Rodlakh's brief reign, this was first hint of disharmony, and the *rabhsai* gave Dolvid a quick, wry grimace, before resuming his public countenance.

Farewells had been an untidy affair, with Kamin-Tolagh boarding ship a long hour later than Shumat, while his ship, picking its way through the throng of vessels, waited its turn to tie up, and with him and his officers at length aboard, idled a further half-hour till it could find a space in the jostle of craft of all sizes in search of a breeze to fill their sails. Heavy oars crossed and interwove, helmsmen cursed, as the largest ships were towed laboriously to mid-channel by hard-rowing longboats in constant danger of fouling their lines.

If not there as *Bôdhrai*, Dolvid would very likely have come down to Owan Sai to see off his oldest friend, Shumat, but as the royal party with its escort rode back up Harbor Way, he wondered whether Âna, whose eye he could not catch, was, like him, beginning to feel a forced element in all this cordiality; Rodlakh, Âna beside him, having parted from the captains with both a formal address and personal good wishes, had remained genially at quayside till the fleet was truly under way. Not to say Rodlakh's feelings were artificial, but time could not be stilled at that splendid hour in Kamsilat when Shumat and Kamin-Tolagh forced their way into a city beset by *jinzal*, desperately defended by Rodlakh; such a day, heartlifting in itself, was not a covenant, but an event. One, perhaps, comparable to when a man in love found his love reciprocated (or as much as accepted), a wondrous moment to shed its radiance on all that followed, but not secure promise of a lifetime's bliss; those heights must be abandoned (coming down gently, willingly, to preclude a later crash) for the plainer lands where most of life is lived. At that level, there were surely unasked questions on both sides behind the constantly-smiling amiability Rodlakh and Kamin-Tolagh maintained. Kamin-Tolagh, as confirmed more than twice by his wry but not lighthearted comments, disliked being left out of so many discussions; as a Royal Captain he obviously would have wanted a larger share in policy-making. While Rodlakh, it appeared, had made his mind up not to hear any gossip about Kamin-Tolagh's not-very-private life, but if the frantic drive of his womanizing, for purely practical reasons and with due allowance made for envy, worried Dolvid, it must be far worse for the private Rodlakh, who added an inherited strain of Gabhani disapproval to concerns both about daytime absences, and the certainty Kamin-Tolagh's habit of plucking and soon discarding varied flowers of the Heartland would eventually create a seething compost of resentment, and where least needed, nearest home.

Not one but two potential voices in the Council of Thirteen would be absent while far-reaching decisions were discussed, but the separation meant relief, at least for Dolvid, from unacknowledged tensions, and Rodlakh's ability to control the Council would be very little affected. When the Council confirmed his captaincy, Shumat, with his distaste for and inexperience in debate, had made plain he expected his seat to be occupied on most occasions by Kizhunai, in the newly-created post of Captain-Counsellor. With the new Patriarch, Dozhusai, now ga-Dozhusai-Arbhali, anxious to prove His conciliatory spirit, Kamin-Tolagh's vote would scarcely be missed. His absence would spare him distress of open conflict with his father, if a question of provincial prerogatives found them on opposite sides.

Against that, allowing Kamin-Tolagh to lead troops to where the *jinzal* were bred made far more likely he would discover his mother's alliance with the breeders, her long years of helping them behind her husband's back, information kept concealed out of Rodlakh's compassionate wish to avoid shattering the family of his new ally — and his distaste for determining a punishment in a crime so inconceivable. That secret was principal reason why Kamin-Tolagh had been excluded from most meetings of those who shared it. Explanation also for the unsurprising opposition to her son's going to the West, which Petakoi, aware of her precarious footing, had not quite dared express to the *rabhsai*.

All the same, as Dolvid had again reminded that morning, besides putting tremendous strain on Shumat, who knew all about how the *jinzal* were bred, and would be riding for days beside an inquisitive Kamin-Tolagh, the decision to keep him unenlightened failed to provide for near-inevitable end of that ignorance, his predictable rancor. When Rodlakh demanded, "Then you think we should tell him?" Dolvid knew but was unable to enunciate the answer; *rabhsayum* could not have all the goodwill and clemency it wanted, and if he had to choose, Petakoi, the guilty one, would have to take her chances.

With so many hard and important choices to be considered, it was deplorably but understandably human to do nothing in this case, hoping the question might never have to be faced, or when it did an inspired solution, not now apparent, would occur. As an angry voice in Harbor Way reminded, this *rabhsayum* had already found controversy. Only the first test of wills between new rule and a privileged minority; Rodlakh had needed little persuasion to agree caution here was no prudence; bold action now was wise, while his victories still resounded and alliances held.

Investiture, wedding, ceremonies of new allegiance, had meant purchase of costly and decorative things, and there was also a need to replace furnishings damaged or looted in the battle fought for the New Residence. Many items could come only from the Craft Guilds, and it had one day occurred to Dolvid a *rabhsayum* dedicated to fairness for all the people should not be handing its riches to those who had persistently excluded Other Races from membership. With Rodlakh's warm concurrence, he proclaimed the New Residence would cease to do business with the Guilds until they accepted change, not through pious promises, but by actually finding and enrolling suitable apprentices outside purely Owani origin. Without a word said, it was understood high officials of the *rabhsayum*, often best customers for luxury goods, would follow their *rabhsai's* example.

In addition, the Guilds, of which there were nine, held their authority under royal warrant to regulate their crafts, award standings of half-master and master, which enabled former apprentices to move from place to place, eventually to become their own employers. At year's end Rodlakh was to determine which Guilds would retain that privilege, commercially of inestimable value, decision based largely on what progress had been made in enrolling apprentices from outside their favored circle.

These soon-maligned stipulations were merely revival of a long-unenforced measure, unearthed by the learned Fornival, legal advisor to the *rabhsayum*. Like so many beneficial decrees, it had been promulgated, well over a century ago, by Plakhsila *Kímukoi*, though in this case, it would appear, with less lofty motives. Architect of Kadon Dinul as it now was, and builder of the New Residence, Plakhsila had become impatient with the slow pace of the work, and used his law to override the excuse of the Stonemasons Guild that they could not find enough apt apprentices. Consulting the rolls of the Guilds, by law deposited at the Bronze Residence, Dolvid found by the end of Plakhsila's long reign a fair sprinkling of names not belonging to Owanil listed among apprentices, and a handful of half-masters, but during the succeeding, reversionary reigns those numbers dwindled, soon almost to vanishing. He wondered what had become of all the skilled Others, and what tactics Guilds had used to avoid bestowing on any Gabhani or Mixed member the full-mastership which, by enabling him to enroll his own apprentices, would surely have perpetuated the reform.

In arguing against its renewal, the assertion of the Guilds, that their disestablishment would lead to a disastrous decline in standards, could not be entirely dismissed; the Guild system was not devoid of all merit. The Goldsmiths, Silversmiths and Jewelers, for example, guaranteed fine-metal content and gem quality, instantly expelling a member who knowingly alloyed his gold or sold flawed rubies as perfect. Though the defiant shout had sounded near their shops on Harbor Way, those were the crafts least affected by the *rabhsai*'s pronouncement. Most were small, family concerns with never above a half-dozen apprentices, specifically exempted from the demands of Plakhsila's decree, since they normally had more offspring, nieces, nephews and other close kin desiring to learn the trade than they had places to fill. In Plakhsila's actual words, such family traditions possessed an "irreplaceable and overriding importance" for preservation of standards.

Of larger Guilds, Stonemasons, Fine-Weavers, Dyers, the last, concentrated near the town of Bathrâd, was worst offender, employing Others in rote tasks, but as far as could be determined from a close study of their rolls, never offering any of them an apprenticeship. Their best defense, as presented by a delegation met with a week ago, depended on their right to protect secrets of their craft. "There are barks and woods we import, but do not name to strangers, *Bôdhrai*," said the woman who spoke for them, the lean and austere Kiravoi. "And other substances, mordants, as we call them, to make our lakes fast."

"Are you saying, the Owanil keep secrets better than the Others?" Dolvid gave a strategic laugh. "That has not been my experience, here in the Residence Quarter — " a predominantly Owani section, notorious for its gossip. He could have added it was from a drunk and garrulous Owani he had learnt years ago of ingredients used in the dyeing trade she had failed to mention here, such as lichens and bodies of various insects.

"The steelmakers of Upper Dakbân have processes they have never shared."

"Steelmakers do not exclude Owanil from their ranks."

"But everyone knows that has always been a Gabhani craft — "

"As everyone will continue to acknowledge Heartland dyeing as a proud Owani accomplishment, no matter who practices it."

"If the Others are allowed to protect their secrets," Kiravoi demanded, tightlipped, "why not your own race, *Bôdhrai*?"

"Then, after all, the Other Races are able to keep a secret?"

"When it is in their interest to do so."

He had her. "Forgive me if there is a point I do not understand, but that being so, isn't it more likely your secrets will be kept by men and women who can become apprentices, and hope to rise within the Guild, than by the same people as day-workers with no hopes at all?"

"The dyers do not underpay their day-workers," a revealing, irrelevant defense against an allegation not made — or perhaps a side-hit against the Fine-Weavers, who notorious employed many poor women and their children in routine drudgery, and paid them a pittance.

But winning debates did not change hearts. Among officials, loyal servants of the *rabhsayum*, the learned Fornival, painstaking, unimaginative Rhunilat and scholarly Faëdhal all had interwoven ties of kinship to the Heartland Families, who in this question (as not invariably) were blood-allies to the Guilds. But it was for Dolvid alone the great landowners kept the familiar charge that in pressing to correct egregious injustice he displayed a hatred of his own race; what was disliked but understood in Rodlakh as ascribable to the slight strain of

Gabhani in his blood — and additionally now, to his outlandish choice of an unmistakably Mixed bride — was unforgiven in him, the renegade Owani.

Whatever the Families invented for his motives, he reflected, as the riding, cheered in through Harbor Gate, clattered on the dark-rose stone of the Avenue, they could not say he was studying selfish convenience; he hoped the Guilds would soon capitulate, and for his own sake could wish they had been left alone. Shortly he would be passing near front gate of the house, to the south side of the Avenue, where he wanted to live with Aëlu, his wife of only weeks.

A new home, but far from a new house, the harmonious stone building had survived Plakhsila's renewal of Kadon Dinul, once belonging to Filat Plakhyali, that great *rabhsai*'s interesting if promiscuous nephew. Later, as the quarter at the head of the Avenue, virtually under the shadow of the New Residence, became the fashionable place to live, the house had gone through some hard times, shared by several tenants and properly maintained by none. More recently, in a time when, for those who chose to live below Market Way and the Disc, prestige belonged entirely to the north side of the Avenue, where Khelagh, most prosperous of landowners, had his imposing mansion, Filat's house had quartered cavalry officers. Yet its situation was superb, far back from the busy Avenue, its run-down but remediable grounds overlooking the Gardens of Kamzhinu, massive old inner walls to the city there having been razed to no more than chest-high, and surmounted with light and graceful fretted stonework: a quaint heirloom stipulation of the freehold acquired by Dolvid was his undertaking to provide if needed armed forces adequate to defend the wall against invaders at that point, and "expeditiously to inform the Captains of the Realm" if unable to do so.

While chances of having to withstand a siege were slight, the practical demands of the house were as daunting, and, in present conditions, impossible to meet. Very few of the needed repairs, to roof and floors, windows, stairs and panelled walls, could reasonably be undertaken in advance of necessary attention to the fabric of the building itself, and to restore its original chaste beauty was nothing less than master-mason's work. With this distinctly personal motive added to his passion for justice, he yearned for the Stonemasons, at present not wishing to be seen breaking ranks with the more intransigent of the Nine Guilds, to quickly offer proof of their better intentions, so he could put some of them back to work. Camped with him in a small rented house, her furnishings from Kamsilat warehoused at Owan Sai, Aëlu, pregnancy not yet generally apparent, was serenely uncomplaining.

4.

"Before evening, according to Rhinval," Shumat told the small, dusty gathering of officers, "we shall reach the edge of Landegh. When we make camp tonight, we'll be only hours from Lunu Jinzalladhiyu."

"I, for one, shan't mourn Landegh," Yaënsilat said, confident he spoke for all. He was the oldest present, perhaps oldest on the expedition, a veteran squadron-leader of Kargul. "They say Dakbân steel is plunged straight from the forge to a snow-fed stream; going suddenly from white-hot to ice-cold improves its temper. Not, mine, Captain."

Gathered about the flat rock Shumat had chosen for meeting-place, everybody laughed, except Rhinval, their captive guide, whose masked expression never changed, and Dorrmas, who had no time for jokes. Without fully knowing why, Kamin-Tolagh disliked the square-framed Master of Weapons; a wonderful swordsman, certainly, but with a brusque, impatient manner.

Here, now, was the furnace, midday on Landegh, and if this was its autumn, Kamin-Tolagh did not want any part of summer. Under a milky blue sky, the wind was where it had been for days, in the northwest, at times gusting to raise clouds of dust and stinging grit, yet while the sun was up, a hot wind. There was no shade. Earlier, in the deep-folded country west of Drin Navuna, the army had been able to make its noon break in the shadow of a beetling cliff or steep-walled gorge, but after two days they had descended into a flatter though tumbled land of parched ridges and arid hollows, where only occasional tufts of pale vegetation relieved browns and greys of the landscape.

Soon after leaving Drin Navuna, they had picked up the trail made by *jinzal*, crude and uneven, but better-defined than expected, though they knew it had been used to bring cumbersome siege-engines trundling against the Colony. In places, hollows had been filled, rubble packed down to something like level, and sharper clefts bridged by rolling in boulders and filling remaining gaps with smaller stones. When the flatter lands were reached, the way often branched into a cluster of narrow paths.

The general direction, though with much meandering, was south and west, leaving that course to avoid a wider ravine or a tormented cluster of bony heights, or, later, to come near spots where, at another season, water was found. Most such places showed signs of improvement, watercourses partially dammed, basins widened and deepened, but at only one was there as much as a faint trickle of water. Forewarned, each man in the army had carried a water-bag slung on his saddle-bow, and the pack-ponies started with heavy burdens of gurgling skins, but on the fifth morning out of Drin Navuna, Kamin-Tolagh judged they must now be at the point of no return; there would not be enough water for the long march back, if their close-faced guide was mistaken about streams and wells ahead, or had deliberately decided he was willing to die for the sake of killing an army. Shumat, enviably serene, agreed with his calculations without showing any concern.

In ideal conditions the crossing of Landegh was said by Rhinval to be a six-day journey, but the expedition was delayed waiting for the return of patrols which, wherever terrain permitted, Shumat sent out to either side, always the mounted bows. Several times they encountered individual or small groups of *jinzal*, survivors or strays from the war by the helms and remnants of body-armor they wore, but in the absence of their masters reverted to their normal practice of hunting, singly or in small packs. They had lost none of their determined ferocity, but the experienced Frontier bowmen, their numbers overwhelming, dealt with them with no loss. They returned to the main force with trophies to show, but Shumat could not share their elation. "Twelve or so *jinzal* killed," he remarked. "All within five miles of this trail — there could be dozens more in all the vastness of Landegh. We were hoping this expedition would make it safe to reduce the garrison at Drin Navuna. Not for years to come, I'm afraid."

Lavsila, given a chance to examine a dead *jinzai*, when yet to see a live one, decided they were, after all, less fearsome in the flesh than rumor made them, but when, early in next day's ride, the vanguard encountered three *jinzal* on the trail itself, he did not ride forward till assured all were killed. Yet Kamin-Tolagh had to admit the man, accustomed to leisured rides in the soft hills and benign meadows of the Heartland, did well to endure the wearing days astride a big *pefrai* of the Household. After sunset, when scorching wind changed in an hour to nagging cold, Lavsila, wrapped in a blanket, teeth chattering, complained incessantly, huddled close to a campfire the scarcity of fuel kept small, but there were gnarled half-Froghul' archers of the Frontier who shivered and cursed as bitterly.

Now, Shumat began setting order-of-march for the approach to the Lunu. Idmas, an effective officer from the Army of the West, asked, "Will we fight there, Captain?"

"There, if not sooner," with a glance towards the silent Rhinval. "To tell the truth, we're not certain what to expect. At or near the Lunu, we may encounter armed men still be able to control some formations of *jinzal*."

"Many?" Gremnivai asked. He was a man of Kargul, and because of his rank, acting under-captain, Kamin-Tolagh had been obliged to make him his second-in-command, though he would have much preferred one of the senior squadron-leaders, Yaënsilat, or from his personal squadron, Freighanai, both of whom had ridden with him in the two great victories of the Jinzai War. Gremnivai, instead, had been with his father in the disastrous Battle of Dônshei, where his sedate mental processes must surely have contributed to Tovakh's defeat. Thick-set, double-chinned, he was seldom seen without headgear, probably because he had lost most of his hair.

Shumat said, "At highest estimate, there can hardly be a hundred *jinzal* left alive, and some, as we see, are adrift on Landegh. But most of us here know at any odds *jinzal* are not to be taken lightly. All we find must be exterminated. Also, there will almost certainly be a number of women."

"*Jinzal* women, Captain?" The incredulous question came from Noldar, leader of the mounted archers, a typical mixture of Gabhani and tribal bloods, whose bowmanship at the Battle of Kamsilat had been prodigious.

"There are no *jinzayul*," Kamin-Tolagh said, one thing he was sure of.

"No," Shumat agreed. "These will be tribal women — of one tribe."

"The weekwife tribe?" a *kímukan* of General Cavalry said.

Shumat did not join the laugh, and outside battle Kamin-Tolagh had never seen him so serious, eyes going from face to face to be certain he was understood. "Not weekwives, and they aren't going to become so. You will all make it plain to your squadron and half-squadron officers, who will in turn make plain to their men, there is to be no association between them and the women of Lunu Jinzalladhiyu. Any violation of this ban will result in severest punishment. There can be no exceptions."

No one wanted to phrase the questions this left hanging in the air, and Shumat went on to give the broadest outline of his battle-plan for investment of and entry into the Lunu, in describing which he had the help of Rhinval, of whom he asked brief questions and received terse answers in the Owanilú, then translating for those who did not speak the language.

Kamin-Tolagh caught himself paying attention to manner rather than matter. Shumat's command of the Old Tongue was fluent if not quite correct; like many Others who, not taught as children, picked up the language in later life, he muddled inflexional endings, and pronounced inconsistently, reflecting a variety of models. As with any educated Owani, Kamin-Tolagh's Owanilú was slightly academic, the form as taught and spoken by the *Atarlum*, preserved, formalized, and to some degree reconstructed on the Island during the long Night of Owan, a language at its best in ceremony and rhetoric, somewhat stiffly bent to everyday circumstances. No scholar, he knew rougher, more vernacular forms had remained cradle-tongues in a few nearly-inaccessible, widely-separated parts of the realm, worn down into dialects so various, a man from a remote western valley of his own province could not understand one from southern Kamanta, though both spoke what they called Owanilú.

Rhinval gave no sign he had any other language, but if he had descended from what had been called a tide-pool of purebred Owanil, left behind when the First Empire receded, Kamin-Tolagh would have expected their language to have undergone its own process of divergence. The answers Rhinval gave were in model Owanilú of the *Mankh'*, every case, conjugation and accent correct. In their chance exile, those who had trained and led the *jinzal* must for centuries have preserved and guarded their language like some perishable treasure, impossible to restore once lost or altered. For how long exactly, he did not know, nor how that strange community connected, as somehow it must, to the legend of the True *Rabhsai* — but that in itself was another puzzle; *rabhsai* as a title was, if ancient by standards of living memory, relatively new in the long span of history, having come into use only with the Return in 2477; anciently, rulers of Owan were styled *Nímurai*, Great Lord, becoming *Nímuraibáki*, Greater Lord, with establishment of the First Empire. If cut off from all contact with the realm, how would the breeders of *jinzal* adopt a title they had never used — and why? But perhaps Dolvid and the others had on their own associated that legend with an attempt to seize power; Kamin-Tolagh might get some solutions to these mysteries from Rhinval himself, but had not been able to speak privately or at any length with the man, who had apparently been told not to answer any but immediate and practical questions. Shumat, while in all other ways as friendly as ever, was even less forthcoming: once again, that galling exclusion from the final, most intimate circle of Rodlakh's *rabhsayum*, failure to extend the last measure of trust — and as he arrived at this familiar point of rancor, Kamin-Tolagh was obliged to attend once again to the current subject, and found he was being asked to lead their main striking force, his own Karguli contingent, augmented with six additional squadrons of cavalry, and one hundred mounted bows. Shumat himself, with about a third of their total strength, intended to maintain a position to guard against unexpected developments, and dispatch reinforcements where they were needed.

"As at Kamsilat," Shumat said, "the bows, wherever feasible, will engage and reduce the *jinzal* at long range, with cavalry held ready to protect the archers when the *jinzal* charge.

Ashamed of his doubts, Kamin-Tolagh was suffused with a warm feeling of comradeship. He startled, perhaps offended the pompous Gremnivai by putting an arm behind the powerful shoulders of Noldar. "Aye, these little tigers were worth a half-squadron apiece in the war. However, if there is a flat floor to the Lunu, as you say, it'll be good to be where we can deploy our lances again. Even Household men grow tired in time of riding ceremonially, head-to-tail." This, with a grin, was meant good-naturedly, a traditional gibe at the *rabhsai*'s glittering guard. Everyone knew they were in fact superbly-trained fighters, and Kamin-Tolagh was, after all, their captain. Still Dorrmas, whose entire career had been Household, chose to be touchy.

"Not much ceremony about it," darkly, "when we took the New Residence back from Kargul."

Other officers of Kargul stiffened instantly, but Kamin-Tolagh said sweetly, "Let us not begin recalling those unhappy days."

Prompted by a thunderhead frown from Shumat, Dorrmas concurred. "As you say, *Asai*." Once more, Kamin-Tolagh enjoyed the effect produced by his unexpected mildness, but Dorrmas could not resist a double-edged return of courtesies:

"The cavalry of Kargul knows how to fight, as we saw at Dônshei, poorly led as they were." He had fought there, as had Shumat, on the opposite side to Gremnivai, or to Kamin-Tolagh's father.

The remark about the Residence was forgivable in response to Kamin-Tolagh's jocular taunt; not this, a calculated piece of baiting. As he bristled, Shumat forestalled him, very impressive in his quiet steeliness. "Dorrmas, with the mixed forces for this expedition we can prove a new age has begun. Kargul shed blood — Kamin-Tolagh *Asai* himself shed blood — at Kamsilat, to save our *rabhsai*; that blood, as Rodlakh *Rabhsai* says, should be enough to heal older wounds. Ordinary troopers who fought on rival sides at Dônshei are sharing their food and their campfires; do they have to set an example for their officers?"

Dorrmas was correctly contrite. Gremnivai, however, belatedly muttered, "The worst captaincy at Dônshei was not bred in Kargul, but in the bosom of the Household." He meant, Bolan, but was tactless as well as stupid; what a fool the man was, Kamin-Tolagh thought: *bred* in the *bosom*!

Shumat held up a hand. "Enough. I am sure Dorrmas would want to regret any offense he may inadvertently have given."

With little choice, Dorrmas mumbled assent, nodding to Kamin-Tolagh in a manner not distinguished for its graciousness, and he waggled a dismissive finger. Shumat could have hoped for a happier resolution to his conference.

Mid-afternoon brought an ambiguously stirring sight. The column had been descending crosswise over a single vast tilted slab of terrain, ten miles wide, its edge seeming to drop off into nothing. Their guide directed them to where the rim fell away less suddenly, and the trail, bending sharply south, curled down into a notch, a distant view of grey hills beyond. They had reached the southwestern corner of the great plateau, elsewhere falling in stark cliffs, almost sheer to brown, rolling plains. The track wound back on itself, and above to the right were remains of tremendous stoneworks, stumps of long-fallen towers, broken teeth of crumbling walls. This, recognized in unexpected awe, must be the last, doomed hope of the First Empire for a stable frontier, that of the Year 1550. Somewhere not many miles to the west, as Kamin-Tolagh could not wait to tell Shumat, there must be the line of Yuval's Frontier, anchored to the head of the Great Gulf, Flamûrai. "Even that was not the farthest extent of Larghai's conquests; there were tributary lands almost to the Western Ocean." The already-legendary name of Larghai, and of his revered monarch, Shâl IV, were invoked in dissent when Yuval, third of the name, realizing he could never have armies enough to subdue all hostile tribes, found a new, shorter line to defend. His great-grandson, Shâl VIII, on his deathbed, was the one to decree a further withdrawal here, to the edge of Landegh.

Shumat was lost among these ancient names, but knew the large outlines of the history. "But this frontier could not be held, though it kept back the tribes another hundred years."

The diminishing-glass of history — it must be a phrase from one of Dolvid's books; it would seem eternal, anything Kamin-Tolagh could make to outlive him by a hundred years, yet against the agelong history of the First Realm, to prolong the life of the Empire by a century appeared at this distance as futile gesture. Farther down, the riders passed near scattered and windworn wreckage from an ancient stone structure of unguessed purpose. Among fragments could be seen fading evidence of vanished skills, crumbling curve of a graceful stair, a section of frieze where carved forms of women and forest animals could yet be discerned.

"Hard to believe all that greatness, all this craft, could come to nothing," Kamin-Tolagh, wistfully. Was this not also *Shud'rai baSibadhum*, the Blossoming Age?"

"You had better ask Dolvid. My people were wild men of the Northeast when yours were building their empire. Dolvid says you had a worse enemy than the tribes here, or *jinzal*, or our

Pir Perus — worse than treachery. The weather. According to
him, the rain stopped coming; Landegh was once a green place
with grazing herds and growing crops."

"Beyond believing," not meaning he disputed it. The
head of the column was moving now into sandy country, with
sparse tangles of thorn, and island clumps of harsh grass; not far
ahead were scattered stands of scrawny trees, but low hills
beyond were scarcely less arid than the plateau they had
descended from.

Shumat was smiling reminiscently. "As boys, we used to
campaign together in the Gardens of Kamzhinu, leading armies
to reconquer the lost West; we were still young enough to think
empires were all glory and renown, nothing to do with profit.
What have you seen out here worth conquering?"

"Armies could lose themselves," Kamin-Tolagh agreed,
without admitting to similar games he had played by the shores
of the Inilu. As Shumat emphasized, the First Empire was of
Owan, not Arbhal, and at ten, Kamin-Tolagh's dreams had been
his mother's, his people, their beliefs restored to their rightful
preeminence under an Owani ruler, a revered Patriarch. That
meant nothing now, although it did occur to him that thirty years
ago it must have been unusual for a boy of Dolvid's pedigree to
have friends with Shumat's origins. As he had told his mother,
that time was past, he could not imagine why anyone would fight
wars or scheme strategies to increase influence of the *Mankh'*,
wealth and power of families such as Lavsila's, or his fat elderly
friend and kinsman, Khelagh. To make an empire for its own
sake, for the splendor of it, because a wide domain was more
glorious than a narrow one — those things he could understand.

"Yet any man could fancy the title of *Nim'raibaki*," he
said.

"Not Rodlakh. He thinks the realm he has is quite
enough for ruling, and as Dolvid says, the people won't thank
him for the pride of empire if they have to pay taxes to garrison
wastelands that show no return."

"Then this has been discussed."

"To be dismissed. Oh, there's no secret the *rabhsai* wants a full report on the state of the Farther West, if only for the security of the existing Colony. We may be going among some of the tribes."

"For what purpose?"

"They are away to the south, Rhinval says," sidestepping a direct answer.

"These women at Lunu Jinzalladhiyu — they would be from those tribes."

"One of them. It is called Man-mani."

"What were they, servants? They gave sport for trainers of the *jinzal*?"

Shumat dabbed again at his forehead. Tired, Kamin-Tolagh thought, with a dark flush to his face except for a pallor surrounding the eyes and above the upper lip, where there were tiny beads of sweat. "They were mothers of the *jinzal*."

"They *mated* with *jinzal*?" Not imaginable.

"No, no, *jinzal* do not mate. They are bred, so I'm told, from two human strains. Only women of the Man-mani can be their mothers, and their fathers are of — another race."

Many strange explanations existed for the origin of *jinzal*; this of Shumat's was at the same time the most farfetched, and the one which answered most questions; their lack of female counterparts or of any mating behavior, their apparent rootlessness.

"The tribe that fathers *jinzal*," Kamin-Tolagh asked. "What is that called?"

"Owani."

"You believe this?" Lavsila said.

"I have to, unless it can be disproved."

"And this has been known ever since the True *Rabhsai* was captured in the war — that long at the least."

"The so-called True *Rabhsai*," Kamin-Tolagh corrected. He began to wish he had not confided in Lavsila, who was perceptibly turning from disbelief in his pet direction, conspiracy.

It was late. The knifing wind was left behind on Landegh, but night was still cold enough to make them glad there was fuel for campfires. From not far away, welcome sound of another comfort, the faint purling of water. They were camped within the loop of a stream running gently but steadily in a deep, terraced cleft, and according to Rhinval there was a week in spring when, fed by melting snows somewhere far to the north, it became a torrent too fierce to ford, and had been seen to overflow these absurdly capacious banks. The notion of floods in this sunbaked country was only another strangeness of the West, where nothing was familiar.

"If we are to accept it requires Owanil to father *jinzal*," Lavsila said. "There must have been a considerable colony of the Old Blood, to sire several thousand of the creatures."

"They are long-lived," doing the sums in his head. "Given enough mothers, twenty men could easily father a thousand in five years."

"Well, but a large settlement of Owanil would make the tale of the True *Rabhsai* much more interesting. A ruler such as Rodlakh, of doubtful legitimacy — if this impostor they told you about was so laughable, why was he not paraded through the streets of Kadon Dinul, for everyone to enjoy? For that matter, where is he now? Rodlakh *Rabhsai* must have tidied him away — the grass will grow greener in the Residence grounds."

"That is not Rodlakh's way." But Kamin-Tolagh was troubled to have learned so late about origins of the *jinzal*, when Shumat, his professed brother-in-arms, had known long ago — even before their great night ride to Kamsilat.

"Say what you will, this One Realm we hear so much about is not going to be yours or mine," an echo of Petakoi. "The *rabhsai*, Shumat, this Dorrmas — they stick closer than any kin, those people."

Shumat, Kamin-Tolagh told him, had been quick enough to reprimand Dorrmas at the midday conference. As he recounted the incident, he was more than ever pleased with his own restraint. "That fool Gremnivai expected me to take offence, as if I would dispute publicly with an officer of my own command."

"Besides, Dorrmas is too lowborn. It might be, nonetheless, he was hoping to taunt you into a challenge. That would give him choice of weapons."

"That is ridiculous," testily, while not failing to note as an abstraction the cogency of Lavsila's distinction; there was not much doubt Kamin-Tolagh would win with his choice of weapons, lances, as Dorrmas with his, swords. "He would not dare fight with me, knowing he would have to answer to Rodlakh for my death."

"Well, yes," at his airiest. "Unless."

"What?"

"Dorrmas had secret instructions even Shumat knew nothing about."

"You go too far," voice low, but letting Lavsila hear danger. "The *rabhsai* is my friend."

"Did I say, instructions from Rodlakh? Dorrmas was with our beloved *Bôdhrai* in the storming of the Residence, also at Dônshei. The *Bôdhrai* is in a position where he could promise Dorrmas freedom from any consequences. He would succeed to your captaincy, not so?'

"And Dolvid's reward?" It must be as what they judged a traitor to and of their own race that the unteachable Heartlanders reserved such a special loathing for Dolvid, although with Lavsila there was a mysterious personal animus as well. Kamin-Tolagh leaned forward to pat his knee, as, huddled, he tried to work out a motive for his improbable conspiracy. "For me, it is far easier to believe Dorrmas dislikes me on his own. He is envious. He was at Dônshei, yes, but that was Shumat's battle, and then Dorrmas was left behind at Kadon Dinul while others went to the war and won fame, including one whose House he fought against at Dônshei, now Captain of his Household. He lacks tact to conceal his feelings."

"All that kind are twisted with envy, and have been for an age. They want handed to them the benefits we won with hard work and skill."

Again, Kamin-Tolagh marvelled at how blandly Lavsila could shift his ground when a position became untenable, or when he found no takers for one of his elaborate theories of conspiracy, the only constant his unruffled superior wisdom. Not Lavsila's but Kamin-Tolagh's own analysis of Dorrmas's character gave him misgivings, as he lay down for a few hours' sleep; tomorrow's almost certain fighting needed cool heads and astute use of numbers, not the heroics of an officer bypassed so far by fame, one who had never before fought *jinzal*. Wanting to demonstrate he could overlook personal aversion, Kamin-Tolagh had given Dorrmas leadership of an important section; the man was, after all, the only under-captain available apart from the unthinkable Gremnivai, who had been fobbed off with the vital task of assuring communications and protecting the baggage-train (otherwise, of keeping out of the way of the fighting-men). If no enemy was encountered before the Lunu was reached, the companies under Dorrmas, entering the great depression by the narrow eastward access, might easily be first to meet any challenge. Earlier patrols had obeyed Shumat's strict orders to hold back from fighting at close quarters, as far as possible letting bows do the job, but Kamin-Tolagh guessed a repetition of that command coming from him would not go down well with Dorrmas. In the morning he would ask Shumat in his final instructions to reemphasize the wise use of superior skills and prudent tactics; no one expected the expedition to fail, and the only way to win distinction was by keeping casualties to a minimum.

When morning came Shumat was obviously ill; he had been up most of the night with vomiting and loose bowels, and was shivering and unsteady as he hoisted himself laboriously into the saddle. Noldar, the Frontier veteran, was sympathetic but unworried, calling the sickness Landegh fever, often striking newcomers to the West; a number of soldiers had suffered similar symptoms over the past couple of days; some blamed the rapid changes from hot to cold, others the flat-tasting water, and there were more elaborate theories to do with *jinzal* or spirits in the dust, but the complaint had never killed or permanently disabled anyone. Noldar sent a couple of his full Froghul archers to hunt along the riverbank for a herb from which, he said, a drink useful against the fever could be infused. When they returned with bundles of what looked like a cress, Shumat, not wanting to wait while water was heated, took a handful, and chewed listlessly on the stems, remarking it had the taste of a well-rusted nail.

Scouts were already riding ahead, and soon the main army was moving off, Kamin-Tolagh with Dorrmas at head of the first main section. Rhinval was also with them, taciturn as ever.

"*Asai*, do you believe this," Dorrmas asked, "about these tribal women giving birth to *jinzal*?"

"Why would anyone make it up?" Kamin-Tolagh, turning to Rhinval asked in the Owanilú for confirmation.

At first he thought the man was not going to answer; he licked his lips and glanced nervously from side to side. "*Certainly*," at last. "*The women were kept all together in a large white building. You will see it; we called it the Hatchery.*"

"What?" Dorrmas, with the suspicious face of one unable to follow.

Making a grimace, Kamin-Tolagh translated for him. Dorrmas too was offended, letting out a curse, but their distaste had different sources, Kamin-Tolagh's the contempt for women implied by the building's nickname, Dorrmas fresh confirmation vermin like *jinzal* were deliberately bred of human mothers.

Near noon at the brink of Lunu Jinzalladhiyu, Kamin-Tolagh paused for a long, astonished look; exact advance description had done nothing to lessen shock. Not valley as its name said, it was indeed clean-edged and abrupt as a vast footprint in crisp snow, oval in shape, a mile-and-a-half along the long axis, east to west. Girdling walls were layered in shades of raw yellow, brown and dusky rose, and the floor for the most part was flat or gently undulating, with denser vegetation, especially at the fringes, than the rim above.

Mid-morning advance scouts had ridden back to report they had come in sight of the Lunu without any encounters, but down in the great depression itself had seen signs of life, smoke of fires, laundry fluttering on lines. Pressing forward, the main force had soon arrived at the place where the ways divided, and Kamin-Tolagh had parted from Dorrmas, earning further displeasure by again cautioning him against unnecessary risks. The descent at that eastward end, narrow and winding, was said to lead direct to the mound where the men of the Lunu had their cluster of dwellings, making it less likely Dorrmas would have *jinzal* to deal with. It also meant Rhinval went with that detachment, to identify important buildings, and Kamin-Tolagh, though reluctant to draw attention to the under-captain's deficiency in language, had to give him a *kímukan* of the Household with enough of the Owanilú to communicate with their guide.

A strange, metallic day, hot with a high cover of clouds and not the least promise of rain. To find the principal among three ways down into the Lunu, Kamin-Tolagh had hardly needed Rhinval's directions, holding to the trail as it followed the southern edge of the depression, till he came to a broad, levelled space from which any trace of vegetation had been removed. Taking his own advice, he ordered his column with care, his personal squadron at the head, lances unslung. With a clear view ahead, he would have placed mounted bows in the vanguard, but they were too lightly armed against the chance of an ambush, and here followed the lead squadron, with the remainder of the cavalry wheeling in behind. All went in fours, which the width of this track, according to Rhinval, would permit all the way to the valley floor.

At the end of a plodding descent with many turns, the force began debouching in another bare and level space, margin of the grounds where *jinzal* armies had trained. At second hand Kamin-Tolagh had heard that training described as a savage business in which dozens of the creatures were killed and maimed, their battles mock only in the sense they had no objective except to teach the *jinzal* formation fighting, and instill obedience to the trumpet signals of their masters, and were halted short of general massacre, those killed providing meat for the survivors.

Across the stony plain, near the north side of the Lunu, were eight long, low, nearly windowless structures, barracks where the *jinzal* were kept, according to Rhinval — those being trained, he amended, when Kamin-Tolagh questioned the size of buildings, not adequate each to house six hundred or so of the creatures; hardly fewer than five thousand had begun the assault against the Colony.

Even so, there was room here for a thousand, and Kamin-Tolagh maintained caution in his approach, ranging half the bows to command the central doorways of the first pair of barracks, silent and menacing under pewter sky. Detached files of cavalry sidled up, and dismounted beside the doors, drawing their swords. First man to kick open a rough wooden door and move warily into the dim was the youthful Kambanal, taken out of Kamin-Tolagh's personal squadron, where he had served well, to replace a squadron-leader lost in the War.

For a brief time near end of battle at Kamsilat, with victory certain, Kamin-Tolagh had ceased to feel the special terror living *jinzal* inspired, and they became simply a loathsome enemy to be destroyed. He had hoped then he was free forever from return of *jin'dazhai*, but it was not so, and in the tense apprehension of the waiting troops, he could detect no difference between veterans of that fight and those who had never confronted the creatures.

After long moments, Kambanal reappeared, with a gesture indicating the building was deserted. As Kamin-Tolagh spurred forward, he saluted with his sword. "Nothing, *Asai*. But it has not been empty long. They left pieces of clothing and equipment behind, and a smell — " he exhaled with a noisy flutter of lips. "Like the lair of a wild beast — worse. Not many wild beasts foul their own living-quarters."

Kamin-Tolagh nodded, and noted the young man's admiration for him was unconcealed. Made brave, another half-squadron had entered the second of the barracks, soon emerging with much the same story. Apparent now no enemy would be found here, though all the buildings had to be searched; growing bored while this went on, Kamin-Tolagh rode eastward to a faint rise, to watch for appearance of the men under Dorrmas at the far end of the valley, as for any sign he would need help.

Leftward along the same low rise — what country folk would call a *tull* — a pair of battered siege-engines were standing forlorn, *zhin'pefral*, wooden catapults capable of hurling large stones over great distances — these, with *jinzai* strength for winding back the stiff throwing arm could outdistance two or perhaps three good bowshots. Similar engines had done still-visible damage to the fortress of Drin Navuna, and might have reduced defended places at Kamsilat to rubble, if more than one or two had ever come into action.

Freighanai, leader of Kamin-Tolagh's squadron, ambled over. "Strongly made," he commented. "They've had some use." Not a lettered man, he had a native shrewdness.

"Funny thing, *Asai*, so far as I have heard, nobody ever thought of using these things in the open field — against a massed cavalry charge, say?"

Kamin-Tolagh half-assented, considering the difficulty of maneuvering the cumbersome things, on their small, solid wheels, their need for a ready supply of rocks, and vulnerability to attack. Nevertheless, if a dozen could be placed horseshoe-fashion on heights, and the enemy then induced to attack across the lower ground they commanded, their boulders would indeed clear some lanes in the advancing ranks.

Behind, search of the barracks was complete. Ahead, across a half-mile of stunted brush, under the glare of the oppressive sky, was the group of whitish buildings Rhinval had said were the women's quarters, standing a little apart, a larger one, of a length similar to the *jinzal* barracks, but taller, with more windows. Horsemen with bright breastplates, the men with Dorrmas, were circling there, and a flicker of colors, yellow, blue, white, could be discerned, washing drying on a line.

Annoying, having undertaken what was supposed to be the most dangerous part, to be here ransacking deserted buildings, while Dorrmas was where discoveries might be made. As soon as he could, having received formal word the barracks were without life, he reassembled his squadrons and headed for the farther end of the Lunu.

His intention had been to make straight for the women's quarters, but the brush, which from above had looked like soft moss on a level surface, was surprisingly hard going, with tough, springy branches close-set, concealing sudden holes or precarious jumbles of rock. Very soon, Kamin-Tolagh was glad to give up the attempt, and turn aside to gain the continuation of the trail by which they had descended, a fair road running along the base of the south wall. Here and there on the cliffs he noted shining streaks where water oozed out, and as they neared the huddle of white buildings he saw they adjoined a stripe of well-tended garden plots crisscrossed with shallow irrigation ditches. Past that was the long building where the washing hung in a low-fenced yard, and rounding the corner Kamin-Tolagh came upon a scene.

Shumat was there, dismounted, unwell, saying angry things to a defiant Dorrmas, also on foot, a bloodstained sword in his hand. Behind him, outside the central door to the so-called Hatchery, were about a dozen men in the Army of the West's scarlet-trimmed tunics, additionally spattered and streaked with blood, as were their breeches. Evidently, Kamin-Tolagh had missed a battle, but he could not imagine a reason for Shumat's rage, unless Dorrmas had, after all, taken unnecessary casualties in close-quarter fighting. No wounded were to be seen.

"Stay here," were the only words of Shumat's he heard, an uncharacteristically curt order, as he brushed past Dorrmas, other men parting to let him go inside. Giving a similar but softer instruction, Kamin-Tolagh dismounted, handed up his reins to Freighanai, and went after Shumat.

A long chamber was divided into small cubicles by wicker screens which did not go all the way to the ceiling. Each enclosure had a washstand, a chest or locker, and bedding spread on the flagged floor. Patches of fresh blood glistened, and at the third or fourth cubicle Shumat was looking down at the body of a young tribal woman. Obviously pregnant, she had been cut down with a dozen sword-strokes, and her blood was still spreading on the floor. He noted a plain silver ring in her ear.

"What is this?" but beginning to guess. Shumat, dull-eyed, acknowledged his presence, but said nothing, going to the door at the end of the chamber.

It led to a similar space, and here were corpses of another girl and a somewhat older woman, also pregnant, also killed by many swords, or many ferocious hacks from one. In the last cubicle was the body of a naked infant perhaps six weeks old, almost cut in half. A male child, and bunched shoulders, thick chest, the abnormally wide mouth, unmistakably indicated he would have grown into a *jinzai*. It was true: they were of human parentage.

"Now, this... " Shumat muttered to himself, his tone conceding there was sense to this killing. Without a glance for

---

Kamin-Tolagh, he opened the next door, and his breath hissed in so sharply between clenched teeth Kamin-Tolagh thought for a moment their leader had been ambushed and stabbed. Stepping over puddled blood, he followed, as Shumat, seldom given to pieties, breathed, "*Zhôl, begetter of pity, hold us in your thought.*"

They were in a washroom with big stone tubs either for bathing or laundry. Women of the Hatchery must have retreated here because there was a way of escape, a back door, giving on the yard with the washing-line. Locked, jammed, or perhaps held from outside, door had failed to open, and more than a dozen women had been butchered, together with an indeterminate number of babies. In a tangled mass, victims had been killed and rekilled, fantastically hacked and stabbed; blood was in rivulets on the floor and ran down from gouts on the walls; even the ceiling spattered by killers driven to a mindless fury Kamin-Tolagh had known in thick of battle, but could not comprehend when turned against defenseless women and children. No doubt who the killers were, and Dorrmas had not even the excuse of having fought in the Jinzai War.

"There was no need for this." Shumat wanted to judge calmly, but sounded as ill as he looked. "Any *jinzal* sons borne by the pregnant ones could have been killed at birth. Some they were carrying would have been girls." Indeed, of infants Kamin-Tolagh could clearly sort out in the muddle of bloodied flesh, two at least were ordinary girl-babies.

Kamin-Tolagh said, "I wondered why a Household man, Dorrmas, chose Army of the West for his lead squadron — men who would have lost comrades in the war — kin, perhaps, to the *jinzal.*"

"Does that excuse this?"

"Nothing does," he concurred. "This was done by design, not on impulse." All the same, while he could not imagine planning or ordering, much less taking part in such a slaughter, there was a pitiless logic if the object was to be certain no *jinzal* could be born in future.

"My fault. The orders should have been clearer."

"You will not discipline Dorrmas?"

A weary shake of the head. "His men will be the ones to cleanse this place, and bury the dead."

Shumat's justice, acknowledging what he considered his own part of the blame. Yet Kamin-Tolagh would find it hard to look Dorrmas in the face without letting contempt show, and he did not see how the man could continue as an officer in the Household, his Household, when they returned.

The gradual slope of the eastern mound was walled, with an arched gate, and the nearly-level space in front of the gate, fringed by stables and storehouses, looked very much like the marketplace it would have been for many small towns of the realm. In fact, to judge by the tall flagstaff by the gate, it must have been a parade-ground, though surely *jinzal* soldiers had not mustered in ranks for inspection and saluted the colors. Its expanse began to alter Kamin-Tolagh's ideas about the number of men who had been here, as did the settlement behind the wall.

It was laid out Owani-style, the east-west axis, the *traëvu* sacred to the Encompasser, here an avenue leading nowhere, lined with scrawny trees of unfamiliar kinds. Where intersected by the way leading up from the gate, high-point of the mound, there was another flagpole, this one in front of a stone building of some antiquity, much in the style, if far short of the size, of the Bronze Residence by Kadon Dinul. Shumat said, according to Rhinval, now not to be seen, it had been called the Great Residence, and had housed the retinue of the True *Rabhsai*, as well as other dignitaries. With other substantial buildings flanking the crossways, it possessed a small but elaborate garden with hedges and decorative trees. For water, there were several wells, and a rill which, originating somewhere in the eastward cliffs, passed under the north-south way in a culvert, and trickled down through the Residence grounds to end in a dark pool with no apparent outlet, bowed over by what a Household man born in Ninkufu identified as lemon trees, with dark, shining leaves.

The smaller houses were well-built and in good repair; the climate here, with no snow and little rain, was no doubt kind to masonry. Though the cavalry had yet to go through every building, no living occupant had been found, and everywhere had the sense of recent occupation. When Kamin-Tolagh, with Shumat, went up the steps to an ornate front door and entered the Residence, he saw a fine coating of dust covered the furniture, solid and old-fashioned, but this was a dusty place, and the people of the settlement must have departed only days ago.

As they settled which rooms they would use while here, Kamin-Tolagh puzzled over that departure, hasty, but with no sign of panic. "They left bedding, some clothes, stores of food, so Idmas says, but there is nothing strewn about or broken."

"As yet," drowsily, "no documents have come to light."

"As if they had warning of our approach. Could they have had spies in the Colony? Or at Kadon Dinul? If Rhinval is an example, any man from here, once he found his way to the realm and picked up enough ordinary language, could pass as just another Owani, and never be questioned."

Shumat merely nodded. With every allowance made for illness, this silence was concealing additional secrets shared by Rodlakh's inner circle. He had shown no surprise when Kamin-Tolagh pointed out the fine wall-hangings here were uncannily similar to those of Heartland weave, prized everywhere in the realm.

In the morning Shumat was much worse. Sweating profusely, he tried to dress, but was overcome with dizziness, sitting on his bed to hear overnight reports of unevent and issue instructions to senior officers, and then lying down. Noldar, the authority on Landegh fever, acknowledged an unusually severe attack, but maintained there was no reason for alarm.

"You are now in overall command," Lavsila said. He had come with the supply-train in late afternoon, and they were now breakfasting in a small, tapestried room of the so-called Residence. "What will you do?"

"Exactly what Shumat would," wondering what the question meant; he had already organized squadron-strength patrols to sweep surrounding country in all directions, while lettered soldiers under Gremnivai's direction were making an inventory of food, feed and miscellaneous supplies in various storehouses, and listing furnishings of value. Legally, after one-seventh had gone to the *rabhsai*, remainder of any proceeds would be shared out as prize-money in amounts proportional to rank, but surely smaller articles had already vanished into cavalry saddlebags. Pilfering was as much a part of armies as the weapons they carried, but ill as Shumat was, he was experienced enough to have made a senior officer responsible for valuables in each of the larger dwellings.

"They lived well enough, these people," Lavsila said. "Carpeting, some good glassware, brocade outshirts... "

"What about women?" Here in the settlement on the mound, little if any female clothing or paraphernalia had been found.

"They could have the tribal women. I imagine they were encouraged to visit the women's quarters, to make more *jinzal*. There must have been about a hundred women at one time." The Hatchery, plainly, had been occupied only by women whose pregnancies were confirmed, and in one of the smaller buildings down below, about two dozen frightened women had been taken alive, "before Dorrmas could find them," as Kamin-Tolagh had corrosively commented.

He said, "Women of their own, *Owaniyul*." The idea appeared new to Lavsila, but as well as fathering *jinzal*, the Owanil here had to perpetuate their own bloodlines. Again, something was not right. There could never have been beyond a few hundred living here on the mound, surely impossible for so small a number of Owanil to have maintained racial purity over, what? fifty generations, sixty? They would have succumbed to the effects of excessive inbreeding, which, Kamin-Tolagh had learned in childhood, was as disastrous for humans as for cattle or horses, always a danger for the Great Families, as could be seen in the feeble-minded Finú and her half-mad sister, Radaghi. But in explaining his understanding of *jinzal*, Shumat had emphasized (half-apologetically, because of who he was talking to) the father's blood had to be unmixed Owani.

"You could ask Rhinval," Lavsila suggested, when he understood what women Kamin-Tolagh was insisting on.

"I have." The man, evasive as ever, had sidled around the question till Kamin-Tolagh demanded whether he had a mother, and Rhinval then admitted there hd been "a few" women of their own race here, and "more, sometimes."

"If this was your command, you could think of ways to make the man become talkative. What would you do if Shumat did not recover?"

The question he had begun with. "He will recover. Why do you ask?"

"Oh, only he is so doggedly determined to finish up here and ride for home, without — " he shrugged — "seeing something of the West."

"Those are our orders."

"Yes, but this place, the Lunu, is better than we were led to expect. Good building, and the wells have no bottom; more could be done if water was used properly. Food could be grown here, if the brush was burnt off — it would make an ideal base for exploration, and you would no longer have to depend on supplies carried across Landegh. You might ride to the Western Ocean, or — you remember the story of the rich gold mine Larghai could never find again? That would be somewhere south and west of here."

"If it ever existed," Hard to believe in a Lavsila excited by exploration for its own sake, and the entry of gold mines put them back on more plausible ground. "Our task here," coldly, "is to eradicate all trace of *jinzal*, and return to our posts in the realm. I am Captain of Rodlakh's Household." Just the same, thinking of the tame business of escorting dignitaries up and down the Avenue, he felt a sharp stab of desire for the limitless unknown whose threshold he had attained. Rodlakh's narrowly constricting orders might be envy of men who would be riding to places, seeing sights he never had: it paralleled what he must already feel for Kamin-Tolagh's varied adventures with women. Although it had been widely noted the *rabhsai*, with power to follow any whim, evinced no desire for women other than his bride. Âna, granted, with her intense animation, diffused a certain dark excitement, but that was a familiar delusion born of desire, that here, at last, was a woman not his sister he would not be bored by after a week putting her through her various paces. A dozen, a score of exquisite moments, and he would be supplying his own spark, till fresher flanks and thighs renewed his dulling appetite.

"I have to work out what to do with the tribal women." There had been airy talk of returning them to their own people, but Rhinval was all vagueness about where the Man-mani were to be found, and for once his reticence might be based on genuine ignorance. The women themselves, speaking a language unintelligible to any of the troops, possessed a dozen words of the Owanilú among them, and could only wave in a variety of directions when asked where they had come from; frightened and tearful, they remained canny enough, Kamin-Tolagh suspected, to hope to ingratiate themselves, and so remain, with the new masters of the Lunu.

Near midday, Idmas, who had taken a squadron out on the north side of the rim, returned to report an important find. Drawn by the wheel and swoop of carrion-birds, he had come to an abrupt natural crevice, where vultures and ravens competed for what flesh was still on the bones of a large number of corpses, easily recognizable from their size, the massive jaws and fierce teeth, as *jinzal*.

Idmas, who frequently seemed to think his actions needed justifying, explained he could not get an accurate count without sending men down into the awkward and malodorous common grave to disentangle the putrid remains, but there were not less than fifty bodies, and perhaps seventy-five, not all full-grown. He had been struck by the curious posture of many, tightly curled, heads touching knees, and the conclusion they had been poisoned was supported by the sight of perhaps a dozen carrion-birds as dead as their final meal.

"Or some unknown disease," Lavsila said, with a shudder.

"Then they all died of it at once," Idmas said. "The ground over there is too rough for wagons, so the bodies were not brought there. My guess, *Asai*, is they were marched there, then fed poisoned meat. If they were in a hurry, the men may have thought the *jinzal* would delay them on the march. Besides, they would have to find food for them."

"They would have killed some to feed the others, as I heard was done in the War," Kamin-Tolagh said. "No, to keep the *jinzal* would make it harder for them to vanish into the wild. Reports and rumors would have led us to them, sooner or later." A hard decision, he thought, sacrificing strength to secrecy; a fighting-band of seventy *jinzal* would make its masters invulnerable to anything short of the full strength of an aroused realm.

"They may have been afraid of their *jinzal*, too, *Asai*. Most of the men who were best at controlling the brutes must have been lost in the War."

These officers Sebhal had brought up in the Army of the West were undeniably impressive; Sebhal's celebrated habit of letting them speak their minds had produced men not afraid to think.

If the creatures had been deliberately killed, and prior estimates of their surviving numbers were accurate, the masters of the *jinzal* had practically accomplished the main aim of the expedition: Kamin-Tolagh did not speak his sardonic thought:

the fair distribution of honors would not be easy with a force that had achieved the death of more unarmed women than of its real enemy. Asked, Idmas said his patrol had been unable to pick up any trail left by the men after ridding themselves of the *jinzal*.

Kamin-Tolagh stood, fastening his tunic. "I had better see for myself. You can take me there? Is it far?"

"An hour. But it's not a pleasant sight, *Asai*. Nor smell."

Glad for an excuse to be in the field, he waved away that consideration, and also gestured Lavsila back to his seat. His matchless bravery with dead *jinzal* was needed less than his assistance with the inventory here. As a true Heartlander, he could unerringly come within a tobhai or two of the fair value of every furnishing — and, as a true Heartlander, carefully undervalue anything he hoped to keep, overvalue what he expected to be sold.

Kamin-Tolagh was just in the saddle when his plans were changed by the puzzling return, after no longer than four hours, of the youthful Kambanal. He had taken a squadron south on what was supposed to be one of the farthest-ranging patrols, searching for signs of any fugitives in that arid country, using his judgment about whether to make overnight camp, but at soonest not expected back till late in the day.

With him was just a file of his men, and as they mounted the slope to the crossways, Kamin-Tolagh saw in their midst a tattered figure in a flapping and soiled cloak, a small man on the back of a small, threadbare saddle-horse, leading a shaggy pack-pony. He had a short, matted beard, and the hair not contained by the hat of woven reeds was tangled and dusty.

Kambanal saluted, and reported he had left most of his squadron under a capable under-officer. He would now ride to rejoin them, but had judged the encounter with the ragged man to be important.

"Your prisoner?"

Kambanal was indecisive. "*Asai*, he said he was riding for the Lunu in any case, so we rode with him to be sure he did."

"Said? In what language?"

Keenly, the stranger looked up at Kamin-Tolagh, who saw the pale eyes and firm, narrow nose of an Owani. "Captain, I speak the same languages you speak, and, I believe, a few you do not." With the sunbaked scoring of his face, the age was hard to guess, though he was not as old as Kamin-Tolagh had first thought; the lean, corded forearms were not those of an old man.

"You have a name."

"Iruvakh. Iruvakh Iribanat-Baëtufi."

"*Asai*," Kambanal prompted. "You are addressing the *Valnim'* Kamin-Tolagh baKargul."

"*Asai*," the man assented, making a half-deference. "Well met, *Asai*."

The sense of absurdity was growing. Asked if Iruvakh had been searched for weapons, Kambanal produced a small, sheathed game-knife, which Kamin-Tolagh promptly had restored to its owner. "Then you are Owani of the realm," baffled how that could be, yet with the distant feeling that with careful treatment this man might be the key to many mysteries.

Invited, then, rather than commanded to join Kamin-Tolagh at the Residence for a refreshing drink, Iruvakh suggested they go instead to the house of the Captain Kemunai, at the eastward end of the *Traëvu*, hard against the cliffs. The water there, he said, was always coolest, and they could also unearth a wine to Kamin-Tolagh's liking. After instructing Kambanal to inform Shumat a captive had been taken, or, if he was sleeping, to leave a written report to be shown to him as soon as he woke, Kamin-Tolagh declined the offer of guards, and let Iruvakh lead the way. The two of them, he thought, must make for an odd sight, tall man on a tall *pefrai*, the short one on a small horse trailing a stunted pony.

Kemunai's house, he was told on arrival, was one of the earliest built, a massy structure of a darker stone, with large windows on the upper level to catch the late-afternoon light.

Within, there were signs the place had been searched and slept in, but the soldiers now were absent at their duties. From the broad front hall an archway gave on a brief passage, doors opening right and left, and led to a cool, bare rearward room crossing the width of the house, its dim scarcely lessened by tall windows on either side. In the rearward wall, dressed stone ceded to an expanse of native rock, and near the center a tiny natural spring spurted into a fan-shaped stone basin, from where it drained, presumably into cellar cisterns. As Iruvakh had predicted, the water was marvellously cold, with a slight, not unpleasant bitter tang.

After they had both drunk, Kamin-Tolagh, with a dreamlike feeling of watching events he had no hold on or power to change, let the little man conduct him up a narrow, curved stair to a small room at the front, meant for reading and writing, simply furnished with plain oak chairs and desk, rush matting on the floor. The other door, Iruvakh said, gave on the main dining-hall, where Kemunai had often entertained. "A man of taste," he commented. "Or he was; it is said he was killed in fighting at Kamsilat."

"True. I was there." If correctly identified, Kemunai had been about the last of the *jinzai*-masters to die, cut down at quayside attempting to escape.

"What, *Asai*, was your part in the fight?"

"With Shumat, we helped raise the siege of Kamsilat, and joined with Rodlakh *Rabhsai* in destroying your *jinzal*."

"Not my *jinzal*," quick to correct. "I was *with* those of the Lunu Jinzalladhiyu, not *of* them. But you, Kamin-Tolagh baKargul, you helped defeat the *jinzal*, and to make this Rodlakh the *rabhsai*?"

"I am now Captain of his Household."

For the first time the little man ran short of the amazing composure he had so far displayed. "*Asai* — " he hesitated. "Would your mother not be Petakoi *Asayu*?"

"And my father *Nim'* Tovakh baKargul, yes."

"But the cavalry of Kargul is here under the colors of Rodlakh."

Kamin-Tolagh laughed. Not a reason for Iruvakh's sudden wariness, and nothing yet explained what an Owani born in the province of Dramal was doing in this place supposedly cut off for centuries from all contact with the realm, but Kamin-Tolagh still enjoyed bewilderment over the change in alignments. He said, "It is a new age, a new generation."

"And I have returned too late."

"Returned from what?" Interrogation had to begin somewhere.

"*Asai*, from the south, the Man-mani country. I persuaded Sranadatta, their head-man, to agree to take back their women, but now it seems a wasted journey."

"Why was persuasion needed? Couldn't the women simply be sent back? With their own people, they cannot have *jinzal* sons, as I understand."

"True," interlacing his fingers, adopting an instructional manner, not for the first time reminding Kamin-Tolagh of an *atarlai* of the *Mankh'*. "Among the Man-mani, indeed, with all the tribes, a woman who has once mated is seen as spoiled for marriage."

"Why?"

"It is their way, *Asai*, as with Others of your realm, at least in country places where Owani enlightenment is yet to flourish. I have known Man-mani women whose fault was to have been raped by Hill Froghul' raiders driven away to starve. They cannot be reasoned with."

Evidently Man-mani was one of Iruvakh's other languages, and when Kamin-Tolagh pointed out the contradiction, that apparently he had been able to reason with their head-man, he laughed.

"By now, I am welcome among the Man-mani — and others of the southern people. No wonder your officer took me at first for a man of the tribes." Iruvakh ran fingers through the unkempt hair. "Going among them so much, I almost am."

"For what did you go among them?"

"For myself, to learn, to teach. But there were things the Lunu required of the tribes — foodstuffs, workers, servants — breeding-stock for *jinzal*."

"Man-mani women, you mean."

A nod, followed by a sad shake of the head. "With our needs from other tribes, I at last made them see fair and friendly dealing was more rewarding than intimidation, but the Man-mani they continued to bully. For countless years, and up to onset of the War, the Lunu maintained an armed company in Man-mani country. All the more unforgivable they should simply leave the women here without protection, to be killed, or perhaps enslaved by some wandering clan." He would have been willing to launch into a lengthier condemnation of irresponsibility, but Kamin-Tolagh insisted on the plain tale.

With news of the *jinzal* armies' unimaginable defeat, he said, many of those left at the Lunu had departed. Not certain whether the new *rabhsai* would act to extirpate the last of his enemy, others had remained, maintaining order among remnant *jinzal*, but with no signs of resuming training or breeding. Iruvakh, coming back from journeys in the tribal Froghushei, had been given permission to negotiate for repatriation of the Man-mani women — here, as often, he asserted he was neither paid by nor under orders of the *jinzai*-breeders, obviously a point anyone in his present position might like to establish, true or not.

"But now they are gone, sooner than was planned. Fresh word must have come in my absence."

"Word from where?"

"From Kadon Dinul, I would suppose, *Asai*."

"Then you had an informant there."

"Indeed." As with the previous question, he gave an odd, assessing look, as if doubting he could be serious.

"My lack of any standing." he resumed, "meant a great deal was kept from me, but even I knew a Captain Shumat was chosen to lead an expedition here, which was to consist of over a thousand cavalry, with our captured *Kímukan* Rhinval as guide.

Here, they had hoped to find additional pack-animals, but in the end, as you see — " he gestured at the abandoned furnishings — "it was a hasty departure."

"Where?"

"*Where?*"

"Where have they gone? What were the plans?"

Now there was no misreading the wry, guarded glance; the man thought Kamin-Tolagh was trying to trap him with questions whose answers he already knew. "Eastward, would you say, *Asai*? They would hope to reach the Island."

"What island?"

"What Island?" Iruvakh stared, and quickly asked pardon for the laugh he had not uttered. "The new age really has come. When I was last in your realm, there might be many islands, but for true Children of Yoëlladhu, only one Island." Piously, he touched a thumb to his heart.

5.

During the next hour, everything Kamin-Tolagh believed he knew was undermined by information outside belief, impossible to doubt. Explanations, no matter how outlandish, that dovetailed with known facts and solved outstanding mysteries could not be rejected, especially as told in Iruvakh's unchanged manner: no oath or passionate protestation would have been as convincing as his furtive, skeptical glances, the wary yet half-facetious tone of a man reciting what he is sure is no news. As the story unravelled, Kamin-Tolagh saw why: as Captain of the Household, joint leader of this expedition, or, bitterest of all, as Heir in Kargul, in any of those three distinct persons he might be assumed to know all of what Iruvakh had to tell.

The Island was *the* Island, Kamanta; Rhinval their guide, Kemunai whose house this was, all who led and most who had fathered *jinzal*, were officers and men of the *Adanum Plakh'*, the Patriarchal Guard. Till his resignation six years ago, Iruvakh himself had been an *atarlai*, one of the *Edhrodilum*, the Growers, and the entire scheme to breed *jinzal*, train them into an army, and use them to install a spurious True *Rabhsai* at Kadon Dinul, came from the *Mankh'*.

"The *Atarlum*," Kamin-Tolagh said.

"Indeed," momentarily conceding part-belief to his ignorance. Not, he emphasized in hasty emendation, the entire *Atarlum*, not even all the *Manadilum*, though it had always been there, in the Teaching Order, where most if not all of its chief adherents had been found. The breeding had begun, it seemed, many centuries ago, probably with the idea of furnishing the Patriarch with an invincible bodyguard, and after as the forceful means for combining functions of Patriarch and secular ruler in one Person, as was said to have been so in ancient days, the dawn of history.   Complete training of *jinzal* proving to be unattainable, the abandoned plan had periodically half-revived through the centuries, and over and again failed to come to fruition.   Sudden mutinies of what seemed well-drilled companies led to periodic massacre of the trainers. The need for secrecy, not only from the realm at large, but from the body of the *Atarlum*, which Iruvakh believed would at all times have condemned the attempt and its objectives, was equally an obstacle; Iruvakh conjectured that the times of the Lunu's revival generally coincided with the tenure of a Patriarch elevated from within the *Manadilum*, always the Order where zealots for a rebirth of Ancient Owan, cleansed of all alien institutions, were to be found.

In latter years, the scheme resurrected itself, he had been told, in reaction to the sweeping reforms of Plakhsila *Kímukoi*, with his determination to curtail the established privileges of the Old Blood, and exclude religious considerations entirely from qualification for high office. With the erection of most of its present buildings, in this period the Lunu Jinzalladhiyu came to look much as it did today. But accession of Banak, first *rabhsai* of Mixed blood, made inevitable the attempt by traditionalists to seize back the power, and in its last stages chief architect and driving force had been the man, for long years *Menadhi*, Head of the Teaching Order, who eventually became the Patriarch ga-Owan-Alladh XX.

"Patriarch no longer," and Kamin-Tolagh saw the irresistible connection to defeat of the *jinzal* armies. "He has retired. His last official act was investiture of Rodlakh *Rabhsai*."

"Can you doubt, *Asai*, His abdication was forced by Rodlakh, under threat of exposure?"

"If what you tell me is true, and if Rodlakh learned it, why would he stop at the threat? This is a story that could bring down the *Mankh'*."

"*Asai*," Iruvakh remonstrated. "Not everyone who stands out against the racial obsessions of the *Atarlum* would wish to see the *Mankh'* entirely destroyed. I never did, and I quit my *atarlayum* rather than be part of assailing the realm."

Yet, Kamin-Tolagh thought, he had been part of it, continuing to act as envoy of the Lunu to the tribes. That he had survived his retirement was due, on his own admission, to a solemn oath (now considered null) not to reveal what he knew, and to the usefulness of his skill with languages — to which could be added his descent from an old family of high standing in the realm, hereditary wardens to the once-flourishing port of Irbat. And all the while Kamin-Tolagh's remorseless mind was obliging him to see how well this preposterous tale fit in with what he had observed for himself, the mystery of Rodlakh's sudden ability to influence the *Mankh'*, beyond any *rabhsai* since the dominating Plakhsila. While no one, till now, had charged he had compelled Owan-Alladh's abdication, Rodlakh was rumored to have been consulted in choice of a successor, a concession with few precedents, and had now promulgated a revised Treaty, which the new Patriarch, ga-Dozhusai-Arbhali, intended to sign, promising every future *rabhsai* a voice in the elevation of a Patriarch. Another clause was said to stipulate reduction in strength of the *Adanum* to the level of the personal bodyguard it had been intended for, and there were whispers about further restrictions on Patriarchal prerogatives. This gossiped supersession of the famous Treaty of the Wind Caves had met with bitter complaint in predictable places, such as Lavsila's circle, although Kamin-Tolagh's mother had been uncharacteristically silent about all these developments. He supposed Petakoi, strategist as well as devotee, was biding her time — and in a dark corner of his brain, remembering her intimacy with Owan-Alladh, another and unthinkable idea began to stir into life. But not even Lavsila, with a conspiracy for every occasion, had been able to suggest the source of Rodlakh's extraordinary power over the *Mankh'*; Iruvakh supplied one of overwhelming plausibility.

Yet still with apparent impossibilities. Stressing how much of what he recounted was first-hand experience, Iruvakh claimed when he first came here, a dozen years ago, it had been in the company of Owan-Alladh, then *Menadhi*, and he had seen him here a dozen times since; in all his account there was constant coming and going between Lunu and *Mankh'* or the Island. Yet all those journeys, and many others, some including arms and armed men, the wives of *Adanum* officers, supplies, even furniture, had to be made in secret; they could hardly have landed at Kamsilat, made their way to Drin Navuna, and crossed the Frontier into Landegh without questions. Possible, Kamin-Tolagh supposed, to cross from the Island and make landing in uninhabited parts of the western shores of Arnan, to find or make a way westward through wild lands only nominally protected by the realm, but in speaking about the flight of the last survivors from the Lunu and their likely desire to reach the Island, Iruvakh had shaken his head dubiously over the difficulties of such a journey.

At this point, his skepticism returned full-force. "Before the War changed everything," with a prim show of patience, "and for centuries, they have come and gone by the way I came here, the ancient road through Kargan baDulfu — " the huge, reputedly impassable range confining the westward taper of Kamin-Tolagh's own province between mountains and Arnan.

"They would have to pass through Kargul," Kamin-Tolagh objected.

"Through Peframi, yes, as I did. The road, as the wise know, begins at the upper end of the Gorge."

"There is a road there, yes, for pilgrimages to the tomb of *Kirova-Kindhri*, in the hills above the Gorge."

"It was not. Not before they needed a new excuse for using that road. *Kirova-Kindhri* died a thousand years ago, and the first hint he was buried anywhere other than the Island, his home, was heard almost in living memory. Has anyone kept count of the devout who went that way, and how many of them returned to Peframi? For heavier supplies to be brought by that road, however, required a powerful ally within your province."

"My father would have told me about such an arrangement."

"Your father, as did your grandfather Tobhan, took an Island wife." Wives, according to Iruvakh, chosen for the *Nim'* so the breeders of *jinzal* would have a dependable friend in the Great House at Inilun Barabhi. The autumn season, Kamin-Tolagh was told, when his father normally went north to hunt with Vinilat of Dramal, was a favorite time for traffic between Lunu and Island — and he did not need reminding his mother had a small country estate of her own by the vineyards of Peframi Gorge, where she spent much time when Tovakh was away.

Kamin-Tolagh tried to treat this with the anger it ought to deserve, but now so many puzzling, remembered things fell into place, oddities recalled from earliest childhood; he was overwhelmed by recognition: his mother's passionate devotion to the *Atarlum*, beyond any partiality she showed for her adopted province; how, when he was nearing manhood his father had told him privately he had never interfered between Petakoi and her Island mutterers, because with skill her friendship with the *Mankh'* could be made to advance the purposes of Kargul. Clearly, the opposite was true. When Tovakh fought at Dônshei to prevent Rodlakh's accession, it was to establish a Protectorate, with himself as Protector, Rodlakh's younger brother nominal *rabhsai*, a plan put forward by Petakoi, with the alleged support of the Patriarch. And all the time they were merely using Kargul as a distraction, till their *jinzal* armies came to sweep away the House Arbhai-Navu, and put a puppet True *Rabhsai* in its place.

His father had been wounded at Dônshei. Fingering the scar along his jaw, he reflected his mother had come near causing the deaths of both husband and her only son.

While Iruvakh could speak about how often he had heard Petakoi mentioned as a staunch ally, more than once supplying arms and equipment from stores of Kargul's own cavalry, how she had remained to this day their informant at Kadon Dinul, Kamin-Tolagh had evidence he had not; the near-hysterical fervor, till now inexplicable, with which she had argued against his riding with this expedition. All overwrought and mainly untenable reasons she had given for him not to go to the West must have been fears for her safety, not his; she was terrified he would discover too much.

If Petakoi had been a chief creator of the Jinzai War, was Rodlakh aware? Her circumspect public behavior in recent weeks, which Kamin-Tolagh had ascribed to his new captaincy, could be read either way, caution of a woman who is afraid she'll be found out, or chastened face of one controlled by the same threat Rodlakh held over the *Mankh'*, public revelation of her crimes. But while Kamin-Tolagh could understand why Rodlakh, feeling the realm still had uses for the better aspects of the *Atarlum*, might prefer to coerce the *Mankh'* with threat of destruction, rather than let loose forces to actually accomplish it, he could not think of any use the *rabhsai* had for Petakoi, or why he would wish to spare his most implacable enemy.

Well, if Rodlakh didn't know, he was not going to learn from Kamin-Tolagh, who would do all he could to prevent anyone else from informing him. The case should be dealt with as a family matter; Petakoi's crimes began and ended with dishonoring the House baKargul, and he had little doubt his father, discovering how he'd been duped over the years, would want to kill her. The other Great Houses would approve, urge it, once they knew what she had done.

Time was no measure of life, and neither were events; he had lived a whole year thronged with different women and affecting him less than this inactive hour, in which his life was not so much changed as emptied of all its most cherished assumptions, setting him adrift with nothing but his own resources, doubtful he would ever trust again.

He had begun still baKarguli, unalterably Owani, and yet newly convinced a realm ruled by outworn ideas of racial purity was a dead ideal. Determined to keep the oaths he had sworn to Rodlakh, he cherished a half-formed idea that by being in the position of real power he would alter his parents, or make them not matter; they would come to seem laughably old-fashioned with their ridiculous genealogies, their nostalgia for glories that never were. Religiously passive himself, he had not doubted his mother's true devotion, nor the sincerity of the *Atarlum* whose aspirations she embraced: she was distressed, he would have said, by the unexpected eclipse of her great friend, Owan-Alladh, but in time would align herself with the new Patriarch's milder principles, which, as a true daughter, she was required to believe proceeded from *aën'modha*, that special, infallible insight of all who occupied the Golden Seat. He had known she was capable of duplicity, but would never have dreamt his blunt, unsubtle father, the entire House baKargul, were mere elements to serve her cold contrivances, just as he could not have imagined Owan-Alladh making cynical use of belief itself: there was no conceivable greater good to justify breeding *jinzal* to use against the realm, only the desire for power at any price.

His decision to join with Rodlakh's allies in the Jinzai War had already separated him from older concerns of Kargul, the *Atarlum*, the frayed and corrupted dream of a restored Owan, and these fresh revelations would affect him less if, at the same time, they had not shown him how far he was from a trusted member of Rodlakh's inmost circle. Not his mother's part, perhaps, but the rest of the story must have long been known to the *rabhsai*, to Âna, Dolvid, Shumat — perhaps down to the lowly level of Dorrmas, and nameless squadron-leaders in the Army of the West — but had been carefully kept from Kamin-Tolagh, without whose bold rejection of the heirloom enmities of his house the war would have been lost. As his father had been dupe of Petakoi and the Patriarch, so he had been Rodlakh's. For what reason but lack of trust had the secret been kept from him? did Rodlakh think he would not have fought against *jinzal* knowing they were the Patriarch's, his mother's *jinzal*? How, too, could they have imagined he was going to be kept in the dark? The appearance of Iruvakh could not be foreseen, but it was almost certain he would encounter somebody who could enlighten him, unlike Rhinval not yet terrified into silence.

He called Shumat friend, Rodlakh his liege. A principle of fealty was that oaths bound both giver and receiver: neither old allegiance nor the new had dealt fairly with Kamin-Tolagh.

Iruvakh, with difficulty, had at last begun to believe his revelations came as news. Curiously echoing Petakoi, he said, "As Captain of the Household, *Asai*, you will need to cultivate your own circle, men and women who can keep you informed."

That was the moment when Lavsila found them. Flustered, he apologized for being delayed; debating the value of furnishings in the great hall of the so-called Residence, he had only just been told Kamin-Tolagh's message for Shumat, which, he was blandly convinced, contained an implicit request for him to join Kamin-Tolagh in questioning the prisoner. The meeting he came upon, so little of an interrogation, was a new puzzle, and Kamin-Tolagh did not say he had deliberately omitted bringing him into this discussion. Now, with Iruvakh showing tedious signs of multiplying anecdotes to demonstrate his long-standing disenchantment with the aims of Lunu Jinzalladhiyu, the interruption came near being welcome.

"What's this you were saying about wine?" Kamin-Tolagh asked.

Sure the soldiers who had slept here could not have discovered the cache, the little man led the way through to the rear of the house, which, because of the backsloping cliff, extended farther than at the lower level. With a manner somewhere between an unctuous host and a Bathrâd stallkeeper displaying his wares, Iruvakh pulled aside a green wall-hanging to expose a stone door. Perfectly balanced on its unseen pivot, bolt pulled back, it swung open at a slight push, to reveal a cool but dry and airy natural cave, where shelves held a bewildering array of bottles, jars and earthen crocks, while wheels of cheese matured in isolation, and fragrant hams and sausages dangled overhead.

Iruvakh reached for a squat earthen bottle, pitch-sealed and stamped with the Bees-wing emblem. "Island wine. Few outside the *Mankh'* have tasted it, except officers of the *Adanum*. A little heavy for some tastes." He passed the crock to Kamin-Tolagh, and reached for a more familiarly-shaped bottle. "This one you'll know, *Asai* — a Peframi Gorge red. This is from Eighteen Lambarr, the hot summer, and just coming into its own."

Kamin-Tolagh, again seized by a sensation of unreality, nodded recognition of the vintage, wondering what bland-faced Lavsila was making of the references to *Mankh'* and Kargul.

Iruvakh found cups, complaining someone had made off with Kemunai's superb goblets of Island glass. From below among the effects of officers sleeping here Lavsila brought kiln-bread, stale, but eatable with slices of ham and cheese they cut. Striking how Lavsila took Iruvakh in stride, oblivious to his ragged appearance, asking minor questions about details of life at the Lunu, what they did for fresh meat, milk, whether they had weavers, cordwainers, armorers here. There was, Kamin-Tolagh learned in answer to the last, a well-appointed forge, for which charcoal had come by the pony-load from tribal country.

One of the rare subjects on which Lavsila could be cogent and even informative was the taming of water, and as he questioned the little man about wells and wind-pumps, aqueducts and terraces, Iruvakh almost visibly resumed the dark-green robe of an *edhradu*. Water, he assented, was everything here.

"I have tried to teach principles of good husbandry to the tribes. At best, it's like trying to cure the bad habits of children who can never be whipped. I show better ways to plant and nurture crops, tell them how they must vary their crops and leave some land idle, but they almost always return to their old ways. With enough water, they could see for themselves how what I teach can work, but any year when what little rain there is fails to come, crops fail, too, and people are going to die, men, women, especially the children first, no matter what method is used for growing."

Draining into Kamin-Tolagh's cup the end of the thick Island wine, very strong, with a faint, not-unpleasant tang of prunes in the aftertaste, Iruvakh used his little knife to pick at the seal on the Peframi Gorge wine.

"There are still the women to be restored to their homes."

"Your officer told me they had all been killed. To tell the truth, I expected no less, knowing what your mission here would be, but it's a waste."

About to protest they had not come as murderers of women, Kamin-Tolagh caught himself, and explained *only* pregnant women and recent mothers had been slaughtered; perhaps two dozen of the *jinz'onoyul* remained, and could be returned to their tribe, as had always been the intent. "You said this head-man of the Man-mani agreed to take them back?"

"At a price," speaking, as they all were, with the increasing care of those who feel they may soon be affected by wine. "To tell truth, I was obliged to offer Sranadatta a quantity of weapons, clothing and food — goods I knew would be left behind when the Lunu was abandoned."

Kamin-Tolagh with a lordly wave agreed, ignoring start of a protest from Lavsila; with the expedition lacking pack-animals to carry back many of the valuables here, they could honor Iruvakh's promise at no loss to themselves.

"They can't go unescorted, *Asai*. In the wilds, the Hill Froghul' — " making a somewhat uncertain swooping motion with his hand — "would snap them up as eagles their prey."

"They shall have an escort. I'll lead it myself, and you shall show us some of your tribal country, and talk your Froghulú to this — " the name eluded him — "this head-man." Kamin-Tolagh was all at once hungry for an adventure which would take him from here, give him some days away from the company of those he'd given his trust to — from Shumat. His life, he perceived, required reinventing.

Iruvakh, repeating the name, Sranadatta, courteously corrected Kamin-Tolagh's remark; the Man-mani language was not a Froghuli tongue. While cups were half-filled with the last of the lordly Peframi wine, he gave a complicated disquisition on different branches of the Froghulú.

"Once," Kamin-Tolagh said, "I knew a little of the syllabary glyphs." For the son of a *Nimu*, he had been considered learned.

"They are not easy," Iruvakh conceded.

"My sister, at thirteen, could speak more than a thousand lines from *Frela'olurai Larghayi* — " the famous Epic of Larghai.

"I myself," Lavsila, having left, and returned with another bottle of the Peframi, "wrote songs in my youth."

"Who didn't?" Kamin-Tolagh said.

Iruvakh considered this. "Not my father. He was never young."

"Mine is just the opposite," Kamin-Tolagh confided. "If a man could become an old campaigner by telling tales for thirty years of old campaigns he had no part in, my father would outdo Sebhal. When he got his battle at last, he had the ground, he had the numbers, and he lost the fight."

"There was treachery, too," Lavsila said.

"I am named in songs of the Jinzai War. I can have any woman of the realm."

"Any?" Lavsila rote-challenged.

"The *rabhsayu* is of no birth. She also would have been killed, if I had not prevented it. Her father's a farmer."

"Yet we must have farmers," Iruvakh, solemnly.

Lavsila said, "Among stores, we found a great quantity of *raminat*-leaves. *Raminat*! You can't tell me that's grown in these parts. There must have been regular dealing between this place and the Island."

Word was brought by a palpably nervous Household file-leader that Shumat was awake, and desired further information about the captive. Leaving Lavsila, who'd had more than his share of the third bottle and was starting to hum, Kamin-Tolagh, after splashing his face with cold water from the unfailing spring, rode back to the crossways with Iruvakh, pack-pony still dejectedly trailing behind. Mid-afternoon and warm, and already the shadow of the westward rim was advancing across the training-grounds of the *jinzal*.

Before preceding Kamin-Tolagh into the Residence, Iruvakh rummaged in his saddle-bag, and produced a small flask. "For your Captain's sickness," he explained.

Shumat was said to have swallowed some broth, and was sitting up in his bed, though his chin was dipping to his chest. At Kamin-Tolagh's signal cough, he raised his head, and shook it like a fly-plagued dog.

"This is Iruvakh," and with caustic emphasis, "formerly at-Iruvakh, *atarlai* of the Edhrodilum."

Shumat's bleared eyes met his, and regarded him for long seconds. "I had my orders."

"You are unwell," Iruvakh, in advance of any salutation. Taking up a bedside drinking-cup half-filled with water, he poured from his flask a slow, brown liquid, unmistakably *ga-raminat*, the sticky, unpleasant-tasting medicine of the *Mankh'*. Shumat, with disgusted face but no apparent fear of poison, swallowed the forbidding dose, and shuddered.

"Iruvakh," Kamin-Tolagh said, "knows the tribe of the *jinzai*-mothers, and speaks their language."

"Man-mani," dully.

"Exactly, Captain," Iruvakh said.

"He is to guide us to their country, so we may take back their women." He was mouthing words with unnatural clarity, as if Shumat was deaf, or half-witted.

"Good. How is it you were left behind?"

Iruvakh began an explanation, once again insisting on the unofficial nature of his standing with the Lunu, but before he could finish, Shumat was asleep. The little man tugged up the blanket to cover the shoulders, and automatically tested Shumat's forehead with the back of a hand less that of a scholar than of a laborer, callused and capable.

"How ill is he?"

"I am not a *ramidu*. The medicine should help him. The fever is slight."

When they emerged from the Residence, Iruvakh suggested he should go to where the women were, tell them to be ready for imminent departure. "It's for the best," he said resignedly. "But this won't bring any rejoicing. A Man-mani woman's life is harsh. They had reasonable treatment here, as brood-mares, not so much for themselves as for the foals they bear."

Seeing Freighanai idle, waiting for orders, Kamin-Tolagh told him to take a couple of men from the personal squadron and act as Iruvakh's escort, whether for his safety or to remind him he was technically a captive being left an open question.

The officers, men from the General Cavalry, had come back to Kemunai's house where they had slept, bringing food with them, including a smoking chunk of meat, about a quarter of a roasted goat. Disconcerted, like guilty stable-boys, when Kamin-Tolagh appeared, they were relieved to find him affable, and shared their food, for which he recompensed them with an indifferent bottle of pink Ninkufu wine, not revealing the treasure-house it came from. Lavsila, dozing, woke to share some of the meat.

"What became of our little rat of the Westlands? He's spent time in the realm? Yes, if you had lived your life at Kadon Dinul, you would know his kind very well."

"What kind?"

"The speech," loftily. "He would wish to pass as a man of true breeding — you hear the same in the Craft Families, brass to true gold, too much glitter. How did he come here?"

"Horseback," bending to loosen his boots. Lavsila's estimate of the man came late, and was interesting for being so badly off-target. Arriving here expecting to join in bullying a prisoner, he had met a serious competitor for Kamin-Tolagh's ear. Kamin-Tolagh smiled privately; Lavsila was jealous.

No, the women were not happy to be going home; some were sullen, others weeping or angry. Iruvakh with what soon became excessive tolerance presided over their marshalling, soothing a woman stridently unwilling to leave behind a massive oak chest, given to her, she claimed, by what she called her husband, an officer no doubt lost in the war. The wrangle was punctuated by throaty wailing of a small girl, her daughter, and a short distance away two younger women were disputing ownership of a shirt or light jacket, and would soon stumble on a fair though nullifying solution, if they continued to jerk, each at one of the sleeves. Others were gloomily going through belongings, deciding what was truly indispensable; the women were to ride pack-ponies, which Kamin-Tolagh had decreed must not be overloaded; the remaining animals would be carrying supplies, including water, and the goods promised the head-man.
    At last resigned to abandoning her chest, its owner untied the lid, and began sorting through its contents. Not everything she was reluctant to part with could be of much use to her; a bright Heartland-dyed kerchief, a pair of slippers made for a large-footed man, and Kamin-Tolagh felt equally assailed by impatience and the oppressive force of sentiment. Men of the implacable *Adanum*, brought here to be stud-bulls to these women, had yet made pets of them. Several, he admitted, slender and smooth-armed with a golden bloom to their skin, would be worth the bedding, if he had not known a *jinzai* infant might be the result; still unimaginable a creature so thick and ponderous could be product of admixture between the small,

slight Man-mani, and his own race, typically slender, among whom Kamin-Tolagh was unusually tall — or, for that matter, such ugliness come from blending two different kinds of good looks.

Lavsila, at the head of the baggage-train, came down from the warehouses and called out Shumat was up, and wanted words with Kamin-Tolagh before the start. Leaving too-patient Iruvakh and a brusquer Freighanai to supervise loading, Kamin-Tolagh rode up the slope and through the gateway. At the Residence, he found Shumat in the kitchens, continuing his breakfast, or beginning a second one. He was shaved, and had the newborn look of convalescence, robust and fragile at once.

He asked, "What men are you taking with you?"

"Four squadrons, and fifty mounted bows." Kamin-Tolagh, seeing Shumat's thick eyebrows go unevenly up, explained: "According to Iruvakh, there are wild men of the hills, who might attack a lesser riding, for a chance at such a prize — the women, that is, as well as the goods we're carrying." Shumat understood without telling that while neither of them believed any number of tribal warriors could succeed against a single squadron of regulars, the object was to avoid casualties by making the force large enough to be sure they would not try.

"How long?"

"With the women, it will be a full two-day journey, perhaps into a third. Allow a week; if it takes longer, I'll send word back. I am taking the Kargul' squadrons." He looked Shumat full in the eyes. "My mother would enjoy the joke."

If he knew about Petakoi, Shumat could not ignore the implied accusation. After fighting down a sudden yawn, he said quietly, "My advice was to tell you everything. Rodlakh *Rabhsai* would not allow it, but I told him I couldn't lie; I'd give a truthful answer to anything you asked. As I have."

"And not a syllable more."

"Tam — Rodlakh's wish was to avoid, if possible, an open breach in your family. He values your service, past and future."

First reply to come to mind was an angry one, that House baKargul could manage its affairs without the solicitude of Banak's brood. That set aside, Kamin-Tolagh said, "Or was afraid to risk confusing my loyalties? Am I still on trial, after Kamsilat? Did he think I might after all approve of what my mother helped Owan-Alladh to attempt?"

"You were never mistrusted. You have my oath, no one for a moment questioned your allegiance."

Yes, but that was easily said. "It is of no consequence," abruptly. "If I am going to be Captain of Rodlakh's Household, I have to be given trust."

"As you are, Tam."

"Not merely relied on to follow the *rabhsai*'s orders. I have to be trusted with his thoughts, as you are, or Dolvid is. Nothing is to be gained by debating this. We came to see the end of *jinzal*, and the *jinz'onoyul*, back with their own people, are no longer a danger. Till you are fully recovered, Gremnivai and Dorrmas between them can arrange patrols and watches — if one doesn't butcher all those the other doesn't prattle to death." He took a deep breath. "As we see, not all cruelties and crimes ride under the banner of Kargul. Dorrmas will make a fine leader of cavalry in our next war against pregnant women and infants."

"Nevertheless, he's a good officer, when his orders are clear." A chill and an authority had come into the voice, and Kamin-Tolagh, instantly ashamed of trying to provoke a quarrel, was too taut with righteous anger to make amends.

"It is of no consequence," he repeated.

After a heavy silence, Shumat started a tentative grin. "I hope you're not taking the Karguli squadron that calls itself the Zelkovani."

"Yaënsilat's squadron," mystified. "No, they're staying here."

"Good." Shumat took a small loaf from the table and broke it. "A man of that squadron, Sedhsilai, I think is his name, has taken charge of the bakehouse — his father's trade, I hear. I never tasted better bread." He took a large bite from one half of the loaf, while offering the other.

Kamin-Tolagh accepted and ate, not because he was hungry, but in some peculiar way to signify his belief Shumat had been against deceiving him. There remained some advice about preventing straggling among the women, and keeping any scouts he sent out in sight of the main body. Their parting, after all, was cordial enough.

At first the direction was due south, on what was called a trail, often hard to pick up on the arid and pebbled plain discovered after crossing a low, brown ridge. The first day, Iruvakh said, was worst part of the journey, through country nearly devoid of vegetation, way bearing well to the eastward of their destination so as to include the one place where, from late winter to early summer, water was usually to be had. There would be none now, but they would find a welcome clump of trees there. That was this region, Kamin-Tolagh thought sourly, where a few trees were an event to be anticipated, like sight of an ancient bridge or celebrated city on roads of the realm. He with Iruvakh and Lavsila had been riding with the lead squadron of bows, the one commanded by Noldar, though they called themselves Galt's Men, after an admired leader, now dead. This happened on occasion; to the very brink of the Night there'd been a legion of the Empire calling itself Larghai's, nearly four centuries after the great captain's death, and there was now a squadron in the Army of the West known as Sebhal's; he wondered whether, a hundred years from now, Kamin-Tolagh's Squadron would still ride with Kargul or perhaps the Household.

Lavsila, to make the ride yet more tedious, had a theory. At first reminding he was no slavish adherent of the *Mankh'*, with all its niggling points of doctrine, he produced the *however*, with the notion, hardly new, that practical wisdom was often embodied in what was taken purely for a tenet of faith.

"If true it is by mating our best to these women that *jinzal* are born — "

"It is," Iruvakh, with finality.

"And how often have we been warned about the dangers of mingling Owani blood with that of lesser races?"

Kamin-Tolagh said, "The women here could say equally it is their blood that is being defiled, and who is to say which is the lesser race?"

"You can't be serious, *Asai*;" Lavsila, genuinely scandalized.

"But certainly," Iruvakh contributed, "it is the Owanil, not so much the tribe itself, who have been vigilant to keep Manmani blood free of any mixture, except with theirs when they wanted *jinzal*." From the back of his small horse he looked up wryly at Lavsila on his *pefrai*. "The opposite lesson might be adduced, sir. Only purest of Owani blood can father *jinzal*, this has been many times proven; if ever there was a failure, it could invariably be traced to a forgotten or unadmitted admixture in the ancestry of the sire. If, then, the *Mankh'* had, for all the years since the Return, encouraged rather than condemned free intermarriage between Owanil and Others, then soon, if not already by now, *jinzal* could never again be fathered."

"Then, after all," another of Lavsila's effortless shifts of stance, "Raëdh may have a purpose, even for these monstrous creatures."

"Oh, I have heard that before, more than once," Iruvakh, bitingly.

A dark island in a sea of roasted and broken stone, the expected clump of trees drifted slowly out of midday shimmer, tall and scrawny with smooth, brown bark and sprays of pale arrowhead leaves, clustered along both sides of a wound in the desert skin, where grey mud baked hard no less than coarse grass and tough bushes, was a sign water came here. In partial shade, they rested, resuming the journey in latter afternoon.

Still their course made no decisive turn westward. Somewhat greener lands, scarcely less harsh, met them with the hills; trail, more clearly defined now, a pale scar winding south, often climbed the skirts of matted uplands. To their left, the riders began passing scattered stands of stunted trees, but beyond and stretching for miles began a bare, blighted country, level, black, in places streaked with what must be salt, but was absurdly like windskimmed snow. Remotely might be the gleam of water, but there was a haze that muddled vision, so land and sky and conjectured sea dissolved into uncertainty.

Late, the sun moved into cloud like dirty smoke rising behind the hills, heralding the coming of evening; Kamin-Tolagh questioned whether their progress was fast enough to reach the intended camping-place before dark. At length, with the sun gone for good, and light beginning in earnest to fail, they accomplished a long, gradual climb, and looked down into what might be marginally a more hospitable country, dreary waste to their left ceding to frequent islets of spiky shrub, patches of what could be enormous thistle mixed with spear-grass. Ahead, trees, though still dwarfed and tormented, were more numerous, and there were grudging stipples of pallid grass. Near foot of the downslope, the trail forked, one way continuing to wriggle southward, while the other made a sweeping loop right, starting to climb before being lost to view in an ascending gully.

On the farther side of the trail's wide curve, Iruvakh indicated a dark meander of bushes and trees, a camping-place used in the past, where there would be water.

Kamin-Tolagh nodded. Guthdar, of the mounted bows, brother of Noldar, enough like him to be a twin, though in fact three years the younger, pointed south to where a thin ribbon of smoke coiled lazily against a pale, luminous segment of yet-unclouded sky. "*Asai*?"

"The Laughing Owl," Iruvakh supplied, a translation for the name of a tribe. Their main villages were a dayride to the south, but these were the borders of their country. "On this eastward side of the hills are five tribes, who call themselves separate peoples speaking distinct languages, though they are really all varied dialects of the Froghulú. In the entire northern Froghushei, only the Man-mani has no Froghuli blood."

This, he noted, accorded with the tradition that when outlying regions of the First Empire began to be overrun by savage invaders, the Man-mani had been transplanted here from west of Flamûrai by the Owani, forcibly displacing a Froghuli tribe, which accounted for the permanent hostility of other tribes for the Man-mani.

"And the hills which are spine of the Froghushei," he continued, gesturing at the densely matted uplands, "belong to the Hill Froghul, who make war on everyone, and are feared by everyone. The land they hold, you see, is too poor to feed them; they scorn tending of crops as unmanly, though they herd some goats. But they can feed themselves only by raiding the valley tribes, east and west. They are short in stature, but for their size as fierce as any *jinzai*, and they can move through dense brush swiftly and silently as snakes. They raid and vanish; the valley tribes think of them as an occurrence, like brush fires, or drought, or a sickness — a misfortune it is useless to fight."

"But they're Froghul, these?" Noldar, with the gleaming interest of someone half-Froghuli himself.

"They are anything you want to call them. Their language, true, is nearer the Froghulú you hear in the Colony, or Lunu Tezh', and they have your skill of shooting from the saddle. They say they can foretell the future by throwing knotted cords — "

"That's a Froghuli way," Guthdar said.

"They claim to be truest, purest of all Froghul' peoples," Iruvakh went on. "But you see, they count descent only from father to son, ignoring the mother. The tribe has no women."

That startled Kamin-Tolagh, but Lavsila laughed. "Then the valley tribes should soon be rid of this plague."

"I did not say there were no women among them. For wives, or, as I should say, for the mothers of their sons, they have always gone raiding, so their blood is really a mixture of all valley tribes. Women they carry off do not count as part of the tribe, and can mother only sons — any girl-children they bear are left on an open hillside to die. They make no settled dwellings, no huts or villages, as even the meanest of valley peoples build. They sleep in tents of sewn goatskins, but seldom stay in any one place long. Strange ways."

"Strange," Noldar vigorously echoed; the exposure of girl-infants had shocked him, and he was now sure these were no true Froghul.

Like the one by the edge of Landegh, the stream when they came to it was a slight trickle given lavish elbow-room within terraced banks. The infrequent rain, Iruvakh said, when it did come, scoured away too rapidly to help the land.

"Wasted," Lavsila said, and Kamin-Tolagh again heard the competitive note in his dealings with Iruvakh. "These people need to be taught how to make water work for them."

"We've tried teaching many things. They are set in their ways, and would have to be bullied into change. With power to enforce their advice, six good *atarlal* of the *Edhrodilum* could transform these lands."

"One man who knows water runs downhill could do it," Lavsila said.

Night became chill and damp, but with unlimited fuel to be garnered from the hillside, they built huge fires, bringing the additional blessing of hot drinks. With a rare show of amusement, Freighanai reported young Kambanal, who had charge of watches, hearing about the fierce Hill Froghul, had boasted they would never dare attack, because even this forsaken place would have heard about the cavalry of Kargul, the fame of Kamin-Tolagh *Asai*.

"Not their kind of fight," Iruvakh said. "Once in the open, they're no match for regular troops, as was seen some years

ago, when a raiding-party tried to stand against a squadron of —
" his mouth shaped *Adanum*, but he discreetly changed it to " —
cavalry. A tile I lost for my bargaining with Sranadatta," he
confided. "In the past, he would do anything to have our help
against Hill Froghul' raiders."

"The valley tribes," Kamin-Tolagh said. "They must
outnumber the hill people?"

"Oh, by far. Hill Froghul are hard to count, but the
Laughing Owl alone must have twice the people." Seeing where
he was going, he explained the valley tribes were often divided
by long intervening miles of wilderness, which, together with
their own rivalries, made alliance difficult, with nearest tribes
commonly bitterest rivals.

"What would they quarrel over," Lavsila wanted to know,
"with so little to call their own?"

"The few things they do have are that much more
precious to them," Iruvakh answered.   "They differ over
pastureland, crops, spices, ownership of livestock, but chiefly
over streams and wells. With what I believed was support from
the Lunu, I did try to foster an alliance, over several years — I
had all the negotiating to do, and that was a wearisome business,
back and forth, with each head-man's exceptions and demurs.
Here in the east, the Chon'la, one of the relatively prosperous
tribes, took the lead. Somehow, the Hill Froghul scented the
forming alliance, and descended full force on the Chon'la. When
merely raiding, they are careful not to give mortal wounds to a
tribe — "

"Very considerate bandits," Lavsila interjected.

"Of themselves. The valley tribes do the planting and
husbanding for the Hill Froghul, and furnish mothers for their
sons. This one time they came to destroy. Food they could not
carry off, they burned; every man and boy, all the livestock they
could find, was killed. The smoke from burning villages and
fields could be seen from fifty miles. The Chon'la can never
recover, and news of the massacre spread faster than fire among
the other tribes. When I tried to reopen the question of acting

together, all at once head-men couldn't follow my pronunciation. At best, it could only have been a defensive alliance. In their hills, they are impregnable."

"For these cowed valley tribes."

A short laugh. "After the rape of the Chon'la, the Lunu demonstrated its displeasure by sending two punitive squadrons up into the hills, to take revenge. After five days' hunting, those who were lucky rode or scrambled out of the brush — of the worst-hit squadron, only nineteen came out, and none of those without either wounds or burns."

"Burns?" Kamin-Tolagh was troubled; the pride of the *Adanum Plakh'* was equal to that of his own cavalry.

"They use fire as an ally. They know the way of winds, and places where they'll be safe. Fortunately for the Lunu's prestige with the valley tribes," with sour irony, "our cavalry, a few days later, surprised a careless band of raiders out in the open, and cut it into dogsmeat."

A question, the habit of military analysis concluded, of depriving them of cover, and closing before they could bring their bows into play; whoever had commanded the men of the *Adanum* had been criminally stupid to send them up where *pefral* would be immobilized, and hostile bows most effective. A few added squadrons, Iruvakh complained, could have been used to coerce the tribes into alliance before the Hill Froghul' could respond.

Except after prolonged and satisfying exertions in bed, he seldom slept longer than a few hours, while Iruvakh, if anything, appeared to need even less sleep; they sat together late, tending the fire. Though he had answered several hundred questions that day, the man was still ready for more; like another product of the *Mankh'*, Dolvid, he retained the *Atarlum* passion for complete explanations, but while Dolvid relished for its own sake the sharing of knowledge, Iruvakh must require the sense of importance he derived from displaying his store of information.

Discussing how potential mothers of *jinzal* were chosen, he revealed it was no simple question of mating Owani to Man-maniyu. "Sons born to that union, are Mixed, certainly, but otherwise like any child. It is when the daughters, or daughters of daughters, again mate with Owani, that *jinzal* sons are born, so my task was to seek out Man-mani women with any trace of Owani admixture, perhaps from half an age back; once the seed of *jinzayum* is introduced in that first mingling, it is passed, mother to daughter, through many generations, and evidently never dies out. That is why the daughters born at the Lunu to the *jinz'onoyul* were always kept track of."

"This, then, would be the meaning of the silver ring they have in their earlobes?" Kamin-Tolagh had noted even the smallest girls wore it.

"The right earlobe, yes." Beaming, Iruvakh reminded him of when he had pleased his *Mankh'* tutor years ago.

He spoke about another mark of identification, about which the soldiery ought to be cautioned. "As well as the four wives Man-mani tradition permit him as head-man, many young women, girls, of the tribe belong to Sranadatta."

"What do you mean, belong to him?" It was grotesque.

"It is their way. To explain in full, I have to tell you about the Sranadatta clan, who rule the Man-mani."

Kamin-Tolagh reached behind him to find a substantial chunk of wood for the fire. Out of the darkness beyond the black gulf of the stream, a weird cry sounded, a screech with a chuckle in it, the *laughing owl* from which the nearby tribe took its name.

In the Man-mani language, Iruvakh told, the word for *law* was "god-thought," and the head-man was able to utter that thought, so within limitations imposed by ancient custom and tradition, will of the head-man became law of the tribe.

Partly because of confused succession arising from the four-wife custom, leading clans had for centuries quarreled and feuded over supremacy. In recent years, the Sranadatta clan, ruthless in their treatment of rivals, obtaining the favor of the Lunu with shrewd promises of cooperation, had emerged as the tribe's sole rulers, and through force, fear, and the accumulation of property, now dominated the Man-mani as no predecessors had.

"The giving to the head-man of unmarried girls — and it must be borne in mind, unmarried with them must always imply, unbedded — has been a practice of the tribe, as return for a favor, to make amends for some insult, real or imagined, perhaps in gratitude for a good harvest. Others are willed to him by their fathers, or come in payment of a debt. With little else of value left to them, many families have given Sranadatta their daughters, and now he owns, I believe, forty to fifty."

"What do you mean, owns them?" irritably. Affronted by the idea, it yet stirred in him an undeniable and voluptuous envy. "He's got four wives, does he also sleep with these fifty others in turn?"

"No doubt he could, *Asai*, and they include the most desirable maidens of the tribe. Remarkable, if you are father of a pretty daughter, how easily you can give offense to Sranadatta, and be obliged to atone. But in the main, the women are simply a sign of his standing. Some become his servants, but for many their ordinary lives are scarcely changed, and they continue to live in the huts of their fathers. He might choose a new wife for himself from among them, or a wife for one of his sons or nephews. Again, a girl might be, as it were, loaned, for the requirements of an honored guest, a high officer of the *Adanum*, or you, *Asai*."

"But that would, by their rules, spoil her for marriage."

"Not these women, not if he says so. No bachelor of the tribe would dare refuse a wife bestowed from Sranadatta's supply, even if she is, by his lights, spoiled a dozen times over. On the other hand, *Asai*, and this is what I wanted to warn you about, one of the girls who bedded with a man of her own choice would without question be put to death."

"*Killed*?" Fathers of Other Race often beat their daughters for being with men, but death was ridiculous.

"You must tell the men of your command, *Asai* — not only to save the girls' lives, but because Sranadatta will be angry if he is made to kill one of his prized maidens."

"Then why do it?"

"It is their way, god-thought. A god here, with the life here, is hard."

"None of my men would take a girl of the tribes against her will."

"With her assent, even at her instigation, they must not."

Kamin-Tolagh's head swam. "But don't the girls know that?"

A resigned gesture. "They are children in many ways; they see only what is in front of them, and fail to keep in mind the consequences. Women have boring lives, and can take a fancy to a newcomer; they have have heard from their mothers, an elder sister, a friend, that most men of the realm are in every way larger than all but a few Man-mani; they want to try that for themselves."

Kamin-Tolagh gave up debate. A man who owned women, not necessarily to sport with, but then would kill them if they gave pleasure to anyone else; women who, aware of the rules, did so, the entire lunacy under the eye, and therefore with the tacit assent of agents sent by a Patriarch constantly praised by his mother as standing for all that was noblest in Owani thought — it was beyond comment. "How, then, can we tell which are the head-man's women?"

"When they become his, often in childhood, two small, shallow cuts are made, here — " touching the point of his cheek. "In time they show as a scar like the head of an arrow."

"He is not much loved by his tribe, this Sranadatta," getting the name right first time.

"The weapons we are carrying are to better arm his bodyguard, and they are not men of the Man-mani at all, and so could not profit by his death."

"If I had understood their intended use, I don't know I would have approved this bribe. I might withhold them, after all."

"If we care about the lives of the women with us, we still need the goodwill of Sranadatta."

"Nevertheless — " Kamin-Tolagh found the taste of retribution in his mouth — "I would enjoy humbling this brander of women."

Morning was abruptly cool and dismal, with a swirling wind bringing now and again the faintest prickle of fine rain, scarcely enough to lay the dust. By the time they had breakfasted and the horses were being readied, the wind had decided on the northeast, soon running the clouds into long tatters.

"It'll be in that quarter for days, now," Iruvakh predicted. "The sky will soon be clear as Kamanta glass. In summer, K'daab's People say it dries up brains, and Man-mani call it a *jinzai* wind; it can blow, hot and dry, for two weeks on end, till anyone might think of murder. It dries the brush, that's certain. A few days of this wind, and any fire that starts must burn till it burns out; it can't be stopped. At this season, it brings cool."

As it did. For the first time, as they climbed up into the pass under a white sun, all the men had their outshirts on, and women were rummaging through their bundles for shawls and cloaks. Brush was denser here, dull green and brown, with outcrops of white rock showing, and in places the dark scarring of fires. The way narrowed, making the going tedious, and clearly the women, as they drew nearer their own country, were doing all they could to prolong any delay.

The sameness of change was bewildering; every turn, each abrupt rise breasted brought a new vista of slopes and domes, with not a hut or a stream or a tall stand of trees, no feature to seize the memory.

Near noon, the column climbing on the curving spine of a long ridge, the leftward embankment all at once fell away, and they had a sudden, startling view of hills tumbling away to the south for many miles, all with a dreamlike clarity, edges sharp and clean in the wind-scrubbed air. A few more paces, a turn right, and Iruvakh pointed to where a cleft drove down between flat crests. "Larghai's Notch. Top of the pass."

"Larghai's?"

"Not an historical name, but that's what our cavalry called it. When Larghai conquered the Froghushei, he may well have come this way. There were forests then."

A ruffle of movement among leading riders, men unslinging their bows and laying them across their saddles. Noldar dropped back to report the column was being watched from cover.

"For the past hour," Iruvakh, from experience, not observation. "The Hill Froghul would never contest passage of the Notch against a force such as this."

"You rode this way alone," Kamin-Tolagh said.

"They are robbers, not murderers. They could see my clothes, and that the pack-pony had no load. The beasts would not be worth stealing."

A forbidding place, nonetheless, heights a massive threat above the dusty trail, and Kamin-Tolagh was not sorry he had brought too many men. Considering what he had learned about the Hill Froghul, the privations they had to endure in this awful country, their frequent hunger, their hardness not moderated by lasting dwellings or women with any influence over them, he murmured, "What soldiers they would make, if they could once be tamed."

Iruvakh came edgewise. "So someone said, an age ago, contemplating *jinzal*."

"They were fools, boys trying to fight as men, choosing swords they can't lift. A victorious army is made of half-squadrons, companies, regiments you know and can direct — " holding up a gauntleted hand to flex. "As you know and can command your own hand."

"I am no authority on armies."

"*Jinzal* have no speech," Kamin-Tolagh expanded. "We saw they could be made to march together, to charge as one, but that is not acting in concert as men can, giving help where it's needed, calling warnings to each other. The best soldiers are comrades with shared memories and shared boasts to live up to — "

"Shared beliefs," Lavsila, piously.

"In their own prowess, yes. They share danger as men with a common objective, not mindless killers." Part of this came out of talk with Shumat and Dolvid, some was new to him as he spoke it, but he noticed Iruvakh glanced at him with new and rather startled respect.

End of the First Part

Kamin-Tolagh

II

6.

Why had all their long dealings with the *jinzai*-breeders done so little to improve Man-mani life? He entered the shabby main village by early light, the stockade enclosing its mound, bundled sticks interspersed with crudely sharpened logs, making a long, saw-toothed shadow on the pebbled valley floor with its sparse grass and pale weed. On each side of the gateway, guards, short men with bows and long shields of stretched goatskin, mounted on a kind of shelf inside the fence, watched but neither challenged nor hailed. Kamin-Tolagh was with Iruvakh, at the head of two squadrons, under both royal colors and his own provincial standard, sky blue with lion depicted. The women, for the time being, had been left below at riverside with Kambanal, who had the other two squadrons and all the bows. Lavsila, his curiosity about the village defeated by indolence, was asleep when Kamin-Tolagh left.

Unaccustomed eyes were stung by sour smoke of cooking-fires. These people cooked outside their huts, often under a kind of flimsy canopy, a plaited roof strung between rickety poles. The dwellings themselves were not much more substantial, though some of the larger huts were raised on platforms, and the mud daubed on wicker walls had been given a wash of lime. Roofs were mainly a tattered thatch; Kamin-

Tolagh did not see glass in the dark window-holes, most closed on the inside with screens of woven reeds.

There were no real streets, only spaces between the irregularly-placed huts, but a well-trodden way ran fairly straight upslope from the gate. As the column jangled on, women cooking or hanging colorless scraps of dismal laundry on poles or under eaves to dry gave dark-eyed stares, and lean goats tethered for milking looked up with even less interest, jaws working without pause.

Iruvakh led the way to the largest of the huts, or rather a structure formed by amalgamation of several, varying in height, age, and skill of construction. At the top of half-a-dozen unequal steps a woman squatted over a quern went on grinding handfuls of grain into meal, but a small child with matted hair, boy or girl, impossible to say, dressed in a ragged smock, left watching the woman to run inside the hut. After a moment a slender young man, taller than many of his tribe, appeared at the reed-hung doorway to greet the dismounted Iruvakh with what must be a courteous gesture, pressing together knuckles of his two clenched hands. Iruvakh replied in kind.

An unemphatic exchange of talk in a language Kamin-Tolagh knew he could never learn, an ear-baffling succession of what seemed the same few mumbling sounds in slightly varied order; Iruvakh's voice when speaking this murky tongue took on a cringing quality unpleasant to Kamin-Tolagh, who was already at the brink of irritation over the reception given him, or lack of one. Last night when they camped Iruvakh had spoken with a couple of passing Man-mani herders; word of the large riding and its purpose had certainly reached the village before now.

After a couple of speeches on either side the young man turned and went back into the hut. The woman on the steps tipped meal into a crude earthen bowl, and put a fresh handful of grain in the quern.

Iruvakh squinted up at Kamin-Tolagh. "Sra-Min-Talla-Tyu," pronouncing it like a name. "A son of the head-man. He says Sranadatta will greet you at Meeting Place."

"When?"

"*Asai*," uncomfortably, "it is not possible to ask that question."

Nearby, Freighanai growled, "Why not? The Captain-*Asai* should say if there is to be a meeting, and when, and where."

Though Kamin-Tolagh gestured for silence he agreed with the sentiment, and his impulse was to quit the village, draw up his entire force outside the gate, and demand this Sranadatta come down to him. Iruvakh was trying to soothe: "He means to honor you, *Asai*. The head-man goes to Meeting Place only to share his god-thought, or to salute another chieftain."

The sloping way broadened to the summit of the mound, a cleared level of beaten earth, far end with a sort of ramshackle pavilion, a raised platform with stone steps at either side and an insubstantial roof or woven canopy supported on poles. Off to his left the ground fell away more sharply, and the village was more populous than he had perceived, slope thickly sown with smaller dwellings, most in poor repair. He remarked he had thought the settlement on the shores of En'Tesh in the Protectorate was poverty, when he landed there during the Jinzai War, but this was far more dismal.

Iruvakh half-smiled, with a tint of condescension. "This is among most prosperous of tribes. Every Man-mani lives under a roof, almost all have household goods. There is a shop — " He pointed at one of the larger huts, close to the head-man's, where stacks of rough earthen pots were ranged against the wall, and mixed odds of poor clothing were hung under the eaves, not to dry, but displayed for sale. Iruvakh explained that while barter was the chief system of exchange, the only one for most of the tribes, here some of the women and most of the beer-makers had handled both bronze and silver coins of the distant realm, brought by soldiers. If any gold was ever in circulation it had been accumulated by Sranadatta.

Turning to watch his squadrons toiling up the hill Kamin-Tolagh saw no matter what its listless air of unhope the village was superbly situated above the broad valley now filled with morning light. Next to the Heartland, or deep-grassed mountain-clefts of his province, the prospect would be dismally barren, but after days of the arid West, and the parched journey from the Lunu, it seemed green and fertile. Outlying dwellings, here and there gathering into something like a hamlet, were broadcast over the valley's ten-mile length, and clumps of bushes and small trees dotted the sparse grazing, which lapped up into the lower slopes of the central hills with their dark, matted growth. Growing-lands, small square plots marked off by narrow strips of untilled earth, were mostly in the flats on both sides of the river — or of its course; like all he had seen in the West its bed was the measure of spring floodwaters, oversized for the much smaller stream it usually contained. Here in the valley the river made a great bow, turning through four-fifths of a circle before bending back to resume its southwesterly flow, finding a gap in low westward hills, beyond which there was a distant view of broad, shining water, Flamûrai, the Great Gulf, A'hwen-Hweng to the Man-mani, Iruvakh said, *hweng* being their word for water.

Kamin-Tolagh and Iruvakh dismounted. At the near corner of Meeting Place was a large well circled by a rough stone wall. Boys and women, mainly young, were gathered to fill jars and pails, the number needing water at this one time disproportionate to the size of the settlement; many were seizing the chance for a closer look at his soldiery. He admired the graceful, swaying walk of the girls, each carrying a tall jar on the left hip. The one he first noticed was marked by the small scar Iruvakh had described, high on her cheek, showing lighter against the sun-ripened bloom of her skin. The young women wore robes folded rather than sewn, a smooth shoulder bare. He had thought the difference in skin-color between the herders they had seen and the women from the Lunu was due to the admixture of Owani blood, but now saw none of the Man-mani girls were as dark as most of the men or some of the older women, and guessed that was because they were less in the sun, working at household tasks instead of herding goats or tilling the fields.

A boy who came sauntering up the hill carried an empty water-jar, but hardly bothered to pretend it was anything but an excuse. The dark eyes were alert, and he had a strikingly self-sufficient manner, a cool assurance remarkable for his age, which Kamin-Tolagh would have put at ten or so. The boy flashed a sudden smile, and it was for Iruvakh.

"Here is Chamya, who would wish to meet you, *Asai* — " Iruvakh startled Kamin-Tolagh by going into the Owanilú.

"Another of the chieftain's sons?" in the same language, assuming, as in the realm, it was a way of talking privately in the presence of Other Races. "With so many wives, he must have a crowd of those."

"That is so indeed, *Asai*," the boy said, in good Owanilú, very much with the *Atarlum* accent. "But I am not of those numbers."

"Step-son to the head-man," Iruvakh dropped into everyday speech. "His mother, Osré-dnë, was widowed when he was six. She was the fifth woman Sranadatta married, and is third of surviving wives. She is no ordinary woman, Osré-dnë."

"You speak of my mother," the watchful Chamya, still in the Owanilú, having caught the name; with difficulty Kamin-Tolagh perceived that here ordinary language was what would not be understood.

"I am saying to Kamin-Tolagh *Asai*, Osré-dnë is rightly famed among Man-mani."

"Even big men," Chamya agreed, "come to her for counsel. My mother teaches them when to plant, which wife to choose. She cannot choose a wife for me," he added.

"You come to fetch water?" wanting only to enter the conversation, but the boy heard it as a slight against his independence, and firmly put down the jar he was carrying.

"I do not need to fetch water, *Asai*; we have women to do that. Soon, I — " he struggled for a word, consulted in his own thick language with Iruvakh, and was supplied with: " — soon I shall *catch the rope*."

"So to be counted among men of the tribe," Iruvakh explained. "a ceremony, a test of manhood all youths must endure. They usually attempt it when they are thirteen, but many fail at first try. Chamya is past twelve."

Kamin-Tolagh reassessed wiry muscling of the boy's arms and legs, and saw he must learn to allow for the short stature of the Man-mani. "What weapons have you been taught?"

"I use bow and knife," face eager. "I was to be shown lance, but those soldiers have gone away." He looked longingly at the massed squadrons. "Also I would wish to learn how to kill with long-sword."

Kamin-Tolagh laughed, and slapped the boy's shoulder, surprising himself with the thought, he would enjoy teaching him. Chamya stood for a minute contemplating the big *pefral*, breastplates and helms of the cavalry. Then, Kamin-Tolagh not offering to give him lance lessons on the spot, he turned and, well-taught (presumably by Iruvakh), took formal leave, courteously hoping so lofty a lord would be content with his stay among the Man-mani. Picking up the unfilled water-jar, he went off down the slope.

Iruvakh spoke about the boy's mother: "It is rare for the Man-mani to give a woman standing; their word for foolish or nonsensical is *woman-thought*, and the respect men give Osré-dnë is unheard-of. It is believed Sranadatta murdered her first husband to get her, and would never set her aside, as he would another woman who did not give him a child."

"The boy — he resembles her?"

"In a way, yes — " for once uncertain. "I know Chamya well, having taught him what he has of the Owanilú, but I confess Osré-dnë is largely outside my experience."

He might have gone farther and admitted the woman rather frightened him; the prim air of distaste was easily read. In part traceable to the *Mankh's* disapproval of anything hinting at prophecy or divination; to Iruvakh's mind there was something uncanny about this Osré-dnë's powers. Kamin-Tolagh wished his sister could be here beside him; these things interested her.

Gripped her, rather; Kamin-Tarú had a marvellous capacity for belief in the unseen and unexplained, portents, messages from the future written in stars, smoke, the acts of animals, conveyed in trances. He missed her happy guilelessness.

By the well some of the ones in between girl and woman had been stealing quick, shy glances at the tall stranger (presumably they knew Iruvakh). One, cautiously indicating Kamin-Tolagh, spoke quietly to her neighbor, and instantly put a hand over her mouth, but what she said caused a quick ripple of high laughter. Despite which her words met with general approval, and Kamin-Tolagh was pointed out to others, girls hiding faces in their hands or ducking away to giggle, not in ridicule, but for embarrassment at their own temerity. The same short phrase was heard over and again.

"What are they saying?"

"*Noh-Sra-Lal-Hin*," Iruvakh answered.

"Which is?"

"A tale — a legend." While he gave, for Kamin-Tolagh's taste, excessive respect to the laws and customs of the tribes, the former *atarlai* was lightly offhand with an alien belief. "*Sra* as part of a name is leader, or captain, while *Noh* before a word means the greatest or most important of its kind. In their tales recalling the Western Ocean, for example, they call it *Noh-Al-Heh-hweng*, Greatest of Waters. *Lal-Hin* is a name, a hero in their lore, He Who Makes War on the Gods."

"They are giving me this name?"

"In the tales Noh-Sra-Lal-Hin is very tall; his name can also signify 'Red-of-the-Rising-Sun' — he comes out of the east, you see, and his hair is red, or bronze, which is rarely seen among the tribes."

Unclear whether the giggling women really took him for their tribal hero, or were merely enjoying his resemblance to the tale. One, the girl he had noticed before with the arrowhead scar, put a finger to her chin, and this too was approved and imitated by the others. Kamin-Tolagh was at once self-conscious about the still-angry scar at the right side of his jaw.

"In one ending to the tale," Iruvakh resumed drily. "Lal-Hin goes off to do battle with the Dark Hawk or Black Vulture — the words are very much the same; it is the name of a cruel god. But Lal-Hin is to come back to the Man-mani, bringing both wealth and sorrow. Your pardon, *Asai*, you have marks of your struggle against beak and claw."

No use trying to determine whether the girls meant only he was *like* Lal-Hin: their language, hence their thought, Iruvakh asserted but Kamin-Tolagh was unable to believe, had no such distinction. "Wanting rain," Iruvakh, continuing to affect *Atarlum* disdain, "they will throw a cup of water at the sky, while pounding a big log drum. To their minds the drum is thunder and the water, rain. They give them those names, you see."

Abruptly laughing and chatter ceased, and the girls drew back against the wall of the well, making themselves small. From below, the hut of the head-man, a small procession was coming this way. At the same time two men of the tribe had gone to the raised platform at farther end of Meeting Place. There with effort they set upright a large slab of worked bronze that had lain unnoticed on the ground, and leaning it against the platform struck it with thick log clubs. Its dull booming proclaimed the coming of Sranadatta.

He was preceded by warriors with shields and longstaffs, swords at their sides, eight of the foreigners Iruvakh had mentioned as the head-man's bodyguard. Sranadatta himself was tall for a Man-mani, wearing a brightly-colored kirtle, a burly man with a short, creased neck and a curious walk, as if he was knee-deep in barley. He passed, making no sign, a few feet from where Kamin-Tolagh was standing; small eyes, a bulged brow and jutting lower lip, all of which characteristics were youthfully represented in the man who walked beside him, his eldest son. Another four sinewy guards, smoother-featured than Man-mani, but much the same height and build, flanked the head-man, and just behind came his eldest surviving wife, a neckless and waistless pillar of a woman, her hair carved rather than combed, so it seemed, into a domed headdress. Her brother beside her, like the head-man, looked to be at the latter end of middle age, though Iruvakh said these people aged rapidly after thirty or so. He now murmured the brother-in-law, Nifra, was a sort of advisor, a *bôdhrai*, to Sranadatta, but having seen the head-man's willful, self-regarding face Kamin-Tolagh did not need to be told he made his own decisions no matter what counsel was given.

A final quartet of guards surrounding two more of Sranadatta's grown sons brought up the rear, one carrying in place of the staff a large, shapeless stuffed bag. When the head-man with his retinue had mounted the platform and they had at last arranged themselves in proper order, this bag was placed behind Sranadatta, who, after a glance right and left, sat, allowing his senior wife to hand him a short wooden stave, and to drape over his knees a square of plain blue cloth.

Alerted by the gong the village had quickly gathered at the fringes of the open space. Women and children were the majority, and most men here were well past their prime, some bent and ancient. By contrast to the lighthearted mood at the well, the feeling now was subdued and apprehensive.

The brother-in-law, Nifra, opened the proceedings. Stepping down, he paced down the middle of the Meeting Place. A few strides short of Kamin-Tolagh he stopped and pressed his fisted hands together in the gesture of greeting, promptly copied by Iruvakh. To him, Nifra, exactly the tentative, sycophantic advisor a Sranadatta would choose, sparse straggle of dark beard doing nothing to disguise weak chin, addressed words which, allowing for the unlovely sound of the language, was conversational rather than formal. Iruvakh's response was brief.

Sranadatta, he told Kamin-Tolagh, greeted them, and invited the visitors to speak with him. He understood Kamin-Tolagh did not have Man-mani words, and asked that he would talk through Iruvakh.

With no doubt they would follow him Nifra had turned and begun pacing back. Pride surged in Kamin-Tolagh, and he swiftly told Freighanai to wheel a half-squadron in eights behind him. Iruvakh did not risk comment, though his face was not approving. As soon as the bright breastplates and big, glossy mounts were aligned across the space, Nifra having regained the dais, Kamin-Tolagh strode forward, Iruvakh having to skip to keep up, cavalry just behind.

They halted in front of the platform. The watchful cunning of Sranadatta's small eyes gave him a face for the remorseless opportunist Iruvakh had described. Nifra, beckoned, bent so the head-man could speak words in his ear, which through Iruvakh came to Kamin-Tolagh as: "Sranadatta would hear about you, your title, rank and position."

Just behind, as if to himself, Freighanai grumbled, "Why is the lord of goats seated, while Kamin-Tolagh *Asai* is standing?"

"Why, indeed," Kamin-Tolagh said.

"It is their way — " Iruvakh began uncomfortably, but Freighanai had put a spark to Kamin-Tolagh's tinder. He had nothing but amazed contempt for how Iruvakh's *jinzai*-breeders had dealt with this tribe, neglecting needs but coddling their customs, instead of first cowing then taking care of them, the grown children they obviously were. The guards ranged to either side of Sranadatta had the watchful, untrusting gaze of killer-dogs, but Kamin-Tolagh knew Freighanai had made the same soldier's assessment as he had, their longstaffs no match for lances, short swords stuck unsheathed through their waist-ties betraying inferior temper with their dull sheen. If these sixteen were enough to keep the Man-mani docile under Sranadatta, a couple of squadrons of cavalry could enslave them in an hour.

"Tell the head-man," he instructed Iruvakh, "I am a great captain of a people much greater than his. Tell him — " as the man began to protest.

Not willingly Iruvakh spoke again to Nifra, leading to a muttered conference on the dais, with Sranadatta's eldest son joining in.

"Why can the head-man not speak direct to you?"

"Patience, *Asai*," Iruvakh pleaded. "These are friendly people, but their ways must be understood."

In the growing muddle of Man-mani talk one thing was clear: he did not need a study of tribal lore to understand intent when kept standing by a seated man whose head was higher than his.

"I am liked by my friends, too," he told Iruvakh. "But I also have my ways." In two strides and a long-legged step up he had mounted the dais to smile down on Sranadatta. Villagers voiced shock, there was a rattle of weaponry among the bodyguard; the excellently-trained Freighanai rapped out an order, and cavalry swords came out of their sheaths with a slithering ring. Sranadatta, on his feet at last, calmed his men, but was still angry himself.

Kamin-Tolagh had not touched his hilt, and he continued to grin down at the head-man, turning away only to offer a hand to help up the reluctant Iruvakh. As he did he heard a rustling noise, wind in autumn treetops, in parts of the world where there were such trees, and an autumn. After a moment he recognized what it was; the name bestowed by the girls at the well was rippling through the assembled tribe, *Noh-Sra-Lal-Hin*.

Lavsila, who ambled in unescorted in late morning, was sorry to have missed that small drama, but acutely disappointed that Kamin-Tolagh, having achieved ascendancy, had not bluntly forced Sranadatta to take the Lunu women back into the tribe.

Their meeting was in the square common room of the so-called Lunu Hut, lower down the hill than Sranadatta's dwelling, not far from the stockade. Iruvakh said it had been made to specifications of the Lunu, five modest sleeping rooms opening off this central space, but building materials, with the method of construction, were Man-mani. Hut-building took place only at the end of winter, when the brief and unreliable rainy season and thawing of snows high up in the hills provided river-mud for daubing the wicker walls, and the sun could then be counted on to bake it nearly to the hardness of brick. Nearby there was another large hut, divided into only two rooms, sleeping space for a half-squadron of Kamin-Tolagh's men and a dozen of the bows. The remaining soldiery was to be housed down by the river, in a stone barracks with adjacent stables, erected earlier for the *Adanum Plakh'*, and much like the plainer buildings to be seen at the Lunu. Extraordinary to Kamin-Tolagh, neither the barracks, immensely stronger than anything the Man-mani could erect, nor this roomy and well-furnished hut, had been occupied by the tribe; not the arrogant Sranadatta himself had dared claim the carpets, comfortable chairs, tables, the glazed plates or the drinking vessels of fine Island glass; these would have surely been marvellous treasures to Man-mani eyes, as would the several real beds: that none of this had been disturbed suggested greater awe for the Lunu than had been displayed toward Iruvakh.

"What are the women going to do, then?" Lavsila asked.

"Most have kin who will take them in. Those who have not can earn their keep fetching water for the larger households, till they find husbands, if they can."

Some, the best-looking, would no doubt be branded with the arrowhead scar. "Husbands? With the overabundance of women here?"

At first puzzled, or affecting to be, by this observation, Iruvakh, after frowning thought, said, "Ah." Women, he believed, were somewhat more numerous than men, but the difference was not nearly as much as appeared from the gathering at Meeting Place. Many men were out of the village herding their goats, and small bands were always hunting small game, or making the journey to Flamûrai to fish. At this particular time a large number of men were away in the south, to gather firewood — a far stronger band than in other years, when the Lunu had lent mounted troops for escort; Iruvakh believed as many as two hundred had gone, to discourage attack by Hill Froghul.

"To rob them of what?" in scorn. "Firewood? Isn't there enough of that, up in the hills?"

"They drive part of their livestock with them," Iruvakh patiently explained. "Then there are ponies to carry the firewood, and the men take small goods, for trading with the southward tribes. The absence of many of his best fighting-men, *Asai*, was what made Sranadatta so anxious to placate you."

"Are you saying if they had been here, he would have defied four squadrons of cavalry?" Kamin-Tolagh was incredulous, though Sranadatta certainly had been swift to swallow anger and turn to blandishment.

"That was not my meaning, no. He knows the Hill Froghul, who keep watch, must have seen the firewood party set out south. With the village short of men who can fight, Sranadatta is hoping you will be here for a while, to protect the valley from raids."

"Why?" Kamin-Tolagh did not see where he had a quarrel with the Hill Froghul, or interest in the wellbeing, the very survival, of the Man-mani. Lavsila agreed. "What use are they? Next time you are hailed as a god, make it a tribe with a ton of treasure to lay at your feet."

"In their tales, the Man-mani once had gold," Iruvakh said. "when their lands were westward, on the farther side of Flamûrai. They must have been subdued for the Empire by Larghai himself — conceivably, the name they give you, *Asai*, Lal-Hin, is a memory of his. Some accounts make Larghai red-headed."

"So he was," Kamin-Tolagh said. "One line in the baKarguli ancestry goes back to Larghai."

Iruvakh did not dispute the point. "Just so. Tall, bronze-haired, a great warrior from the east — "

Lavsila bayed. "You mean these half-wits really think Larghai *Nim'raibakim-dhanai* has returned to them after, what is it, fifteen, sixteen centuries?"

As he had earlier with Kamin-Tolagh, Iruvakh hedged, saying the distinction Lavsila sought did not exist in Man-mani language; all that could be said was the tales and prophecies had not been contradicted. By outfacing Sranadatta Kamin-Tolagh had again given confirmation: since Sranadatta's will was god-thought, Lal-Hin had 'made war on the gods' as he was supposed to.

"What a chance this would be," Lavsila said. "If only the Man-mani had something worth taking from them."

Both men, Kamin-Tolagh decided as, stripped, he washed with cool water, were going to have to be reminded of his ancestry and theirs, Lavsila for his perpetual mockery, Iruvakh for his bland air of superior wisdom. Not to say his habit of behaving as if he had no master; announcing he wanted detailed news about Man-mani doings from an old acquaintance in the tribe he had drifted off without asking leave.

Lavsila, when Kamin-Tolagh came back into the common room, had chosen another of the bedrooms and was apparently napping. With Freighanai not due to report for two hours or so, an opportunity for some overdue reading; from a saddlebag Kamin-Tolagh took a bulky sheaf of pages, part of Dolvid's confessedly hasty draft history of the Jinzai War. Each of the principal captains had been provided with a copy of the pages dealing with actions of which he had been part, inviting suggestions and changes, promising the final work would do its best to reconcile all the different versions.

In a loose dressing-gown Kamin-Tolagh, having mixed ink, sat at the table and made marginal notes with his travelling-pen. Sounds of the village were faint, and there was the occasional fidget of his mount, tethered outside, or Lavsila's. While there were places where his detailed recollections differed from Dolvid's he found his contributions to the war treated fairly and generously; there was no reason why that should surprise him, but it was generosity that came too late: remembering the fellowship of that desperate time, knowing now about the trust his comrades had failed to give, Kamin-Tolagh could have wept. Instead, soon bored by minor details, he lost interest.

Being roused by a light footfall told him he had dozed in the afternoon warmth. As he sat slumped he was being gazed down on by a girl, not older than, well, sixteen, making appropriate allowance for Man-mani size. She was pretty, but what she was carrying had taken her past the guards, a tall earthen flask and a platter heaped with foodstuffs, mostly unfamiliar. These she set on the table, murmuring words in her language, then returned to the entranceway to usher in a small, tanglehaired boy fiercely clutching an armload of flat rounds of bread and a bunch of wilted greens. From the resemblance Kamin-Tolagh would have known he was the girl's brother, without her stream of bullying directions. As soon as he had safely unloaded onto the table she sent him away, then addressed Kamin-Tolagh. She spoke earnestly, as if her intensity would penetrate his ignorance of the language, saying something longer and more complicated than her first brief salute. Among the harsh syllables he thought he caught the name, Sranadatta, which, together with her prideful, circling gesture he took to mean the head-man had sent the food. Kamin-Tolagh thanked her in the two languages he knew, and she appeared to understand it in the Owanilú, making deference in Owani style, and whispering "*Asai.*"

Her robe, he noticed, was finer than he had seen on the women at the well, a soft weave, surely Heartland, which draped fluidly over her rounded hips and between the young breasts; as with the tribal dress, one shoulder was left bare. She was the most winning of the Man-mani women he had seen, with small, even teeth, very white, and large, long-lashed brown eyes; her hair was lustrous; hardly surprising that Sranadatta had made her his, with the arrowhead scar high on her cheek.

This was not the first time she had waited on a guest here; she knew where plates, forks and knives were kept, and set them on the table with a drinking-cup. Earlier Kamin-Tolagh had declined the offer of servants, made through (if not by) the head-man's eldest son, Sranya-Dalhitta; he considered himself part of an army in the field, but it was very pleasant to be helped by this lovely girl. She occupied herself determinedly with knife and fork, cutting small pieces of an unidentified meat to put on his plate. Iruvakh had passingly referred to poisoning as part of Man-mani politics, and Kamin-Tolagh supposed he should have the girl taste first, but would have felt foolish conveying the idea to her. Sranadatta, in any case, would not dare it.

The meat, probably goat, was overcooked but eatable, snake less repellent than it looked before being cut up small, and the very salt fish parching enough to send him for deep draughts of the pale, ambiguous drink. The bread had a coarse texture he enjoyed, but the Man-mani attempt at salad greens was a failure, chewy and bitter. A wizened and tasteless peach he did not enjoy, but there was a section from a small, dusky melon like none he had ever tasted, rich and perfumy.

With the scent and movements of the girl, he began to feel his waxing restlessness, the warm, familiar tingle of anticipation; after taking more of the marvellous melon he cut another piece, speared it on his fork, and held it out to her. The eyes became huger, and she shied away with a smothered giggle. Kamin-Tolagh caught at a remarkably slender wrist, and tried to force the fruit on her, desisting only when she twisted her head away in torments of embarrassment. Eating the piece of melon he waited till she turned back to face him, then pointed to himself, saying "Kamin-Tolagh."

She remained too self-conscious to attempt understanding. He tried it twice again, but dark eyes remained perplexed. From a doorway Lavsila asked, "Shall I try?"

Still rumpled from sleep he came to the table, tasted a bit of fish, shuddered at snake, then, pointing to Kamin-Tolagh, enunciated "Noh-Sra-Lal-Hin." He had made Iruvakh repeat the name many times till he had it right.

Joy of comprehension came at once, and the girl agreed with avid noddings: "Noh-Sra-Lal-Hin." A spate of her own language followed, illustrated with self-effacing gestures.

"She wishes to endorse," Lavsila suggested, "that her people agree, you are truly Noh-Sra-Lal-Hin, and she altogether unworthy of the privilege of ministering to the human side of your earthly nature." He smirked. "You did not think she was sent only to bring you food?"

Kamin-Tolagh's wakened blood wanted to accept this reading, but the scar of ownership was unignorable. "She is Sranadatta's, by rules of the Man-mani."

"Did Iruvakh not say they were known to honor a guest this way? I have been waiting for someone to flatter me."

Kamin-Tolagh looked for confirmation to the girl, greedily watching talk she could not follow. At that moment, Freighanai, slightly ahead of time, came to make his report.

The hint of reproach was barely detectable; he had just been reprimanding the door-watch for letting the girl come in unguarded. Letting that pass, he reported the squadrons safely installed in the barracks by the river, and a rotation established for the various watches here and there. At a loss for more, he recommended a lance-drill in the flat next to the barracks, for men not assigned to guard-duty. "They can't be left idle here, *Asai* — too many distractions, you see." His eyes were very plainly not going to the Man-mani girl.

Kamin-Tolagh recommended men and their mounts rest today. "Hold your lance-drill tomorrow — we'll be here another day or two."

"Very good, *Asai*." After a mournful moment Freighanai brightened with a new inspiration. "We'll have equipment inspection. I saw some badly-wrapped hafts on the ride. Being in the field's no excuse for letting equipment go, just when it ought to be in top condition."

"Leave word with the guard where you'll be every hour, in case I need to find you in a hurry."

"I'll be back at the other hut here, after inspection. Not expecting trouble, then, are we?"

"In unfamiliar country, it's as well not to lose touch. Be sure the other squadron-leaders have the same orders." With no one likely to ride off on an adventure of his own this was exaggerated caution, and Kamin-Tolagh recognized the man's reference to *distractions* had brought him to this overdone display of efficiency and vigilance.

As Freighanai gave his salute Lavsila ostentatiously stretched and yawned. "I would be no worse for a breath of air. May I ride with you, Squadron? With your leave, *Asai*." His deference was massive, shod in iron.

Like all the officers Freighanai was happier when Lavsila was not trying to play soldier, but his face was mute as they turned to go out into bright afternoon sun.

The girl contemplated the remains of the meal, uncertain whether she should clear away. Kamin-Tolagh, half-convinced she had been sent for his use, made one final attempt at the naming ritual, putting both hands on his chest and saying, "Noh-Sra-Lal-Hin." With a looping gesture of continuation, he waited for her answer.

She put a hand to her breast and said, "Siv'loi."

"Siv'loi?" He pointed.

"Siv'loi," she agreed, delighted.

That could not be her tribal name, but must have been given by someone from Lunu Jinzalladhiyu — a soldier, not one of the *Atarlum* proper: no *atarlai* would make that mistake. In the Owanilú, flower was *sivu*, but the diminutive, which meant flowerlet, a blossom from a spray, took the soft aspirate, *sibh'loi*. The girl's name was a typical mispronunciation of an illiterate Islander. The thought she had already been under a soldier, most likely an officer of the *Adanum*, gave want fresh urgency. As she reached for the flask to refill his cup he ran a hand down the slight back, and let it rest on the soft slope of her bottom.

Her shyness went away. Turning, she put a hand without hesitation under the flap of his dressing gown and inside his thigh. He kissed her mouth and the pleasing junction of neck and shoulder, making her wriggle. Half-squatting she tilted back her head, mouth wide, as if already entered and nearing ecstasy.

Ready with all three fists (as horse-breeders of Kargul said) he found the arrowhead brand in his eyes again, and annoyed himself with a final querying of her, touching the scar, "Sranadatta?"

"Noh-Sra-Lal-Hin," laughing, lunging up to kiss and bite. His lips were dry, and his mouth.

He had stopped keeping count of his beddings, aware of censorious, envious, amazed, admiring rumors putting them in the hundreds, some said thousands. Unchallengeably more than most men enjoy in a lifetime, but he could not remember a partner as gleeful as Siv'loi, so entire in pleasure; she was a kitten drunk on purring, for whom each touch impossibly adds to an ecstasy already absolute. Yet her honeyed body followed an innate pulse and was not untaught; she was good at this game, and her feral abandon nevertheless made use of intuitive rules to ensure every happy enhancement for them both. He did not need a bridle, but was glad to postpone fulfillment while she helped make anticipation into such an exquisite poignancy.

They did not need a speech in common, though Kamin-Tolagh did talk, voicing what came into his head, overripe endearments from absurd romances, bald cudgels of campfire bragging, sentimental promises and fierce threats about what would come next. Her few ejected noises were language the world understood.

After varied grapplings and doughty feats Kamin-Tolagh drowsily considered this self-refreshing marvel of skins and exploration. Siv'loi was passively watchful, and he guessed she meant to creep away when he fell asleep; he contrived a complicated tangle of legs and arms, knowing he would wake wanting more of her. He thought he could never be bored with newness — newness for him, not an outright beginner; he much preferred women who had been schooled. Apart from all other advantages, they could judge how skilled he was.

"Kamin-Tolagh *Asai* — " awake swiftly and completely, like a cat, he knew Iruvakh's voice, but numbers of feet were clattering, and there was a babble of urgency.

Disengaging from Siv'loi who was waking blurrily, he found dressing-gown and slippers, and pulled aside the coarse hanging in the doorway. The light had dimmed, but through a window-hole where the woven screen had been raised he could see the fading red of evening. Two ordinary troopers of his personal squadron were by the outside door, and there were five men in the middle of the common-room, Lavsila the calmest. Freighanai was there glumly watching the agitated discussion, chiefly between Iruvakh and two of those closest to the Man-mani head-man, the counsellor Nifra, and the eldest son, Sranya-Dalhitta, who, first to see Kamin-Tolagh, tried to convey his tale in very faulty Owanilú, not improved by contributions in Man-mani language from his uncle (or step-uncle), interruptions by Lavsila, eager to show he was the one who could tell the story most clearly.

Kamin-Tolagh commanded silence in a voice to make meaning unmistakable. In abrupt quiet he went to the table and poured a cup of the pale drink. After a swallow he pointed at Iruvakh. "Tell me."

Disregarding a frequent need to hush the two Man-mani, it was fairly simple; Hill Froghul' raiders were coming. A herdsman searching for a strayed goat and going farther up onto the hillside than was prudent had been lucky to avoid wandering into the midst of forty or fifty Hill Froghul, coming from southward, leading their tough little ponies through thick brush on the flanks of the ridge. A pure raiding-party, armed and provisioned, but without their women or their goats. Their march was unusually careless: their lack of vigilance and imperfect use of cover had saved the Man-mani herdsman from detection and sure death. After staying hidden for a time he made for home, and again almost stumbled into the raiders where they had camped for the night, above the main valley only a few miles short of the village. Making a wide, fearful circuit, the man had brought his story to Sranya-Dalhitta just half an hour ago.

General opinion was, the Hill Froghul did not mean to attack the stockaded village, hardly proof against a siege and obviously vulnerable to fire, but strong enough when defended to discourage assault; pickings were easier down below. Within the big circling bend of the river the Sranadatta clan had an enclosure with storehouses for foodstuffs, and space for livestock; when, as now, there was a shortage of men for defense, most of the goats and many ponies were driven there at nightfall.   The opening, facing a little north of east, was furnished with a triple line of fences, gateways staggered left and right, but there was only a single line of palings where compound followed riverbank.   True, the sharp slope of the bank would help defenders, but as Freighanai remarked, at the present level of the river, a six-year-old child could wade across without difficulty.

If the Hill Froghul had observed the soldiery, Iruvakh reasoned, they certainly would not contemplate a raid; they must have been well to the south, laying in wait for the annual woodcutting expedition, and on seeing its numbers had changed targets, reasoning the Man-mani valley would be stripped of its best fighting men.

"If they made camp so early," Kamin-Tolagh said. "They must mean to sleep now, and attack in darkness, past midnight."

"Not these, *Asai*. So far from their home, they will wait for dawn." Iruvakh explained the Hill Froghul believed when they died or were killed, the life-spirit left the body, but could begin an afterlife only if it could return to the man's birthplace. For this reason, if they could, they eschewed fighting by night, afraid spirits of the killed would miss their way in the dark.

Lavsila was about to give a guffaw, but seeing he was alone changed it to an indeterminate noise, succeeded by a cynical grimace. Neither of the Man-mani present liked that Iruvakh and Kamin-Tolagh had been using ordinary language; Nifra kept trying to put points to Iruvakh, and Sranya-Dalhitta used his halt Owanilú to demand, "Has it been said to your lord what my father's wishes are?"

Iruvakh went into the same language to explain: "Sranadatta has asked the horse-soldiers of his honored guest, with their long weapons and their body-armor, be marched and countermarched in the valley, for the hill-men to see, so they will abandon their raid."

Sranya-Dalhitta nodded agreement, while Freighanai, getting straight who understood what language, confided, "More like *ordered* than asked, *Asai*, when they met me by the gateway." He stared at Iruvakh. "I said, not a trooper will put his boots on without the Captain's word."

"Good." Kamin-Tolagh turned to the head-man's son, "Why? For what am I to do this? Your father is aware I came here with one purpose, to see to the return of the women."

Not trusting his Owanilú, Sranya-Dalhitta spoke to Iruvakh, who translated: "His father has said the women will be accepted. For the sake of friendship he makes this request. It would cost nothing, *Asai*." The last plea was Iruvakh's addition.

Kamin-Tolagh's mind was racing at various levels. Uppermost was dislike for the ruling clan of this tribe, intensified contempt for cowardice that thought only of frightening away their enemy with a display of force; their best men might be away cutting wood, but the Man-mani could surely muster several times the half-hundred of the raiding party. He pictured that band, almost sauntering into the valley, anticipating little fight from a tribe cowed in advance, a gift for his troops, many of them blooded against *jinzal*, supported by excellent mounted bows, better-horsed by far than the raiders. The question remained, why should he risk Kargul' lives to help pig-eyed Sranadatta hold on to his goods?

"What shall I do with his friendship?" he demanded, but Iruvakh was no longer paying attention; with Nifra and Sranya-Dalhitta he was looking past Kamin-Tolagh, to where at the bedroom doorway Siv'loi stood a long moment, naked and yawning. Someone had brought a rush lamp, and in that light her skin was a dusked gold, pale scar on her cheek plainer than before. Nifra, advancing in a menacing crouch, poured out a stream of what could only be invective.

"What is this, *Asai*?" Iruvakh demanded.

"This," coldly, not ready to concede the right to question him about his women, "is Siv'loi." The girl had backed away, letting door-hanging fall, and Kamin-Tolagh roughly grabbed the shoulder of Nifra, who was ready to follow the girl inside.

"Their Sranadatta," Lavsila explained, as Nifra continued to rail, "sent this girl for the use of Kamin-Tolagh *Asai*."

"Your pardon, he did not," Iruvakh tautly corrected. "*Asai*, did I not warn you about this?"

"Ask him," Lavsila challenged. "Or ask the girl." Siv'loi, partly clad, had reappeared, and blandly ignored Nifra's stridency, coming to Kamin-Tolagh, her lovely, sleepy face trusting.

With promptings from Sranya-Dalhitta, Nifra went from abuse to abusive interrogation, Siv'loi replying calmly.

Iruvakh pursed his lips primly. "He tells the girl Sranadatta will have her life. She says, you are Lal-Hin, over any head-man."

"Noh-Sra-Lal-Hin," Siv'loi reechoed, tilting her chin defiantly. Nifra's voice rose again, and he lifted a hand against her. Kamin-Tolagh, with a half-step, locked eyes with the older man, and the upraised hand stayed, then wilted, an early blossom struck by frost. Siv'loi leant into Kamin-Tolagh's chest.

"Say, if harm comes to this girl my vengeance on the Man-mani will make Hill Froghul raids into fleabites.

"Well?" Iruvakh was merely staring.

"*Asai*, how can I say such a thing? This is a bad business, but to deal with laws and customs of the Man-mani in that spirit can only poison all future dealings with the tribe."

"What dealings?" Kamin-Tolagh gathered he was to let them butcher his bed-friend for the sake of diplomacy. "To obtain breeding-stock, your masters, perhaps, were obliged to deal as equals with Sranadatta's offal, these men who bravely brand women and come bleating for help against a handful of raiders. Do you think it matters to me or to my realm if the Man-mani is destroyed, or destroys itself? We should welcome it; no *jinzai*, certainly, could ever be bred again."

Sranya-Dalhitta was trying to guess what was being said, but also doing his best to assess how his father would come off in a trial of wills with this new chieftain. "Sranadatta," he said, "is not maker of law. Only says law."

Though the man's Owanilú was not up to expressing the thought, it put Kamin-Tolagh on familiar ground; orders are orders; he could remember a servant in his childhood, about to give him a flogging prescribed by his father, making similar noises, and his mother used the Will of Raëdh in much the same way, to deny responsibility for expedient cruelties.

He was calm and he would not have Siv'loi killed. He cradled her in the crook of his arm. "Tell Nifra, then," to Iruvakh in a measured tone, "whoever hurts this girl makes war on me. Tell him, unless he can give me the word of Sranadatta no harm will come to Siv'loi, my troops will stand by and watch what Hill Froghul can do. If she is harmed, we shall feel free to take or destroy anything the raiders happen to leave."

Iruvakh sighed, and his small hands made futile gestures. "Again, *Asai*, let me remind you their minds are different from ours. God-thoughts are what they are: they do not have conditions."

"Gnats' milk. Sranadatta knew all about conditions when he demanded food and weapons as the price of taking back the *jinzai*-mothers. This, too, is a bargain — except if they wanted nothing from me, they still would not touch Siv'loi. Make that clear." While Iruvakh mustered phrases he led the girl to the inner room, and indicated she should go back to bed, and stay there. A flirtatious look over a bare shoulder as she complied, and he used signs and a light kiss to say *when there is time*. It would have been *now*, with only littlest permission of mind to his primed body.

With a rapid exchange going on among Iruvakh and the two Man-mani, entirely in their language, Lavsila said confidentially, "You do recognize you have more-or-less undertaken to help them against the Hill Froghul, if they promise the girl's safety? Suppose Sranadatta planned this as a trap — sending the girl, guessing what would happen, then denying she was meant for you."

Typical Lavsila, combining desire not to have been mistaken about Siv'loi in the first place with habitual love of the devious, a strained explanation of the inexplicable: why would Siv'loi would be so eager to bed, knowing it could mean her death? As Iruvakh had said, Man-mani were strange children in much of what they did. But how could Sranadatta guess Kamin-Tolagh would care whether the girl, once enjoyed, was to live or die?

"How am I *trapped*?"

Lavsila shrugged it off. "But you mean to use your troops against these raiders?"

"At some point," offhandedly. Freighanai was shuffling his feet, bored with debate, and Kamin-Tolagh touched his shoulder. "Should we frighten off the Hill Froghul, as the Man-mani heroes ask?"

Hardly a real question. Freighanai laughed without mirth. "If they haven't heard we're here, *Asai*, we wouldn't want to spoil their surprise, would we? That place, you know, where the river bends — " He went on to describe how, where the bow of the river began, the force of spring floods had cut away at the bank, widening the bed, so with the water low there was a broad dry flat where, beneath the bank, a hundred men and their mounts could easily be concealed.

Kamin-Tolagh was beginning to have a taste for this business. "Would you give me five tobhal for each raider we kill, if I offer a plakhi for every one that escapes?" Those odds came to twenty-four to one.

"Very generous, *Asai*," Freighanai, with a sudden grin. "No."

"No quarter, then?" Lavsila, with all the bloodthirsty relish of the armchair warrior.

Iruvakh had said Hill Froghul rarely let themselves be taken alive, unless wounded to helplessness (and then the vengeful valley tribes usually killed them), but Kamin-Tolagh had learnt fighting *jinzal* the high cost of having to battle on past victory to extermination. "No," he decided. "We'll give survivors the chance to surrender." They could strip their prisoners, send them home naked to impress their people with the prowess of their new adversary — but what would be the object of such a demonstration, when in a few days he and his troops would be gone forever? The *rabhsai* had made it clear he had no ambitions for conquest in the West.

Though he might change his mind, if he could talk with Iruvakh, if he was aware such a man existed, one who could find his way through the maze of tribes, knew their languages and customs, not to say how feeble they were. A new protectorate in the Farther West, from what Kamin-Tolagh had seen, could be maintained with a couple of squadrons and a cluster of tribal auxiliaries, if these Hill Froghul could be brought to heel, or shattered. The question was, apart from the increased security it would provide for the western borders of the present Colony, how would it profit the realm? Rodlakh, who wept after winning at Kamsilat seemed in some way ashamed of his astonishing courage and proficiency in war, and certainly, as long as he had the cold advice of Dolvid, would not see expansion of his realm as a glory in itself. Perhaps he had no sense of glory at all.

Iruvakh had reached what passed for accord in his debate with the two Man-mani. "Nifra," he reported, "for the sake of your help against the Hill Froghul, is ready to give his word this girl will come to no harm at his hands, or the hands of any Man-mani."

"Is this to be trusted?" choosing the Owanilú so the men of the tribe could follow. "Does Nifra speak for the head-man?"

Sranya-Dalhitta was swift. "Nifra does speak here for my father. This is to be our — " he looked to Iruvakh for a word.

"Your pledge, your solemn pledge."

"Pledge," Sranya-Dalhitta echoed, and spoke in an undertone to Nifra. The older man came forward to speak, to chant what was evidently an established formula, ending by touching fingers to his forehead, then to Kamin-Tolagh's.

"So we do *pledges*," Sranya-Dalhitta redundantly explained.

"Say to your father," Kamin-Tolagh told him, perfunctorily imitating the brow-touching ritual, "with us, such oaths are death-questions, and if this one is broken the wrath of your gods will be as nothing next to my vengeance."

"*Asai*," Iruvakh protested. "These words, so spoken, are binding."

Nevertheless, the girl would remain here, Kamin-Tolagh decided, and he would spare men to stay on guard at the hut, Hill Froghul raid or none. He would never trust Nifra's weakly cunning eye, while Sranya-Dalhitta's veiled smugness was disquieting. Though it might only reflect satisfaction over the counter-pledge of assistance against the raiders.

"Was this so hard, then?" he challenged Iruvakh when the two Man-mani had gone to report to the head-man, their surreptitious backward glances leaving Kamin-Tolagh to reflect that pledges and alliances had done nothing to increase trust.

"When laws come in conflict with appetites, *Asai*," Iruvakh, with *Atarlum* sententiousness, "it is never easy. Not for Nifra; this is his tribe, and Sranadatta his law, but the girl is his daughter."

Kamin-Tolagh shuddered. In everything he had read or heard about the Farther West the implacable enemies had been heat and thirst, and he was damp and chilled, wishing not for cool water but a warming drink. He wondered what had become of the drying wind, supposed to blow for days on end, though Iruvakh, true, had described the climate as somewhat moister west of the hills, the mornings later, with those hills blocking the early sun. Full heat of day was needed to dissolve the layer of dank mist that clung to the valley floor, eerie insubstantial wreaths in the darkness.

Next to him the leader of the frontier bowmen, Noldar, grunted softly, kicking stiffness out of each leg in turn. Behind, the flat sheen of the river had just begun to reflect traces of color coming into the sky, but the broad terrace under the bank was absolute darkness, and though there were slight sounds of restlessness in horses, murmurs of talk, no one could guess over a hundred men and their mounts were waiting here.

"Will they come, *Asai*?" Noldar, not for the first time, testing the tension of his bow. They were on an earthy shelf halfway up the bank, where they could keep watch. The Man-mani, as represented by Nifra and the Sranadatta clan, were certain the raiders would come here, but Kamin-Tolagh suspected they were simply making sure their own goods and livestock would be protected; the Hill Froghul could with impunity plunder outlying huts and storage-sheds, till full daylight made patrolling practicable for troops new to this country.

Morning was crawling in; an hour ago had been first hints of lightening, but only now was the rim of sky where the black hills were lower turning to a watery pink and yellow, making it possible to pick out stunted clumps of bushes, and up to the left the vague blur of the village, where other eyes were vigilant.

A shattering goat-bleat came from the compound behind, just across the stream, and was answered by distant others. Noldar put a blunt hand on Kamin-Tolagh's arm, breathing, "Something moving, there." Off to the right, where a straggled line of bushes marked a slight trough, leading to a place where the riverbank was lower. Straining, Kamin-Tolagh thought he could make out bobbing grey shapes.

"On foot," Noldar murmured rapturously. "They've come on foot."

As the cavalry, at Kamin-Tolagh's quiet order, began swinging into the saddle, downstream there was the plash of wading men, and dark shapes of the raiders were plain against the brighter water. The foremost had already reached the fence, and defenders in the compound were running heavily to that place; there was a half-squadron of cavalry to stiffen the spines of the Man-mani defenders. The clash of weapons came.

Urging his *pefrai* up the bank just behind the mounted bows Kamin-Tolagh laughed for joy. Already in a fight at the compound fence hotter than anticipated, the Hill Froghul had no chance to make effective use of their bows, and long knives were no match for lances and swords. In moments, fifteen or so at the rear of the raiding party, never attempting to join the main fight, tried a retreat for the distant cover of the hills, but were caught between pursuit and the downhill charge of his personal squadron, led by Freighanai with a relish unusual for him. He had been disgusted to be given defense of the village, and seized with both hands the opportunity for action. Kamin-Tolagh barely took time to shout him a greeting before wheeling back to where the main fight was all-but finished: also issuing from the village, a band of Man-mani led by the two eldest of Sranadatta's sons were making their contribution by cutting the throats of wounded and disabled Hill Froghul. It took the serious threat of cavalry lances to make them desist, and then Sranya-Dalhitta, remounted on his small, mangy horse, rode at Kamin-Tolagh, shouting angrily in bad Owanilú, demanding whether his men would bind the wounds of prisoners, and see them fed.

"No good," he bawled. "Hill men do no work. Kill them, kill them all."

Kamin-Tolagh felt a rush of murderous disdain for his unwanted allies. All the same, the Man-mani at the compound fence had shown fight; five had been killed, and about twice as many wounded. There were wounds among Kamin-Tolagh's men, and more to their mounts, and it might have been worse, including some deaths, except the enemy arrows had nothing but fire-charred points, which bounced off helms and breastplates.

Steel-tipped arrows from those powerful bows could have pierced body-armor.

Victory was made complete by return of Talfoyan, leading a string of captured ponies. Hidden farther down the valley, his squadron, at the first sounds of battle, had ridden as instructed to the place where the raiders had made camp, guided by the herder who had first spotted them. There, Talfoyan had killed four of the men left to hold or guard the mounts. Two or three others, he believed, had escaped into the brush, but he had kept to his orders and made no attempt to hunt them down. Kamin-Tolagh had given this job to Talfoyan for that reason, no matter what his dislike of the man's sour face and rancid manner. Another more dashing officer, such as Kambanal, might have forgotten orders and lost lives in a chase where bows could outfight cavalry.

In all the count was thirty-three enemy dead, and eight prisoners, none unwounded. The crushing victory left Kamin-Tolagh with less contempt for the adversary than for Sranadatta's Man-mani. Men of his who had fought *jinzal* spoke admiringly of how the Hill Froghul, surprised, caught in the open, outnumbered and outweaponed, had fought bravely; among cover, Kamin-Tolagh confessed to Freighanai, or on terrain less favorable to cavalry, he would not want to tackle them with any less advantage in numbers. Though little if any taller than most Man-mani, they were thicker-set with strong legs, and their broader, flat-nosed features made them a great deal like the bowmen under Noldar.

The small knot of bloodied prisoners enclosed between two squadrons, captured ponies strung behind, made for a ramshackle triumphal re-entry into the village, but this time Kamin-Tolagh could not complain about his reception. Most of the village was crowded at the gate or along the walls beside, and as he rode in a small boy wearing what must be a month's grime tipped his shaggy head back like a baying dog and howled out, "*No-Sra-Lal-Hin.*" At once, the cry was taken up on all sides.

Kamin-Tolagh was instantly drunk. Not even the ride into Kadon Dinul after the Jinzai War had been so heady; that he had shared with other heroes, and the capital, not able to imagine how nearly their realm had gone under, was chiefly hailing a new *rabhsai*, only secondarily the victors of distant battles they had been told about. Whereas the Man-mani had witnessed this fight, and knew from experience what they had been saved from.

He deserved their admiration, he decided, if not for the one-sided fight, for his exact reading of enemy intentions, and firm adherence to plan, as if he had commanded for both sides, so obediently had the Hill Froghul done what he expected.

Not seeing Sranadatta, he called to Kambanal the troops would assemble up at Meeting Place, where he meant to wring some sign of gratitude from the head-man. For that he would need Iruvakh, and waving the squadrons on he swung aside at the Lunu Hut.

A strangely nervous Lavsila appeared in the doorway. "We hear you won, *Asai*. The girl — she's gone."

Kamin-Tolagh, swiftly out of the saddle, pushed past him, and almost ran down Iruvakh just inside the common-room. Imploring calm, he confirmed the news. "She kept saying she was needed at her father's hut." Not admitting danger, certain No-Sra-Lal-Hin would keep her safe, she had repeatedly tried to wheedle a way past Iruvakh or Lavsila, one of whom, with a pair of soldiers, had remained in the common-room all the time, with four other guards outside. Eventually Siv'loi had gone back to bed and pretended to sleep; a body as small and lithe as hers would have had no trouble negotiating the window-opening in the early morning dim.

Kamin-Tolagh could not blame anyone, except himself for not placing men outside each of the hut's windows, but that did not lessen his anger.

"Why would she go to her father's hut?"

"*Asai*, it is her place."

Recalling Nifra crouched in the passionate venom of his abuse, Kamin-Tolagh stopped trying to understand. "Have you been there? Or to Sranadatta, to remind him of his pledge?"

"I was just about to go to him. We only discovered the girl was missing when Lavsila thought she should share in our food."

"Come with me."

"Where, *Asai*? — " but following him out into sudden full sunlight, and continuing to scuttle behind, making weak pleas for patience, as Kamin-Tolagh strode up the slope. He was making for the head-man's hut, but up at Meeting Place he saw seven or eight of his soldiers, dismounted and clustered about something on the ground.

As he approached, they fell back, except for young Kambanal, who actually interposed himself, trying to prevent Kamin-Tolagh from seeing what was there, the naked and gorily mutilated body of a woman, a girl, of Siv'loi. As revulsion and rage rose, Kamin-Tolagh had space for fervent hope the bloodiest of many wounds, nearly severing the head, had been the first, since none of the lesser cuts would have caused immediate death. His mind dwelt on the trusting docility when he led her back into the bedroom, where, not long before, he had felt the young thighs, nuzzled the smooth throat, been pleased by the tiny, clever hands — all stained wreckage, smeared face a ruined mask of terror.

"Who did this?" He straightened slowly.

"The body was here when we came," Kambanal, voice unsteady.

"Somebody is going to feel pain," Kamin-Tolagh vowed. For idiotic reasons of his own, Iruvakh was still trying to placate, but could not meet Kamin-Tolagh's eyes.

Going the length of Meeting Place, avoided by his men and the Man-mani following them up the hill, he stooped for the heavy, battered bronze plate, and setting it upright against the steps banged furiously with his sword-hilt, filling the village with its dull booming. Freighanai, last to leave the battleground, had now appeared, and Kamin-Tolagh mastered himself enough to issue terse instructions for his squadrons. Then the dam of sanity was swept away by a new flood of red rage, and he beat at the bronze again, hearing his breath sob hoarsely in his throat. Villagers were gathering from every side, and it occurred to him his men would not disobey if he commanded a charge against them, old, young, women, children, a general massacre, and then the village burnt to the ground. His anger might then begin to ebb.

"Their laws, *Asai*," Iruvakh stammered. "No one has anything but horror for this killing, but I warned you from the first — "

"Their laws! I shall give them the laws swords bring. The girl's father — did he not pledge a solemn oath? And while I was fighting their battle for them — this?" He had made a few steps back in the direction of Siv'loi's remains, and found he could not bear the sight. To a file-leader standing near he snapped, "Cover the body." The man was at a loss, and Kamin-Tolagh jabbed a finger at the hut Iruvakh had called a shop, where together with the clothing under the eaves a large oblong of rough cloth was hung, meant, perhaps, for a bed-covering. Hastily dragged down, it was brought and draped over the huddled corpse.

Sranadatta's bodyguard was just breasting the rise, followed by the head-man in the midst of his male kin, including three grown sons, no Nifra. The head-man's face was warily angry.

There was no plan but confrontation. Before Sranadatta could mount the dais he bellowed, pointing at the covered body, "Who ordered this?

"Interpret, curse you — " to Iruvakh. Sranadatta was making a furious retort, and Sranya-Dalhitta a gesture of dismissal.

Iruvakh's face had gone chalky. "He demands, requests to know who has sounded the assembly-gong, which only he — "

"*Demand* of him — " Kamin-Tolagh stopped. Dismounted as he had ordered, his squadron had come up about him. Seeing their bare blades Sranadatta's bodyguard had also drawn. Two of them, standing together, were obviously brothers, and their swords were stained with blood. The bodyguard had taken no part in the fight against the Hill Froghul.

At once he recalled the wording of the oath spoken by Nifra and subscribed-to by Sranya-Dalhitta: the girl would come to no harm at the hands of a Man-mani. The bodyguards were not of this tribe, they were — was it Hwenala? Foreigners, anyway, and so Sranadatta had carried out his vengeance while keeping to the letter of his son's pledge.

Instead of fanning Kamin-Tolagh's anger, perception of this duplicity brought him an icy calm, no less murderous. Not pure ignorance he was dealing with, but a brutal and infantile cunning. Stupid, like most cunning; how could head-man imagine his ruse would deflect Kamin-Tolagh's fury? But Siv'loi's determination to go back to her father's hut shared in the same inexplicable childishness. Sranadatta, voice shriller, was, by his gestures, protesting sounding of the gong.

"Tell him," startling Iruvakh with the steely quiet of his tone. "I am not here to answer questions, but ask them. Those two men of his guard — there, with bloodied swords. I want them surrendered to me, so they can be interrogated about who gave orders for the killing of Siv'loi."

Iruvakh opened his mouth, but for the first time did not tell Kamin-Tolagh how unheard-of his demands were. He looked to one side and the other, as if seeking his accustomed neutral ground, and yet it was in Kamin-Tolagh's mind poor Iruvakh was at last very close to irrevocable choice. He had been of the *Atarlum*, yet contrived to be aloof from the aims of Lunu Jinzalladhiyu, gone among the tribes without being of them, and had constantly tried to stand as he was standing now, sideways-on, so as to emphasize his position as a mere interpreter between Kamin-Tolagh and the Man-mani. It would not do: whoever did not condemn the killing of Siv'loi would be the enemy.

Sranadatta's sons had clambered up on the platform, and as two of them helped him up he continued his harangue.

"He says he is the law," Iruvakh, flat-voiced. "Speaking through him the gods have said the girl who was his has not been. She shall not be spoken of."

No answer was possible. Kamin-Tolagh told Freighanai, "We'll seize the two with the bloodied swords, there. No needless killing." His men moved forward, and he made straight for the nearer of the two. As if he had dreamed it all, days ago, he knew exactly what would happen. The man warded him off with his shield, at the same time stabbing low at Kamin-Tolagh's body. He turned the thrust with a cocked wrist, and used a short-armed backhand to slash the shield aside, as two of his squadron seized the man. The other was already a captive; the cavalrymen, with experience last spring of controlling hostile crowds at Kadon Dinul, had surged forward to neutralize the bodyguard by weight of numbers. There were protests as the captives were dragged down from the platform, but only one of the guard, goaded by Sranadatta, tried to interfere, springing forward as the troops disengaged. Blades rang, and the man was clutching at a gashed wrist, his damaged short-sword in the dust.

Sranadatta was purple, hurling invective and obviously exhorting his guard, his clan, the village as a whole, to fall on and overwhelm the blasphemers. But the guard was cowed, Kambanal's squadron in the saddle, ready for any move from the crowd, who could have been watching the Burantal Marionettes, for all they seemed likely to interfere.

"It is god-thought, the law," Iruvakh translated.

God-thought! How was it different from the *aën'modha* claimed for and by the Patriarchs? Kamin-Tolagh recognized his contempt for Sranadatta had fused with the anger he had for

Owan-Alladh, another devious tyrant who made special enlightenment an explanation for letting loose murder.

"Tell him, it is law no longer."

"*Asai* — " Iruvakh was at a loss. "That cannot be said. The words would be *god-thought is stopped*."

"Tell him that," signing to Kambanal to begin his advance. "Say I bring new gods."

Amid dust with the dense-packed troops, huddled group on the dais around the almost-apoplectic head-man, ring of expectant villagers, there was a freakish ebb in the confusion of noises, a moment nearly silent, so that Iruvakh's rendition of Kamin-Tolagh's words rang out, a proclamation.

The Man-mani gave a gasp and a sigh of wonder; a woman's voice came clear, "Noh-Sra-Lal-Hin!"

Many more took that up, and other things were being shouted, certainly not acclaim. But the abuse, unmistakably, was not for Kamin-Tolagh's presumption; it was directed against Sranadatta, as if the village had only just discovered how much they hated their head-man with his alien bodyguard, his greed and despotism. Threats were hurled, and Kamin-Tolagh abruptly thought he might have to use troops to prevent Sranadatta from being torn in pieces.

Now the words the man screamed were filled with resentment, as his face with fear and hatred; not hard to guess he was trying to reverse a turned tide, either to cow his people or to direct their rage against the usurper, the law-scorner.

All his sons had long knives out, and Kamin-Tolagh's eye was held by the sly face of Sranya-Dalhitta, plainly making an assessment. Added voices were joining the denunciation of Sranadatta, and the son's gaze swept the hostile crowd. To Kamin-Tolagh's astonishment and quick horror Sranya-Dalhitta, with the same unfeeling proficiency he had displayed in murdering disabled Hill Froghul, drove his blade into his father's heart. The head-man looked comically affronted, almost spoke, stiffened and died, Sranya-Dalhitta letting the crumpling body slide from his blade, which he held aloft, dripping blood. "Noh-Sra-Lal-Hin!" he shouted, and his further frenzied words had a mixed reception from his own people.

"We shall be brave and free as once we were," Iruvakh supplied in an expressionless tone. "Our slavery is over."

"Noh-Sra-Lal-Hin," one woman in the crowd sobbed out.

"This is not altogether what it appears," Iruvakh added in a more natural tone, as if in quiet talk over *raminat*. "Myanachë, youngest of Sranadatta's wives is the woman Sranya-Dalhitta wanted: his father took her from him."

Clearly, this was not proper vengeance, much less justice, for Siv'loi's killing. The two other sons had not given a clue how they felt about their father's murder, standing with blades immobile, eyes on Sranya-Dalhitta. The bodyguard frozen in shock, Kamin-Tolagh and a wedge of his men pushed through to mount the dais. Behind, Kambanal displayed intelligence with his cavalrymen, anchoring on the right and wheeling inward from the left, so the front of the dais was swept clear, with bodyguard hemmed in by the dismounted squadron.

Before Kamin-Tolagh could think of what to do next Sranya-Dalhitta dramatically fell to his knees beside the motionless body of his father, actually kneeling in a puddle of his father's blood. His two brothers, sheathing their knives, also abased themselves, but when Sranya-Dalhitta, presumably making a present of the murder to Noh-Sra-Lal-Hin, tried to hand up the gory knife, Kamin-Tolagh struck the back of his hand. Various sorts of self-interest, he perceived, could come into the making of new gods.

"Noh-Sra-Lal-Hin," the villagers were chanting. He could not see the covered shape of Siv'loi between the horses of Kambanal's squadron; she was as if already forgotten, assessed by history as the cause of events more important than she was.

"Noh-Sra-Lal-Hin," the Man-mani exulted. He needed time and talk to make it all clear; at this moment the tribe was absolutely his, and he had no idea what to do with it. There was merit to his earlier, angry notion of extermination: like Dorrmas after the slaughter at the Hatchery he could claim it was all to the good, making certain there could be no women to mother *jinzal*, not again, not ever.

7.

"You must give them a new head-man." Iruvakh had at last stilled most of the hubbub outside the Lunu Hut by telling admiring villagers Noh-Sra-Lal-Hin must have silence for thought, his god-thought. Short of armed force there was no way of making the curious and the wonderstruck go home, but while not even whispering was kept out by the flimsy walls, talk was now possible for those inside.

"Who is their choice?" Kamin-Tolagh asked.

Iruvakh made an impatient noise. "You must see, *Asai*, no choice made within the tribe can stand, without the endorsement of Noh-Sra-Lal-Hin. You have broken their old gods. If cruel to our understanding," he lectured at his most *Mankh'*-like, "the ways of their gods have been clear to the tribe, and with them the Man-mani have survived. For the moment, the idea of change has them excited, but without something new to put in place of what is gone, they will soon be lost. Sranya-Dalhitta," pedantically, "is undeniably among the best of the tribe. He will assuredly take his father's youngest widow for his wife. His half-brothers will follow him."

"He killed their father."

"That could be seen as justice. You yourself, *Asai*, have no doubt Sranadatta ordered Siv'loi's killing; his death could be called a just execution."

Not for the first time Kamin-Tolagh was reminded of his mother's shameless talent for giving acceptable names to expediency. If Iruvakh had really given up *atarlayum* over a plan to assail the realm with *jinzal*, he failed to see why; the man had no conscience. Everyone must know why Sranya-Dalhitta wanted his father dead. "He is not going to succeed the man he murdered," with finality. "I may let him live." The casual assumption of life-and-death powers here was altogether satisfying. His blood-hunger of an hour ago was dulled, but he was going to have executions, and soon; real ones with cold ceremony, dignified demonstrations of justice.

"Sra-Min-Talla-Tyu is very able for his age — "

"Why can we not consult the woman you say the Man-mani listen to?" There must be choices aside from the Sranadatta clan. "The mother of young Shamya."

"Chamya," Iruvakh corrected, and bared closed front teeth to demonstrate the first sound — very difficult, but no harder to say, he insisted, than the *j* in *jinzai*, also a borrowed sound not found in either language of the realm. The difference was, one was hummed, the other only breathed. All this instruction plainly helped Iruvakh master his irritation over what he perceived as Kamin-Tolagh's toying with the Man-mani future.

"I mean it," Kamin-Tolagh, in his levelest manner. "You tell me this woman is seen as wise."

"Osré-dnë. But men of the tribe would never ask the help of a woman, any woman, in choosing a new head-man."

"I bring new gods." Struck by a thought, Kamin-Tolagh chuckled. "If only the boy were a few years older he would make a fine head-man, with his mother sitting beside him, if the woman is all you say."

Iruvakh's lips tightened further. "This is not Kadon Dinul, where ceremony reigns. Chamya has not yet caught the rope, and if he had, the Man-mani head-man has to be a hunter, a proven warrior. That is why Sranya-Dalhitta, after all, may be best choice. His father's bodyguard, for a start, will follow him — "

"His father's bodyguard no longer exists." They were, in fact, being held by the troops. Unsure of what he wanted with the tribe, Kamin-Tolagh was obstinately determined no one would benefit from parricide: he meant to prevent marriage between Sranya-Dalhitta and the father's widow, Myanachë, though he could not stop them bedding together — only a difference, however, if the Man-mani had some sort of wedding ceremony.

"Indeed they have, *Asai* — " comfortable again, explaining. "They speak pledges, a small animal or bird is sacrificed. The bride's father gives the groom a glowing coal from the cooking fire at his own hut, which is then given to the bride — "

"And the bride," Lavsila conjectured, happy to find something to say, "scampers off to her new hut to start a cooking fire with the hot coal."

"Just so," Iruvakh gave his congratulatory beam, and went on to tell how maidens of the tribe, usually at their first moonsblood, were given marriage-tongs for the ritual of the coal; mainly crude and simple implements, they were among the few things beyond clothes ever owned by women, and often passed down from mother to daughter. There were, he added, other parts to the ceremony after first bedding, by which the man claimed the woman for his unshared own; to Kamin-Tolagh it meant Sranya-Dalhitta's standing with the tribe would be greatly diminished if he was unable to proclaim sole possession of Myanachë.

Most Owanil of the realm were repelled by the claims made by ordinary Mixed men about their women. But under Owani influence, those had become, except in remote parts, little beyond habits of speech, with no standing in law and diminishing force in everyday usage, nothing approaching this actual life-and-death ownership of Man-mani women Iruvakh could talk about so coolly — the set of mind that had led to the butchering of Siv'loi.

"I bring new gods," grimly. "Does that distress you? is it not more than time someone did?"

Iruvakh was all-but wringing his hands with vexation. "Time, whose time? *Asai*, you speak about consulting a woman to help choose a head-man, about disbanding the bodyguard, changing marriage-customs — how can you enforce these things?"

"He is Noh-Sra, whatever-it-is, isn't he?" Lavsila had spoken Kamin-Tolagh's god-name well enough earlier; this was another sample of his contemptuous posing.

Iruvakh turned on him. "For the present, the Man-mani will do as they are told by Lal-Hin. But a month, two months from now, when they begin to forget there ever was such a visit?" He struggled to sound as reasonable as he could. "The ones you dispossess, *Asai*, will deny Noh-Sra-Lal-Hin came here, they will say it was a mistake, or a fraud by those who wanted to seize control of the tribe. They will point to the unnatural new ways you brought — the better you succeed in bringing change, the bloodier it will be when the old customs come back — the clan of Sranadatta will not accept their eclipse, once the force that deposed them is gone."

"I might stay for a time," offhandedly. "I do not like the Kadon Dinul winter." If he shocked his listeners, he startled himself, not the words, but recognition they could be true; there was nothing waiting for him back in the realm, except to confront his mother with her guilt, Tovakh with his gullibility; except sourness toward the *rabhsai* who had withheld truth about Lunu Jinzalladhiyu. None of that was urgent. He began to recall his earlier, idle thoughts about a new protectorate here in the Farther West.

"The *rabhsai*," forestalling Lavsila's inevitable comment. "Will come to understand the unique opportunity here to extend the borders and prestige of his realm — these Man-mani are mine to mold — we can train them, make them fighters enough to stand up to the Hill Froghul. The whole West could be transformed, at practically no cost. Shumat — " once again anticipating Lavsila — "can't say anything about use I make of my own troops, men of Kargul; the bowmen from the Army of the West we shall return to him."

"You are Captain of the Household, Rodlakh's Household," Lavsila said.

"Leave of absence." Rodlakh must surely recognize his deception of Kamin-Tolagh left him the debtor.

"Why would Rodlakh want to spend his treasure *transforming the West*?" Lavsila began questioning how the men would be paid, not quite daring to say if the *rabhsai* held, as was predictable, that they had ceased to be the realm's responsibility, Kamin-Tolagh's father could yet more justifiably maintain they were no longer acting as provincial cavalry.

Lavsila's habitual opportunism was here surpassed by Iruvakh, who said reflectively, "With the name of Noh-Sra-Lal-Hin to invoke, it might finally be possible to get them to change to better methods of husbandry. Poor soil as it is here — " he returned to his teaching manner — "yield could be doubled, quite easily, really quite easily. Just a single growing-season, with means of enforcing my advice, and they would see what I have told them is true — there is nothing harder, *Asai*, than to make these tribes leave the ways they learnt from their fathers."

"These, the customs by which they have survived?" Kamin-Tolagh mocked, "Foolish to an outsider, maybe, but to impose change is dangerous. We must not do anything hasty — "

"*Asai* — " fumbling self-importantly for a distinction. "I am not speaking about lore which is as it is for its own sake, but of proven means of increasing yield, and guarding against drought — "

"We all have points too important for compromise," corrosively. "With you, crops badly planted, with me, murder of innocent girls — for some things, our ways, the ways of Owan, are not merely different, they are better, twist words however you try."

Iruvakh struggled, and his discomfiture either coincided with or brought about inexplicable change in Lavsila, whose face adopted an expression of complacent knowingness, as if deciding he was part of a clever conspiracy, his eyes virtually saying out loud in Kamin-Tolagh's direction, *I see what you are up to.*

What he imagined as other (and evidently more cunning) than Kamin-Tolagh's stated intentions was a subject that would have to wait: Iruvakh's guard was beaten down; time for the kill. "I have not studied the tribes as you have, master, but if you want to teach new practices, the worst ally you could find, surely, is this Sranadatta brood, who have accumulated what wealth there is. Who would be less welcoming to change of any kind?"

"Foolishly so," Iruvakh admitted. "Wealth, anywhere, must begin with the growing of food: our prosperous Heartland could have no weavers or dyers, no goldsmiths, cartwrights or scribes if every man and woman spent all their time producing the food needed to live. Till a people comes to where only part of its numbers can provide food for all, there can be no standing armies, no songmakers, no fine builders — "

"No priests," Kamin-Tolagh taunted.

"Say, rather, no scholar-priests. The poorest tribe has some species of belief about the unseen, and most have men adept at interpreting the signs, honored for that. Like Nifra."

"Or women, such as Osré-dnë, mother of *Chamya* — " biting down hard on the initial sound. Iruvakh's point about food as the beginning of all wealth had struck him with the force of a truth never considered, but there was no time to linger over it; he wanted the woman brought here.

She matched none of his expectations. In Lunu Tezh' last spring, during the Jinzai War, he had met one of the wise women of the Froghul, a *well-woman*, as they were called, a dark, impressive figure ancient as the earth. He'd had dealings, too, with *raf'yalul* of western Kargul, who could see, so they claimed, into the future, and sold charms against disease, danger, pain; they were not necessarily old women, but spoke in a high-flown, riddling way that set them apart; about Osré-dnë there was nothing to proclaim special powers. Age was unguessable; with her oval face, full lips and smooth, polished brow she was certainly above thirty, surely less than sixty; he supposed she might be considered beautiful, but there was nothing there for him, none of the playfulness he needed; the gaze was forthright, but the dark, alert eyes her son had inherited were filled with canny calculation.

She began with a deference to Kamin-Tolagh and a wordy appeal; Chamya, dressed in what must be his best, translated with Iruvakh's help. His mother was glad to have answered this summons, and asked Kamin-Tolagh to make it so Sranya-Dalhitta would not have bestowing of her. As his father's heir, Iruvakh explained, he would have the right to choose new husbands for his father's widows, one, presumably, being already chosen. Once again, it staggered Kamin-Tolagh the crudest rules of the most primitive tribe could fail to debar profiting from murder. "Tell your mother, she has nothing to fear. Sranya-Dalhitta will have no voice; Noh-Sra-Lal-Hin does not permit it."

Chamya, with evident relish, translated. Osré-dnë nodded her approval, and her next remark echoed Iruvakh: "My mother says, but the Man-mani must have a new head-man."

She was not wasting time with a pretence of mourning her husband. "In that," Kamin-Tolagh said, "we would hear the thoughts of Osré-dnë, to help us choose."

This proposition flustered Chamya, who fumbled for a start on his translation. "Men," Iruvakh confided, "do not ask women for advice, not directly, not ever, not even an Osré-dnë."

Kamin-Tolagh gestured impatiently. "They must learn new ways."

Perhaps with his own plans in mind Iruvakh bypassed Chamya's struggles, conveying Kamin-Tolagh's meaning to the woman. She too was taken off-guard, muttering what translated as her unworthiness to advise such greatness. When she sounded the name, Noh-Sra-Lal-Hin, Kamin-Tolagh wondered whether he really detected a veiled glint of irony: was it conceivable she had made up her mind to take maximum advantage of the legend, not for a moment believing it had manifested itself in Kamin-Tolagh?

He threw out an easier bait to her opinions: "I am told with the clan of Sranadatta to lead them Man-mani have prospered."

Osré-Dnë gave a look to Iruvakh as if identifying the source of that report, and abandoned her abject pose, eyes brilliant with scorn.   "The clan of Sranadatta," Chamya translated, with shared conviction, "has surely prospered. In the day of my father's father, less food grew in the valley, but every man, if not robbed by Hill Froghul, had enough to last the winter. In those days robbers came from outside the Man-mani." On his own account, Chamya added, "Today, *Asai*, most have to choose between bondage and hunger."

Iruvakh, without apologizing for his former sympathies, explained it had been Sranadatta's practice to supply foodstuffs as a loan during lean winter months, against a promise of double repayment. Inevitably, paying off these loans had led to a worse shortage the next winter, and grower after grower had ended by forfeiting his small lands to the head-man, and becoming his vassal.

"I was beginning to think the Man-mani had learnt nothing from their long association with Owanil," one eye on Lavsila. "But this Sranadatta was sharp as any Heartlander, with his loans and foreclosures."

"Do not believe Dolvid's eternal rant. The Families do not make loans on such extortionate terms.   If Heartland smallholdings have been lost, it is because they were poorly farmed. That patchwork farming is always inefficient; when the little garden-plots are incorporated into workable farmlands, more food is grown, everyone prospers."

"Especially those who do the *incorporating*." Kamin-Tolagh enjoyed baiting Lavsila, but these were not his real interests; he did not care who controlled the land, there or here, Lavsila's cousins or Chamya's uncles, listening only perfunctorily as Iruvakh tried to explain how fairer shares of better harvests could be realized. He was additionally distracted by sounds of a new altercation outside, not far from the hut, men's voices rising in anger.

It would be a mistake to settle the question of the new head-man too swiftly, since anyone he chose, no matter how compliant to begin with, could rally opposition to the drastic changes there were going to be. "We shall name a new head-man," loftily, "when the matter can be fully considered. For the present, my counsellor here is Osré-dnë."

Before this was wholly translated, Kambanal, coming from outside, poked his head into the room with an apologetic cough. "Pardon me, *Asai*. The leader of the Man-mani, who is so good at cutting throats of wounded enemies — the one who stabbed his father — "

"Sranya-Dalhitta. Well?"

"He is here, *Asai*, with a small crowd of kin, and other rabble, demanding — " there was more than a hint of caustic emphasis on the word — "*demanding* to speak with you." Kambanal imitated the man's imperfect Owanilú: "*not right woman and boy brought while big Man-mani men wait for speech with Noh-Sra-Lal-Hin.*"

Kamin-Tolagh went to the young officer, and with a touch of ceremony removed the squadron-leader's insigne from right side of his outshirt, where it signified acting rank, and refastened it over on the left, where it was permanent. "This you have earned," cutting short stammered words. "We have adequate forces here?"

"*Asai*, they don't breed many heroes. Squadron Freighanai is just down from Meeting Place, and Squadron Talfoyan has his men at the gate. There won't be any visitors you do not summon."

Kamin-Tolagh found he could appear decisive by reaching a decision. "Tell Sranya-Dalhitta there is to be a meeting, where Noh-Sra-Lal-Hin will give his judgments, an hour from now. At Meeting Place, for the whole tribe."

After Kambanal went out, and Kamin-Tolagh reannounced the meeting, Chamya said, "Shall I sit in the high place with Noh-Sra-Lal-Hin, next to my mother?   Before, because my father was not Sranadatta, I was below."   For stepsons, Kamin-Tolagh saw, different customs expressed the same complaints everywhere. He had been joking when he spoke of Chamya as a fine choice for head-man, but now he wished in earnest the boy was just a little older, and had caught the rope, whatever that was.

Chamya asked, "Are we to have feasting? Goats are ready for killing, and roasting-wood cut."

Iruvakh was shocked. "The murder of Sranadatta cannot be marked with celebrations."

"But victory, my victory over the Hill Froghul, deserves applause. Yes. After judgments, a feast."

He was beginning to enjoy himself again: here was a world he could move like a puppet with a twitch of his finger. Osré-dnë merely nodded when told about the feast, and showed no particular emotion of any kind to hear she and her son would be accommodated here at the Lunu Hut. He would like to see her thoughts.

After Iruvakh left for the Meeting Place with Osré-Dnë and her son surrounded by a heavy escort, Kamin-Tolagh was alone for a moment with Lavsila, who grinned. "What will you do? leave the Karguli banner flying over the village, tell them you will be watching from afar?"

Kamin-Tolagh was baffled, till he recognized what was behind the earlier conspiratorial looks: Lavsila thought talk of staying here through winter was a sort of bluff, or decoy. He could hardly offer a plausible reason why Kamin-Tolagh would lie, but neither could he imagine what there was to keep them here. Whether he would stay was conjectural.

"You are squandering all the goodwill you have gained," he warned. "Our young *rabhsai* will be angry."

"He will thank me in the end. I shall send Rodlakh a letter, explaining my purpose, the unique opportunity there is here."

"Yes, a unique opportunity to train fighting men, with the tribe that mothers *jinzal*? I am merely pointing out how it will appear at Kadon."

"No one is forced to stay. Those who wish may return with Shumat's forces."

"What inducement to stay can you offer your troops?"

"There are men who have fought *jinzal* beside me, men with loyalty," hoping that was true. As for Lavsila, he could go or stay, it did not matter. Once again he had demonstrated how an excess of cleverness could make a man stupid.

In the common-room Freighanai was waiting. Table was covered, the floor cluttered with offerings, mainly fruit, brought, Freighanai said, by those who wanted to lay them at the feet of Noh-Sra-Lal-Hin.

"Girls, mostly, *Asai*," stooping to pick up a smooth-skinned golden melon. "This one, *Asai*, has hair almost to her waist, dimples when she smiles. Slender little thing, but plenty of shape to her." A married man who, even after long separation from his wife, seldom looked at a woman for himself, Freighanai, with most of Kamin-Tolagh's squadron, took personal pride in his leader's reputation. With Siv'loi scarcely cold the thought of new conquests might seem tasteless, but Kamin-Tolagh had to admit Freighanai was right; the girl, if she had lived, would soon have been replaced. "You'll have to point her out to me," he said, so as not to disappoint his officer.

"Some of the men, *Asai*, they're wondering, the young ones, specially, if that about the scar still holds, the ugly who was supposed to own them being dead and all."

This needed care. As Lavsila implied, Kamin-Tolagh did not have much to offer his men for reward, and if they stayed till spring he could not ask them to behave as fish among willing young women inclined to see them as heroes, slayers of the Hill Froghul. Yet quite aside from conflict with the Man-mani bachelors, there was the danger of fathering a whole new generation of *jinzal*.

Most rules he could formulate instantly; for the feasting tonight, watches must be arranged to let all the men take part for a time, but no drunkenness would be tolerated. No women were to be taken against their will, and no married women, the wives of those on the firewood expedition, however willing.

"Understood, *Asai*," Freighanai murmured.

"I shall not accept excuses such as *she would not be refused, she came to my bed of her own choice*; no wives are to be had — and none of the women we brought from the Lunu —
"

"With the silver rings," Freighanai nodded, touching his own ear.

"Women who were called Sranadatta's are free to make their choices. But you had better warn the men they may be here longer than we had thought."

He watched for reaction. Freighanai adopted one of a soldier's traditional faces, resigned, perversely proud of anticipated abuses. "*Asai*, when they told us two months for this business, most of us guessed half a year. It's the way."

Some of them, part of the Karguli force seconded to the Household while Ban-Sila still reigned, had already been away from their homes almost a year. "Men who form friendships, if they give presents to their new friends, it must be their own property, not cavalry stores."

"They know that, well enough, *Asai*."

"Do they. After ten days at Kamsilat before we went to Kadon, the only things they had not given the Colony women were their breastplates and saddles. If I see a woman of the Man-mani with a new blanket, or using harness-leather for a belt, I shall find out who her friend is. Make that known to the men, too."

"Very good, *Asai*."

"One thing. Do you have a man who could make a clean job of cutting off a head?"

"With a sword, you mean?" Freighanai pondered. "Well, Vakhsilai, that boy giant of a file-leader in Talfoyan's squadron. He looks as if he could take the head off a bullock."

"We need him, at once."

Muttering had greeted pronouncement of sentence on the two men who had killed and mutilated Siv'loi. Iruvakh said there was no remembered example of a man being put to death for killing a woman; he could recall the case of one sent to live outside the tribe for six years after killing his mother, but a man who killed a woman who counted as his property, or commanded her death, was seen as unfortunate rather than wicked, like a farmer obliged to put down a sick or injured animal. These, moreover, as they tried to protest, had acted only under orders. Still, they were not Man-mani, making their unjust execution popular with the tribe, and in the event interesting to watch. At a sign from Kamin-Tolagh the brawny young Vakhsilai stepped forward, sword already bared, to where the two men were on their knees in front of the raised platform, hands bound behind them. Two steps back, a quick stride forward, blade whirling, and the first head flew, trunk falling sideways, neck gushing blood. A curious sound came from the watching villagers, gasp, groan, sigh and murmur of triumph all at once. From glances among his soldiery Kamin-Tolagh guessed there had been wagers on whether Vakhsilai could do it in one stroke.

Made over-confident, he struck high when it came to the second man, finding too much bone: it might be his sword had lost the fineness of its edge. Though the victim toppled forward, he let out an agonized scream, and a second stroke, then a third, were needed to sever the head. The youthful executioner was caught between pride and apology; the Man-mani had fallen to silence, and the two heads lay nose-to-nose, as if conferring. Soldiers carried and dragged away the four parts, and someone had foreseen the need for sand to strew on the puddles of blood.

Removal of the corpses released the tongues of the Man-mani; the buzz and ripple of discussion came, many eyes turning to where the clan of the late head-man had taken up their stand, Sranya-Dalhitta prominent in their midst; they had arrived in a clump, but made no attempt to mount the ceremonial dais. Long knives remained sheathed, though there had been restlessness when they saw Osré-dnë and Chamya beside Kamin-Tolagh.

Kamin-Tolagh's sentence was a shock for all the tribe, but for Sranya-Dalhitta was bound to be seen as a personal affront. Iruvakh had warned it could provoke desperate deeds, and Kamin-Tolagh answered, "I hope so." His cavalry was ready, and at three places on the fringes of the Meeting Place Noldar's men, carefully instructed, had bows in their hands. An excuse for annihilating the whole troublesome *Sra*-brood was exactly what Kamin-Tolagh thirsted for, the more so when he noticed the slight, wisp-bearded Nifra, whose ambiguous oath had enabled butchery of his own daughter.

A pallid sun was settling into layered haze above Flamûrai as Kamin-Tolagh, through Iruvakh, called for silence, and announced Noh-Sra-Lal-Hin gave the Man-mani new laws.

Sranya-Dalhitta spoke loudly to anyone nearby, words which Iruvakh translated as: "What are new god-thoughts without a head-man to speak them?" His half-brothers boisterously agreed, but while it sounded rebellious it gladdened Kamin-Tolagh; his authority was being confirmed in the act of protest; this plainly conceded he alone could make a new head-man.

Still through Iruvakh he began his lawgiving with what everyone there could see as an assault on the pretensions of the Sranadatta clan; no man was to profit from murder, or could take possession of goods belonging to the man he had killed, nor his lands, nor any title that was his. Nor could he marry the widow of his victim.

He was using ordinary language of the realm, which no one in the tribe seemed to understand at all, translation slowed by the difficulty of the thought — and, plainly, Iruvakh's nervousness over the effect these words would have. Thus, Kamin-Tolagh was able to observe the unconcealed glee of Chamya, the mounting outrage of Sranya-Dalhitta, who at the last clause burst out with an angry cry in his own language.

"He says, *false trade*," Chamya informed Kamin-Tolagh.

"False *dealing*," Iruvakh amended. "*Treachery*, or *betrayal* — yes, betrayal."

Voice overburdened with bitterness and angry rejection, Sranya-Dalhitta, in his faulty Owanilú, called out: "Noh-Sra-Lal-Hin! I, I am to be head-man. New law after." His half-brother, Sra-Min-Talla-Tyu, translated this for the tribe, and the only response was scattered jeering from boys and one or two old men. Most women, greater part of the assembly, looked away.

It was Osré-dnë who, with arms outstretched, exhorted the Man-mani to hear the new ways brought them by Noh-Sra-Lal-Hin. Suddenly moved to real passion, or with a new-found talent for creating effect, she made the god-name into a trumpet-call, and the stir of excitement and anticipation this caused led Kamin-Tolagh to expect tumultuous approval from the women for the first of his pronouncements: the days of owning women were finished; not father nor husband nor head-man from this time could call a woman his property.

After an uncomprehending stare, Chamya made heavy labor of conveying these words, and his translation was met by near-silence. Even women marked with the arrowhead scar showed no sign of gladness, but were, if anything, more perplexed than the men, some uttering despondent little whimpers.

Iruvakh failed to conceal smugness. "Do you wonder, *Asai*? Women here have always been property; the terms *daughter* or *wife* include the idea of ownership. Slavery may appear better than nothingness."

"Say," Kamin-Tolagh instructed him, bypassing the baffled Chamya. "*No man can own a woman, just as no woman can own a man.*"

Reluctantly, Iruvakh spoke. A general catch in the breath, and then a burst of laughter; by far the most successful joke Kamin-Tolagh had ever made. Young boys slapped at each other, old women covered their mouths to laugh, girls pressed knees together as they giggled with their friends. The men of the Sranadatta clan did all they could to prolong the merriment, making derisive gestures, dry voice of Nifra prominent, forcing a harsh, sarcastic laugh.

"As I told you, *Asai*," pettishly. "This to them is as silly as if it were to be declared men could not own horses, nor horses, men."

"Silence them," determined not to let annoyance show.

Iruvakh turned back to Osré-Dnë, who had given no sign of amusement, and now raised her hands, reminding the tribe, it must be, that Noh-Sra-Lal-Hin spoke to them.

"Nothing," Lavsila confided in Kamin-Tolagh's ear, "can be done with such ignorance. You will need whips, not words."

Kamin-Tolagh, passing on from the hilarious issue of women as chattels, now gave a series of specific judgments which were, as intended, blow after blow at the Sranadatta clan, disbanding the remainder of their foreign bodyguard, cancelling debts, delaying inheritance of the late head-man's property, either lands or goods, till it could be determined which had been unlawfully acquired.

This was the critical moment, and Kamin-Tolagh took swift glances at his senior officers to be sure they were alert. The former bodyguard, disarmed, encircled rather than held captive by Kamin-Tolagh's men, were at the foot of the platform, and from the right Sranya-Dalhitta and his following began pushing in that direction. Quite aside from prestige, they must feel they had no chance of dominating the tribe unless they kept their armed servants. Without need for orders a double-file of dismounted cavalry moved to interpose; the second son, Sra-Min-Talla-Tyu, went angrily for his knife. Kamin-Tolagh made a one-finger signal, Noldar's bow twanged softly, and from at least thirty paces ruffled the man's hair with an arrow, which ended sticking in a pole of the canopy. Noldar quietly fitted a fresh arrow to his string, his men watching him for a sign. The next arrow would wound, followed by a killing volley, but in that throng Kamin-Tolagh had not expected the warning shot so close. He could almost wish the calmly expert Noldar had made a slight error, provoking the fight that would exterminate the Sranadatta clan. As was, they were frozen in place, merely observing while the bodyguard was led away.

To hooting on all sides, especially from the women, who began to see Noh-Sra-Lal-Hin meant what he said. In the tumult Sranya-Dalhitta preserved what dignity he could. At a quiet word from him, his people, with sullen stares of resentment for the tribe they had hoped to inherit, made off down the slope for the head-man's hut. That dwelling, too, they would have to yield, but for the moment Kamin-Tolagh motioned his men to let them go; Osré-dnë, he noted, watched the retreat with undisguised satisfaction, lips slightly parted, eyes thoughtful.

A cool wind roused and swirled, carrying the musty and acrid odors of this place; Kamin-Tolagh took in the scene, the ragged people and their tattered domicile, the eager face of Chamya, unguessable thoughts behind the smooth self-containment of the mother, and marvelled at how he had to remind himself how unfamiliar everything was; he had mislaid his sensation of strangeness, vanished, he guessed, at the moment when he learned about his mother's complicity in the breeding and training of *jinzal*. When, rather, he tried and failed to disbelieve it; after that, between expectation and reality there could be no gap wide enough to astonish him.

"Let the fires be lighted," he commanded. The piled wood stood ready.

He had noticed Chamya briefly scowl over disbanding of the bodyguard, who were to be sent back their own tribe. "Why should that displease you?"

"Noh-Sra-Lal-Hin speaks his will —" the boy forced a submissive expression. They were seated side by side on the dais, Osré-dnë gleaming nearby. Senior officers had joined them, and Lavsila had found another of the girls formerly Sranadatta's, taller than Siv'loi, and with about a dozen words of the Owanilú, all amusing. Other women and sometimes men of the tribe kept bringing Kamin-Tolagh choice bits of meat, sweet fruits, grain cooked with spices into a gluey mass, cup after cup of thin, flat beer. Flickering flames and many rushlights gave a cheerful, dappling illumination.

"Hwenala," Chamya cautiously offered, "are Man-mani enemies. They want the *n'dwatta* lands, and we should take them, and fight for them."

Iruvakh's tilted ear did not miss the chance for a dissertation. What the Man-mani called *n'dwatta*, he explained, was a spice, variously named among the tribes of the Froghushei as *tvathi*, *dhako*, or *dao*, the most usual name east of the hills, when it travelled there. Prized by all tribes, it was said to produce a pleasant lightheadedness when swallowed in quantity, or with its smoke when burned on a small, hot fire. Iruvakh could not confirm that claim, since he found the spice, hot and sweet at the same time, quickly cloying, its smoke unpleasantly pungent. It came from the tiny, hard fruit of a plant which grew here and there in somewhat moister spots along the westward slope of the hills, but in quantity in only one place, a small valley south of here, to which both Man-mani and the Hwenala asserted an ancestral right. He said, the Man-mani, but in recent years the spice had, with everything else in the tribe, become practically private property of Sranadatta and his close relatives. Since it was one of very few commodities with value in trade, the dispute with the Hwenala had in the past been a bitter one; at present possession of the spice vale was precariously shared, but no Man-mani leader had accepted that as permanent, and for the past year or so Sranadatta had been trying to whip up his people for a new round of the perennial war, accusing the Hwenala of violating the peace.

"There is *n'dwatta* in this," Iruvakh, scooping up three fingersful of the cooked wheat mash.

Clearly, the unwarlike Man-mani would have been particularly reluctant to fight a war to benefit no one but their acquisitive ruling clan, but Kamin-Tolagh could not see how retention of the Hwenala bodyguard entered the question: Chamya's complaint seemed to be against the folly of giving back to the enemy better than a dozen good fighting-men, originally brought here in an exchange of hostages. Evading the boy's natural partiality he went into ordinary language to ask Iruvakh why the two tribes, with Sranadatta gone, should not share peaceably in the spice valley and its proceeds.

"Your own province, *Asai*," complacently, "has for years clamored for return of the lands called Paowanu Loi — "

"Kovilanu," giving the original name, "is Kargul's again; I won it back when I agreed to help the *rabhsai* in his war."

"Still, many years of bitterness could have been saved, if the region and its revenues could have been shared between Kargul and the Paowan."

"Kovilanu is ours."

"That is much what the Man-mani would say about the spice valley. And the Hwenala, I do not doubt."

That irritated Kamin-Tolagh; the Kovilanu had never been a disputed region till wrenched away from its province after the War of the Widowed, but he was sure Iruvakh would continue to insist on the parallel.

He let the subject drop. All the soldiery, not merely the loftier ranks here on the dais, were being pampered by the Man-mani, and there were signs of quick-ripening friendships, touchings and the challenges of eyes. Enforcing the restrictions he had listed for Freighanai was not going to be easy. Through Iruvakh he asked if Osré-dnë could watch out for the *fidelity* (as Others called it) of married women whose husbands were away.

She said something sardonic, with a dry laugh. "And the horse-soldiers, *Asai*," Iruvakh supplied. "Are they all without wife?"

Having had the temerity to give this reply the woman was watching warily to see how it was received.

He decided to smile. "Tell her, no, but none of the soldiers' wives can come here and find their men bedded with other women. Lal-Hin, tell her, does not care about *chastity* of Man-mani wives, but wishes to avoid anger between his tribe and hers."

"I do not have a word for *chastity*," Iruvakh complained. "Not one that does not include the very principle you are trying to banish, the idea women can be property."

"Say it how you can."

It took longer, but Kamin-Tolagh felt undeniably flattered when a nod by Osré-dnë obviously acknowledged good sense in what he said. She agreed, according to Iruvakh's translation, to be "mother-in-law to the whole Man-mani," and with Kambanal assigned to her was soon moving among feasters, saying words to sober overexcited young wives.

Lavsila looked like taking his lissome catch back to the Lunu Hut. Kamin-Tolagh knew Noh-Sra-Lal-Hin could have any woman for crooking a finger, but he was too weary; he had been up since well before sunrise, and had fought many battles, of which the one with the Hill Froghul' raiders had been much the easiest.

Yet as the great cooking-fires burnt down to a steady red, permitting the white silences of innumerable stars to appear above, Kamin-Tolagh wished after all there could be a woman, not so much for bedding as to have been beside him through the day, applauding his deeds, his unexpected flair for so much other than war. Not the simple Siv'loi, who would be memorable mainly in what her murder had provoked. His sister, perhaps, Kamin-Tarú. But she took his success for granted, and what he wanted was astonished praise for talents newly revealed. No, not Kamin-Tarú; someone else.

Near dawn there was a bungled attempt to set fire to the Lunu Hut, and presumably to kill off Iruvakh, Chamya and Osrédnë, as well as Kamin-Tolagh with several of his senior officers. Three men with piled brushwood absurdly tried to reach the back wall unobserved while carrying a blazing torch, and were challenged from the shadows of other huts by Noldar's bowmen, who shot two of the firesetters when they made to run. The third man escaped, possibly wounded.

As light grew one of the dead was identified as a cousin of Sranya-Dalhitta's. At about the same time the head-man's hut was found to have been abandoned by all except what Lavsila called "a selection of new widows." Here, Iruvakh said, he was quite wrong; the women left behind were none of them wives or former wives of Sranadatta or his sons.

Very soon Talfoyan rode in from riverside to give a sour-faced report; at half-dawn, he said, men had come to the compound storehouses, wanting to load what they said was their own food and feed onto pack-animals. "The Man-mani fools there would have let them, but my men roused me, and I went over with an extra half-squadron and put a stop to it, told them they must take it up with yourself, *Asai*, at a decent hour, I had no authority to let such quantities be carried off. That same lordly young swine, it was — Sran-hitta-something, is it? — he tried to make out he didn't understand plain speech. *Is mine, is mine,* he kept saying, but these princes of the dustlands soon sing softer when they see hard steel. He looked swords at me, but if he'd touched a hilt he would have been wearing a lance in his navel. He'll come to that in the end, I don't doubt."

"You did well," Kamin-Tolagh said, hard as it was to give praise to a manner so surly.

Iruvakh, newly risen, shook his head, observing the food did in fact belong to the Sranadatta clan.

"We must send it after them by pack-train." Together with fourteen surviving Hwenala guards, the deposed ruling family, after failing to move Talfoyan, had made off southward; their one success was to have stolen the hill-ponies captured from yesterday's raiders.

Iruvakh's opinion was, they would try to make allies of the Hwenala, perhaps recognize the permanent Hwenala right to the spice-valley in return for restoration to power over the Man-mani. Chamya's eyes flashed bitter contempt for this conjectured treachery, but Kamin-Tolagh could not make it add up: if the Hwenala with their famous dogs had not been able to seize all the spice-lands before now, how could the slight reinforcement of about twenty Man-mani fighting men, plus return of fourteen of their own, improve their chances against the Man-mani protected by regular cavalry?

"They'll wait till we have gone," Talfoyan, with a covert look at Kamin-Tolagh; the soldiers had heard rumors he meant to stay, and were beginning to wonder how long.

Kambanal, who very nearly blushed with self-consciousness when he had a comment to offer, reminded them about the return of the wood-cutters, expected any hour. "In my understanding, *Asai,* most of the best men of the tribe were with that expedition, and I suppose some of them must belong to the Sranadatta clan — "

"Sranya-Dalhitta will want to claim all of them," Iruvakh
predicted.

He made his best attempt, intercepting the woodcutting
party about fifteen miles south of the village, and giving a
garbled account of happenings, taking credit for victory over the
Hill Froghul, blaming death of his father on traitors who had
allied themselves to Kamin-Tolagh, the false Noh-Sra-Lal-Hin.
Unfortunately for him, the woodcutters had already heard a
plainer account from some families returning to outlying homes
after taking refuge at the village when the raid threatened.
Except for the dozen or so of the Sranadatta clan, or their
direct dependents, the men, Kamin-Tolagh thought, would hardly
have joined Sranya-Dalhitta, never mind if they believed his
story; why would they fight, making alliance, as he intended,
with the hated Hwenala, in order to restore the father's
despotism? Outnumbering Sranya-Dalhitta's current following
by four to one, and including many of the tribe's most warlike
men, the bulk of the woodcutting party, not fooled, could not be
cowed, either, and the two groups parted in bad temper, but
without open fighting. Sranya-Dalhitta's strength increased only
to about fifty, including the former bodyguard.
A leader with the woodcutting party, Dilana, unusually
large-framed and burly by Man-mani standards, a cousin, he said,
of Osré-dnë, was brought to Kamin-Tolagh at the Lunu Hut, and
with Iruvakh's help spoke of sending men southward at once to
seize Sranadatta's parts of the spice-lands, make them truly Man-
mani again. For this, he begged the help of the horse-soldiers.
Clearly, swift defeat of the Sranadatta clan was desirable, but
Kamin-Tolagh was reluctant to let cavalry of Kargul be seen as
the ready tool of Man-mani needs, and was not at all certain this
Dilana did not mean simply to succeed Sranadatta in controlling
the *n'dwatta* business.
Lavsila was seated at the table, amusing himself making
rough sketches for wind-driven pumping devices to bring water

up from the river and irrigate lower slopes of the valley. Without looking up he said in a conversational voice, "According to Iruvakh here, the other tribes of this region would never accept Man-mani domination — the Hill Froghul would be less hated. Do I have that right?"

"Man-mani," sententiously, following Lavsila into the ordinary language of Arbhal, "will always be outsiders, interlopers from across the water."

Once again Kamin-Tolagh had to take a sharp glance at Dilana to be sure he had not understood: the lifelong habit of putting private talk into the Owanilú was hard to forget. He said, "I hear too much of that *always*. The tribes will accept what they have to. The Man-mani have been this side of the water for a thousand years."

"With assistance from their friends at the Lunu."

Kamin-Tolagh made an impatient gesture, but Lavsila's point was readily expanded-on by Iruvakh: the Hill Froghul, having carried off women from these parts, must have a strain of unacknowledged Man-mani blood, but the Man-mani despised voluntary admixture with the other tribes, who, despite their inability to ally against the Hill Froghul, recognized their languages as related, and were to an extent intermarried. They would be much readier to combine against a Man-mani given ascendancy by Kamin-Tolagh's forces, once left to fend for itself.

"A wonder to me," keeping the same elaborately casual tone, "the Lunu did not take control of this spice all the tribes are supposed to be so keen on. It is the first thing I would do."

A part of Lavsila's new game of Iruvakh-baiting, no conflict, a dovetail, rather, with Kamin-Tolagh's sudden conviction that if there was to be war with the Hwenala, his men must defeat them, not in alliance with the feeble Man-mani fighting forces, but alone, so a settlement could then be dictated to both tribes, not victor and vanquished but equally subordinate to his wishes. He had no hold on the other tribes comparable to his recognition by the Man-mani as Noh-Sra-Lal-Hin, but control over the spice they all used should give him leverage.

"You would have grounds for your own war against the Hwenala," Lavsila said. "If they give refuge to Sranya-Dalhitta and his crew, who made war on you. You can demand the Hwenala hand them over as prisoners — "

"They will refuse." Iruvakh insisted. "No tribe of the Froghushei could comply with such a demand. It would lose all standing."

"Of course they will refuse," Lavsila agreed in a bored tone. "I may not know what this tribe or that does to keep away evil spirits, but I know men."

This was direct imitation of Kamin-Tolagh's earlier rebuke to special claims of expertise: Iruvakh might have taken offense, if he had thought of it, but obviously was struck with how this changed situation could be made to serve his long-standing dream of ending famine here. He began to expound on how the two things were related, the constant threat of Hill Froghul raids and the slowness of the tribes to adopt improved methods of growing their food. Not only that all the tribes to an extent had the hopeless feeling raiders would inevitably take away any increase they achieved, but all their fears fueled and confirmed each other; mutual suspicions prevented alliance against the common enemy; constant fear of famine left all obstinately hostile to any change in how they planted or tended their crops, and their traditional methods were wasteful of energies better used in concerting a defense against raids. While the old masters of the Lunu Jinzalladhiyu had provided protection, and made preventive war against the Hill Froghul, they had never given wholehearted support to Iruvakh's attempts at forming a coalition of the tribes.

"I have said it for years, alliance, if it came, would have to be imposed, till its benefits could be plainly seen — as with good growing-practice."

Kamin-Tolagh laughed. "My mother would recognize you. I grew up watching how blandly she could change horses — oh, I am not saying you lack constancy," he assured the man, who was about to express outrage. "Neither did she. She had her goals, perhaps still has them, and anything will do to advance them — as I now know, to the extent of letting loose an army of *jinzal* on the realm."

"*Asai*, I stood aloof from the purposes of the Lunu. I had other aims, better ones."

"Exactly. You want to bring safety to the Froghushei, so these poor savages can learn to feed themselves. For that you were willing to be an ally to the robber, Sranadatta, and when he was killed you wanted me to sponsor his son, who murdered him. When I declined that, you saw how the name and powers of Noh-Sra-Lal-Hin could, after all, change the Man-mani, make them your tool, but if not that, it will suit you just as well if we use armed force to achieve the cooperation of the tribes. I thought my mother was singlepurposed, but you make her seem as lightminded as Finú."

After a struggle Iruvakh recovered aplomb. "*Asai*, you have not told me your aims in staying here in the West, beyond making something of these tribes, but as I have said, nothing can be done with this or any people till they learn to feed themselves in peace."

The Man-mani, Dilana, had been watching all this talk with dark, puzzled eyes. "Shall I tell the men to be ready to march south?"

For the Hwenala there was no need to issue Lavsila's ultimatum; the marsh-dwellers began the fighting, and with an attack (if it could be called that) against regular cavalry. The action was fought near and partially within the shallow valley where the *n'dwatta* was harvested, the armed horde of the Hwenala having driven the Man-mani spice-gatherers from their ramshackle dwellings at the valley's northward fringe.

This was two hours' riding south and west of the Man-mani country proper, and only one of the tribe was with Kamin-Tolagh as guide, Chamya, who rode a small hill-pony; the great *pefral* went at an easy canter so the mounted bows could keep pace, and the boy was under strict orders to stay well clear of any fighting there was.

The main body of Hwenala, hard to count in its straggling order, but some hundreds strong, made straight for the oncoming cavalry, and sent their dogs ahead, a couple of dozen lank yellow beasts with matted hair and long heads like a big lop-eared rat. Conceivably, in the past, the mangy beasts had caused panic among enemy on foot or mounted on pack-ponies: here, their masters shouting them on, not one ventured nearer than twenty-five paces from the advance of war-trained horses. The foremost of the dogs, coming hard, made a splay-footed stop, let out a high-pitched howl, and when he bolted they all did. At the same time arrows, too raggedly released to be called a volley, began falling short of the cavalry, though from the flanks, where various small bands of Hwenala were mostly waiting to see how the main fight went, one shot reached a *pefrai*, and weakly bounced off the animal's hide. The Hwenala, though slighter in build than their Man-mani neighbors, appeared a little apter for war, but their bows were limp little things they pulled only to their chests, and again the arrows had no real tips, only fire-charred points. "With a lucky hit," as Kambanal said afterwards, "they might injure a duck."

At a nod from Kamin-Tolagh, Noldar's bows sang in unison, eight or ten of the main enemy force fell dead or wounded, some cast down their weapons and raised their empty hands. Dozens joined the headlong retreat of their yelping dogs, while against the remainder who stood to fight Kamin-Tolagh led the cavalry, lance-points serried as in a drill. One man who mowed at him with a crude spear, iron point lashed to a rough stick, he spitted; dropping lance he went across for his sword, and by the time it was out the battle was good as won, many of the enemy throwing themselves down and covering their heads, others scattering as they could.

The melting-away of the Hwenala revealed, at what had been the heart of the fighting force, a knot of momentarily more determined men, bawling at the others to stand up and fight, men of the Sranadatta clan; Kamin-Tolagh recognized the eldest half-brothers, Sranya-Dalhitta and Sra-Min-Talla-Tyu, and others of those who had stood with them at Meeting Place, but could not see the man he most wanted to meet, Nifra, who had not less than concurred in his daughter's ugly murder.

Despite defiant noises, the renegade Man-mani very swiftly decided they could not stand up alone to two squadrons of cavalry, and as they also fell back Kamin-Tolagh shouted to Kambanal these were the men to pursue; there was little point in hunting down the fleeing Hwenala. He himself spurred after Sranya-Dalhitta, who made a swerving retreat through clumps of growth. When a quick glance over the shoulder convinced him he could not outrun the *pefrai* he turned, jumped aside into brush, and aimed a cut with a battered sword, which Kamin-Tolagh warded in passing, then wheeled his rearing mount to cut down Sranya-Dalhitta with a crisp backhand to the throat. The man was very likely dead before his body hit the ground.

Not long after Kamin-Tolagh was rejoined by Kambanal near the middle of the valley, where no live enemy bearing arms was visible. In routing six to seven hundred of the Hwenala — though many were never engaged — Kamin-Tolagh's forces had suffered mainly minor wounds to men and mounts; one of Noldar's archers had been struck in the neck by an arrow, but though bleeding copiously the shallow wound was nothing near

mortal. Of the Sranadatta clan and its adherents eleven were
dead and twelve captured, most of those wounded, though there
were also three women discovered sheltering in one of the little
Hwenala storage-sheds, even cruder than those of the Man-mani.
Nifra had not been seen, neither had the woman, Myanachë,
cause of bad blood between Sranadatta and his son, and Sra-Min-
Talla-Tyu did not appear among either dead or captured.

Dismounting for a breather Kamin-Tolagh's eye was
caught by a lank, weedy plant with sprays of small flowers
exactly the clear, pale blue of Kargul — the color of their banner,
or facings on their cavalry-tunics. At that moment Chamya, still
watched over by a lancer, came up. "That, *Asai*, is the *n'dwatta*."

Kamin-Tolagh thought, yes, but the Man-mani name was
not what the spice would be called now he controlled it; of the
string of names recited by Iruvakh the one which stuck in his
mind was the sonorous one used by the eastern tribes: *dao*.

He broke off one of the blossoming heads; each star-
shaped, the eight to ten flowerlets formed a starlike spray. "An
emblem," he remarked to Kambanal. He meant, Kargul's color,
the star made of lesser stars to signify confederation, the *dao*
itself, recognized and desired by all the tribes, who would have
to come to him for it.

Kambanal, however, also dismounting, was furnishing
another interpretation. "*Sibh'loyil*," he murmured with a rapt
expression, "flowerlets;" then, careful to mispronounce in the
singular, "*Siv'loi*. A touching emblem, *Asai*."

Tears were threatening in his eyes: Kambanal had been
the one who had tried to prevent his captain from seeing the
mutilated body of Siv'loi. Instantly, Kamin-Tolagh decided to let
him have his fable. In romances there were heroes who wrought
vast deeds in commemoration of or vengeance for a lost love,
and while Kamin-Tolagh doubted any such warrior had ever
existed in real life, Kambanal's misreading of what he meant by
the flower-emblem surely held greater unifying power than the
prosy notion of helping scarecrow tribes defend themselves and

grow twice as many beans. "Here in the West," he agreed with Kambanal, "we shall ride under a standard with this device, the Siv'loi Banner."

Lavsila said, "A confederation? Do the other tribes want the *dao* spice so much they will bow to your command?"

"No, the *dao* is only a sign. Some will join us to get security against the Hill Froghul. Some we may have to rap over the knuckles, as we did the Hwenala."

That campaign, such as it was, had ended after Kamin-Tolagh's squadrons rode to the marshlands where the tribe had their mean dwellings, often concealed in high grasses and reeds. Their wretchedness at last let Kamin-Tolagh understand what Iruvakh meant by the relative prosperity of the Man-mani. A desultory exchange of arrows cost the Hwenala another dead and two wounded, without damage to Kamin-Tolagh's forces. The main cluster of huts was found deserted, the Hwenala having hidden in the marshes, with their dogs for company. Not much point to setting fire, Noldar's suggestion, the dwellings small loss to their owners, mainly mud-daubed reeds, hardly as substantial as the one Kamin-Tolagh as a child had made with his sister, playing in the marshes by Inilun Barabhi. On the second day, seeing Kamin-Tolagh's men had not eaten those already captured, the Hwenala began venturing out of hiding, and through one of the former bodyguards, who spoke in the Man-mani language to Chamya, reported the remnant of the Sranadatta clan had fled south, with the again-widowed Myanachë now at the side of Sra-Min-Talla-Tyu, working her way, as Lavsila commented, through the entire family. The tribe southward, the Gudi-la, more numerous than the Hwenala, were herding people holding dubious sway over wide stretches of sparse pasture, and not renowned for their hospitality, although the Man-mani woodcutting party had passed their claimed territories without unfriendly incident.

"Meanwhile," Lavsila wore his tolerant face, "thanks to Kambanal the tale of your immortal love is spreading through the squadrons like a plague of crab-lice. You know the girl's body is unburied? Stay upwind of the remains. The Man-mani bury their dead in the gulch here, behind the village, but they do not mark the places, and Kambanal stopped them. He said, all on his own, you would want the burial done with proper rites."

"Did he?" not amused by Lavsila's tone. As with a physical wound, it was one thing when the sufferer made light of it, quite another when a bystander did.

"It will do no harm, a funeral appropriate to the deathlessness of your feelings for the tragic Siv'loi. You have to live up to the flag you have given them." Women of the Man-mani, using cloth the cavalry carried for repairs to their tunic-facings, had sewn the Siv'loi banner after Lavsila's drawing, sky-blue five-pointed stars on a white ground, ten small ones clustered about a larger, the whole design also making a five-pointed star.

There was another rite Kamin-Tolagh wanted first, for which he had men building gallows up at Meeting Place, but he was conscious of time slipping away. "I must ride for the Lunu Jinzalladhiyu, to inform Shumat what we are doing."

"He will try to stop you."

"We cannot know that."

"He is under *orders*. The *rabhsai* expressly forbade adventuring in the West."

"Shumat is aware actions must adapt to circumstances — Rodlakh could not guess the whole Froghushei could be tamed at so little cost, as now we see it can. Besides, what was this entire expedition but adventuring in the West? What if, at the end of a year, less it may be, I can present the *rabhsai* with a new empire ready-made?"

"The *rabhsai* disavows all desire for empire." They had been through this before. "Our beloved *Bôdhrai* has said, let us bring the benefits of law and learning to those who already acknowledge the *rabhsai*, before we look for new territories to tame. You have sworn oaths."

"Oaths that include the realm's welfare." He was debating, not with Lavsila, but with what was probably an accurate representation of Kadon Dinul's views. "This is a chance that comes once in a thousand years, and we lose it if not grasped in time. The Man-mani are like a floating twig caught on a stone, not much in itself, but enough to begin the damming of a river. By the time this can be explained to the *rabhsai*, it may well be too late. I must be allowed to exercise my own judgment." All of this became true as he spoke. He was using the discussion as a rehearsal for what he would say at the Lunu, but was aware an important element was absent, his genuine liking and admiration for Shumat; it would not be comfortable face-to-face with his comrade, fellow-victor of the Jinzai War.

"Don't go. You have said you cannot keep Noldar and his bows with you — have him carry your written message for Shumat — for the *rabhsai* by way of Shumat. Or I would carry it; Shumat has no authority over me."

He was deliberately dangling the possibility he might not remain here in the West, wanting Kamin-Tolagh to ask what his plans were, perhaps to woo him. Except that he was someone to talk to, it did not much matter, and Kamin-Tolagh spoke instead about reasons he had to return to the Lunu, the things there he must collect, not excepting the two remaining squadrons of his cavalry, with one valued officer, the reliable Yaënsilat. Gremnivai, nominal second-in-command of the Karguli contingent, could be expected to have grave doubts about Kamin-Tolagh's course. He had grave doubts about everything, and Kamin-Tolagh would welcome the chance to be rid of him — he wished the glum Talfoyan would go home, too, but the troops were needed; with a squadron left to guard the *dao* valley, and need for another here at the village he was very soon spread thin.

"I am still young," Lavsila, abruptly. "My father's fields are not going to vanish. There are things I can do here: Iruvakh knows what and when to plant, but he can't make it rain. The water there is must be managed."

Kamin-Tolagh took pity on him. "The salary is poor, but I'll be glad if you decide to stay for a time."

Not far to the south, in sight of the village, beyond where the river swung west, Kambanal had noticed a small, conical hill, hardly more than an oversized hummock, which Kamin-Tolagh approved for the burial of Siv'loi. The place, appropriately part of grazing-lands claimed by Nifra, the girl's father, according to Iruvakh already had religious meaning for the Man-mani, in an undefined way associated with fertility. Notably, he no longer tried to insist such things could not be interfered with, and effectively gave sanction to the funeral rites, a strange mixture of Man-mani and *Mankh'*, the former *atarlai* chanting a *kolukezh'*, two young women, friends of the dead girl, performing a posturing dance, strange rather than solemn. Two full squadrons and a throng of villagers watched in silence, as Kamin-Tolagh, with the feeling he was participating in a puppet-play, turned the first spadeful of earth.

His mind was mainly elsewhere, on the morning's executions at Meeting Place. Though capital punishment had become rare in the realm, hanging was the traditional method, and the right way to tie the knot, to make death was certain and reasonably swift, was still surprisingly common knowledge. When he was a boy Kamin-Tolagh had seen the hanging of two soldiers of Kargul who had robbed and raped, and remembered the furtive tension of the occasion, somewhere between guilt and pleasure.

Of nine captured men of the Sranadatta clan one had died of his wounds and another was too weak for hanging and had to be garroted; three of the former bodyguard brought the number up to ten, and they were hanged in two batches on the frame

Kamin-Tolagh's men had erected, the rough platform they stood on being toppled when the nooses were secure. They did not kick, as was always said; in the short time they remained alive they worked their feet as if trying to step up onto a support that did not exist. From each batch, because of greater strength, a fiercer will to live, or a badly done knot, one man went on dancing and making noise till, at a nod from Kamin-Tolagh, a strong cavalryman grasped his knees and gave a downward wrench to end the struggle.

Except for Osré-dnë, whose face gleamed with satisfaction when she translated Kamin-Tolagh's explanation of his justice, the assembled Man-mani, though they listened attentively, did not let much emotion show, and the actual hangings were watched in a closed silence. Iruvakh officiously explained they were puzzled by the cold ritual when this same Noh-Sra-Lal-Hin had prevented them from killing wounded enemy in the heat of a fight. They were apprehensive, too, about these unfamiliar laws.

"Aye," Freighanai agreed. "They are glad to see the last of Sranadatta's brood, but they're wondering who might be next."

"Let them wonder," obscurely reminded of his mother.

Pain and death, he reflected, watching as six men of the tribe slowly manhandled to the top of Siv'loi's burial mound a big, rounded, whitish boulder found nearby, with which the grave would be sealed, were strangely trivial except when one's own; he could use them, but had no shared feeling when they came: over the killing of Siv'loi his emotions had been anger they dared do this to his chosen woman, horror over the bloody mess they had made of a perfect thing he had been pleased by. When the grave, with a last heave of the big stone, was covered, Kamin-Tolagh, well coached by Lavsila, proclaimed this place, till the end of time, would be called Kaf'loi Siv'loyani, Siv'loi's Hillock, not only a memorial to the murdered girl, but reminder of the rule by law and justice the crime had brought the Man-mani.

All the men of the escort, tough *péfrapravádal* of Kargul, their camp-talk bawdy as any, knew Kamin-Tolagh's reputation for letting a woman go as casually as he took her, but no one gave a knowing wink during the solemnities; not his personal squadron, not even Freighanai, appeared remotely like breaking into laughter; Kambanal was in a trance of tragic exaltation, eyes bright with manfully restrained tears. Yet he, too, though he might have read too many romances, was a good soldier and would make an excellent squadron officer: endlessly odd how so much that was useful could be strengthened with the rule of damp sentiment. Nevertheless, between the hero-captain Kambanal was inventing, and the Man-mani's Noh-Sra-Lal-Hin, Kamin-Tolagh would have to fight for freedom to perform any act not dictated by expectations.

8.

Though learning to be less certain about most tribal subjects, Iruvakh remained dogmatic about where Kamin-Tolagh should sleep; here at the Visitors' Hut, not the head-man's, which still stood for the powers of that office. "*Asai*, it can only lessen your standing if they come to you with head-man questions — disputed ownership of a goat, an argument over water, the proper place for a dung-heap. As I have said, you must give them a head-man, and soon."

"Why not Osré-dnë?" Lavsila, at his sketches, cheerfully, "She seems to be running most things. Her idea, they say, to have a rope-catching, the day after tomorrow."

Iruvakh shook his head. "She only reminded the men of the custom, when war threatens, to have as many as can try to catch the rope, so to give the tribe added warriors." The woman, however, since being chosen to speak god-thoughts of Lal-Hin, had rapidly consolidated her standing, and was being consulted on practically any issue affecting the whole tribe.

"What war threatens?" Kamin-Tolagh demanded. This particular rope-catching was news to him, but he recalled it as a test of manhood. "I have subdued the Hwenala." They kept to that Man-mani name, not what the marsh-dwelling tribe called itself.

"Chamya, since then, is an authority on god-thoughts of Noh-Sra-Lal-Hin, and I believe he has told men of the tribe you mean to lead them in war to rid them forever of the Hill Froghul."

The tone was skeptical, but Kamin-Tolagh did not explain. He had told Chamya, if the tribes could cease fighting among themselves, learn some discipline, they would never have to fear raids again. That had been while riding south, before seeing how the Hwenala fought, or failed to. The boy's dreams of being a great cavalry captain had changed it to the idea of imminent war.

"It is said I am too young for the rope-catching," the boy said, eyes on Kamin-Tolagh.

"If said you were old enough, could you catch the rope?"

"It is a difficult and dangerous test," Iruvakh protested. "Many boys older and stronger than Chamya are injured."

Chamya was assessing calmly. "I could not be sure to catch the rope; there is luck as well as strength and skill. But there are older boys with smaller chance than I."

"You would want to try?"

"If it could be permitted."

"Then you shall attempt it — " warning Iruvakh with his eyes not to object further. "Noh-Sra-Lal-Hin permits it."

"You say, if he were to catch the rope he would be in every way a man, no different in standing from a man of thirty with a wife and children?" The boy had gone to give the news to his mother.

"That is the rule of the tribe. Membership in a ruling clan such as Sranadatta's is a separate consideration, and special skills in warfare or animal-healing merit additional respect, but as far as I can ascertain, once the tribe has acknowledged a boy's manhood, then they *see* him as a man. Small as Chamya is, if he can survive this test no Man-mani will ever again think of him as a boy."

"Survive?" An ominous choice of words.

"Succeed in it, I mean to say. I have never heard of anyone dying at a rope-catching, though no doubt there will be some nasty wounds, and broken bones, too."

"Can Chamya do it?"

"He is quick," Iruvakh, doubtfully. "Agility, perhaps, can compensate for strength."

"And determination," picturing the boy's dark, fervent eyes, the set of his jaw. He was not quite twelve, but Kamin-Tolagh had a plan he could not reveal, since it would make failure ten times worse if Chamya were to fail at the rope-catching. If he succeeded, Kamin-Tolagh would make him head-man.

Lavsila suggested, "Could word not be passed, if Chamya succeeds it will please Noh-Sra-Lal-Hin?"

"No," Kamin-Tolagh was certain. "If we cheapen the test, it is bound to be known by everyone."

All the same, when the morning came and he understood the test he could almost wish he had listened to Lavsila, or to Osré-dnë, who had been opposed to her son's candidacy, mystifying Iruvakh, who said Man-mani mothers generally were avid to see their boys win manhood.

The day began in overcast, and though it brightened, a layer of tenuous cloud remained to veil the sky, filtered light making watery shadows as Kamin-Tolagh with an escort rode to the rope-catching place, a short way south and east of the village. The wind was pressing steadily off Flamûrai, and he could not tell whether he was wearing too much or too little, a slight sweat on his body quickly becoming clammy.

Much of the village was already gathered on the shelving hillside, scoured bare, not far short of where the climb began in earnest to the dark central range. For a change, men were in the majority, many faces new to Kamin-Tolagh, but women and girls were scattered among them, and there was also a tight knot of women standing apart near the head of the slope, Osré-dnë emotionless, mothers of those who would attempt the test, recognizable by the slender fresh-cut rods they were holding. According to Iruvakh the candidates who failed would have a ritual beating from their mothers to add to the bruises of defeat, a ceremony to proclaim they had not won their way out of childhood: no woman would dare raise a hand to one accepted as a man.

Chamya was at the crown of the hill, small and frail among about eight or nine others, all older, a couple as old as fifteen. Like them he was wearing the simplest tribal dress, loose shirt and a breech-clout, and the boy looked a little chilled.

A course was marked off, mainly downhill, though not smoothly or uninterruptedly so; stakes driven into the ground where it levelled into the valley showed the distance, said to be *two furrows*, however that might be measured, the rope, once caught, must be kept hold of. Near the stakes ten or dozen of the older men had taken their stand, presumably as judges.

There was no signal to begin that Kamin-Tolagh saw, but a cluster of young men stood out, most not more than a year or two beyond this test themselves, one carrying coil of rough and hairy but strong rope the tribe used, though evidently did not make. The occasion was serious — solemn, according to Iruvakh — but that did not prevent chuckling comments by onlookers, as the wielder of the rope, well-muscled, measured off a free end, and began swinging it to and fro. Behind him three others took the rope's tail, spitting on hands, making half-winds on their forearms, testing their holds with sharp tugs against each other.

Four of the candidates had formed a line facing the rope-wielder at a distance of eight to ten paces. The swing of the rope was very deliberately lengthened inches at a time, and then, a fisherman making a cast, the brawny one sent the rope-end looping. All four of the candidates grabbed for it, and it was caught by a slender, long-legged boy with a thick mane of dark hair. At once the four at the other end went bounding away, yanking at the rope, and before he could make his grip secure the boy, stumbling, lost it. Spectators gave an expectant murmur, and three boys stepped back to leave the lanky one alone. By making a catch the candidate won the right to go on till he had attempted the full test.

The next throw had more snap. The boy caught it above his right shoulder, and immediately dropped it again, not trusting that grip. Next, the rope came looping low, and he made only a half-hearted stoop for it; Kamin-Tolagh could not tell whether the faint jeer from the onlookers was meant for the boy or the one casting the rope. The next came whistling, striking the boy what must be a painful blow near his jutting shoulder. But the end went coiling about the upper arm, and with a fast lunge he had the rope two-handed.

The hauling team gave their quick, unison jerk, but with a leap the boy stayed on his feet. Headlong down the dusty slope the four went plunging and the boy bounded and skidded after them, elbows tight to his sides, hugging the rope to his body. The rope team stopped, started, paused, and with a ferocious tug began again. The boy, stumbling sidelong, tripped on a rock-projection, lost his footing, but held on to the rope. Keeping head and upper body clear of the ground he was dragged brutally across the punishing terrain. When the hauling team made another unwarned stop he thrust a knee forward, and nearly managed to stand, but the runners were off again, and he was twisted around, back of his head bobbing down dangerously near juts of bleached rock. In trying to wrench back to a forward position he lost left-hand grasp of the rope, and in the final flatter but bumping stretch of course, to a groan from the watchers, he was jolted loose, rolling to lie face down not ten paces from the finishing stakes, past which the hauling team galloped, shouting.

After a still moment the boy raised his head, and gradually got to his feet. Kamin-Tolagh saw him as he limped back up the hill, one side scraped raw from hip to lower calf, feet bleeding, arms and wrists bruised and bloodied by the rope. Nevertheless, he took his place among candidates again; evidently he was permitted a breather before trying once again.

Another boy replaced him in the initial four. At second throw, one who must surely have tried and failed in the past, biggest and strongest-looking of all the candidates, somehow contrived to get the rope wound around his waist, and when the haul began his experience could be seen in how he anticipated sudden stops and jolting starts, the swift changes in direction and speed; he ran and bounded in a low crouch, trying to keep the line taut throughout. In those final treacherously pitted, rock-studded yards he stumbled, or slithered on a loose stone, but though he fell heavily, gripped the rope at the pit of his stomach, and was dragged past the stakes to acclaim from the watchers.

After him another of the bigger youths tried twice and failed badly, the second time crashing heavily on his back and lying a long time with wind knocked out. Chamya thus took his place as one of the waiting four.

His shorter reach was a disadvantage, and in the end he was seventh to catch the rope and attempt the course. The six preceding were evenly divided between success and failure; two more had finished the course, and one of those who had failed, though battered, waited for another attempt. One of the youths admitting defeat appeared to have broken a wrist, and Kamin-Tolagh saw his mother barely touched him with her rod in token of a beating, by contrast with the other, who, already bleeding, was given ten resounding strokes by his disappointed mother. She was a head shorter than her son, and her weight must be scarcely half his, but he accepted the beating in a passive cringe.

Finding Iruvakh standing nearby Kamin-Tolagh leaned over in the saddle to ask what happened to youths who were unable to catch the rope when they were fifteen, or sixteen, older; were they doomed to count as mere boys all their lives?

"That is rare, *Asai*; when it is plain to everyone he has reached his manhood a way is found of letting him succeed, with not a word said. Some, on the other hand, are killed."

"Put to death?"

"Great Hrafi, no. Although boys are not supposed to take part in war, the rope-catching is forgotten for one who fights well, particularly if he is wounded. When there is war with another tribe, or raiders come, an older youth will sometimes attempt rash deeds, seeking his manhood."

"I have heard of such things, even in Kargul," drily, but he was thinking if he had known about this before he might have invented a few feats for Chamya in the brief war with the Hwenala, and saved the boy this ordeal — though in fact he suspected Chamya would disdain such an evasion of the test.

Just then, seeing a flatter cast of the rope, Chamya darted forward to take it with both hands, but dropped it at once after surviving the initial jerk from the four handlers. As the other three candidates stepped back to give him his attempt he shot a quick, confident look at Kamin-Tolagh, then rubbed palms on his shirt to dry them. Heightened expectation, a sense of keener attention could be felt, as if a change had come in the weather; there was no one in the tribe who did not know this was Chamya, son of Osré-dnë, chosen companion of Noh-Sra-Lal-Hin.

The next cast of the rope Chamya ignored as too high, and the one following struck him above the knees, but he made no attempt to catch it, only shuffling his bare feet a little; Kamin-Tolagh admired the boy's distilled calm and complete focus. A third cast, snapping venomously, he had for a moment, but too near the end, and dropped it like a hot coal. A low mutter of comment could be heard.

Again the rope came with a crack. Not flinching Chamya let it strike him in the ribs, and as the end curled behind his back seemed to have ample time to take the rope two-handed, whirling swiftly so as not to be spun off-balance by the first big tug. Three or four nimble steps kept him upright, and there came another jolting pull, as the team plunged downslope, gathering speed and swinging from one side to the other. Clearly, there were to be no concessions; if anything the haulers were more determined than ever to make this a real test. They stopped, and then were off again, Chamya trying to keep slack out of the rope; the thumping jerk of their resumed gallop took the boy's elbows away from his sides, and Kamin-Tolagh's own arm-sockets ached as the arms stretched straight.

Lean-muscled, Chamya had the pliancy of green hazel, and was near success. He had bad luck; a flat-topped stone he used for footing tilted sideways just as the rope-handlers gave a new, massive pull. A groan came from many throats; Chamya was down, rope snaking away. Osré-dnë stood motionless, face carved of cold stone, while her son picked himself up, called something to the team with the rope, and toiled back up the hill, small and self-contained.   A nodding of heads and sage murmuring among older tribal men made Kamin-Tolagh review what he had seen, and realize the boy had let go the rope on purpose so as not to be dragged. That showed confidence, but a body so spare must have limited resources, and while avoiding serious injury Chamya had expended himself; another try or two and he would not be able to lift his arms, unless the skin of his palms betrayed him first. He was studying his hands as he made his way back to the starting-place, and there stooped for a double handful of soft dust, sifting it away, then brushing palms on the front of his shirt, where they left muddy streaks, dust wetted with both sweat and blood.

He waved away the other three boys, indicating he would continue. A fresh team had taken up the rope, and as he turned to face them a young man below gave a shout of encouragement. Evidently a breach of tradition; while a few took up the cheer, most hissed them to silence.

Kamin-Tolagh tried to catch Chamya's eye, but he was altogether in the world of the rope and its thrower. The first cast came low to his left, but he reached for it, and was off again with the same dancing blur of feet, anticipating the halt, agile to skip by a jagged outcrop when the run swerved. Willing success, Kamin-Tolagh gripped and twisted his reins, but the team was unrelenting, using every tactic of cunning and strength to shake Chamya loose. Themselves stumbling on the broken ground the four went for the finish in a reckless stampede, a last huge jerk sending the boy headlong to the ground. Again a groan came from the spectators, but with catlike swiftness Chamya brought up his knees to clamp on the rope, and disappointment changed at birth to astonished acclaim, as, wound to the rope with the fierce hunger of a strangling vine, he was dragged bumping past the stakes, and the rope-handlers came running back to raise him to his feet, bestowing affectionate slaps of congratulation.

Kamin-Tolagh tugged on his reins and picked his way down the slope. The circle of Man-mani well-wishers fell back, and Chamya looked up at Kamin-Tolagh with a proud but otherwise unreadable expression. "I am a man, *Asai*."

Between them, this had added meaning. A week ago, when they were in the Hwenala country, Chamya, without a word said, had come to Kamin-Tolagh in the night. It seemed axiomatic to him Kamin-Tolagh would want it, and he was not inexperienced; at a guess, another of the many things taught him by Iruvakh. Kamin-Tolagh, who had not had a boy, nor wanted one, in the last six or seven years, was surprised by the excitement he found in the lean body, so little like a girl's, and by his quick affection, again quite different from what he felt when pleased by a woman, not a rush of sentimental tenderness, but an untangling of feelings already there, the happiness it gave him to help and to instruct Chamya, the anticipated pleasure of teaching him to ride a *pefrai* and handle a lance, his admiration for the boy's eagerness and hope. Kamin-Tolagh did not think he could be in love with a boy of the tribes, but to the extent he was it was like falling in love with his own younger self, when all the world was thrilling possibility, boredom and betrayal unknown.

Since then they had bedded together twice without fuss: for Kamin-Tolagh, while pleased to have Chamya's firm nakedness beside him, he did not yearn for that, as when for a while a particular woman had become necessary to his happiness: in their daylight contacts there was affection, but nothing of either caresses or endearments. When he noticed Chamya's muscled legs or the dexterity of his hands, to remind himself of intimacy was strange, and he was no more excited by sight or the idea of the boy's body than by his own: there was nothing of that rush of blood (joy, astonishment, and an enjoyable fear together) when he glimpsed, remembered or imagined a particular woman's thighs, shoulders, hair; it seemed he was not really *anib'anuli*.

For Chamya too this was plainly a logical occurrence, not a statement of lifelong preference: too soon for him to have much idea about women, but in Kamin-Tolagh's bed he talked about Man-mani girls and his future wiving, and at this moment, having caught the rope, he was plainly telling Kamin-Tolagh a boy had seen to his pleasing, but men did not bed with men. After passing regret, as for anything that could never happen again, Kamin-Tolagh was mainly glad; he had been uncertain how it accorded with the dignity, the remoteness of Noh-Sra-Lal-Hin.

"*Asai* — " Iruvakh reproached. "When one of these tribes lacks a head-man or a ruling clan, it becomes a struggle for power from which only the strongest and deadliest emerge — proven warriors, hunters, the cunning killers."

"I have said before, they must learn new ways." Actually, Kamin-Tolagh had yet to encounter a Man-mani to fit Iruvakh's description; not even the deadly Sranadatta and his sons were a match for the most ordinary soldier of the realm.

"Plakhsila *Kímukoi*, it is true, began his reign at twelve," Lavsila said, for once in perfect agreement with Iruvakh. "But you are not at Kadon Dinul, Tam, where you can declare a protectorship, and the fighting men follow rank because that is the law."

"This is not a whim," he could easily have shouted, abruptly angry. Did they think him stupid? Chamya had acquired new standing as the only Man-mani companion of Noh-Sra-Lal-Hin when the Hwenala were subdued. A Man-mani willing to learn, he would have the help of his mother and her prestige in day-to-day affairs of the tribe —

"And you can control him when it is needed," Lavsila supplied. "Perfect, if it can be made to work."

In the morning he presented Chamya with a saddle such as the mounted archers used, to put on the pony captured from the Hill Froghul. With help from his mother in finding the thought, and Iruvakh in speaking it, Chamya, while delighted, offered that the gift would be much envied.

"No matter. You will be envied anyway. If Chamya is a man, can he be head-man of the Man-mani?"

Iruvakh's mouth betrayed resigned exasperation, but he murmured in her language to Osré-dnë. Chamya's unfathomable eyes assessed the seriousness of the question, and after all the energy expended by Kamin-Tolagh in beating down the objections of his two main advisors, declined the offer. "Not yet. Rope-catching is not enough; there are other Man-mani who have done deeds in war."

Quite admirably, the boy waved off what was obviously a strong attempt by his mother to change his answer, but listened to her when, with the familiar face of canny calculation, she had a longer and less strident comment. "My mother says, Noh-Sra-

Lal-Hin need not make a head-man yet, but who is to own the valley where *n'dwatta* grows, and what is to be done with lands Sranadatta stole from the Man-mani?"

In short, Kamin-Tolagh translated for himself, Osré-dnë would willingly do without the head-man's title for her son, if she could get control of the former head-man's wealth. But the power to bestow that wealth was too important to let out of his hands.

"As your mother says, those growing lands were taken unjustly by Sranadatta's clan, but the question who is to have them can cause quarrels in your tribe. Only Noh-Sra-Lal-Hin can be above the feuds of the Man-mani. As for the *dao* vale, that, too, must remain in the hands of the one who has the swords to defend it."

Osré-dnë's face remained expressionless while this was relayed to her, but her son said, "Will Man-mani, as you have said, *Asai*, be taught how to be their own swords?"

"In time." Kamin-Tolagh considered Chamya's earnest face, and decided the rope-catching really worked: yesterday the boy would have been eager for nothing beyond mastery of lance and warhorse; overnight, his concern was for the tribe. "The young men of the Man-mani will find time for the arts of war, when they learn better how to grow their food."

Iruvakh, recognizing this came from his little lecture, beamed affably in anticipation of getting his way at last.

Nizhadh, a leathery, tough little officer who had fought with a striking, composed proficiency in the Jinzai War, had been left with the squadron watching over the *dao* valley, and now rode in bringing a little mounted delegation (as it turned out) from the more southerly tribe, the Gudi-la. One at least knew Iruvakh, who could speak their language — their dialect, he said, of the Froghulú. Having heard about the humbling of the Hwenala they had come to assure the Master of the Horse-Soldiers he had no need to come to their country seeking the last of the Man-mani traitors, already turned away by leaders of the Gudi-la: they were believed to have continued up into the hills farther southward, waterless places where even the Hill Froghul did not go, and only a few wretched wanderers were to be found.

Kamin-Tolagh thanked the men, but made them thoughtful by saying he would, nonetheless, soon visit their tribal lands, since all peoples in these parts were going to concert their defenses against Hill Froghul' raids. Iruvakh had said the Gudi-la had the likeliest fighters among the western tribes, and were undoubtedly the best riders, yet with their herds necessarily dispersed wide over sparse grazing, obviously vulnerable to raids.

"Are they afraid I shall subjugate them?" Kamin-Tolagh asked, after the men, declining further hospitality, had begun the return journey,
"They are beyond that. Their coming to you as they did shows they already accept your power. Their fear is you may set the Man-mani over them."
"Why would I do that?"
"What would make them think so? *Asai*, the name the other tribes hear you called is a Man-mani legend, and the banner you have chosen is named after a woman of the Man-mani; to find you they ride to the chief village of the Man-mani, one of whom was your close companion when you warred on the Hwenala. They may not care about rival forces in the distant realm, but they do know horse-soldiers resembling yours for generations have defended Man-mani interests, and their oldest fear, beyond doubt, is that foreign cavalry would help the Man-mani defeat and dominate them all."
He was laughing without joy, and the sour eloquence of their first encounter returned. "In reality, the last thing the Lunu

Jinzalladhiyu would have wanted for the Man-mani — either conquest of, or true friendship with the other tribes. With alliances, when I complained they were dragging their feet, the high ones at the Lunu used to nod and smile, tell me to keep trying; only quite recently I realized my foolishness: for generations all men the Lunu sent here must have been instructed to discourage the idea of a secure peace, because that would bring about intermarriage, and threaten the supply of Man-mani breeding-stock for *jinzal*. All these centuries the *jinzai*-breeders were diligently fostering Man-mani dislike and contempt of other tribes, belief in its superiority, the necessity to avoid admixture with lesser peoples of the region. Naturally, the other tribes were suspicious; how could they tell the Lunu was not going to help its favorites conquer the whole Froghushei? Or now, by the same token, that you have not begun to?"

"I did not subdue the Hwenala for the Man-mani," but he recognized how the conquest, and particularly the subsequent hangings, would appear. Here in the Farther West he was his own man as never before, and it irritated him he had to keep demonstrating he was not controlled, by Shumat, or Lavsila, Iruvakh, now the Man-mani.

"We shall reoccupy the Lunu." It would give him the needed distance, so he could become master of all the tribes impartially.

"Will that be permitted?" Iruvakh meant, by the realm.

"Shumat must be gone." Advantages were beginning to multiply, and Kamin-Tolagh wondered why he had not thought of it before. Favored officers would have comfortable houses there, and ordinary soldiers, on a rotating basis, could share quarters more like proper housing than anything the Froghushei could offer.

Lavsila said, "I shall not mind sleeping in a real bed again, but when Kadon Dinul hears Lunu Jinzalladhiyu is back in business — "

"It will not be Lunu Jinzalladhiyu. We shall have servants from the tribes there, but no Man-mani women." Only for Man-mani was Kamin-Tolagh a demigod of legend, and he would keep his special place here, but he would always be worried about chance-bred *jinzal* so long as his men, almost all unmixed Owanil, were quartered in the village.

Lavsila was meditative, not saying what was obvious; Kamin-Tolagh's thoughts were no longer compatible with a brief stay here in the West, the year or less he had spoken about. Empire was starting to be a serious business.

9.

In a week when winter, still weeks away. could be felt in gusting winds from the northwest, lashing Kadon Dinul with cold squalls of rain, unexpected visitors arrived from the south, five men, seafarers and traders from the distant Hrin lands. Though Hrin traders came quite regularly to the southern port of Thenimala they generally stayed only long enough to exchange their cargoes for goods of the realm, and Dolvid could not say when a Hrin had last been seen in the Heartland. Their leader, Iolfrant, alleged they had come to offer respects to the new *rabhsai*, but would take the opportunity to discuss trade — a polite reversal, it might be suspected, of their real priorities.

The Hrin had been recognized by and long ago loosely allied to the old realm of Owan, but their territory had not been part of the Western Empire, and remained elusive; no extant map showed its precise whereabouts, and the few written references were sketchy, filled with conjecture. Not a raw tribal people but a genuine nation, with large cities and skilled crafts, their lands, the Hrinani, had been rumored as awash with treasure, but other more credible reports said their riches came only from the working of fine metals, which they had to import. While fine and enormously expensive examples of the goldsmith's art were occasionally offered in trade, the ramshackle appearance of the seagoing Hrin vessels and shabby clothes of their crews hardly proclaimed inexhaustible wealth. Their soils were said to be fertile, but their climate must be ill-suited to growing grain, for which they were always ready to trade sweet fruits and their crafted metals, sometimes lengths of fine brocade or other costly cloths of cunning weave.

Iolfrant, who had come to the Bronze Residence with a letter of introduction from the military commander at Thenimala, was a mid-aged man, solidly built and of moderate height. He had the regular features, prominent forehead and receding chin evidently typical of his people, his straight black hair just long enough to cover the ears, and he wore a handsome brocade tunic over breeches of natural linen. His manner was dignified and a shade forbidding; he spoke a passable Owanilú, and had complete command of the ordinary language of Arbhal, shaming Dolvid, who had not a word of the Hrinanilú. At the man's courteous request, he arranged to take Iolfrant for audience with the *rabhsai*.

These were anxious days, no news from Shumat since the report, now twenty-five days old, describing arrival at the Lunu Jinzalladhiyu and successful overcoming of the remnant *jinzal* there; doubly anxious for Dolvid, whose wife, Aëlu, was due and past due to give birth; the estimated date was over two weeks past. It was hard to keep his mind on the realm's affairs, but Aëlu, though this would be her first child, was quite unperturbed. With capitulation of the Guilds over the apprenticeship issue, noisy and dust-raising work was proceeding on their house, and at Rodlakh's insistence Aëlu was here at the New Residence, installed in the Personal Suite.

Meetings in the General Audience Hall, frowned over by the famous Oak Wall carvings, were apt to be solemn, and with the *rabhsai* still just a little inclined to take his tone from the manner in which he was addressed, the opening exchange of greetings was very stilted. Iolfrant then put a series of polite questions which displayed surprising knowledge of the realm and its affairs, about the Jinzai War, the victory at Kamsilat, and the recent change of Patriarchs. He even asked how the campaign in the Farther West was progressing. Rodlakh was smilingly confident the expedition would soon be successfully concluded, and Dolvid admired how well the young *rabhsai* was learning his job; he was as worried as Dolvid about the lack of news.

"Concluded," Iolfrant echoed. "Then, *Rabhsai*, you have no intention of maintaining a standing force there in the Farther West?"

Dolvid, before Rodlakh could answer, reassured him the realm had no territorial ambitions, and there was no need for uneasiness, if the expedition came near lands where the Hrin had an interest. This attempt at a better idea of exactly where the Hrinani might lie was a failure; Iolfrant glazed over, and said it was very difficult to approach his unwarlike homeland, except by sea. No doubt, he said sweetly, for that reason they had not had the privilege of being part of the First Owani Empire, long ages ago.

Embarrassed the man could be so well-informed about Arbhal when his own notions of the Hrinani were so vague, Dolvid sought partial excuse in Iolfrant's smug evasiveness, in tune with long Hrin traditions of reticence to the point of secrecy concerning their customs and beliefs, how they were governed. Iolfrant described himself as a trader, but admitted his title, *Hrithust* (or something near that), meant both provincial chieftain and priest; he added self-deprecatingly he was one among a number such. Not forgetting the resplendent brocade coat, everything about the man, his ease with the *rabhsai*, the extreme deference he was given by his fellow-mariners, suggested a leader of greater consequence than he cared to reveal.   Long ago, according to accounts, the Hrin had acknowledged no general overlord, no *nimúrai* or *rabhsai*, but were largely ruled by their *atarlal*: there was some sort of connection between the callings of *atarlai* and goldsmith, but when Dolvid tried to discover how much of this was true today, Iolfrant gave his recurrent bland smile and said he knew very little about metalworking. At this meeting he had presented Rodlakh with a small but exquisitely crafted golden brooch or cloak-fastener, and a hair-clasp for the *rabhsayu* of similar workmanship. He seemed to think he was the gainer when he received the *rabhsai*'s return gift, a very fine hunting knife of Upper Dakbân make, with ornamental hilt and an inlay sheath.

"My people — " Iolfrant alarmed vigilant guards by unsheathing the knife to admire the edge, "do not have steel to match yours," but when Dolvid tried to lead this into a discussion of Hrin military practice, and his people's enemies, past or present, he again turned the question aside.

His proper subject, trade, would very soon bore Rodlakh, and when he began expounding a desire to contract for an assured supply of wheat over a long term, perhaps seven years, Dolvid, prepared, cut Iolfrant short. The proper place for this discussion, he said, would be at the feast in Iolfrant's honor, tomorrow night at the house of Khelagh, Dolvid's former father-in-law, certain to be attended by all the important corn-dealers of the Heartland, of which Khelagh himself was biggest. Dolvid, whose present standing with the Families was less than cordial, would not be among the guests.

"Any agreement on the scale you envisage," Rodlakh interposed, "will be subject to consent of the *rabhsayum*."

"Understood," Iolfrant, recognizing his interview was coming to an end. "I had intended, in any event, to ask for the *Bôdhrai*'s guidance as to prices and terms."

"You realize," Dolvid cautioned, "Advice is all; I cannot take direct part in negotiations." Having already been bullied by the new *rabhsayum* in the eternal fight to ensure sufficient food at prices all could afford, the big landowners had to be permitted a compensatory opportunity to try fleecing the Hrin.

"I wish them luck," Rodlakh with a laugh when Iolfrant had withdrawn. "I doubt he needs much advising."

They had moved to the Great Window Chamber. Probably because there was no chair of state here to be deferred to, Rodlakh chose this place for his informal meetings and discussions, but his preference could make for a squinting ordeal late in the afternoon of a fine day with sun flooding through what was said to be the largest single sheet of the crystalline Island glass ever forged, the west-facing Great Window. Today, with the Avenue dull but shiny under frequent flurries of rain, the room was pleasant, high-ceilinged, clothed in fine stone of pale rose and dove grey, floating in space.

They were joined by Âna, the *rabhsayu*, who had been meeting with a delegation of tenant farmers from her own country, the Lower Paowan. She asked at once about Aëlu, and sympathized with Dolvid's anxieties at the same time as she dismissed them. What she said was true, Aëlu could not have better care; the new Patriarch, Himself from the Healing Order, had put a trusted *ramidu* on constant call, and there was also the calming presence of Morú, formerly a well-known midwife. Years ago, when her husband Untimarr, the master-carpenter of Burantal, had been steward on his estates, Morú had said she would aid in delivery of Dolvid's sons and daughters. Those children had not come, that was another marriage, Aëlu's unborn child was not Dolvid's, and Morú no longer practised midwifery, but she had made the journey from Burantal unasked, to offer her services out of friendship and in fulfillment of her old promise.

It was far from certain she believed he was not the sire; he guessed there was widespread conjecture on the point: Dolvid wafted innumerable apologies in the direction of the real father, the late hero, Sebhal. As a matter of fact Dolvid had met Aëlu for the first time only about thirty weeks ago, but that had been when he played a part in her rescue from the fabled fortress-city of Drin b'Afon; inevitably there was romantic speculation, which the child's belated arrival would do nothing to dispel. Indeed, when Dolvid offered any help he could give during delivery, Morú answered, "Nay, Master, you've done your part," a stock phrase, no doubt, for dismissing the ineptitudes of well-meaning fathers.

When Âna heard about Iolfrant's purpose she said for the realm to contemplate export of large quantities of foodstuffs was madness, only making it harder, considering the rapacity of the big dealers, to see their own people provided with food at affordable prices.

"On the contrary — " Dolvid was little huffy, as always when there was failure to give him credit for any subtlety. In their greed for new and profitable business, the magnates, after bitter objections, would have to accept as a condition that the *rabhsai*, at any time when shortages or rising prices threatened hunger at home, could abrogate his approval and claim, at low market price, goods intended for export; in order to protect their profits they would work hard against that extremity. They were already worried about the effects of a new law rammed through Council, nominally the *rabhsai*'s, although all the Heartland families, remembering the *Bôdhrai*'s old zeal, called it Dolvid's Law, by which large proprietors could be compelled to lease growing-lands they allowed to lapse into disuse for three years or more, including farms they had acquired through foreclosure. At the same time, low-interest Treasury loans were made available for small farmers in danger of such forfeiture, and to aid in a new beginning for those dispossessed in the final, grinding years of the previous reign. This was the reason Dolvid was not invited to Heartland feasts; the magnates were already grumbling privately that with proliferation of new or restored smallholders, a multitude of minor harvests next year would have a depressing effect on the prices they liked to set. In these circumstances, their desire to make money off the Hrin would if anything make likelier they would produce enough to avoid hunger here.

Short of patience for the ceremonies of *rabhsayum*, Âna was normally indefatigable when it came to real work; she did not hide dissatisfaction with how slowly injustices were eliminated from the realm, but this morning's meetings had left her unusually exasperated; to Dolvid's eye tired, with a trace of soot under the eyes. He wondered whether she might be in the early stages of pregnancy. Dolvid discovered he was admiring Âna's hand resting on the arm of his chair, as if he was noticing for the first time the clean boning, the competent perfection of the fingers. He was forever being wonderstruck by a different aspect of Âna, the dark hair at her fine neck, a laugh, her quick grasp of new ideas, her deft management of differences with Rodlakh, brilliance of her eyes when her passions were engaged. He had not anticipated — he could surely say, they had failed to anticipate — the ferocity of their continued effect on each other, meeting virtually every day after witnessing and in some quaint way conferring blessings, each on the other's marriage to a demonstrably suitable partner. Recently for Dolvid there had been resurgence of deliciously crude and fascinatingly specific physical desire: he supposed when he and Aëlu could resume their beddings this would calm back to simmer, but not the unwavering wish for the intimacy of thought and feeling to which his few wondrous minglings with Âna had been key. None of this contradicted or in any way amended his deepening affection for Aëlu.

As Rodlakh, for the hundredth time, was wishing out loud he had gone in person to the Farther West and so avoided this ordeal of waiting for news, Dolvid, for the fiftieth, explaining without conviction lack of word might only mean there was nothing out-of-the-way to report, with Shumat not wanting to expose messengers unnecessarily to the dangers and rigors of Landegh, a girl, a servant to the Personal Suite, made a shy entry. After deference to the *rabhsai*, she turned to Dolvid. "Your pardon, *Bôdhrai*, it is Lady Aëlu. Mistress Morú says her labor has begun. In earnest, she says."

At a quick nod from Rodlakh Dolvid rose to follow the servant, and Âna, barely aware she did it, reached to give his hand a comforting squeeze.

The Bronze Residence, separated from the ceremony of the New by Harbor Gate and the length of the Avenue, was where Dolvid's routine daily work went on. He rode there in another cool and blustery morning with an entirely unjustified feeling of personal accomplishment, leaving behind a complacently pleased wife and a large, loud foster-son, whose name would be Sedukh, preserving memory of his male lineage. He was, presumably, heir to overlordship in the Colony, although hardly likely to come of age in time for direct succession. His grandfather, Saidhan, now nearly 88, was eager for word; Dolvid's first business was to dispatch the news by fast-messenger for Kamsilat; Sedukh would be Saidhan's last grandchild, and only one in male line, though through his late daughter he was grandfather also to the *rabhsai* and his younger brother, Orbanak.
    "Of all things," Dolvid remarked to Elamirr, his newest apprentice, "I would never have expected to act as father to a *rabhsai*'s cousin."
    "Master?" Elamirr was naturally puzzled; the strangeness of it had only now struck Dolvid, grandson to a chandler and once a dockside porter in the run-down port of Irbat, but the young man knew nothing about those origins, and to him Dolvid was the dignitary of the realm he saw; Owani, and therefore born to privilege.
    Yet Elamirr's people, irked by the zealous pedigree-keeping of the Families, had their own regard for blood-relationships. When Untimarr and Morú had come to Kadon Dinul they brought eager Elamirr with them, and he was a nephew of their family friend Nentirr, master of the celebrated Marionette Guild of Burantal. Since the half-dozen leading

families of that city were much intermarried, Elamirr must be related, not too distantly, to Untimarr as well. He was tall, good-looking, in his early twenties, not shy about his accomplishments, which included ability to read and write in both languages. Dolvid, wanting a few capable assistants to train, trying especially to find qualified or teachable candidates of Other Race, liking Elamirr's evident energy, had offered him a post. Ambition was there, too; the readiness and unsurprise of his acceptance suggested this had been in his mind from the first.

At Dolvid's invitation Iolfrant came to the Bronze Residence for a meeting with Âna's uncle, Sett, advisor for commerce to the *rabhsayum*. A fascinating encounter between two astute men who chose to hide behind an apparent softness. The Hrin visitor, in what had once been the Main Audience Hall, looked about him like a person not unaccustomed to fine buildings, and asked if this had not been the Great House of the *rabhsai* who reigned one hundred years.

Ninety-three was the exact count, but Dolvid was newly impressed by the *Hrithust*'s detailed knowledge. "Plakhsila, who built the New Residence," he confirmed, "was last to hold state here. After," once again fishing, "this was for several years a library, as indeed it still is, a working library; the true collection is on the floor above this. It is our regret we have no examples of writings of your race, sir. If scholars of the Hrin, among which you are surely one, could come here to study and teach, our two peoples might benefit by the increase of mutual understanding."

"Our writings, you see, *Bôdhrai*," apologetically, "are poor reading for one not of the Hrin. Almost all are commentaries on what you, I believe, would call *Mankh'* matters; many are secret. Besides — " there was a momentary loss of Iolfrant's airily dismissive manner; his voice hardened and his eyes gleamed. "Some books are filled with lies — not all Hrin yet see truth whole." Like one who thinks he has said too much, he hastily retreated back into offhandedness. "Most of our texts," he said, "to you would be very tiresome, I fear."

"Still — " Dolvid began. The quick glimpse of Iolfrant's passion had reminded him of an early chronicler who had written of the Hrin as amazingly disputatious on religious questions: "*it is said they will go to killing over meaning of a single phrase.*"

"Tiresome — do I use the word properly? Speaking of differing customs, *Bôdhrai*, in my country, when we agree to buy a considerable portion of a man's harvest for an agreed number of years, that man will set a price reflecting his appreciation of a guaranteed income over that term."

This complicated sentence must refer to Iolfrant's meeting, at last night's feast, with a coalition of leading growers and dealers in grain, led by Khelagh. "This would also be our normal practice. I think you would find it so if you were to speak with individual growers, one at a time."

"Ah," Iolfrant, sagely.

Sett arrived, a little out of breath from negotiating the steps up to the second level. Roundfaced and plumpish at forty-odd, he had managed to remain uninfected by the epidemic of marriage which swept through the realm after the Jinzai War. He had a warm greeting for Iolfrant, and Dolvid was soon fascinated by the professional talk between the two, easygoing, even careless-sounding, but focused and astute on both sides. Hearing an outline of Khelagh's proposal, Sett at once saw the Hrin were being overcharged for cartage from the Heartland to Thenimala, where their ships would come for the cargo, and recommended Iolfrant have his goods delivered to warehouse at Kanzan Tâl, from where carriers were easily hired. "What you need," he told the *Hrithust*, "is an agent to act for you here." He was going through a short list of names when one of the scribes, Orimat, came to tell Dolvid there were important dispatches. A messenger had ridden up with them from Owan Sai, where a ship had docked by early light. They had made good time by fast-messenger from Drin Navuna where the dispatches were written, or at least addressed, in Shumat's looping hand, just five days ago. Presumably that meant the expedition had completed its task and returned to the realm, but before finding out, Dolvid sent the messenger on to the New Residence to inform the *rabhsai* there was fresh word from the West, and he would be there very shortly. Watched attentively by Elamirr, he then broke the seal.

"Not bad news, Master?" Elamirr, seeing his face change.

"Not a battle lost, at any rate." He was not going to satisfy the young man's curiosity, not before Rodlakh had the shocking news with which the dispatch opened: Shumat had returned to the realm without Kamin-Tolagh baKargul.

A long dispatch, partly in cypher, although Shumat, never entirely confident with a pen in his hand, kept saying he would defer detailed explanations till they could be given face-to-face.

"He could have been here by tomorrow in the evening, if he had left when this letter did," Rodlakh complained. No giant feat of intellect was needed to guess the *rabhsai*, explicably devastated by the tale Shumat had to tell, found it less distressing to be annoyed with Shumat.

"What further is there to explain?" Âna demanded. "Kamin-Tolagh has broken his oaths, used threat of force against his agreed commander, and is acting contrary to the stated policy of the *rabhsai*."

Shumat, Dolvid put in, had in fact had behaved very reasonably, returning to where his troops and animals could be resupplied, and remaining where he could set out again at once if decided Kamin-Tolagh must be brought back by force. "Or however we determine," not closing off any possibility. Kamin-Tolagh, he agreed with an irritable Rodlakh, had exceeded, contravened his orders; over and again the *rabhsai* had made it plain he did not want conquests, any extension of his influence in the distant West. But one tribe of the Froghushei, hailing him as something near a god, had fallen like overripe fruit into

Kamin-Tolagh's hands, and now, according to Shumat's cautious secondhand account, he had apparently subjugated another, or brought it to heel, at small cost or none; he might be forgiven, surely, for regarding these as circumstances not foreseen in his orders, and for wanting to hold onto the unexpected prize, till there could be fresh instructions from Kadon Dinul.

"What is the use to us of new dependencies in the West?" Rodlakh demanded. "You do not believe we should support him?"

Dolvid went slow. Where Kamin-Tolagh had stumbled into sudden, small, uncertain empire was divided from the realm by several daysworth of stony wilderness, but the same was true for the port of Narn in the far northeast. What had made Narn worth maintaining as part of the realm was the import of shuzi. "If there was gold to be dug, or anything else of value to us — " The thought had Dolvid wondering again about the position of the Hrin lands in relationship to the northern Froghushei, where this tribe of Kamin-Tolagh's was. None of the old maps, impossibly crude or self-defeatingly ornate, made when the tribes of that quarter were either incorporated in or tributary to the Empire, had shown the entire Froghushei Peninsula, noting only there were mountains and "harsh high lands" to the south of the tribal lands; the Hrinani, also said to lie east of Flamûrai, the Great Gulf, might occupy the southern portion of the same peninsula. That would account for *Hrithust* Iolfrant's evident nervousness about armies of the realm in the Farther West: while he could not have heard so soon about Kamin-Tolagh's adventuring, likely, if they were among the Hrin's northern neighbors, he would know the whereabouts of the tribe that furnished breeding-stock for *jinzal*.

Nothing, as Rodlakh said, indicated Kamin-Tolagh had found anything of worth in the West; Shumat made passing reference to his having gained control over some sort of spice used by all the tribes, but there was no suggestion it would have commercial value in the realm, and none that Kamin-Tolagh was looking for anything but adventure.

Âna had a harsher view. "Said another way, he is loose in the West with control over the tribe used for breeding *jinzal* — he may have secret instructions from his mother."

"She is a resourceful woman," Dolvid said. "But I do not see how even Petakoi could arrange to have her son hailed by a tribe of the Farther West as a demigod, a fulfillment of prophecies." In his mind was Shumat's cyphered account of Kamin-Tolagh's double bitterness over what he had now learned; impossible for that to be a pretence.

"Where is she now, have you heard?" Rodlakh, before Âna could make a rejoinder.

Dolvid did. While she had started north with her husband Tovakh when he went to Dramal for the autumn hunting, Petakoi had taken a ship at Irbat and was now on the Island, either on her family lands, or with her old friend and ally the deposed Patriarch, Owan-Alladh XX, who was living in retirement at or near Drin b'Afon. It was quite clear she had become fearful of what would happen if on the expedition her son, as was predictable, found out about her knowledge and support of the aims of Lunu Jinzalladhiyu, and had gone to where she would be safe, equally from the wrath of her husband.

"This advisor of his, Irovakh, is of the *Atarlum*," Rodlakh worried.

"Of the *Edhrodilum*, the Growers. Iruvakh, I think it should be; Shumat misspelled, or misheard the name."

"You know him?"

"Of him, if it is the same person. I had heard he was dead, but his case was quite famous when I was in Irbat." Sons of leading families were often sent to the *Mankh'* for a year or so of training in one skill or another, and from time to time a boy of good birth would catch the infection of belief and elect to remain with the *Atarlum*; if there was dismay their families could never let it be seen, since all those of Old Blood paid no less than lip-service to piety.   Iruvakh was only son of the hereditary, pompous Warden of the Port of Irbat, Iriban Baëtufi, who, rumor was, when he heard of Iruvakh's intent to join the *Edhrodilum*, had shut himself away in private and taken out his anger on the books of his library, till then a celebrated collection. In public he would speak of his son's choice with a fixed and rigid smile.

"I doubt Iruvakh would know any more than we do about breeding *jinzal*."

"But the opportunity is there," unhappily.

"Shumat," Âna said, "should have seized Kamin-Tolagh when he came back to Lunu Jinzalladhiyu to announce his intent. He had the numbers."

"As he says — " not certain whether she or the *rabhsai* had read right to the end of the dispatch — "He was more than reluctant to begin what would have become a killing between comrades of the Jinzai War. He fought the Battle of Dônshei, but it was a nightmare for him, men of the one realm riding to kill each other, both sides under royal colors." As ruefully reported by Shumat the reappearance at Lunu Jinzalladhiyu of Kamin-Tolagh, with only part of his forces, was less the reporting-back of a second-in-command than something between visit of a foreign potentate and a raid; as it happened the Kargul' forces left behind had been duty-squadrons for that day, meaning they had the task of guarding the stocks of food, feed, and equipment, as also the treasury, while the other troops were on patrol or resting, so Kamin-Tolagh was able without opposition to claim what he considered his share of supplies. He had even taken time to have a follower count out to the tobhai what he computed his men were owed in pay, acknowledging the men of Kargul ceased to be in the realm's service (their wages therefore becoming his responsibility) at the moment he declined Shumat's direct order — a piece of punctiliousness that put Dolvid's teeth on edge, occurring as it did in midst of a lengthy debate during which, while his men abstracted the needed supplies, Kamin-Tolagh continued to maintain the *rabhsai* was certain to confer retroactive approval on the tribal adventure. Knowing Shumat as he did, Dolvid saw it must have been for him a painful scene.

"Kamin-Tolagh," abruptly, "swore personal loyalty to me."

"You saved his life at Kamsilat," Âna said. Meant as additional reason for grievance, this unexpectedly softened Rodlakh's bitterness.

"I helped save his life — in a place where he would never have been, except riding to our rescue." He shook his head. "But I thought he loved being Captain of the Household above anything. He was cheered wherever he rode; at the investing the acclaim for Kamin-Tolagh outdid mine. Do you think he will think better of this enterprise of his?"

The wishful question was meant for Dolvid, but Âna was quickest. "How can he ever again be a royal captain? He has broken his oaths, disobeyed a direct command, gone against stated policy of his *rabhsai*. Shumat," she repeated, "should have detained him."

"There would have been deaths," Rodlakh said. "If Kamin-Tolagh were killed or wounded, it would be the end of all our efforts to make Kargul a true part of this realm."

"Hopeless. Conspiracy and deceit are their mother's milk." Not hard to understand Âna's distaste: with plenty to resent she had genuinely tried to be friendly to Kamin-Tolagh, and now felt individually affronted. But if deceit was to be the subject, the four of them — Rodlakh, Âna, Shumat, Dolvid — were not beyond reproach. It made Dolvid's part harder; he did not want to be in opposition to Âna — nor appear to be defending Kamin-Tolagh, who had acted, at best reading, irresponsibly. At the same time, precipitate action could turn a small adventure into a permanent and dangerous rift.

"Let us not say *hopeless*," he urged, "before we have a chance to question Kamin-Tolagh."

"About what?" Âna asked. As *rabhsayu* she was gentler than before, conscious of dignity, but at times, for anyone who remembered her in the late days of Ban-Sila's ugly reign, the old, dangerous vehemence was occasionally visible just under the surface.

"Any captain, any half-squadron leader who had been seen to exceed his orders would be permitted to explain himself." Taking up the dispatch Dolvid pointed out two separate places where Shumat, though skeptical, was obliged to concede Kamin-Tolagh appeared genuinely convinced his actions, as the *rabhsai* would come to see, were for the realm's benefit.

"What benefit?"

"That question, *Rabhsai*, was heard a great deal, when your father sent forces to rescue Narn in '28. Even if the expedition had not brought back shuzi, it would still have made Shumat into a soldier, and a captain for the realm."

"But Shumat was following orders, not defying them."

This debate had brought them closer to bickering than any other issue of Rodlakh's brief reign, but Dolvid had kept trying to edge the *rabhsai* away from personal affront and in the direction of conciliation: what might well have begun in one young lord's hurt vanity could be made into disaster by another's. Unconsidered use of force in an attempt to seize Kamin-Tolagh in the midst of the distant tribe he had made his was likely to be costly in itself, but more so in reopening old wounds. "We should bring Tovakh into our consultations."

"Tovakh!"

"He can't have heard yet about what his son has done. He may well have his own arguments against it; that is his provincial cavalry wandering in the West, but if we were to act too soon, and kill men of Kargul, he would be obliged to side with his son. He, and the whole realm, must see you do not have any new quarrel with Kargul, only a difference with Kamin-Tolagh."

Rodlakh, after a moment, nodded agreement: the idea this was a new and yet-more-devious Karguli conspiracy could not be sustained, and if to consider alliance with the old enemy,

Tovakh, to help deal with his son, their comrade in the war, was odd, it was no stranger than that collaboration had once seemed.

"Perhaps he would let us use Kargul's back-door to the West — " the secret mountain way long used by the *jinzai*-breeders. Dolvid's idea was that he, with relatively small escort, could make his way to Lunu Jinzalladhiyu: with its assured water-supply and the well-built houses Shumat described, Kamin-Tolagh or some of his men were certain to come there. Or else Dolvid could find a man to guide him all the way to tribal country. Noldar, for example, an old comrade-in-arms, who had been there with Kamin-Tolagh, but returned to Shumat's force.

Challenged on the point Dolvid could not have denied he relished the prospect of adventure; with Rodlakh he regretted having had to exclude himself from the expedition, sight of so much hovering on the borders between history and legend. Nevertheless, he was logical ambassador to a man with whom he had negotiated successfully in the past; he could not tell whether Kamin-Tolagh actually liked him, but thought they had each other's respect.

Rodlakh, to be sure, envied those who had ridden to the Farther West, maybe an unseen element in his swift, decided veto. "Kamin-Tolagh has been given a royal captaincy, and is our subject. If there is to be a meeting, he must come to us."

Since neither he nor anyone else had an idea how that could be brought about at present, discussion stuck at this point. Rodlakh did concede he would be willing to go, or have a representative go, as far as Drin Navuna, but not one step outside his realm.

Aëlu said, "On behalf of princes, do not be conciliatory too soon."

"Even Rodlakh?"

"Even him." She was sitting up among pillows, though she had already been up briefly more than once, and was determined to be out of bed for good tomorrow. "No one is proof against the sycophancy a *rabhsai* breathes in, day after day. You must give him a chance to put his pride up on stilts — encourage it. When he sees he is being absurd, then you can be ready with the reasonable course, but let him think he is the one relenting."

Aëlu was enjoying herself, as she did at these times. She would seldom if ever give her opinion on an issue, only comment with a certain detachment, often wittily, on how a matter was being handled. Her realism sometimes dismayed Dolvid, who would like to believe her wrong about Rodlakh; he wished he could deal with the *rabhsai* in complete candor, without any strategy, but knew that had not happened today. "He is stubborner than he used to be. But he is torn in two; he gave more than a captaincy to Kamin-Tolagh. His love."

"Kamin-Tolagh might rather have had his frankness," Aëlu suggested. About Rodlakh's final position she said: "How is Kamin-Tolagh to know what the *rabhsai* expects, if no one is allowed to go to him?"

"No one with rank enough to flatter him; Rodlakh does not mind if we send a message, with a squadron-leader or under-captain for courier, expressing the *rabhsai*'s displeasure. That is the half of him that would give Kamin-Tolagh every opening to recant; he wants me to draft a letter to make his disapproval unmistakable, while not slamming shut any doors. But Kamin-Tolagh is going to think it just a way of bringing him where he can easily be arrested. I shall have to persuade Rodlakh to give guarantees against that, and there will be another struggle. Much simpler to send a representative with power to negotiate direct."

"You," she guessed, not having been told that part.

"No danger," before she could protest. "I was completely safe with him at a time when we were at war with Kargul."

"If only Kamin-Tarú would ride with you again — " eyes filled with mischief.

"Simpler yet," ignoring the teasing, "if it could have been stopped before it began. With Rodlakh, I defended Shumat, knowing how he would shy away from starting a new civil war, but as a matter of fact there is a way he could have stopped Kamin-Tolagh, without killing a man, if he had been ruthless enough. Kamin-Tolagh had dry wilderness to cross, and only lances for weapons; the mounted bows were not his to command. Shumat could have threatened to shoot the animals in Kamin-Tolagh's pack-train, and if that failed, to begin shooting the *pefral* from under his squadrons. Those archers Noldar leads could do it easily without touching a man, and from a range where Kamin-Tolagh could not mount a charge against them. Reduced to lancers on foot, miles from the nearest water, he would have to surrender."

Aëlu gave her exaggeratedly wide-eyed look. "Could you have done that?"

"I could threaten it." Whether he could have actually given the order to begin killing horses was another question; he would have hoped the threat would have been enough. The question of what to do with a captive or penitent Kamin-Tolagh would have to be faced some day, but Dolvid did not anticipate that distasteful moment: Heir in Kargul, hero of the Jinzai War, admired throughout the army, greatly popular with the public at large, judging and punishment of his insubordination could only be an embarrassment for Rodlakh's *rabhsayum*, popular only with half a dozen resentful girls of the Residence Quarter.

"You don't fear he is acting at his mother's instructions, nor that he will breed *jinzal* for himself."

"No."

"Then he is on the loose in the West with, what, four hundred men?"

"Three hundred odd. A part of his men and his most senior officer, Gremnivai, declined to follow him. Of course, he has Lavsila," grinning, but at a private joke.

"What real harm can he do the realm?" a question Dolvid had put in different words to Rodlakh.

"Chances are strong he will soon grow bored with his little empire in the dust," Dolvid said, "and be obliged to ask the *rabhsai*'s pardon, and permission to come home."

"Well, then?"

She meant, why, at the same time as he tried to keep Rodlakh calm, was he letting this business so obsess him. A good question.

A deep breath. "You know I am anything but fey. Last spring after seeing Kamin-Tolagh I knew he had to be brought into alliance, if possible friendship, with Rodlakh. Not just because, as it turned out, we needed all his help to defeat the *jinzal*. I had observed him at the head of troops, seen him beside Âna, listened to him debate the wars with his father and Bolan, and — " Dolvid shook off the chill on his shoulders, and came near saying, never mind; it would have been comforting to laugh away a dreamlike episode he had resisted admitting to himself.

Yet with Aëlu he was safe. "I have never had such a feeling: I could see they were born adversaries. If not friends, they would have to be mortal enemies. They were already rivals for Âna, though neither knew it — Rodlakh at that time was still annoyed by her, while Kamin-Tolagh was only puzzled by the simpleton he was bedding."

Aëlu smiled briefly, and remarked Kamin-Tolagh would not pine, and in fact had spent little time languishing over such a loss: the fresh conquests he had crowded into his fairly brief time back at Kadon before and after the investiture had if anything surpassed his former legend.

Dolvid let that drop; when he spoke about Âna with his wife he had to keep close watch on his voice, and he was not going to suggest the urgent quality of Kamin-Tolagh's recent

---

womanizing only confirmed Âna's persistence with him. In this case no more than a symptom: Rodlakh and Kamin-Tolagh, alike in many superficial ways, were or could come to be live emblems of incompatible human tendencies. To say light and dark, good and evil, was unjust to Kamin-Tolagh, caricature by over-simplification: great cruelties had sometimes been committed in the name of what Rodlakh would see as the general welfare, while men such as Kamin-Tolagh who strove only for expression of their own desires and whims could make gestures of magnificent generosity; impossible to guess how either would end in the eyes of history. All that was certain was the difficulty each would always have in fully understanding the other.

He was churning too many words out of what had been an intuitive perception, a vision coming to one who did not give credit to prescience.

"What I am afraid of is unseen start of a duel that will not stop short of death, for one or the other. Or both." At that, his wholly unsuperstitious wife made a warding gesture learned at the *Mankh'*.

10.

Waking made Kamin-Tolagh realize he must have slept. Too weary to clamber inside, he had lain down on top of his sleeping-bag, but someone had covered him with a light blanket, become faintly damp to the touch. That, with the grey morning, made him afraid the weather had changed, a disaster for his plan, but as he got to his feet, buckling on sword-belt, he felt the breeze on his cheek, out of the same quarter, and the day was drab only because the sun had not yet risen; across featureless flats to the eastward, brightening sky showed no cloud.

Rising from his squat by a small, flickering fire, Nizhadh held out a cup of warming drink. A short, strong, square-framed man, another of those who had won swift promotion to acting squadron-leader in the Jinzai War,, no deep thinker or student of strategy, he was resourceful in a fight, very quick to see where his contribution could be most telling. Wordlessly he passed over cold meat and a hunk of coarse bread, and Kamin-Tolagh was glad to join in desultory talk with stiff and yawning soldiers; when the sun woke would be soon enough to be a prince again.

A brief winter had passed, by normal standards hardly begun; there had been cold nights at turn of the year, dustings of snow on the heights, but while fields and woods were somnolent, the nakedness of true winter did not come to lands never far from bare, and therefore no sensation of rebirth when, after a short rainy period, spring was deemed to have arrived.

Through the cooler time, Kamin-Tolagh's influence, by its own momentum, had extended over the eastward tribes, leaders of the scarecrow Hwenala and numerous Gudi-la acknowledging his authority as readily as his own Man-mani. Plans for making a new army from the tribes had gone less easily. The assumption all the men would be able to ride was mistaken, while those who could manage a horse were hard to convince they must use stirrups to be effective mounted fighters. Once in the saddle, all, though the youth of the Man-mani were worst, tended to behave as dogs off the leash, riding in wild circles, whooping at the novelty of being able to stand in their stirrups, cuffing at each other; there were many collisions and falls, broken bones for both men and mounts, one man crippled from a trampling after being thrown. Among the tribes, any success in fighting had always been due to individual daring, strength or skill, and the collective discipline that made armies work was a suspect alien system. So, at first, was the idea that once in the ranks, a man could not decide to wander off to tend crops or animals, or repair his roof; against this habit Kamin-Tolagh had to threaten and then carry out some floggings; whipping, though now rarely used in the *rabhsai*'s armies, was fairly common in training provincial cavalry, especially of Kargul, and the ordinary soldiers had no reluctance to use the lash as it had been used on them.

Differences in language were the first difficulty to be overcome, and since most Man-mani were already able to mispronounce a few words of the Owanilú, training for all the tribes was conducted, and orders given, in a simplified, soon debased, form of that language, for which the Man-mani name was generally adopted, *Hwanió*, which, while it sounded like a corruption of the word *Owanilú*, was at the same time, according to Iruvakh, their term for foreign things in general. Some of the Karguli soldiery, especially the city-bred, had to be taught a little of their own ancestral tongue, while those from remoter parts, habitually despised for their rural ignorance, found good use for the worn-down dialect of the Owanilú still a cradle-tongue in

isolated valleys of Western Kargul. The simplest Karguli
trooper, no matter what his origins, had here become part of a
ruling class, though riding on patrol, drilling, and helping to train
raw levies, able now to have all his other hard work performed
by boys and young women of the tribes; a measure of these
people's poverty was how they attached themselves to the Kargul'
soldiers merely to claim their leavings, table scraps, strips of
cloth from mending breeches, needles with ends of thread, small
parings of boot-leather, waferlike slips of harsh army soap
(though this the Man-mani had learned to make for themselves,
boiling goat-fat in water strained through ashes).   Horse-
droppings, feed sacks, bent nails and fragments of metal from the
forging of horseshoes or arrowheads — everything was a prize
for those who had so little, though despite Kamin-Tolagh's
warnings against either theft of cavalry property or its use by
soldiers to purchase services, some good blankets and usable
lengths of cloth and stirrup-leather filtered into tribal hands, as
did a few eating utensils, used mainly as planting-tools.

Planting, or the manpower to accomplish it, was subject
of ferocious disputes with Iruvakh, whose complacent, *Mankh'*-
flavored arguments were worse than a toothache, and as hard to
wish away. At the particular time when the urgency of Kamin-
Tolagh's military needs competed for the same men with
Iruvakh's agricultural schemes, he was irked to be told yet again
all other success was dependent on better growing, and without
improved yields, the time Kamin-Tolagh wished to devote to
training armies would all be taken up by the hunting and
gathering of food, tending of herds; so long as they worked dawn
to dusk merely to feed themselves, there could be no tribal
squadrons.

Oddly, a degree of accommodation was achieved with
Kamin-Tolagh's angry retort, less than compromising, `Then
teach the women!' In fact, Iruvakh discovered, women were
often readier than their men to try new ways, or perhaps that the
men were less inclined to be instructed by one who could display

neither wife nor weapon. But there were drawbacks, too; as Iruvakh noted, a man of the tribes, taught good seeding-practice in place of their traditional and wasteful broadcasting, or how to start plants in a small, well-watered bed before setting them out in the fields, could then teach others, but what women learned could be passed on only to other and mainly younger women, while some, under threat or actuality of a beating from husband, father or brother, were forced back to old ways. Here as everywhere, Iruvakh lectured, the familiar, fallacious principle, *it was good enough for my father, and my father's father*, never took into account all those prematurely dead for whom it had not been good enough.

He had to use men, also, for much of the heavy work involved in cutting back steep slopes into terraced, water-grudging steps, and with limited skills for supervising above three or four men at a time, Iruvakh scarcely needed Kamin-Tolagh's exasperated instruction to restrict those efforts, for the time being, to the Man-mani, where he had authority of his own, and in case of resistance to orders judged foolish or unnecessary, could invoke the name of Noh-Sra-Lal-Hin. "Surely," Kamin-Tolagh, tartly, "if these practices are all you say, other tribes will soon copy what works for the Man-mani."

Iruvakh's pained admission that with all his improvements in place, final word remained with the weather, with water or its lack, was countered in theory by the grandiose projects of Lavsila, beginning with wind-driven devices to pump water from the river to the top of the new terraced slopes. He made detailed, surprisingly practical drawings, but would have to have pipes, and either for those or the more complex moving parts, Kamin-Tolagh doubted the army had a smith accomplished enough, despite the well-equipped forge at the Lunu, and a considerable stock of bar iron and bronze. Lavsila's other idea, to go high into the central hills and tap sources of water at present wasted racing down deep-scoured crevices or lost in malodorous patches of bog, would require less skilled work, he insisted, metal or even wooden channeling and stonework, a fair amount of digging, but he had no solution for difficulties of the brush-choked terrain, no answer to where men could be found without disrupting other plans.

He protested it would need only a couple of work-parties, each of about fifty, the most that could be supervised, kept together, and supplied, but when Kamin-Tolagh asked how they were to be protected from the Hill Froghul, whose water they would be taking, answered vaguely the workers could be armed, and a handful of regulars would then be enough to make the hill-men timid.

Kamin-Tolagh would have disputed this point, but Kambanal jumped beyond to a less answerable objection, enquiring courteously how, if the work could be completed, they could guard five, ten, fifteen miles of aqueduct and artificially excavated water-course against the hill-men. who could block or destroy it in a different place anywhere along its length every day. A thousand men, with no other duties, would hardly be enough to make it safe and keep it flowing.

The disconcerting of Lavsila was a spectacle Kamin-Tolagh never grew tired of; the man's arrogant certitude was a bubble made for bursting. Yet his least-cherished scheme, so straightforward he almost disdained to expound it, was simple, feasible, and promised genuine benefit, as well as changing the appearance of the main Man-mani valley. Where the river swept out its three-quarter circle, the place where the cavalry had waited in ambush for the first Hill Froghul raid, the banks, already deeply cut back, were dug out further, deepening the course, sacrificing part of the grazing land in front of the fenced compound. Excavated earth and gravel was used to build up the banks here, large stones to begin damming the stream where it resumed its southwesterly direction. For a month, this resulted in nothing more promising than a dusty scar, slow to fill, but when rain joined with the melting of remote snows to swell the river, a broad reservoir was formed. Below the partial dam, the flow was greatly reduced, and would no doubt cease altogether when the hot months came, but this was very much the Man-mani river, bending farther to the westward and flowing uselessly through white and yellow flats where nothing would grow, before reaching Flamûrai above the marshlands of the Hwenala; no one would be deprived by its damming. Years ago, according to Iruvakh, nearer the village some of the better growing-land had been adjacent to the stream, but the Sranadatta family had steadily accumulated title to it, letting it all revert to pasture for their own animals. Having seized all assets of the former ruling clan, Kamin-Tolagh began parcelling out that land to those families who contributed a son or a husband to his soldiery, but the rest was kept as common grazing.

Near end of winter, the need for armed men in the saddle grew greater; there were minor raids by Hill Froghul, and Iruvakh warned to expect more, as stocks of food everywhere ran low; at this season, when little stored grain was left, the herds became principal target of the raiders.

The southernmost tribe, the Gudi-la, suffered most from these spring raids; the slopes in their lands, below the line of the dense brush, supported something approximating open forest, with contorted pines and scrawny oaks which kept their tiny leaves all year, and the Gudi-la kept pigs and some oxen in addition to goats. Much of their herding was done on horseback, making the tribe apter to cavalry training, and this year, when a party of near fifty Hill Froghul came to round up and drive off swine, they quickly found themselves in a running fight with newly formidable Gudi-la, who outnumbered them, and despite losses succeeded in heading off the raiders, preventing their retreat long enough for the arrival of Karguli cavalry under Kambanal, whose squadron had been patrolling a few miles north. About half the raiders were killed or captured, and all the pigs were saved, except one hit by a stray arrow, which was roasted on the spot for a triumphant feast. A splendid demonstration of strength in alliance, and Kamin Tolagh was happy to have a fresh batch of prisoners to flog and then set free so they could carry home tales about the new hardness of their traditional prey, but the victory was marred by the first death among his own forces, a man of Kambanal's squadron whose horse had stumbled in the charge, throwing him to the ground in the midst of the enemy.

Iruvakh, when he heard of this action, and other widely scattered incidents where Hill Froghul alone or as part of small parties were killed or driven off, made a prediction the tribes eastward of the central hills would suffer an increase in raiding, and in the rainy season Kamin-Tolagh was sought out by leaders of the Laughing Owl, most numerous and influential of those eastward peoples, who made it plain they spoke also for the remnant Chon'la, virtual vassals since their decimation by the Hill Froghul.

As usual, Kamin-Tolagh was treated to a dissertation as to how the Laughing Owl differed from all others in their tales, practices and beliefs, and once again they seemed to him drearily like the rest, short, ill-fed, drably costumed and uncouth. He still let Iruvakh amuse him with details of tribal ways, but no longer gave them any weight; the man had a vested interest in preserving the lore that made him an authority, and the learned were always in love with the notion of immemorial, unchanged customs, but even at Kadon Dinul there were many who made no distinction between the ritual of *Shuda'sai*, descending from time before history, and the Pledgings, inaugurated by Banak within living memory of the aged, honoring both equally as ancient observances. For people without written records, lucky if they saw fifty, anything older than a grandmother had origins lost in time, and as for *unchanging*, that was easily disproved; men were ready to abandon the most hallowed of their ways when threatened with starvation, dispossession, painful death or serious inconvenience.

The Laughing Owl, then, were the same as all so far, trying to get the benefits of Kamin-Tolagh's protection, without giving anything in return except useless vows of friendship. Having gone through similar negotiations with the western Gudila, Kamin-Tolagh scarcely needed Lavsila's written list of conditions for the alliance, acceptance of his general authority, and that of Iruvakh in farming practices, supply of young men for military training — to which he added *abolition of all abhorrent tribal customs*: according to Iruvakh, in years when the harvest was failing the Laughing Owl performed revolting mutilations on from one to a half-dozen selected youths, the few over the years to survive this becoming objects of general ridicule, dressed in cast-off women's clothing and given the most menial household tasks.

On this point the talks ran aground, and the tribal elders rode away, but after an eight-day interval, during which, as he later discovered, the Laughing Owl suffered widespread raids by the Hill Froghul at a heavy cost in livestock and women, they returned and unconditionally acquiesced in his terms.

Kamin-Tolagh, who had meant his high-handedness to discourage or at least delay acceptance, began to be uneasy, and his embarrassment was completed when, within days, three more of the main westward tribes asked to be included in the alliance, the Jai from east of Larghai's Notch, with their related neighbors the Anga-Jai, and the haughty southern Ntara-golal, who, according to Iruvakh, because of their peculiar marital customs, possessed no words for *uncle, aunt, nephew* or *niece*, all offspring under one roof being considered brothers and sisters with multiple (and in fact closely related) fathers and mothers. He had no choice but to welcome these new submissions, though his armed forces were completely inadequate to offer safety to so many widely-dispersed peoples, or so much as come to their support when attacked; it was over fifty miles from Larghai's Notch to the lands of the Ntara-Golal, a long, dusty trail remaining judiciously a distant bowshot clear of heavy brush, down which entire length Kamin-Tolagh soon sent a couple of squadrons to visit the southern tribe, a mere gesture in the face of an enemy able to move swiftly in cover, and emerge at any point to raid outlying storehouses or snatch up isolated livestock, vanishing into the brush as suddenly as they had come. Nor, with so much territory to guard, could he spare officers and men to make a serious start on training tribes to defend themselves. Failure to curtail the raiding could, he knew, begin the swift unravelling of the entire coalition, as yet no more than the illusion of collective strength; if that happened his would not be the first empire ruined by trying to digest too much new territory all at once; the ancient, broken watchtowers at the edge of Landegh were there to tell that familiar story.

One dank day at the head-man's hut of the Man-mani, where the still, moist air held in and sharpened the eternal odors of burnt goat-fat and musty humanity, Iruvakh remarked it was hard to believe how quickly all these lands would dry to tinder, when the parching Jinzai Wind began blowing out of the northeast, and the season of fires arrived. First, he said, the brush of the east-facing slopes would burn, and the tribes on that side, normally upwind of the fires, had little to fear. Here on the westward side the moisture lingered longer, but when the flames began crossing the summit, they brought threat to the valleys where the tribes dwelt and livestock was pastured.

Lavsila, proud of how his reservoir was filling, said, "Here, we have water to fight fires, now."

Iruvakh laughed, as near open scorn as he came; the two men disliked each other, and worked fractiously in harness; Kamin-Tolagh could not decide which exasperated him most, Lavsila's absolute contempt for all the tribes and their ways, or Iruvakh's refusal to condemn the ugliest or most absurd customs. "Water! You would need all Flamûrai to fight a brush fire in front of the Jinzai Wind when it has been blowing five days — the only thing to stop it is bare ground with nothing to burn, and that, too, can be vaulted over. Five hundred paces downwind from the flames it can be hot enough to singe your eyebrows, and I have seen flames overtake a deer at the run."

"On hillsides the fire is fiercest?"

"That is where its fuel is."

"And our enemies." A new use for alliance was starting to stir in Kamin-Tolagh's mind.

Iruvakh assessed him. "They are fire-wise. The Hill Froghul live with fires; they can tell at a glance whether they are in danger, and which way to fly. You would have to burn the whole of the hills to burn them out; each time they would move to where your fire would not come, and when they guessed your intent, move with their goats and their horses to where the fire had already been."

"Not if the whole of the hills were burning at one time." Kamin-Tolagh's ability to picture how the lands lay had been greatly improved by the revealed talent of Dubovai, a young half-squadron, who had come shyly to show him maps he had drawn recording all the journeys of the troops, with distances carefully calculated, and features of the terrain clearly indicated; provided with a travelling-pen and small squares of parchment, Dubovai had become Kamin-Tolagh's official mapmaker.

Where he had slept had once been heart of the Chon'la country, and the delayed revenge of the Chon'la was at hand. Men and women of the vestigial tribe had an encampment nearby, closer to where scrubby pasture with scattered clumps of brush vanished into the dark and tangled growth of the hillsides. As the Chon'la wakened, they built their main campfire up into a blaze, flames pale in the white-gold light of sunrise. Farther back in the flat, Kamin-Tolagh had his half-squadron of lances in the saddle; Chamya, now able to manage a *pefrai*, was with them, and a handful of the younger but more disciplined Man-mani, almost ready to pass for soldiers. All eyes watched Kamin-Tolagh for the sign.

Half an hour past sunrise was the set time, and if all had gone well this same scene was taking place at roughly five-mile intervals, north to where the road began its climb to Larghai's Notch, back south through Laughing Owl country and the long journey to the fringes of the Ntara-golal lands, nearly fifty miles in all. Iruvakh was down there, having been too exhausted to ride back when Kamin-Tolagh had; remarkably, he had spent six long days in the saddle journeying the whole length of the proposed fireline, using five different languages or dialects to explain, cajole, threaten and persuade at Kamin-Tolagh's behest, and then to go through it again with each set of tribal leaders, to make sure they understood the plan must be exactly adhered-to, all for sake of a scheme he utterly opposed — exactly as he had made himself useful to the *jinzai*-breeders, whose aims he deplored. Not really humility, this need to serve, but the reverse; pride in his mastery of languages and grasp of tribal thinking made him want those skills to be used, regardless of ends.

Kamin-Tolagh was aware how dangerously thin his fighting men were distributed, parcelled out in half-squadrons too widely separated to give each other rapid support. Parties of Hill Froghul were known to be lurking well down these eastward slopes, alert for opportunities to plunder; while Kamin-Tolagh was away in the south, a large band had carried out a brutal attack on a hamlet of the Laughing Owl clan known as K'daab's People, and escaped virtually unscathed; their numbers might be enough, with bowmanship, to defeat a half-squadron of regulars, which would be both an irreplaceable loss and an irretrievable blow to prestige. Kamin-Tolagh's main hope was a reasonable supposition the hill-men would do all they could to evade serious fighting so long as they believed they could carry out unopposed raids elsewhere, yet he found it uncomfortable to reflect a large such elsewhere was over on the westward side of the hills, left worse-defended than the east.

It was time. Swinging into the saddle of his waiting *pefrai*, Kamin-Tolagh signed to the tribesmen waiting by their blazing fire. Silence converted to a harsh-voiced babble, they at once seized flaming brands, and fanned out in the direction of the upslope. Kamin-Tolagh turned and jogged to where his men were waiting, and when he turned a low line of flame was already creeping at the base of the dark brush. A bird fluttered, worked wings twice to stand still against the persistent breeze, then banked into a turn to head for deeper cover; Kamin-Tolagh recalled Iruvakh's lament for the animals a general fire would surely destroy; there were large rabbits and strange round-eared foxes, wildcats and the rumor of rare leopardlike creatures; farther south some deer and horned wild sheep, many snakes and unfamiliar, small burrowing animals, at this season the eggs of the early nesters, as well as the goats and hill-horses of the Hill Froghul. Wars were won, Kamin-Tolagh had told him, by captains who can induce an enemy's ally to change sides, and the deep cover of these twisted hills had been their adversary's staunchest friend.

Lazily, the brush-fire was building, while men, women and some boys were working to extend its line, no longer needing to return to their original fire for blazing material. A short way from Kamin-Tolagh, Chamya abruptly cried out, and gestured eastward, to the wide belt of barren and arid land, where, less than a mile distant, a dust-cloud was rising.

"Horsemen?" hand going to his hilt.

The Man-mani youth shook his head. "Wind," *shavurai*, a great wind. The dust tattered and thinned, nothing at its heart, and then came the assault of flying grit, to sting faces, and force eyes shut, as the warm wind came in a rush. It grabbed at the growing line of flame, and quiet, creeping fires burst into brilliant blossoms and leaping blades of flame, while a great, bloodshot furl of smoke rolled before the wind. After jumping back from the initial ferocity, the tribal fire-setters were infected by madness, cackling and yelling as they scurried to encourage the lateral spread. From where they had begun, a vast yellow and orange arrowhead, white hot at the center, drove up the hillside, and half a mile back the noise was tremendous, a deep, rolling roar under fierce crackling, punctuated by sudden, startling bangs. Fire leapt from top to top of clumps of small trees and higher stands of brush, while lower it ran as a flooding river of dazzling heat, consuming the slope with an undreamt velocity; nothing, as Iruvakh had said, could withstand or outrun such ravening greed.

After that first gust the wind remained brisk, and some of the fire-setters were taking risks when they ignited great bundles of brush and ran, holding them downwind at arm's length; if nothing worse there would be burnt hands and short-lashed eyelids today. In places, others of the tribes beat or stamped at small spurts of fire contriving to creep back against the wind, no real threat to grazing-land, nor to the northward huddle of Chon'la huts with its flimsy stockade; this fire had fuel inexhaustible in front of it.

Hard to judge when the protective cavalry should begin to move northward to keep pace with the firesetters. The foremost of those, still wildly excited, were soon to disappear beyond the jut of a brush-clad outthrust shoulder, but Kamin-Tolagh knew with everything going precisely to plan, there must be a four-mile stretch open behind him, a gate, closing slowly, through which their enemy could escape — only with no way of guessing the full extent of their danger, the Hill Froghul would see it, rather, as an opportunity for some pillaging. He waved Nizhadh on at the walk with the regulars, all but a half-file of lances, which he himself led, together with Chamya's small group of Man-mani, to the crest of a slight rise, from where he could observe both north and south.

Excitement of the fire, tension of waiting, had everyone fidgeting in the saddle. The breeze surged, the roar of burning deepened, and well upslope Kamin-Tolagh observed a high dome of brush, not less than a quarter-mile beyond and above the main blaze, erupt all at once in flame, made tinder, he supposed, by the scorching wind, then ignited by fiery airborne particles. Chamya shouted, but not at that spectacle; he was pointing southward, drawing attention to a distant, fat column of smoke bulging up on the far side of a main bastion of the central hills.

"Yaënsilat," Kamin-Tolagh said, the officer in charge of fire-setting there.

He had given strict orders each section should spread its flames only in a northward direction, but seeing how well his firesetters were progressing, Kamin-Tolagh contradicted himself, collecting a few stray tribesmen, and conveying to them with gestures they should work the opposite way. With them went a small contingent of Chon-la warriors, armed with bows, no match, he suspected, for those of the Hill Froghul.

A guess too quickly confirmed. The Chon'la had progressed, spreading fire, a couple of hundred paces in the new direction, starting to mount a long slope, when arrows flew from the brush just ahead, and stocky, broad-shouldered figures appeared, blades flashing in the sun. At the same moment from northward, where the tail of his cavalry had just passed out of sight, there came the short, stabbing note of a signal trumpet proclaiming enemy had been sighted.

With no time to debate decisions, Kamin-Tolagh dispatched one of his few men of Kargul at the gallop to find Nizhadh, and bring back a report. With the others, and Man-mani headed by an eager Chamya, he made for the fighting he could see.

Except the fight was over; firesetters and their escort, leaving several dead and wounded, were scattering before Hill Froghul, of which about a dozen were visible, though others could easily be hidden in the brush.

Yet they themselves were not interested in a battle; a few careless arrows came in the general direction of the oncoming riders, but the bowmen were not going to make a stand; having perhaps understood the implications of the fire, they meant to disperse into the lowlands. A reasonable choice, but it gave the

Chon'la bowmen a chance to rally; they were quite equal to aiming arrows at a retreating enemy.

The nearest made an attempt to withstand Kamin-Tolagh's undermanned charge. He quickly sworded down one knife-wielding fighter, but as he wheeled to take on another, who avoided the lance-thrust of a cavalryman, Kamin-Tolagh's stirrup was seized by a man who had been crouched among bushy growth, and before he could lean away for a backhand slash he felt a sharp pain in that leg. A jarring shock, and his assailant's hands slipped from the sidling *pefrai*; he saw the man's throat had been pierced through by the light lance Chamya carried, and had now released.

"My thanks," Kamin-Tolagh called, but the boy was away with a whoop, and out of the saddle, knife drawn, to bowl over and finish another Hill Froghuli brought to his knees by an arrow-shot. Hoping, perhaps, to make a prize of Chamya's mount, another came in a bounding run, and Kamin-Tolagh quickly spurred his *pefrai* to cut in front of Chamya, and down the attacker with a cleaving stroke that nearly severed the head. Other fights called for his intervention, but Kamin-Tolagh spared time to help and half-haul the boy back into the saddle, telling him to remain mounted, and stay clear of further fighting.

"Lal-Hin bleeds." True; a hand pressed to the outside of the left leg came away red and sticky, not a dangerous wound, and treatment could wait, but Kamin-Tolagh wondered if he was imagining the mockery he heard, as if Chamya was saying *all the Man-mani will see, as we do, Noh-Sra-Lal-Hin is only a man.*

Arrival of Kamin-Tolagh's makeshift contingent had turned the fight, and what most amazed him was the clemency of the Chon'la, satisfied to make captives from a tribe that had treated theirs so savagely, instead of hewing them down as they tried to capitulate. One of the lancers of Kargul was giving chase to a scuttling enemy, who turned too late to use his bow, and was ridden down. That was the end here.

Breathless, Kamin-Tolagh's message-rider returned at the gallop to report a small group of enemy to the northward had easily been subdued, and had evidently intended surrender when they emerged from concealment, ten or a dozen Hill Froghul including two women and a boy-child, who had narrowly escaped roasting, some with scorched clothing and singed hair.

Chamya eavesdropped, eyes gleaming. "More prisoners," he gloated with a vulpine face. "They should give good sport tomorrow."

"They will not," sharply. With others, the boy had greatly enjoyed the hangings after the cowing of the Hwenala, but must understand the difference between arrested traitors and prisoners-of-war. Loftily as he could, as a mortal who bled when he was stabbed, Noh-Sra-Lal-Hin proclaimed: "Only if fresh fighting breaks out, and men cannot be spared to guard them are those captured in battle killed in cold blood."

"Today," Chamya parried, using his mother's trick of abandoning an awkward topic, "I am *péfrapravádai*."

In the heart of the Laughing Owl country the squadrons reassembled, afternoon dulled by smoke across the face of the sun. The two northermost firesetting parties had worked north to south, and so the rendezvous was ten miles short of where the climb began to Larghai's Notch; by noon there were two full squadrons collected, and Kamin-Tolagh considered beginning the ride back to the other side of the hills, not waiting for the rest. With the westward tribes, somewhat less than two-and-a-half squadrons of regulars with about an equal number of tribal auxiliaries, Man-mani and half-trained Gudi-la, were guarding all the wide lands towards which the Hill Froghul were being driven by fire. Talfoyan was in command there, and would in his dour way do his best, see to it livestock was not pastured far afield, and ordinary men of the tribes had their weapons to hand, but if large numbers of Hill Froghul' survivors could assemble, there might yet be a war to fight, with losses in both men and *pefral* he had no means of replacing.

He decided in the end to stick to the plans, and in mid-afternoon Kambanal rode in with a weary half-squadron, having encountered a larger number of the Hill Froghul, which he had broken with a charge, hunting down, killing or capturing most of the rest, though he had lost two men to bows. "Finding the sly little *jinzal*," he said, "before they can let loose an arrow or two, is no easy task, *Asai*." He spoke fingering a deep dent in his own breastplate.

Additional losses had occurred among allied tribes, but so far as was known no considerable body of enemy had escaped into the lowlands, and forty miles of hillside were set afire. There was no direct report from the southernmost country of the Ntara-golal, but Kambanal had observed dense smoke rising there; those three half-squadrons would assemble under Freighanai near where Kamin-Tolagh had begun the day, and remain here in the east for a time, carrying out patrols.

With no chance of reaching Man-mani country before morning, he permitted the new arrivals brief rest, and all the troops had food. From the fenced village of K'daab's People, children and young women came out to stare, make friends, beg bits of bread and dried fruit. The wind blew gently but steadily, and miles away fire climbed the blackened and blackening hillside. Far above the tallest of the heights an immense cloud of smoke mounted, the broadening top as if sheared off, an abrupt, mysterious flattening. Kambanal, following Kamin-Tolagh's gaze, said, "Like a great anvil."

"*With these flames*," Kamin-Tolagh softly intoned, glad to be beside the one man he could rely on to disseminate his legend, "*In this furnace, upon this anvil, an empire is being forged.*"

Good words, but only words, he pondered, as they rode steadily through latter afternoon. If burning the hills defeated the Hill Froghul, if it only set them back so he could have a respite in which he with the training of armies and Iruvakh with the teaching of husbandry could bring the tribes nearer safety from their two main enemies, hunger and raids — three enemies, really, if you considered the squabbling, one with another, that confederation under Kamin-Tolagh made ineffectual — empire here was as good as won, and as Shumat had asked, months ago, to what purpose? To hold sway over rocks and dust? nothing here for him to reward his soldiers or add to his wealth — on the contrary, he was contracting debts, making his men promises out of his own pocket, and could not envisage them content to be made into landlords, not if he turned all the tribes into tenants, and gave the Kargul' a thousand acres apiece of arid and grudging land.

Nor could he anticipate a triumphal return to Rodlakh's realm, if he brought only tales of victory in battles, nothing but distant skirmishes at Kadon Dinul; his hailing by the Man-mani, submission of the Hwenala followed by the other tribes, success against the Hill Froghul, epic burning of the hills — if the grand result of all this turned out to be a temporary halt to tribal bickering in Northern Froghushei, it was not enough to set against his defiance of Rodlakh.

In time, Iruvakh said, surplus foods, with the *dao* spice, could be traded to the Hrin. Thoughts began to dwell on those southern workers of gold, handlers of gold, about whom even Iruvakh was ignorant to an extent which embarrassed him. One reason for the pride of the Ntara-golal tribe was that their leaders sometimes communicated with each other by means of brief writings incised on pieces of wood, and the system they used was clearly derived and simplified from that of the Hrin, a hint their lands, the Hrinani, were not as inaccessible by land as they liked to assert. Dealing with such renowned seamen, Kamin-Tolagh would never have means to challenge them on the water, but if, say next year, he could build an effective army out of his confederated tribes, a surprise attack by land could bring profit: they were said to be unwarlike, and if too much for him to conquer, the Hrin might be held to ransom, made to pay a tribute in gold as the price of being left in peace.

Pausing near the foot of the Notch to water the horses, they rode on in twilight whose advance was hastened by the thick screen of smoke over the westward sky, although from here all sight of the fire was obscured by the steep slope of blackened nearby hills. There had been talk of making camp below, but Kamin-Tolagh was determined to be back with the Man-mani by morning, if it meant spending a chilly night up in the Notch itself.

At dusk, moving steadily up, they came to the place where the trail bore leftward along the spine of a minor ridge like a causeway. Where the nearby embankment abruptly dropped away, the lead squadron, with no order given, halted as if turned to stone, a low murmur of wonder coming from the men.

It was the fire. At its closest, frenzies of flame that lunged and scrabbled at branch and leaf, but receding to a broad river of gold, meandering away to the edge of the visible world, dimming stars that behind its smokes had begun to prick the darkening sky. At its back, the blaze had left pools and ponds of flame, brilliant and numerous where it had recently passed, thinning and dimming as the eye travelled back downslope, orange to dull red, and where a current of wind gusted the scarlet brightened again to yellow, yellow to white, entire broad sweeps of country glowing with the beauty of embers in a forge under the bellows, a many-layered radiance that pierced to the heart like music.

"Great Hrafi," Kambanal whispered. "There is a sight we will not soon forget."

Kamin-Tolagh was wearing spare breeches borrowed from a long-legged youthful file-leader named Niburai, much his build; Noh-Sra-Lal-Hin did not return to his Man-mani stained with his own blood. He had expected greater rejoicing at his return; the village emerged from its huts and came down to the stockade gateway to call his legendary name, but as Chamya soon discovered and reported, they were unhappy and fearful over the unprecedented quantities of smoke which dimmed the morning sun; before dawn tongues of fire had crept across the distant summit to begin their downward journey, and villagers were talking about taking their few belongings across the river to certain safety, if it meant watching the village burn.

"What they will be watching," Kamin-Tolagh said, "is Hill Froghul' survivors, occupying their huts. Fire won't reach the village." That was the experienced opinion, eight days ago, of Iruvakh, who had, however, reserved the right to change his mind, if the parching wind, now reduced to a faint stirring, had lifted the moisture from the westward slopes, or if it resumed with its former force.

"The village must stand to arms," he told Chamya. "As many as can be of the men should form bands for hunting the enemy. Don't worry," he reassured. "The Hill Froghul will be weary, and discouraged after a night running from the fire. I shall allot cavalry to each Man-mani pack, but the enemy must be captured, mind, not killed, unless they try to fight."

"*Asai*," Chamya asked, eyes meeting Kamin-Tolagh's. "Am I to be the one who orders this?"

Suddenly, a defining question. They were dismounted outside the head-man's hut; Osré-dnë was on the steps, showing no readable emotion at her son's safe return, while behind her in the doorway Imyë, current favorite among the serving-girls Osré-dnë picked and instructed was repeatedly going tiptoe in her delight at seeing Kamin-Tolagh again; she had the soft prettiness of her tribe, but there was something else, a forgotten mingling in her bloodline, perhaps, tautening the features. Oddly, though Imyë was duskier, she reminded Kamin-Tolagh remotely of Âna — not the *rabhsayu*, but Âna as he had first found her, posing as

the half-simple daughter of an obscure farmer, and took her —
but here was no time for bedding this girl, who in her own right
knew how to please.

He saw the hunger in the eyes of Osré-dnë, guessing, not
for the first time, that she understood more of the Owanilú than
was admitted. Chamya was waiting for his answer: a full season
since he had caught the rope, and while apparently true, as
Iruvakh had declared, he had thereafter been accepted as a man,
Kamin-Tolagh had continued to see that less as a reality than as
an affectionate Man-mani family joke, but not derisive, a kind of
warm chuckle. They were still without a head-man, though clear
where the power rested, in the sheath of Kamin-Tolagh, who had
kept the seized lands of the Sranadatta clan in his personal gift,
and made tribal decisions without need of a Man-mani
figurehead.

Now it would be known, the boy proudly knew, he had
come to the aid of Noh-Sra-Lal-Hin in battle, and with that test
passed, he was in effect asking, *if in every sense a man, why not
head-man, as once you asked me to be*?

Kamin-Tolagh felt a sudden surge of pride in what
Chamya, under his tutelage, had become. He put a hand on the
boy-man's shoulder. "The Man-mani shall be summoned by
Chamya to Meeting Place, where their new head-man can tell
them what they must do to be rid forever of their ancient enemy.
You shall speak to them from the raised place."

"Are you to be there?"

"Noh-Sra-Lal-Hin shall stand behind Chamya, who has
been his right hand in war," in best ceremonial style. "As shall
Osré-dnë the Wise, counsellor to the wise."

Having perhaps unnecessarily given this news to his
imperturbable mother, Chamya with a brash grin translated her
comment: "She says, Chamya does not need a guard of men
from the Hwenala." In fact, the small group of Man-mani youths
who had been his companions for this expedition would need
only the smallest sign from him to become his devoted followers;

since they were at the same time military levies under Kamin-Tolagh's orders, they would help preserve desirable ambiguity about the extent of Chamya's independent authority.

That afternoon, and for the next three days, as the diminishing fire crept nearer inhabited western valleys, Hill Froghul began to emerge, singly, in small groups, at times maintaining an ordered band, some driving their goats. When cavalry appeared, they tried to run, or stood in a semblance of fight, but most had stopped hoping for anything beyond escaping the fire, and gave themselves up with something resembling relief. The closer flames approached, the more desperate the condition of the Hill Froghul became; long flight, loss of animals and all other possessions, lack of food, destruction of the lands they had always counted on for refuge, heat, thirst and the eternal smoke all conspired to leave them dazed, broken in spirit. Filthy, lacerated by retreat through pathless brush, many with scorched clothing and burns severe or slight, they staggered empty-eyed from cover, hardly appearing to care whether they would be slain by the patrolling horsemen, or the valley tribesmen, made brave as lions by sight of their diminished enemies.

Most were made prisoner by the cavalry and their auxiliaries, with their swifter mounts and stronger discipline; there were no means of telling how many murders were done; when there were no regulars with them the tribal hunting-packs seemed to encounter a disproportionate number of Hill Froghul who, though hopelessly outnumbered, refused to surrender and had to be killed to the last man (and, often, woman), but as Lavsila did not fail to point out, it would be natural for even an exhausted enemy to believe they stood a chance in a fight against the despised valley tribes, unaided by disciplined soldiery. Natural, too, Kamin-Tolagh conceded, for men who had suffered all their lives from the depredations of these raiders, losing, maybe, friends, wives and daughters, as well as livestock and foodstuffs, to seize this opportunity for revenge. Also, people never very far from starvation would be less than enthusiastic about taking captives who would have to be fed — although, as Lavsila said, the valley tribes had in fact been feeding these Hill Froghul for years.

The fourth morning of the fire began in unseasonable heat, and from the northeast the breeze sprang with renewed vigor. Pockets of fire that had seemed to be dying arose into new life, and approached inhabited places; eastward of the valley where the *dao* spice grew a spearhead of flame came roaring down a brush-clad ridge to threaten outlying Hwenala dwellings, but of all western tribes the Hwenala were least afraid of fire; their flimsy huts were easily rebuilt, and they could retreat into the sanctuary of their marshes. Kamin-Tolagh rode down that way to see the danger, and was greeted by news that well to the south the Gudi-la were fighting fire in their woodland pasturage. Minutes later word caught up with him bushes were burning very near the Man-mani village, but by that time the Jinzai Wind had altogether and abruptly stilled. Moister air was pressing in off Flamûrai, with immediate and obvious effect on the appetite of the fire, which could be seen to settle back, a great, fierce beast all at once overcome by sleep.

What was to be its final surge, however, drove out those of the remaining Hill Froghul who had evidently hoped to survive in the remnant margins of unburnt brush. Among these were the worst cases yet seen, blistered hands and faces, eyes swollen nearly shut, while those who had escaped serious physical injury were hobbling, trembling wrecks of men, half starved, and wholly shattered in spirit.

With one exception. Kamin-Tolagh had taken his stand on higher ground where he could at the same time watch the creeping progress of the flames threatening the Hwenala, and keep an eye on slopes leftward, with particular attention for a brush-choked gully as yet unreached by fire, an obvious refuge. Smoke was again streaming overhead from fire no more than a long bowshot away, and out from the gully a man strode, nearly swaggered, followers appearing piecemeal till they had become a band of about thirty or forty, a handful of women and children with them. Paying no attention to some rag-tag Hwenala hunters who were gathering and wondering if they should risk a demand for capitulation, the Hill Froghuli leader made straight for Kamin-Tolagh.

While all the tribesmen behind him had their bows slung, blades sheathed, this foremost carried his short, broad sword in front of him, both hands on the blade. The half-squadron of Kargul closed in to challenge his progress, but Kamin-Tolagh, who perceived this man was seeking honorable surrender in the fashion of civilized people, waved them back, allowing him to approach. He was somewhat taller than most of his tribe, with a powerful upper body, rather bowed legs as had all the many Froghul' peoples, very black eyes in a blunt, wide-mouthed face, deeply scored but not suggesting great age. Next to Kamin-Tolagh's twitching *pefrai*, he halted, handed up his sword hilt first, and gave a regular military salute.

"Tau-Suaka of the Froghushei yields, making no conditions for himself, but asking his people be treated in good heart."

A rehearsed speech, and behind its formalisms could be perceived a mind coolly assessing chances, not a man to offer himself as sacrifice if he believed it would be accepted. But the calculation of it was not what made Kamin-Tolagh blink in surprise. Tau-Suaka had addressed him in ordinary language of the realm.

Not the mystery it appeared; as a youth the Froghuli had made the transit of Landegh, crossed the Frontier, and served six years with the Army of the West as a mounted bowman. This would have been at the time when Saidhan, in enduring dispute with Kadon Dinul about permitted strength of his army, was sidestepping the question of *pefrai*-mounted cavalry by raising unauthorized formations using small hill-horses. Tau-Suaka had gone, like many others — though very few from so far — because of hard times here in the West, and so as to learn how disciplined armies fought. He was a rarity in having kept to his initial resolve, and returned to his own lands and people; to Kamin-Tolagh, as even more to Lavsila when he heard the story, it was inconceivable a man who had experienced the relative comforts of Colony life, attained rank of file-leader, learnt the pleasure of having a little money and something to spend it on, could come back to the hardships, crudities, the sheer tedium of existence in those hopeless hills. Tau-Suaka said simply, "I shot my first arrow there, *Asai*," and Kamin-Tolagh felt a searing stab of desire for the cool green valleys of western Kargul, their deep grass and ice-fed torrents, the shadowed pine-woods above Inilun Barabhi; what was he doing here in this overbaked land?

"How is it," he asked Tau-Suaka, "you have not taught the ways of the army to your people?" They had come back to the Man-mani village, but not to the head-man's hut, which would now be Chamya's. After expressing eagerness to see the fire-setting operation, Lavsila had stayed in what was now called the Visitors' Hut, and took part in the interrogation.

Tau-Suaka gave his typical shrug. "They're ignorant, *Asai*. When there's to be fighting, we choose a leader for that time. His is the plan, but after the fight, no more captain." Warming to the theme, his manner became confiding. "Men without masters can't be marched and drilled. If the fight is three days away, they must have their goats with them. They're not much other than animals themselves. At Drin Navuna this was otherwise." He took a large drink from his mug of Man-mani beer.

By recognizing the shortcomings of his own people, the man seemed to claim closeness to his new masters; Kamin-Tolagh had met with this kind of attempted ingratiation before;

though distasteful, it could be useful. "We have collected and caged some hundreds of these near-animals of yours. What shall we do with them? They cannot be kept here." Iruvakh, before the fire was started, had said that, and he was right. Captive Hill Froghul, all ages and both sexes, though most by far were male, were being brought together at the warehouses and surrounding compound across the river, not needed as a keep now there would be no more raiding. But not even the magic of Noh-Sra-Lal-Hin could reconcile Man-mani — or any other tribe — to the threatening presence of their ancestral enemies.

"What?" Tau-Suaka agreed. "Surely they can't go back, all that is cinders. But how can we be fed? You will have to kill us all."

"You surrendered, when you might have fought to the death."

Slyly, "I am a soldier, *Asai*, a prisoner-of-war; you took my blade when I offered it up."

"Is this a place where those rules hold? The valley tribes have not seen much mercy from yours." This was sparring; he certainly had no intention of losing the Hill Froghul, when not exhausted, blinded and demoralized by their flight from fire, the only real fighters he had seen in the West. They had a place in his plans, not one to please the valley tribes.

"They say there is a lord who makes new ways here, men from tribes who have always fought ride together, knee by knee. He is going to make bare lands green, and change the shape of hills, he makes a lake where there was no lake — "

"News travels in the wilds," Lavsila commented.

"My people have said to me, Tau-Suaka, this lord can make the wind blow when he wants one, he commands rain — they're like children, *Asai*; they were never soldiers, and believe silly things. What this new lord can do, I say, is stronger; he causes men to do what he desires. Everywhere, there are leaders and the led — those I brought out of the fire would have been lost without me to drive them."

"Then Tau-Suaka, Tau-Suaka, or one like him, could make the hill people drill, or dig, or anything we wanted?" True enough the man was out of the ordinary, proud that among those he had led to safety were his infant son, and — he had stumbled on the alien word, for which his dialect had no equivalent — his *wife*.

Calculation returned. "No one else is *like* Tau-Suaka, *Asai*. From the Notch to the high desert, all clans speak of me. But not all love me. Some have to be killed before new ways are understood; the rest, whips are needed to drive them. But with someone who knows them, to choose the leaders under him, they could be made to dig or drill, or anything else they are told to do."

Lavsila went into the Owanilú, which Tau-Suaka would not understand; it was very little heard in the Colony. "*What do you have in mind?*"

"*To teach them, first, to obey*," not ready to reveal more. "*Your plans might be feasible, with enough hands for digging, now the hills are safe from ambush.*"

With Tau-Suaka's dark, expectant gaze going from face to face, this launched an unnecessary debate; Kamin-Tolagh had no real intention at present of initiating Lavsila's scheme for tapping water up in the hills; too many guards would be needed to prevent the Hill Froghul from escaping once back in their own country, however blackened. In any case, as Lavsila did not fail to argue, the work should have been accomplished before the rains. At last, Kamin-Tolagh reminded him of the relatively modest idea he had when they first came to the West, irrigation at the Lunu so crops could be grown there.

"*Using these men?*"

"*You will not be without protection. There is less need now for patrols; some squadrons can remain at the Lunu, on a rotating basis, to guard and train our new allies.*" In formation riding, that was; there was nothing men of Kargul could show them about bowmanship. Addition of four to six squadrons of mounted bows would let him think seriously about plundering the wealth of southern lands. *"Better,"* he said, *"if the Hill Froghul are trained away from the eyes of the valley tribes. Our men will see it as soft duty, there at the Lunu, with real roofs over their heads by night."* But the place, he thought, was going to have to be called something else; Lunu Jinzalladhiyu no longer existed. He would ask Kambanal, who had a gift for naming.

Belatedly, he noticed Lavsila's odd, questioning look. *"What is it?"*

The perplexed expression deliberately deepened. *"I thought with defeat of these raiders, we had accomplished more than you set out to do. The* rabhsai's *patience is not endless. How long do you mean to stay here in the West, then?"*

"Later," waving off the question, and to Tau-Suaka: "If I give you their training, is there an oath your people swear that will bind them to my service?"

"Give me the job, *Asai*," earnestly. "Let me break and remake them, and you'll see loyalty your Great Banak would envy."

It came to Kamin-Tolagh that to be a leader of his undisciplined people was no new ambition for Tau-Suaka; burning of his homelands, the shattering of his tribe, had become for him an opportunity to realize a long-standing aim. Nor had there been any sentiment, or anything but vanity, in his determination to save his woman and their child. This became clear when Kamin-Tolagh, having allowed that Tau-Suaka could stay overnight for further discussion at the Visitors' Hut then counter-suggested he might prefer to be with his wife and son, who were in one of the compound storage-sheds.

"No, *Asai*. They are safe under a roof, they have food. Men who lead men should be together."

"Here," Kamin-Tolagh, near anger in his determination to let the man see the limits of his proposed power, "In the West, the law is mine alone. I decide whether captives are to be fed and housed, or tortured and starved. I reward the faithful and punish the guilty."

"One lord, *Asai*," Tau-Suaka, fervently. "That is how it should be."

Men lived, Kamin-Tolagh reflected, able to take pride even in how abject they could be, but he was not going to let himself forget these Hill Froghul had habitually left their newborn daughters to die.

By night the smokes overhead thinned, and before dawn there was a light rain, laying like dust the lingering fears of the western tribes. By morning light, the great hills were dark and dead, with wraiths of smoke or steam hovering; a sobering sight, but Kamin-Tolagh had succeeded beyond expectation. Tau-Suaka, no more than Iruvakh, would or could not give any estimate of Hill Froghul' numbers before the fire, and how many had died in the flames would never be counted; some might have survived in pockets of brush inexplicably bypassed by fire, but no one could see how they could go on living in the charred hills, and there was unlikely to be enough of them to threaten the peace of the lowlands. Just short of three hundred were captives, but the number was sure to go higher, when Talfoyan returned from his hunt in the south, and Freighanai from the far side of the hills.

Kamin-Tolagh, seated, a foot up on the oak table, was cleaning and rebinding the stab-wound on the outside of his thigh, when Lavsila came in from early sword-practice with some of the younger officers down by the river. So he called it, but his style was a not-very-private joke among the soldiers, a series of attitudes with the sword rather than real sequences, *as if he is posing for his portrait*, Kamin-Tolagh had heard a scornful file-leader say.

"All the Kargul' squadrons are full of rumors. They say you told Kambanal you were going to hammer out an empire on the anvil of the tribes, or some such. They want to know what it means."

Kamin-Tolagh did not correct the text, though his original was more elegant. "It means what it says. The whole Froghushei is mine."

"For what, Tam? These men have families, homes in Kargul — some of them have not seen their wives in more than a year."

About to dispute the calculation, Kamin-Tolagh saw it would be true for those squadrons who had been attached to the Household at the end of Ban-Sila's reign, and remained with him in Kadon Dinul after fighting in the Jinzai War. "They are soldiers."

"Provincial cavalry, Tam. Most of them, when they enlisted, did not expect to cross the Kôbh — oh, a fortnight at Kadon, maybe, during Great Pledging, escorting your father. You have squadron officers who could count on sleeping in their own beds, when they did not have night-duty at Inilun Barabhi. I talked with a half-squadron who has a year-old son he has never seen."

"When did you become their spokesman? You can go and find your own bed any time you want, if you think you can get across Landegh whole." Unfair to be angry with Lavsila for a question bound to be festering among the men of Kargul; he was first to ask it aloud, but had not invented it; how long would they remain here in the barren West? But he did spend too much time gossiping with the officers, trying to make a crony even of Talfoyan, and Lavsila's nature was to probe at sore spots like an idle child picking at his own scabbed knee.

"They are anxious. Six at least of the officers have asked me what I can tell them about your intentions. Not only that they miss their homes; they worry what Kadon Dinul is making of your absence — they are afraid if you come under the *rabhsai*'s displeasure, they will suffer, too. Some believe you will be outlawed. Everyone knows Rodlakh forbade adventuring in the West."

"Outlawed?" Kamin-Tolagh anticipated annoyance on the *rabhsai*'s part, but this was absurd. "Rodlakh would have lost the Jinzai War if I had not come to his assistance. We may quarrel as brothers do, Rodlakh and I, but — oh, you have never been in battle, you cannot know how it is between two men who have waded shoulder to shoulder through blood."

"I do know men can have friends, but rulers only policies. Rodlakh has had brothers to quarrel with before; they are all gone, except one, and he would exile Orbanak without a second thought, or have him executed, if he came to be a threat to his *rabhsayum*."

Again, pure Lavsila in its innuendo; two of Rodlakh's deceased brothers had been lost in the disastrous Tan Lughsai fire, the third murdered by a madman; Rodlakh, singularly mild for the fighter he was, had not harmed anyone to obtain his power, nor sought retribution against those who had opposed him — had apparently concealed Petakoi's guilt to avoid the question of her punishment.

"The *rabhsai*, when he warned against adventuring in the West, could not have foreseen what is happened here — we have won with a handful of men what would have taken years for thousands by plain conquest."

"What have you won? At Kadon Dinul, they will only see you have placed yourself over the tribe that mothered the *jinzal*, and have reoccupied the place of their fathering."

"We shall give it a new name."

"What new name? "Lunu baSiv'loi?" This was ironic; plainly he did not think a change of names would impress Kadon Dinul.

"Abu Ninusai," not one of Kambanal's several suggestions.

"Ninusai?" The name meant, roughly, `New Province-place.'

"Rodlakh, after he has reprimanded me for exceeding instructions, will not refuse the gift of a new province for his realm." Thus, obviously, making moot the question of his defection from the Household, since he would be first _nimu_.

Lavsila, as all the Heartland Families Kamin-Tolagh had dealt with, fancied himself law-learned, and did not fail to observe a man could not at the same time be Heir in one province and _nim'_ for another, as when Daënakh, when marrying his cousin, Leghayu of Ân, had been obliged to cede succession in Nîv to his younger brother, Laënakh. That could be negotiated, Kamin-Tolagh told him, abruptly relishing the thought that if Kamin-Tarú replaced him as Heir in Kargul, there could come a time when his new province was united with the old.

For Lavsila, the question remained; what profit was there in acquiring these new lands, for a realm which already had one barren and empty province — a reference to Asekh in the east, which, though named among the Six Provinces, had long ago lapsed from that standing, and had no _nimu_, no seat, and no fixed population. "Rodlakh's question, then," loftily, "will be just what your men are asking — what is there here? _What does it add to his realm?_ is the same question as _why should they want to stay here?_ No good land," he expanded, "no cities, no money, and nothing to spend it on if it came — women to sport with, yes, but not women the young men would choose to be mothers to their children."

"No one," pointedly, "will be under compulsion to remain here. When the Lunu is renamed, I intend to call together all the officers, and tell them anyone is free to return to the realm; they will give the same choice to their men. Those who choose to stay will be required to take a new oath, to my service, not my father's."

"At risk of being called rebels in the realm."

"If so, only for a time, till Rodlakh sees we are no such thing. I must have complete allegiance, not grudged service."

Again, this was meant to be taken personally, but Lavsila remained doggedly detached. "How many do you think will choose to stay?"

His tone guessed, very few. "Enough." not sharing his long, anxious assessments. The troops, he reminded Lavsila, were not Heartlanders of pampered birth, needing constant diversion; what the propertied called boredom was simply life for most people, and for these men not very different from what they would expect as provincial cavalrymen — more stimulating, assuredly, than if they were stationed at the lonely cavalry post where the old road crossed the Nibhfoi into Nîv, or as part of the Peframi garrison. Of officers, he needed men like Freighanai, Nizhadh, the youthful Kambanal and elderly Yaënsilat; no chance Talfoyan would stay; his passionless efficiency would be missed, but not his sour manner; most of the half-squadron officers and file-leaders were young and unmarried, not yet urgently concerned, that they would fail to discover suitable wives among the willing girls of the tribes.

"For married men, those who wish, we shall find ways to bring their wives and children here. We have enough small houses at what was the Lunu."

"Will that be permitted?"

"I permit it. How can it be prevented? Is there a law against leaving the realm?"

"The women and children would need an escort. There would be a law against reentering the realm, if those who stay are exiled."

"Laws are as good as the power to enforce them." He had heard from Iruvakh about the back way into his province, and did not see what Kargul — what, eventually, his father — could do about the unwarned appearance of fifty or a hundred *exiles*, fully-armed cavalrymen.

"Besides — " he enjoyed watching Lavsila's face hunt for an expression, somewhere between respectful wonder and suave skepticism. "We shall have cities, and grand houses and all the life of the realm. Builders, carpenters, may come from the realm, but the Hrin are said to be stonemasons to equal our best — a century ago, in the time of Dromladh Gabh'Owan, seafarers brought back tales of great stone palaces and temples in the Hrinani."

"How would these builders be paid?"

"Gold," Kamin-Tolagh replied. "Hrin are very fond of gold."

Lavsila, interest kindled, tried to read his face. "Where will the gold come from?" and struck by an inspiration, "Has the hill-man, Tau-Suaka told you something?"

"We shall have gold," allowing Lavsila to think whatever his fancy suggested.

"When you offer your squadrons the choice of returning home or serving here with you, do you mean to tell them the same? Gold to be had here could make all the difference, to men who, as you say, would be lucky back home to find the money for their first year's seed when they retire to farming."

"Just so," drily, and to mock the implicit claim of indifference: "You, certainly, can return to the realm with no blame, with nothing but my gratitude. You have important concerns in the Heartland, I am aware."

"When will this be? When will you release those who want to go home?"

"Almost at once. The sooner I am rid of half-hearted service, the stronger we shall be for the future."

"What about my irrigation for the Lunu — for *Abu Ninusai*?"

"We have your drawings. If you run over the details with Iruvakh, we'll get it done."

"Iruvakh! Oh, a good man with plants, I do not doubt, but with anything new, he will decide half-way it is too difficult, and end by having water carried to the plots in sieves, after the ancient and interesting custom of the half-monkey tribe, who keep their wives in jars, and hold the world began when the giant lizard farted."

"Well," resignedly. "This venture will not live or die on the question of growing crops there. I suppose you will think about choosing a wife, when you go home."

"When I go home — " frowning on the thought, trying furiously to find a reason to stay that did not violate his air of aloof nonchalance. "I was first to suggest there were reasons for your staying here in the West."

11.

Dolvid, when Elamirr arrived at the Bronze Residence, was poring over a document, and the young man instantly took note of, and asked about the new decoration suspended from Dolvid's neck by a slender chain, a fine gold representation of a fat-bodied spider, with small rubies for eyes.

"This," with slight ceremonial exaggeration to cover genuine pride, "is, and will remain, rarest of all honors; it can only ever be displayed by the four who wear it now. It was given by Saidhan *Asai*." Fatigue, and the winter, had kept Saidhan from crossing Arnan to see what must be his last grandchild, Sedukh, but then, late in spring, Âna gave birth to his first great-grandchild, an Heir for the realm, a son named Lambakh in remembrance of Rodlakh's favorite brother, lost in the Tan Lughsai fire. Nudged by his wife Doleni, or out of his own eagerness, Saidhan decided they could not wait for the Midsummer Pledging to visit Kadon Dinul. For the past three weeks they had been staying at the New Residence, but over dinner at the house at last partially inhabitable for Dolvid, Aëlu and the child, on the exact anniversary of Aëlu's rescue from the fortress of Drin b'Afon, Saidhan had bestowed this Golden Spider, designed for those who had led the desperate climb up the citadel cliffs. Six had been in that vanguard, but two died in subsequent battles; other than Dolvid, surviving recipients were two Colony men, Sarnak and Guthdar, and one from Lunu Tezh', Haun, living at Kamsilat, partly disabled by the wounds he had received in the fight at Drin b'Afon.

Aside from this touching gesture, it was alarming to see how Saidhan's ability to concentrate was sapped by his feebleness; he was in his eighty-ninth year, a respectable but not exceptional age, in view of his descent. For an unmixed Owani ninety was considered a normal lifespan, but many lived beyond one hundred. Possibly, refusal or inability to give full expression to grief had helped age Saidhan, who had outlived his son, his daughter, and eight grandchildren, bearing each loss with a grave dignity no one doubted masked deep and bitter sorrow. But he had enjoyed seeing both the boys, for whom a generation had contracted down to the five months separating them, Sedukh already moving out of anonymous babydom, a large, strong child who would inherit his father's square, powerful upper body.

Noticing the cover for the dispatch Dolvid was studying, Elamirr shook his head. "I still marvel a letter from a *nim'*, addressed to the *rabhsai* under provincial seal, comes first to you."

"The *rabhsai* wishes it," bundling the sheets, and reaching for his outshirt. "We must take this one to the New Residence."

"Is it bad news from Kargul, Master?"

Not to divulge the contents of a letter yet to be seen by Rodlakh, Dolvid appeased the curiosity of his apprentice with a generality: "Tovakh is anxious we concert policy regarding his son before the Council meets at Pledging time. He wants his anger known."

"Or his pretended anger?" Together, they went down the steps to the small side entrance.

"In this case, it may well be real enough. Kargul failed completely in its bid for power; influence has become the limit of their ambition."

"What influence can Kargul have at Kadon Dinul?" Elamirr demanded.

Dolvid did not like the scornful tone. "Each province has its voice, if only for being a part of the realm." Outside in the small court, Dolvid's horse was saddled and a half-file escort of Household waiting; the mount Elamirr used, not yet stabled, was soon brought.

"The influence of a province," Dolvid enlarged, as they mounted, "can take many forms — the needs of its people as they make themselves felt, the power and prestige of its *nimu*, his seat at the Council of Thirteen. Tovakh and Petakoi, but I think particularly Tovakh, hoped Kamin-Tolagh's royal captaincy would give Kargul a special voice, ready access to the ear of the *rabhsai*. Now he sees his son as having fecklessly squandered that advantage. No, he does not need to feign annoyance."

They passed the Spear of Yoëlladhu, and rode in at Harbor Gate under a pleasant late-morning sun. The Avenue of Treaties was preparing itself for the midsummer weeks and the Great Pledging, the first of Rodlakh's reign, the headlong manner of his accession and the Jinzai War, marriage and the afterrumbles of civil strife having postponed it by a year.

To be a Great Pledging, the midsummer observance required the presence of the *rabhsai*, and a meeting of the Council of Thirteen. Banak's intention when he inaugurated the observance sixty years ago had been to hold it at each provincial capital and at Kamsilat in the Colony in a seven-year cycle, but during his failing years the final three Pledgings before his abdication had all been at Kadon Dinul. With his son, Lambarr, the *rabhsai*'s appearance at provincial seats became increasingly erratic, and the practice lapsed altogether during the mercifully brief but seemingly endless reign of Ban-Sila, who had seldom left Kadon Dinul. Rodlakh intended to restore Banak's original plan; he meant to journey frequently in the realm, but the Great Pledgings would make sure no longer than seven years would elapse between his visits to any capital, and Banak's shrewd inclusion in the roster of the by-then phantom province of Asekh gave the *rabhsai* an open year, with the option of returning oftener to a province where the need was seen. Among benefits, this made it harder for provincial magistrates to abuse their positions unchecked; at the Great Pledging all those who believed themselves victims of injustice could petition the *rabhsai* directly, and any decision in which prejudice, vested interest, or inadequate knowledge of law had played a part could be reversed by Rodlakh, as magistrate of magistrates, or by one of his sitting deputies, this year, Âna, Dolvid, and the learned Fornival, *Bôdh'loiki* for Law, who could cite complex codicils to arcane ordinances, age-old precedents and obscure exceptions as Dolvid could the lyrics of his favorite poet, Bronal, and with much the same affection.

Pledging Week, which culminated in the midsummer observance, *Shuda'sai* to those of the Old Belief, had its lighter side, puppet-shows, conjurers, dances and other entertainments, story-tellers, fortune-tellers and trinket-vendors all in the open air; booths, tables and small stages were being erected along both sides of the broad Avenue, portable charcoal stoves for the food-sellers. Dolvid told Elamirr: "It will be good to see your uncles again," both because he liked the men, Nentirr especially, and because performances by the Marionette Guild of Burantal were an event he had first been enchanted by at the age of seven, and showed no sign of outgrowing.

Elamirr only grunted. "The weekwives will be at their greasy trade, too, I suppose — " with all the apparently ineradicable Gabhani repugnance for what they, like others, were not averse to enjoying.

A man known by sight, a Harbor Way shopkeeper setting up his stall not far from the Disc, waved and called out, "Ho, there, *Bôdhrai*. How's little Sedukh, then?"

"Strong as a young ox, I thank you. We are looking for a lance his size."

"Will he lead the Army of the West?" another bystander, a stout woman, loudly enquired.

"Not before he has his teeth — " raising a laugh. Next to him, he noted the face of Elamirr, considered handsome, showed less than unqualified approval. "They are a sentimental lot,"

Dolvid conceded. "But a little byplay doesn't do much harm. Lambarr *Rabhsai* was always ready for banter, with a crowd or a single citizen."

"Rodlakh *Rabhsai* does not banter."

"Not his way. But when sallies come, anyone can see he does not take offense." Rodlakh, in fact, delighted in the broad humor of the street, and would often repeat in private a quip he had overheard; Dolvid and Âna together were working hard to persuade him to let the public see more of his relish.

They came to the New Residence, and passed in by the Pefrai Gate, making their way through the courts on the south side. As they dismounted in the Court of the Ram, Dolvid waved a greeting to his old acquaintance, Norlum, the stablemaster, and nodded to a pair of green-clad *atarlal* of the Edhrodilum, about to mount placid-looking horses.

"Petakoi of Kargul," Elamirr remarked, on the curving stairway up to the entrance, "is said to be very thick with the *Atarlum*."

"Not this present *Atarlum*. Her old ally is in retirement." Under its new Patriarch, the *Mankh'* was working harmoniously with Rodlakh's *rabhsayum*.

"Yet the *Mankh'* is the *Mankh'*, always."

Dolvid did not let a sigh be heard. Any assistant who was useful must do more than respectfully mouth back his own views, but he hoped this youthful dogmaticism would soon amend itself; Elamirr had not yet earned the right to such fixed opinions. Understood, he had been sixteen or so, buried in a provincial town, when the fanatical Owan-Alladh XX came to the Patriarchate, and so had no means of recognizing that catastrophe for what it was, a nightmare interlude between two humane and tolerant occupants of the Golden Seat, made worse by the unrepeatable accident of the *rabhsai*, Ban-Sila, who was that appalling Patriarch's most faithful pupil. A young man of Elamirr's heritage could also be forgiven for seeing in the

Atarlum nothing better than the historical inspiration and instrument of Owani oppression, and it would be part of that upbringing to believe Petakoi's fascination with politics was unnatural in a woman, who should keep to childbearing and household affairs. Kadon Dinul and the two Residences were places made for the curing of such a narrow outlook.

Reaching the Personal Suite, there was an instant reminder of how foolish it was to generalize about attitudes as they came from parentage. Konir was there, another young man of Mixed origins, and an upbringing not very different from Elamirr's — except the younger sister he had would have made it difficult, if not risky, to relegate women's interests to kitchen, nursery and sewing-room. Konir was two or three years older and over a head taller than his more celebrated sister, and resemblance was at first sight faint — but then a dart of the mobile, intelligent eyes, firm set of his chin, would bring a striking reminiscence of Âna.

He was laughing together with Rodlakh, who enjoyed the ready wit of his brother-in-law. Like Saidhan, Konir had come to Kadon for a first sight of the child, his new nephew.

"You are early, *Bôdhrai*," Rodlakh said. "Not bad news, I hope?"

With a rocking motion of his hand Dolvid indicated he was carrying neither imminent doom nor the excuse for feasting.

"Konir has been telling me how the tax laws as written make it hard for even a wealthy farmer to plant except what brings an immediate return. He has some thoughts about variable taxation, which may chime with what you were saying about this same question last year. You should get together, and see if you can think of ways to encourage the planting of crops the realm needs, which do not show a profit in the first season."

"Trees, for example, *Deghi*," Dolvid said.

"Exactly, *Bôdhrai*," Konir leapt in. "The extreme example, but, yes, trees above all. If every farmer of the realm

with a hundred acres could afford to put just eight in oak and ash
— "

"Eight acres of a hundred might be too much to ask,"
Dolvid said. "And beech, at first, would hold out hope of a
quicker return, at least as firewood. Planes, too, put on flesh
fast."

An enduring obsession. Wide swathes of the land held by
the *rabhsayum*, Dolvid had pointed out, would make poor
farming, but could perhaps be turned into flourishing forest over
the next fifty or sixty years.

Delighted to find a fellow-enthusiast, Konir began citing
figures for the relationship, here in the Heartland, between fuel
needs and idle acreage, till Rodlakh softly but quite firmly
suggested they would do better to discuss this at dinner, to which
Dolvid was asked to bring Aëlu. At once, Konir took the hint,
asked leave, and withdrew, pointing a finger at Dolvid to
reaffirm their appointment.

Rodlakh murmured approving assessment of Konir, as he
waved Dolvid to a seat beside his, beckoning Elamirr from
outside the circle of talk, where he had been standing with
respectful but faintly bored anticipation. He came forward and
arranged himself at a small table, ready, if needed, to make notes,
and Dolvid hoped the man would come to recognize crops and
harvests as statecraft, too, as much as Tovakh's sentiments about
his errant son.

An odd, self-contradictory letter, in a sprawling hand
certainly not of a professional scribe, quite possibly Tovakh's
own. He gave formal notice he wished the forthcoming Council
meeting to consider Kamin-Tolagh's case, and without a pause
predicted imminent collapse of the `foolhardy venture in the
Farther West,'* in part because of the recent return to Kargul of `a
large part of the cavalry our son commanded, including some of
his most senior officers.'*

"We spoke of bringing Tovakh into our discussions on his
son," Dolvid wryly reminded.

"What is he about?" exasperatedly. "He writes of being allowed to deal with Kamin-Tolagh's punishment as a provincial matter, and in the same breath admits it might yet require action by the Army of the West to bring him to heel."

"I have independent confirmation," cautiously, "for some of what Tovakh has to say." All his comments or conjectures would be based on information he was hesitant to reveal in Elamirr's presence, but Rodlakh, understanding, gave a slight nod of assent.

This was not one of the happier aspects of being *Bôdhrai*. When Kamin-Tarú had unexpectedly arrived in Kamsilat just before the outbreak of the Jinzai War, she had brought with her Mansi, a serving-woman from the Great House at Inilun Barabhi, who, on her own initiative, before returning, had offered to keep Dolvid informed of happenings there. Her price was a bargain, and the opportunity for keeping watch on the source of so much trouble for the realm could not be declined. She had a kinsman who ran a cartage business from the Karguli seat through Zelkova, ending at Kanzan Tâl, and so was able at little risk to send regular reports, receiving her stipend by the same route.

"My source at Inilun Barabhi, then, confirms sixty or seventy of Kamin-Tolagh's men have made their way back to Kargul, by a little-known road." This was the secret path through the mountains of western Kargul, formerly used by those who oversaw the breeding of the *jinzal*. "They included officers, Talfoyan among them."

"He is?"

"A squadron-leader; he got his squadron in the Jinzai War. Obviously, a loss to Kamin-Tolagh, but he still has a number of officers who did well in the war — Freighanai, Yaënsilat — and Tovakh neglects to mention his son gained back almost as much as he lost; virtually an entire squadron defected from the provincial cavalry to join him. Also some of the men with him have now been joined by their wives and children, so collapse of his little empire may be farther off than Tovakh predicts."

"Yes?" Rodlakh to Elamirr, who was barely holding back speech.

"Your pardon, *Deghi*, but if Tovakh *Asai* is so opposed to what his son is doing, how was all this permitted?"

"It was not," Dolvid replied. "By the time Tovakh heard about it, both his cavalry and the families were gone. That would explain his anger, and also his insistence some other army than his provincials will be needed to bring his son back to heel — any pursuit he makes could end merely by further reinforcing Kamin-Tolagh."

"Why would men, soldiers, break their sworn allegiance," Elamirr asked the world in general, "to go with this adventurer?"

Rodlakh turned up his palms, but Dolvid said, "Kamin-Tolagh led them to victory at the Lunu Tezh' Gate, and at Kamsilat; Tovakh to defeat at Dônshei. These are just boys, in dull provincial service, who hear about Kamin-Tolagh's new triumphs, and want to be part of the glory. Notwithstanding Tovakh's predictions, we hear most if not all the tribes of the northern Froghushei have acknowledged Kamin-Tolagh's authority. My informant says there was big talk about gold to be had, though no one saw any. From the Hrin traders, who, naturally, have an interest in what happens in that part of the world, we hear he is teaching the tribes how to fight as soldiers."

"I wish I knew what the fool had in his mind," bitterly. "And his father, too. He admits Kamin-Tolagh has violated his oaths to me, but seems to expect us to give him back to Kargul, after using royal forces to take him prisoner."

"Even in his anger, he does not want to see his son tried for high treason." Dolvid could only deal with the questions asked, though plainly the real problem for Rodlakh was that Tovakh, by tabling this for Council, was forcing the *rabhsai* to consider publicly decisions he had not yet worked through in private: his deep sense of personal betrayal was emotion, not policy. "Except the capturing might be more difficult than it sounds, it could be the best outcome. I, for one, would not want to prosecute Kamin-Tolagh for crimes so far away, not unless his father could be among the judges." Dealt with as a family matter, it would not become a grievance to unite the Great Families, Kamin-Tolagh's cousins, against Rodlakh's *rabhsayum*.

Rodlakh nodded instant understanding, but Elamirr was outraged. "Surely, *Deghi*, he must be hunted down and put to death? He is the worst kind of oathbreaker. We should make an example of him."

Before answering, Rodlakh raised a wry eyebrow at Dolvid in a conspiracy of tolerance. "Kamin-Tolagh was yet to swear any oath to me," smiling mournfully, "when he rode breakneck to Kamsilat, where this realm was near dying." He put a hand on Elamirr's shoulder. "You will have to forgive those of us who have seen too much death if we are slow to embrace it as the answer to hard questions." He was almost fatherly, although in fact slightly the younger.

That, in substance, was the end of this first discussion, but Rodlakh set a second meeting for later in the day, when Âna could be with them, and Shumat; Dolvid suggested Fornival should be available, to comment on the legality of any move they contemplated.

He had stipulated on call rather than actually present so they could speak freely about secrets still kept, such as the long-term help Petakoi had given the breeders of *jinzal*. For the same reason he left his assistant behind, but when he saw Rodlakh again, now in the small Private Audience Chamber, the *rabhsai*'s first words were, "Where is Elamirr, then?"

"At the Bronze Residence." Elamirr had imperfectly disguised disappointment at his omission. "I thought you would want to talk without constraints." Shumat and Âna were already seated at the oak table.

"Well, true," misunderstanding.   "It is always stiffer outside our little circle. But Elamirr has to learn; he will do very well with a little of the roughness rubbed off. You must not try to do everything by yourself — we need you too much for what is vital."

Dolvid forbore to ask what could be more important than today's subject, or to point out he had been the one to hire Elamirr. "I have thought of a new way to increase my leisure. You will recall, *Rabhsai*, for part of the two preceding reigns, I held a post never given a formal title, a sort of quartermaster to the province." Created, largely at Laluvoi's instance, in a time of widespread hunger, to maintain food supplies at a fair price, in part by acquiring stocks of grain and feed, and by discouraging hoarding, against which Dolvid had requested and been granted powers of seizure. As Dolvid slipped from favor with Ban-Sila, the post had been transferred to Bolan as Captain of the Household, who had gradually turned it into a nightmare instrument of oppression, using bad troops trained only in brutality to enforce compliance exclusively against smallholders. "Of itself, *Rabhsai*," he argued, "the post was no bad idea, and would be better extended to the realm at large."

"If a good man could be found to administer it," Rodlakh demurred, very nearly Dolvid's own words, over a dozen years ago, when he had first heard the function proposed.

"Konir," with a slight deference to Âna. "As son to Konat he has the knowledge of farm-management, and as brother to the *rabhsayu* would carry the authority needed. It would give him the opportunity to study his ideas about variable taxation, and, if they prove feasible, to help in drafting the laws."

He heard Âna give a slight, sharp sniff, and saw her make a face, but when Rodlakh turned to her she admitted, "We might do worse, if you swear I don't have to be there when he talks an hour about marsh-drainage, or south-facing slopes." Apparently Konir had other enthusiasms besides trees.

"Offer him the post," Rodlakh, with a genial nod. To Âna he said lightly, "At Konatstead, this *rabhsayum* is going to be bracketed with Kanavakh's, if I take any more of their children." She, Dolvid thought, looked careworn, having had a hard pregnancy and difficult labor with Lambakh.

They turned now to the main subject, and Dolvid had fresh news; only two hours ago he had received another message coming from Kargul, addressed to him as *Bôdhrai*, and deliberately delayed so he would first be informed about recent happenings in Kargul and the Farther West. That phrase was in a terse explanatory note from Fretasi, a woman of good birth in Kamin-Tolagh's service, writing from his country estate in the western part of the province, and the letter itself was from Kamin-Tolagh.

"Signed by him, that is. The hand is the style used here in the Heartland, so the penman is Lavsila, who probably also collaborated in some of the phrasing."

"But if Kamin-Tolagh put his name to it... " Âna said.

"Oh, I have no doubt the sentiments are his." He could not predict how Rodlakh was going to take Kamin-Tolagh's message, with its blithe, almost naive blending of would-be conciliation and appalling arrogance:

Greetings, Bôdhrai,

You will, I hope, understand it has for many reasons been difficult for me to re-establish communication with the Residence; numerous great and small matters have required my attention, the more urgently in that for me and my tiny company of men, the tribes here had become as metal hot on the anvil; hesitation would have risked missing the chance, not to occur again, of forging a unity otherwise beyond the powers of great armies. That unity is accomplished fact.

As became clear to me at my last meeting with the Captain Shumat, no one lacking first-hand experience of this unique moment could appreciate its implications; if I was unable to persuade a friend and esteemed comrade-in-arms, who was here in the Farther West, that new games need new rules, what hope was there Kadon Dinul could understand in time? Yet rules are only made for what is known or can be imagined, and any enterprising leader betrays his highest duty if he fails to recognize the case where the letter of his instructions must be contravened in order to seize an unimagined opportunity. Please assure the Rabhsai, Bôdhrai, *he has no loyaler subject and Captain than Kamin-Tolagh baKargul, and I stand ready today to do his bidding, except only, we of Abu Ninusai cannot acquiesce in any decision which would entail relinquishing the territory over which our arms and strategy have won control.*

On the contrary, Bôdhrai, *it is my most cherished desire these conquests become part of the* Rabhsayum *of Rodlakh* Deghi, *a second Colony, if you will, like the present Colony enjoying the effective standing of a full province, ruled by an hereditary* Nim', *of which I myself would be the first. I would willingly renounce my standing as Heir in Kargul, so as to conform to law. In this new province, for which the name* Kargusai *is proposed,* Rabhsai's *Law would be observed, with certain exceptions, to be determined, so as to accommodate various long-established tribal practices.*

Some time may elapse, Bôdhrai, *before Kargusai can hope to contribute significantly to the revenues of the realm, but we expect very quickly to attain better than self-sufficiency in the growing of food, and the military needs of our territories will cost the* rabhsai *nothing; we would expect to share equally with the Army of the West responsibility for keeping safe and open the main line of communication, across Landegh. The realm in general, and the present Colony of Telnavu with the Lunu Tezh' Protectorate especially, will benefit greatly from our assistance in, as it were, cutting of at the source the attempted incursions which the Army of the West has spent so much time and so much of the realm's treasure in preventing, so the continued existence of a military force here in the Farther West will make it safe to reduce the size of that Army, or to make forces available for joint actions with my own.*

These, and many other details, Bôdhrai, *can await our agreement on the general principle here outlined, of my modest new Empire becoming a part of Rodlakh's* rabhsayum. *While the expanded dignity and glory of that realm, and of the* Rabhsai's *person, are never far from my mind, it should be said my greatest satisfaction in subduing these western lands has been in bringing the rewards of our law, justice, learning and skills to those who, without them, have lived lives of unimaginable poverty and ignorance, and so helping to fulfill, in the measure granted me, the Promise of Yoëlladhu, which is, equally, the offer Great Banak extended to all peoples of goodwill, and which I do not doubt his grandson will be pleased to renew.*

May I ask you, Bôdhrai, *to extend my personal devotions and respects to Rodlakh* Rabhsai, *to the* Rabhsayu, *and greetings to others of my friends and colleagues, not least the Captain Shumat and yourself; we who rode, a year ago, in the great race to Kamsilat, should never be other than friends and allies in the same cause.*

With all happy personal wishes,

Kamin-Tolagh

"He stands ready to do my bidding," sourly. "*Except* he will not obey my primary orders."

Shumat said, "'We of *Abu Ninusai*'?"

"At a guess," Dolvid said, "a new name for the Lunu Jinzalladhiyu, to reassure us about his intentions."

"You think he has reoccupied the Lunu?"

"If the men of Kargul are going to have their wives with them, they will not be under canvas, or in the huts of the tribes; until he can find builders, Kamin-Tolagh needs the comforts of the Lunu, as you described them."

Shumat made a doubtful mouth. "A poor place to defend. A couple of hundred men could seal off the entrances, while siege-weapons on the rim reduced its dwellings to dust."

"Are we thinking of making war on Kamin-Tolagh, as his father wants us to?" Âna, without giving a hint of her opinion.

Rodlakh, whose head had bowed as if in contemplation, looked up sharply. "We are several steps away from making that decision."

"I would hope so, *Deghi*," Shumat said. "If force is to be used to bring Kamin-Tolagh to heel, it's going to need some planning, and some collecting of supplies; it'll take more than a couple of squadrons. More than a couple of dozen."

Rodlakh said, "But didn't you just say... "

"I said the Lunu, or the Abu, if we're to call it that now, would be simple to invest; if we were lucky enough to catch Kamin-Tolagh there it would all be over; without him there's no, what? Kargusai. But he is aware of that; once he goes to earth somewhere among his tribes — " Shumat shrugged to express uncertainty about how it would go.

Dolvid asked, "What about his proposal?"

"I have not asked for a wider realm. He makes this argument he is bringing the benefits of our wisdom to distant peoples, but they could learn from us, if they desired, without submitting to our rule. Would you add a new province to the realm, if it could be done?"

"No," after getting his thoughts in order. "Not now, when there is so much to be done for the realm you already rule. Once accept the Froghushei as part of a new empire, and we would have to make all the land between there and our present borders safe for trade and travellers, and secure the borders of Kamin-Tolagh's Kargusai. Beyond there is the Minshei, southward the Kufshei, northward Tufani — lands on lands, as many as two hundred tribes or nations, and, I suppose, a thousand small wars, quarrels over borders, over water, grazing land, gold, disputes over beliefs. Each people you agree to protect has to be brought into the empire, and every people you include in the empire has to be protected — a thousand-and-a-half years ago, Larghai, it is said, had a sight of the Western Ocean, but the Empire the Shâls founded there was too much of the West to digest; in the end the land could not feed the soldiers needed to hold it; that is how the Night came." Speaking of the Ocean, he glanced at Shumat, who was nodding agreement, but saw in that plain face no recollection of their childhood, when he and Dolvid, two for whom no one would have predicted fame, used to send imagined armies marching to remake the Empire.

Shumat said, "*When empires can no longer keep ancient enmities in check, they have lost their only valid reason for existing.* You said that," just as Dolvid was about to ask who he was quoting. "At Sebira, in '28."

Âna, quietly, "The question still is, *jinzal*. We sent an expedition to make certain they would never be bred again, and here, once again, we have *jinzai*-fathers, men of the Owani, living with *jinzai*-mothers, the — "

"Man-mani," Dolvid supplied. "But we could make absolutely certain there would never be another *jinzai* born only by exterminating the Man-mani — or the Owanil, neither of which we are willing to attempt — "

"Are you suggesting I put a halt to the massacre too soon?" Shumat demanded. He had been unable to come to terms with the atrocity committed by a force under his command, and was uneasy in his dealings with Dorrmas, rigidly opposed to making his acting-Captaincy of the Household a permanent one by formally degrading Kamin-Tolagh.

"No, no. I was going to say, in a curious way, Kamin-Tolagh, if I understand what he is doing, may eventually make it impossible for *jinzal* to be born. According to those who bred them, not only must the father's Owani bloodline be unmixed, but that of the mother a mixture only of Man-mani with Owani; the Lunu must have taken great care, all through the centuries, to make sure the Man-mani did not intermarry with other tribes."

Shumat said, "I am told Irovakh made a great to-do about the difference between the Man-mani and all the other tribes there, which, he said, still regarded them as foreigners."

"In the document we discovered, Kanavakh called them a tribe of the Kufshei," Dolvid was unable to resist a fascinating bypath. "He was only repeating what he had been told; by his reign, I think they had lived a long time in the northern Froghushei, but at some point, before the Night of Owan, they must have been moved there from their original home in the Kufshei, when the Empire began to ebb, and the *jinzai*-breeders could no longer keep themselves or their breeding-stock safe, so far to the west.   But beyond all distinctions of custom or language, the Lunu must have done all it could to keep the Man-mani as a people apart — and now, by taming the other tribes, Kamin-Tolagh has all-but ensured they will be mingled with the various Froghuli peoples.   The seed of *jinzayum* will be irretrievably lost."

"How soon?" Âna, pointedly.   "Assuming Kamin-Tolagh is not breeding *jinzal* of his own.   The men of Kargul with him must pride themselves on the purity of their Owani blood."

There was a sting in this, and even Rodlakh winced a little, for Dolvid's sake.   Dolvid said, "He would not dare. He does not have the secret of their training.   If he had, how soon could he have any number of *jinzal* to trouble us?   They are fully grown at twelve or thirteen — how many of the *jinzai*-mothers survived?"

"Twenty-two rode with Kamin-Tolagh back to their tribe," Shumat said.

"And if each could be made to bear an average of ten live children over the next fifteen years," Dolvid calculated, "And all the *jinzal* survived, by then, there would be at most two dozen *jinzal* big enough to fight."   In reality, the number would be smaller; he had learned from the former breeders it was impossible, with the most skilled trainers, to prevent growing *jinzal* from fighting each other, often to the death.

"More, surely," Âna, also counting.

"Half the children born would be girls; *jinzal* are only male.   The girls could become, in their turn, *jinzai*-mothers, but that is added years in the future — let us raise this issue ten or a dozen years from today, if Kamin-Tolagh remains loose in the West.   But I do not believe he, or any rider of Kargul could ever wish for a *jinzai* army."

"Petakoi — " Rodlakh began, and corrected himself.   "An Islander who married into Kargul.   Go on."

"*Deghi*," Shumat said, "Kamin-Tolagh thinks even men who fight with pikes or bows are an insult to the glory of a *péfrapravádai*."

"Everything Kamin-Tolagh does is for the honor and glory of Kamin-Tolagh. Very well, I agree," Âna unexpectedly added. "He would not begin breeding *jinzal*. He is too vain of his own prowess."

Admirable, how she could admit a change of heart with so little fuss.

Shumat resumed: "If we discount *jinzal*, then, Kamin-Tolagh with his armed tribesmen is no immediate threat to the realm's security." Belatedly, finding himself on alien ground, he tried to make this seem a completed statement, but the slight emphasis on the final word betrayed him.

Rodlakh did not miss it. "Prestige, you mean to say, mine, is the main public consideration, then: except for how to reply to Kamin-Tolagh's letter, we are back to our question before it arrived, our official position with regard to his disobedience, and Tovakh's determination to raise the matter in Council." Âna shifted impatiently in her seat, but did not comment.

"Tovakh needs to be challenged," Dolvid said. "Made to say exactly what it is he wants from you, *Rabhsai*, and told what cannot be. The only practical object of discussing this case in Council would be to proclaim Kamin-Tolagh's formal outlawry: he would immediately cease to be Heir in Kargul, and you would have the disposition of his person; he could be barred from reentering the realm, exiled to the Island, put to death, at your sole discretion. These consequences Tovakh, notwithstanding his fury, would like to avoid, but I have spoken with Fornival, and he confirms, as I thought, there is no such legal state as conditional outlawry; the assurance Tovakh wants cannot be given."

Rodlakh laughed shortly without joy. "I am plotting how to prevent what I ought to welcome, the Great Families on my side against one of their own, who has insulted and defied me.

Why should I not let Tovakh trap himself into renouncing his son?"

Tempting, except in doing so, Rodlakh would also be trapped. Shumat complained, "But he also wants to say what the Army of the West will do."

"To fight a war, in short, his war. If anyone's pride is injured, it is mine, but I am not as eager as Tovakh to see good men killed and crippled for the sake of revenge."

"I take it, *Rabhsai*," Dolvid stressed, "you would not want to be forced into irrevocable action against Kamin-Tolagh, certainly till we have had a chance to reply to his letter, reiterating your stand against new domains, and giving him the opportunity to repent."

"Repent!" Âna echoed. "Not the first word I would connect to Kamin-Tolagh."

"Repentance comes in various shapes and sizes." Rodlakh had a moment of pragmatism. "They say Shâl I repented, don't they, when he witnessed the destruction of the Vrobhan Empire? That was a change of heart, but when I was in the south, I had a strict tutor, a nephew of Doleni's; at times when I had mischief in mind, just the thought of his length of stirrup-leather could make me repent. We might make Kamin-Tolagh obedient, if we cannot hope to make him virtuous."

That struck Dolvid as a great gain for sanity. He pointed out all this could be conveyed to Tovakh, the inevitable consequences of his denouncing his son, and how such a premature move would negate the *rabhsai*'s hopes for a less formal settlement. If Tovakh persisted, since he could not hope to get the votes in Council, his only achievable object would be to embarrass the *rabhsai*. "We shall meet as only eleven." Ten would sit down, the *rabhsai* counting twice, while Orbanak was not yet old enough to sit as *Nim'* of the Paowan, and Kamin-Tolagh's place as Captain of the Household would be vacant.

"The Great Families will not go against Tovakh," Rodlakh said. "Well, Saidhan will support us, but Dramal, Ân and Nîv will vote with Kargul."

"Not necessarily," Dolvid assured him. "I can see Daënakh of Ân in private when he comes, and hint we must save Tovakh from his own anger; cooled off, he would not thank those who help him to what his bad temper will give; a son who by law cannot be his heir. Ân might abstain, and his brother in Nîv would follow his lead; the *Atarlum* will either do the same or vote with the *rabhsai*; Tovakh can count on only two votes, including his own, and you will have five certain, perhaps six."

"Five?" That was obviously too few for comfort, the votes only of those present at this meeting.

"Seven, at absolute need. I am assuming Fornival will sit as consultant; by tradition he will not vote on a question where he advises."

"But the point," Âna, briskly, "is to prevent it coming to a vote at all — to convince Tovakh he will be the one embarrassed, and that there are better ways to proceed."

"Exactly," noting admiringly that without an added word she made it clear she was only summarizing a position, not endorsing it.

There was one more associated piece of business; the Hrin. The week after Shuda'sai, Dolvid would be riding down to Kanzan Tâl, for a meeting with the *Hrithust* Iolfrant, arranged by the Hrin's new agent there. "The *Hrithust* has to come all the way up from Thenimala, so I thought I could save him a few days. The Hrin, I gather, are puzzled about Kamin-Tolagh. You see, they have no *rabhsai*, only a number of provincial overlords, and knowing our system, they could be skeptical Kamin-Tolagh is acting without the support of Kadon Dinul. How near he is to their borders I cannot say, but they are worried, it appears, by all the troops he is raising and training."

Shumat said, "But there must be more Hrin than all those tribes put together. Thousands more, tens of thousands."

"Perhaps more than that. They are close-mouthed people, but when Iolfrant was here, he let slip an opinion Kadon Dinul must have as many people as the two largest cities of his *onhritha* — that is, province — combined. There are at least three other provinces."

Sharing in the general shock the Hrin could possess such numbers, Shumat pursued his point: "Then how can Kamin-Tolagh's few hundreds make them nervous?"

"They are not a fighting people. When I have talked with Iolfrant, he has expressed admiration of our military discipline — awe would be a better word. Also, there are, allegedly, deep religious differences among the various provinces, preventing united action."

Rodlakh said, "I cannot believe Kamin-Tolagh's folly would reach as far as an attack on people who so much outnumber him, no matter how unwarlike."

"Men usually find more war in them than they thought," Shumat put in laconically, "defending their homes. But Kamin-Tolagh must have offered his soldiers rewards more substantial than dust and glory."

"With your leave, *Rabhsai*," Dolvid resumed, "I would like to explore an alliance with Iolfrant." Obvious next step beyond trade agreements, perhaps helping Kadon Dinul keep a closer eye on Kamin-Tolagh's doings, at a small investment in men or money.

"What do you mean by alliance?" Âna was first to ask. "You want to send troops to help stiffen the Hrin?"

"Not squadrons," before Shumat could complain they had none to spare. "We might send competent officers to help them raise and train their own cavalry; the Hrin are said to have excellent horses, though no *pefral*, as Iolfrant longingly admits."

"We shall not sell them *pefral*," Rodlakh said.

"That goes without saying."

"Who could we send so far?" Âna wondered. "To live among a people about which we know next to nothing."

Dolvid turned to Shumat. "Would you say, volunteers could be found?"

"Will you give me a quarter-hour?" Shumat grinned. "In the Household, the General Cavalry, the Army of the West — Kargul's not the only place that breeds boy idiots with a thirst for adventure. In your twenties, with no one to worry about except yourself — I would have jumped at it, wouldn't you?"

"We did."

With the *rabhsai*'s cautious endorsement of exploratory overtures to Iolfrant, and request for early drafts of replies to Kamin-Tolagh and to his father, they began not so much concluding as suspending their gathering, since they were all to be together again at dinner, with the addition of Konir, Aëlu, and Shumat's wife, Manda, gradually overcoming her shyness for such occasions.

Dolvid left by way of the Oak-Wall Chamber, and Âna came swiftly after him to tug at his sleeve. "I ask pardon."

He saw at once where her contrition belonged. "I am Owani. Nothing I can do will change that. I try my best to be an Arbhali of Owani extraction — and hope, like anyone else, I shan't be blamed for the worst crimes of my race."

She flushed slightly, and murmured, "*Y'olagh am.*"

"Between us, *Rabhsayu*, what is your objection to the appointment I proposed for your brother?"

"I have none," she said, but wilted against his level gaze. "Am I so easy to read?"

"Not to everyone," meaning proudly, as she instantly knew, anyone else.

"Konir, when he travels, forgets he is a married man, a father — or that is what Purnis, his wife, says. She doesn't like me — it is not proper for a woman to argue with men about men's concerns, or, unmarried, to travel with men, or read books other than romances; she believes I encourage all my brother's worst — what are you laughing at?"

"It may have escaped your notice you are *rabhsayu*. Your brother's wife now tells anyone she can get to listen how she always said you were no ordinary girl, and many's the time you've sat there in that very chair, drinking your camomile milk — "

"Comfrey and mint," she corrected, and made a face, not over that, but in recognition of inescapable eminence.

They stood a moment reluctant to let each other go, and Âna found a topic. "One thing — Kamin-Tolagh came in person to Kargul?"

"Was rumored to. My informant says it was both confirmed and denied, but I cannot imagine a squadron of Tovakh's cavalry being won over by anyone less."

"Did he see, or try to see, his sister?"

"Kamin-Tarú, the last I heard, is at Inilun Barabhi, with her parents. I am sure he did not go there."

"But he offered to renounce succession in Kargul," thoughtfully. Clear how her thoughts were going; Kamin-Tarú would replace her brother as Heir to the *nimum*; if he really believed Rodlakh would accept his conquests as a new province, he could be thinking about some day ruling Kargul as well, through his devoted sister.

"I should go there."

"Where? Not to the Farther West."

"I have negotiated with Kamin-Tolagh before; he trusts my word. No matter what is said in a letter, there is room for misunderstanding."

"I heard somebody talking about young fools who hunger for distant adventure. In his letter, Kamin-Tolagh calls himself still loyal, and if that is so, he does not need a high official to persuade him to follow his *rabhsai*'s clear instructions. If he is being deliberately deceptive, we do not need to present him with an invaluable hostage. Dolvid, friend, we are not suing for favors from him, and all the realm has to see that. Your answer to his letter should be carried by a squadron-leader, a *kímukan* at most. What is there to negotiate?"

He was silent, and she gave him a long, curious look. "You don't think we should take Kamin-Tolagh's protestations at face-value?"

"No. But I do not believe he will give up and come meekly home, either. That leaves us a choice of three courses; we can leave him running loose in the West, fight a war to capture or kill him, or find a procedure to bring him back within the law. All bad choices, but the third is the one I dislike the least." Not to Âna could he speak of his recurrent nightmare, Rodlakh and Kamin-Tolagh duelling to the death.

There were other worries in the realm, besides the House baKargul. During the coming Pledging, the new Council of Sixty would be meeting for the first time, a body drawn from throughout the realm, ten members for each province with the Colony, men and women of standing but without larger power in the realm; there would be no magistrates, tax-assessors, no army officers, no cousins to the Great Families, but city elders, landowners, a few artisans — the process of selection had varied from province to province, and was at best flawed; only the low esteem in which they held the new council had kept the provincial overlords from filling all the places with their puppets, but one of the first questions for the body to consider was how future members could be more fairly chosen.

A year ago, hunting for ways to make his rule more broadly answerable to the people, Rodlakh had enthusiastically endorsed the innovation, and Dolvid had worked hard to bring it about; in the end even Kargul agreed to send its ten, on the understanding the part of the new Council was only advisory. That was how it was to begin, but the original plan had been to have the Council of Thirteen gradually agree to delegate part of its powers to the Sixty, with a long-term view to making the two bodies approach equality. As the year passed, however, and Rodlakh learned his trade, his interest in the new Council had steadily waned, and he had scarcely commented on its progress, on the detailed rules for its composition, or on the search for an appropriate meeting-place. Two days ago, after consultation with Fornival, Dolvid had told Rodlakh that under a law of Banak's reign, if they only called it a Pledging Council, many of its recommendations not impinging on prerogatives of the provincial overlords could, with the *rabhsai*'s assent, become law without further reference to the Council of Thirteen, yet there would be no legal reason why it should not become the Permanent Pledging Council, and meet regularly throughout the year.

Notwithstanding his own year-old remark the Council of Thirteen could be made to share power only "by stealth," Rodlakh all at once found this slightly circumventive proceeding distasteful; the intent of Banak's law, he said, was clearly to speed the settlement of petty disputes, land boundaries, or whether the pastry-cooks could have the standing of a guild, freeing the proper Council for larger issues. "Besides," he added, keenly disappointing Dolvid, "do we really want to risk antagonizing the Council of Thirteen, when it is working so well for us? We should go slow in making changes."

Men who ruled, Dolvid reflected, are different. Different even from the men they were themselves, before they came to power.

When, at dinner, he repeated that out loud, Aëlu, with more-than-usual asperity, criticized him, not for the thought, but for stopping there; he was thinking, she told him, as an historian, merely observing events, rather than a *Bôdhrai*, who could cause or alter them.

Chastened, at her instigation he gave notice of some property-law questions, knotted in their complexity, for the Council of Thirteen to consider, including amendment to the Law of Inheritance, which seethed with exceptions, special cases, and bundles of uncodified precedents such as Fornival alone loved to wallow in. There were legitimate reasons for seeking changes in the law, and especially to discourage or where necessary prevent the redivision of an already-divided inheritance, practices which gave limited but unfortunate support to an otherwise purely self-serving assertion, the perennial claim by the large Owanil land-owners, that the smallholders they swallowed up were victims, not of predation but of suicide.

With the Owanil, undivided estates were an established tradition. Those connected, especially, with Kargul and Telnavu tended to maintain inheritance in the male line, while the majority, the Families of the Return, those who came back from the Island with Plakhat Gabh'Owan, normally followed primogeniture irrespective of sex, but both groups were alike in maintaining that integrity of their holdings took precedence over the needs of younger sons and daughters, who had to be content with minor tracts, houses, or cash bequests.

Following the habit of the old Gabhanil chieftains, most of the Others, by contrast, punctiliously shared out their lands among offspring — or rather, sons only — typically more numerous than those of the Owanil. While this custom might represent a praiseworthy fairmindedness, and avoid much of the sulky discontent of younger children so typical of Owani tale-telling (and not unknown in Owani life), it could in a couple of generations result in a preposterous patchwork of holdings; one reason for the frequency of intermarriage among already much-related families was the attempt to tack together farms out of impractical shreds of inheritance. There were two brothers near Nivu Din, with a landed grandfather on each side of their descent, each brother owning two widely-separated seven-and-a-quarter acre farmlets on the north side of the river. The elder also possessed a further three-and-one-third acre plot two miles downstream on the south bank, and both had other odd holdings a two-hour ride on the far side of town. Lunatic as it seemed, this was not the worst case; there were formerly-prosperous farms in prolific families where as much land was now taken up demarcating boundaries as was left for tilling, and cases where, with a family unable to agree on the division of belongings, the only solution was to sell the house and its contents and divide the proceeds, so cherished heirlooms ended in the hands of strangers.

Since all inheritances had to be proved at law, Dolvid had an idea something might be done by empowering magistrates to enforce joint-tenancies or monetary settlements in lieu of real property, where strict adherence to the terms of a will would result in holdings too small or too scattered to be profitably farmed. Yet any legal intervention would require safeguards and discretionary provisions, guided overall by a regard for the traditions it sought to modify, and, as Aëlu credibly predicted, be so tedious for the provincial overlords, they would gladly cede debate to the Council of Sixty, and could be induced to agree the results threshed out, approved by the *rabhsai*, would become law, without further debate in the Council of Thirteen, in itself establishing a precedent. They would be readier still, she forecast, to relinquish any voice in the equally vexed question of *Common Gleanings*, jocularly called "Berries, Mushrooms and Kindling," the defining and codifying of prerogatives till now ruled by unwritten law and local practice, so as to balance traditional public right to cull the fringes of cultivated fields and pasturage against the need of landowners to protect crops and livestock.

Though Aëlu's strategy worked, the early results were less happy. Presented with their first opportunity to make law, the Council of Sixty was unable to reach agreement on any text for the *rabhsai*'s signature. The composition of the new Council retained a bias, though not a racial one, favoring landed interests, resistant to change, and Dolvid, presiding over their early sessions, was disappointed if not surprised to see the same spirit of indomitable self-interest at work as in the Council of Thirteen. In some ways, as he remarked to Aëlu, worse; these new lawmakers had yet to learn how to make compromises and strike bargains. "Give them a wagonload of wheat, a dozen head of cattle, and a disagreement about prices, and most of them could dicker their way to a deal. When it comes to law, no one wants to be first to give a fourthing."

"Isn't it true, where they cannot reach an agreement, it will be settled over their heads in the Council of Thirteen?"

"In the end, it is bound to be."

"Are they aware of that?" Aëlu, without a blink advocating coercion.

At the moment, a delayed threat, the Council of Thirteen having dissolved, their meetings and the jockeying that surrounded them dominated to a depressing extent by the presence of Tovakh, absence of his son. Barren entertainment could be found in Tovakh's irreconcilable desires, to make his anger known but avoid embarrassment, to have the whole realm see Kamin-Tolagh as its primary concern while at the same time acknowledging it as a family matter, best settled by Kargul without outside interference. Beyond a resolution officially "deploring" Kamin-Tolagh's acts, nothing, predictably, had been accomplished, but Rodlakh admitted to sharing Dolvid's feeling the mutiny, or rebellion, or whatever they were going to call it, was taking time and energy from questions of larger long-term importance. Only that day, after a private meeting with Dozhusai, the Patriarch, Dolvid had the duty, particularly unrewarding for one of his birth, of telling Rodlakh they were going to have to make an emblematic concession to the *Atarlum*, or risk making Dozhusai the isolated figurehead over a rebellious *Mankh'*.

"Does He not command there?" turning surprise to humor.

"I told Bolan, years ago, it is not an army. The Patriarch commands the *Adanum Plakh'*, but lances are not much use for enforcing ideas — "

"What about Enlightenment, *aën'modha*?"

"Everyone pays it lip-service, but the man who became Owan-Alladh XX was able to maintain his own following through long years of a Patriarch to whose policies they were completely opposed — One, they said, who had yielded too much to your grandparents."

"As we know, there would be some to say it was yielding too much to allow the Other Races should have any rights beyond a dog."

Dozhusai, though, was well beyond that position. Former progressive Patriarchs had agreed in principle to the idea all races, not merely the Owanil, were included as Children of Yoëlladhu, and shared in the Gift, in contradiction to the ancient claim the Gift — which was to say, the realm and its riches — was intended for the Owani race alone; Dozhusai had agreed to make the change plainer, and guard against the kind of reversionary policies which over and again had reasserted the special rights of the Owanil, by altering the wording of traditional texts, to include explicit references to *men and women of every race* as beneficiaries of the Mercy of Aëlovoi, the goodness of Zhôl. He had, moreover, promulgated versions of the emended texts in ordinary language, and was encouraging their use.

"All this no less than startles and often alarms those who have had the *kolukezhal* and the Lesser Responses by heart from childhood." Dolvid himself, approving their aim, found the new versions flat and colorless next to the familiar rich cadences of their Owanilú originals.

"They'll get used to it," Rodlakh said.

As they would, but Dozhusai's present concern was over disaffection within the *Mankh'*, which Dolvid additionally feared would ally itself to and provide a religious prop for all those Owanil, the Guilds, the landowners, who felt threatened by new policies. "As always, there are those who stand to gain by exploiting discontent, but also some genuinely afraid of being deprived of their whole heritage." He had in mind, for example, old Faëdhal, a good friend and staunch *Rodlakhani*, who had nevertheless asked anxiously if there was anything in the rumor use of the Owanilú would be forbidden, even within the precincts of the *Mankh'*, or Prômsilakh, normally among the more responsible of the Heartland growers, who had wanted to know if it was true a crippling tax was about to be levied against *ga-Yalum*, the ancient Owani practice of consecrating their fields in service to Aëlovoi.

"How is justice served, if we create a climate in which sane and judicious men can begin to ask such questions?"

"What, then?" Rodlakh asked, or challenged. "Are we going to change our minds about the Guilds, or land-reform, just when we start to see some success?" The Stonemasons and even the Dyers were actively seeking apprentices of Other Race, while according to the Treasury foreclosures on smallholdings were greatly diminished.

"Those are measures I designed, *Rabhsai*. Of course I do not think we should go back on them." As an Owani he could never outlive the need to reaffirm his dedication to justice.

"But at the other end, an apparent concession can be made, without compromising any of your reforms. Too much has been said about how the Second Treaty restricts the Patriarch. It is good," quickly, reading Rodlakh's face, "to have it seen the *Mankh'* can no longer be a private realm, free from all responsibility to the *rabhsayum*, but not to so weaken the Patriarch that He cannot control the *Mankh'*. What is needed now is a well-publicized meeting with Dozhusai, ending with

confirmation of His prerogatives in purely religious questions —
His right to send His *atarlal* wherever they are needed or desired,
His sole right to try an *atarlai* on any criminal charge, exemption
of all under His authority from a general levy, and of the *margul*
from taxation — "

"Those points are not in question.   They were left
unchanged from the Treaty of the Wind Caves."

"Yes. In fact, you give nothing. But their reaffirmation
at the end of what looks like bargaining will give Dozhusai the
appearance of a victory."

"Of having outfaced me, that is to say." He shook his
head. "Only if it is made plain these are no new concessions."

It was not always such heavy going. "Could we not say
instead, only that the *rabhsai* welcomes this opportunity to
clarify these ancient rights?" Without room for someone to
imagine the Patriarch had won something, there was no object to
the exercise.

Rodlakh gave him a short smile. "You are better at these
games than you care to admit."

12.

Once travelled, the astonishing mountain road, back door into his own province, haunted Kamin-Tolagh's mind, not only for the skill and daring that made it cling to precipitous walls and challenge forbidding heights. It was a connection back to the realm of his beginnings, to be seen as either a lifeline ensuring eventual safety, or a tether to limit his ambitions. He would use it again, perhaps only for another swift raid on his province, but if his empire failed it might be a way to safety. Again, if Rodlakh decided to put an end to this adventure in the West, it would surely be by that route he would to launch his attack, or one of two simultaneous attacks, the other by the Army of the West, crossing Landegh.

Any notion such an assault could be imminent faded, as fierce summer heat came early; no one could be so stupid as to open a campaign in the Farther West when conditions were at their worst, water vanished. Installed in what he knew was the relative comfort of the Abu, Kamin-Tolagh found it hard to contemplate any decisive action; under this pitiless sky it would be easy to let an empire fall to pieces from simple indolence.

With Tau-Suaka, nevertheless, ruthlessly lashing his own people into a fighting force, and life here, since arrival of the handful of wives and children from Kargul, settling into a routine, Kamin-Tolagh at last goaded himself to make the ride, with a half-squadron, to the head of Flamûrai, the Great Gulf, where patrols had come regularly. Not far from the westward rim of the depression, where the way for the tribal country made its sharp bend to the south, another trail continued in a westerly direction, faint but not hard to follow, crossing many sandy ribs in otherwise featureless terrain, till, confronted with a higher, bonier ridge, it declined the challenge, crept in a long curve northward, and vanished into a desiccated, dirty grey flatland. Iruvakh, on his shabby pony, indicated they should continue to parallel the line of the heights, and after a wearisome hour on searing salt-flat, they struck what seemed the ghost of a broader and better-made road, or signs left behind as it had sunk gradually into the earth, curving in from the northeast, and climbing to find a saddle in the barrier ridge.

"This, I believe," Iruvakh said, "is part of what was once *Zhanurai bi-Nímuraibákimai*, the Great Imperial Road."

"Also called Moon's Road," Lavsila, flippantly. "Though I cannot say why; I do not think it went to the moon."

"The name was given," Iruvakh said, "by a songmaker of the Blossoming Age, to flatter Yuval III, when Empire was at its greatest; from its western border to the Eastern Ocean at the city we now call Narn, was a moon's riding, from full to full — a month of dayrides."

Rodlakh, Kamin-Tolagh reflected, would be able to make the same boast, if he took the offer of a new province. *Why would any ruler refuse?* was a frequent thought, but Kamin-Tolagh could not guess whether Rodlakh would accept, and was not really sure he wanted him to. His true future was on the green shores of Arnan, not here in the West, but if the *rabhsai*, through Dolvid, made him counter-offer of amnesty for his crimes were he to return, he would not accept it, not yet, with so much unfinished here, not if Rodlakh were to let him resume captaincy of the Household; in that realm he could do nothing that had not been done before.

The ridge negotiated, with a first distant and doubtful sight of the Gulf from the summit, the way resumed a direction south of west, descending gradually in a more folded country. At one point a narrow, waterless gulch was crossed on piled rubble, and Iruvakh pointed out the flank of weathered cut stone visible at its base, and squat shapes, barely recognizable as remains of pillars, flanking the trail on either side, all that was left of a bridge built in the reign of Shâl IV. Then, these were populous lands, so the chronicles said, with wooded uplands and pasture below, and those accounts gained faint plausibility when, with the sun high and the heat crushing, Iruvakh led them aside from the trail, winding down into a small, steep-sided ravine, where there was a slight, clear trickle of water, and a dozen trees. In cooler months from the Abu to Larghamit, the ancient, ruined city at head of the Gulf, was a fairly easy dayride, but in the long summer days, with a dawn start, this halfway point was a good place to rest and wait out the hottest hours in shade, shade and silence. Kamin-Tolagh thought of boyhood summers at Inilun Barabhi, lying among reeds, or, later, in the hills above his personal estate, pausing to let his horse crop woodland grasses; the drone of insects, pipe and chatter of birds, snap and crash of a larger animal, startled and plunging for deep cover. Here, summer was still, the occasional scuttle of a lizard, faint stirrings of horses and men only emphasizing the sparseness of life.

With most of those not on watch, Lavsila, after light food and cool wine, slept in shade with a blanket spread on soft sand, but Kamin-Tolagh kept Iruvakh awake with questions about the Hrin. Aside from long-standing curiosity about the ancient port, the strong chance of encountering Hrin had caused Kamin-Tolagh to make this ride today, the eve of midsummer. Kambanal, in charge of a patrol, had reported seeing one of the ramshackle-looking vessels of the Hrin beached near the head of Flamûrai, and had been given the message they were interested in trading for *dao*, which they could no longer obtain from the Hwenala. But according to Iruvakh, at this time of the year, Hrin would always be found in the vicinity of Larghamit, near where was an isolated hill regarded as a holy place by many different peoples. "We called it *Kafai Zhaëli*, Zhôl's Mound. But it has a dozen names. Men and women of the Tufani, for whom it is Center of the Earth, made the journey there three summers ago, farther than you came from Kadon Dinul, *Asai*, and over worse roads, or none; they were weeks on the journey, but it will be sixteen years before they come again, according to their own count; they are great star-watchers." He did not, perhaps could not, explain the connection.

Hrin, or part of them, called the mound Hill of Shrines, but anything one clan of the Hrin held to be a sacred necessity was, according to another, a deadly insult to the gods.

Iruvakh gestured at the dozing Lavsila. "Some brought up, as I surely was, in the Old Faith, find it easy to make fun of Hrin religion, and the more one learns, the more there is to mock. The question to be asked, *Asai*, is not whether we, men of Owan, can understand, but whether we can teach ourselves how serious these questions are for the Hrin; without that, nothing can be judged about them, ever."

"He is of the Heartland. To them, any belief not held by an Owani within a half-dayride of Kadon Dinul is ridiculous."

When they resumed the ride day was still very warm, but the sun had preceded them into the west, to vanish behind distant, high mountains as they breasted a long, gradual climb, and looked down on shallow water at the head of Flamûrai. Under softened, latening light, the scene was unreal; by contrast with the stark mountains straight ahead, the nearer hills to the north of west were a milky blue deepening to soft purple, and long, rippled shores shelving to burnished water had the texture of velvet. Built an age ago of the brownish rock that showed in outcrops hereabouts, what remained of the old imperial city kept a memory of the regular plan of its streets with the east-west axis that was an Owani badge, lines and snags of masonry, a few substantial walls still standing, broken but erect pillars of what had been a splendid eastward gate, all mellowed by time and the light.

"I had heard Larghamit was a port," Lavsila said. The twin-hulled vessel drawn up on the shore was quite three hundred paces from where the ruins began.

"It was," Iruvakh agreed. "You see the line, there, of a stream, once a much greater river, greater than it now is at the spring thaw. The sands it brought down, washed back by tide, evidently laid down fresh land between the port and the Gulf. The Paowan River, over yet longer time, did much the same at Kadon Dinul, which was once its own port, but came to need Owan Sai." He pointed out where great wharves, almost entirely submerged in sand, could be seen, well above highest point now reached by the tide.

The mapmaker, Dubovai, reins in the crook of his elbows as he made notations with his small pen, pressed forward to ask Iruvakh if he knew where the frontier set by Yuval III had run. "Was it the bank of the river, Master?"

"Part of the city was west of the river. I think the low ridge beyond. You can see what is left of fortifications along its crest."

Kamin-Tolagh scanned the line of the ridge, easily imagining the anxious watch kept by defenders towards the higher hills beyond, from where enemies eventually came in numbers too great to be turned back.

Where the ridge tapered down, nearing an arm of Flamûrai, a conical hill stood somewhat apart, Kafan Zhaëli, stone shape at its crown no broken watchtower, but a shrine, dedicated to Zhôl in the waning days of Empire; Lavsila was genuinely offended to learn that in the names of their gods, other peoples lit fires or made offerings there. Iruvakh said the Hrin had a number of their shrines on slopes of the mound, and thought he had done well to discover from that secretive people there was another such hill in their home country. So their gods could never be entirely captured or seduced by an enemy, each shrine they dedicated at home had its counterpart here. "Their shrines, they say, are not to gods, but those who have touched gods."

Lavsila said, "A careful people, if they form shrines like bills of sale, in duplicate."

Kamin-Tolagh said, "Do they make a special claim on this place?"

"Not the Shâls themselves claimed ownership of the mound."

"Time somebody did." Lavsila expounded an idea of charging tolls for access.

The standard Hrin features included prominent brows, virtually non-existent chins, and unpronounceable names, so Kamin-Tolagh forgave himself for not remembering whether the two they met with on the shore were the same as those Kambanal had reported encountering a few days ago. The taller and less meanly-dressed man, who spoke the ordinary language of the realm without mistakes or hesitations, said they were of *Hrithust* Iolfrant's following. "This is my vessel," with a gesture.

Seen close, still unbelievable as a serious craft, more a child's drawing for a seagoing house than anything Kamin-Tolagh would call a ship. Two closed wooden hulls the shape of long, light boats were joined by a large platform, a windowed wooden structure to the aft occupying about half its surface. Forward was a second hut, smaller and lower, and four or five roughclad men of a similar chinless aspect were erecting the mainmast, warping it to iron eyes projecting from what could only be called the front wall. The entire deck appeared to be fastened to the hulls only by many lashings of hairy rope, emphasizing the look of a hasty temporary assemblage of chance-found parts — and yet in these craft the Hrin made their vast, daring voyages, to unmapped southern lands, and as far as

Thenimala in Ninkufu, where this master, Huolafidn, said he had often been.

He was not only follower but cousin to the *Hrithust* Iolfrant, and had an expansive, ingratiating manner. readily volunteering his journey had among its purposes midsummer dedication of a new shrine on behalf of his *Hrithust*.

Dvasslo, his slender companion, offered: "In our tongue, *Hrithust* means much what *atarlai* does to you."

Iruvakh, very courteous: "Am I correct in supposing it also means much what *nimu* does in the realm?"

Before the smaller man could respond, Huolafidn bowed. "For his followers, the *Hrithust* is that, and nothing else."

"We were told," Lavsila said, "you were here to talk about trade."

"Ah," Huolafidn made a negligent gesture. "Trade is the Hrin way — in our tongue, we call it our *tveyusta*, especially for the happy who know the *dveyust-ranga-hrindan* to be written in shape of the skies." His companion, clearly inferior in rank, followed him in what must be a pious gesture, a circling backhand wave of a rigid right hand.

"Forgive me, sirs," Huolafidn resumed, "if these things are not spoken in your language. Hrin ways are not easily understood — " his smile became still sweeter. "Our ways are important only to ourselves, and so it should be. Trade, yes. We hear, as the world hears, new *utveyuodn* have come to these parts, as we see to be true. The *Hrithust*, my kinsman, has asked me to offer his greeting to the Lord Of Kargul, who has come to rule these lands."

"I am he," Kamin-Tolagh said.

After a flicker of doubt he could not disguise, Huolafidn, again followed by Dvasslo, made full deference in Owani style. "Pardon me, *Asai*. You are, then, Kamin-Tolagh *Asai*, burner-of-hills, Noh-Sra-Lal-Hin of the Man-mani, *jinzai*-victor, master of seven tribes, and lord of the double harvest?"

"I am," gravely, though counting the remnant Chon'la, he made it eight tribes, while the last title was somewhat prematurely conferred. He wondered from which tribe the Hrin had heard it. Their friends, the Hwenala, perhaps.

With scarcely a pause for descent from this high ceremonial style, Huolafidn asked about acquiring wheat. Since Iruvakh had described the Hrin lands as well-watered with a stable climate and good growing-season, this seemed odd, but so was everything about them. They had shown no alarm, for example, at the approach of two dozen armed men; the workers on the boat were armed with short swords or long knives at their sides, but had hardly spared a glance for the confrontation on the foreshore; except for a tiny ceremonial dagger worn centered above the waist, their richly-clad leader was unarmed.

The idea of exporting foodstuffs, with the fear of famine scarcely banished, should have fascinated Kamin-Tolagh, but the details were tedious to him; he did not know the price of wheat, nor whether it was sold by weight or measure. Iruvakh was permitted to respond, and did not dwell on the difficulty of feeding their own peoples, but suggested the Hrin ask again, next year. The meaningful glance for Kamin-Tolagh was to remind him that Iruvakh had mentioned a few times it would be desirable to acquire seed for what he called winter wheat, for places where there would now be water for an autumn planting.

Huolafidn emphasized the Hrin would pay well for wheat, which at present they brought in their ships all the way from Thenimala, but the guarded expression of Dvasslo made Kamin-Tolagh suspect the subject had been raised as a way of finding out about progress of his food-growing schemes. The question about *dao* was again deferred when Dvasslo, edging around his point, asked obliquely for an outrageous concession; unless his mastery of the language had failed, he was proposing Kamin-Tolagh's domains should trade only with *Hrithust* Iolfrant, and his lesser ally, the *Hrithust* Svedion, turning away all other Hrin ships.

As Iruvakh had warned everything would be, a religious question: Huolafidn explained that Svedion, like Iolfrant, admitted the truth of the *dveyust-ranga-hrindan*, while the rest of the Hrin, mostly mired in the false *tveyusto-hrid-minyist*, were not to be trusted. Unlike his own, he was prepared to reveal some details of the erroneous creed, so as to expose its absurdities, but Kamin-Tolagh, appalled that the sagely nodding Iruvakh was willing to hear it all, cut the recital short.

"These things, as you rightly say, are important only to yourselves. My tribes have many different beliefs; we do not permit disputation, nor do we decide one is right and another wrong. In trade, all those willing to buy or sell at a fair price will be welcome. While in our territory," as afterthought, "they will be subject to our laws."

When Dvasslo asked about extent of that territory, Kamin-Tolagh, continuing to improvise, for the first time laid claim to Larghamit, and its surrounds up to the ancient boundary of Empire; it would be necessary, he saw, to keep a small garrison here, a rotating half-squadron, which later could be tribal troops under a Karguli officer.

Dvasslo moistened his lips. "Would this, *Asai*, be taken to include the Hill of Shrines, which you call Zhaëli?" As if setting a trap, and Kamin-Tolagh, who had been struggling to think who this shifty little man reminded him of saw the resemblance was not physical, but one of temperament; Dvasslo was a Hrin Lavsila.

"Access to the Mound — " disappointing his own Lavsila, "as anciently, will be guaranteed to all who call it holy. All the shrines will be protected from desecration, and here, too, no disputes of faith will be permitted. If you mean to dedicate the new shrine for your *Hrithust* tomorrow, your rites must take place beside our observance of *Shuda'sai*."

No matter what their intolerance for other Hrin, those of Huolafidn's standing had taught themselves diplomacy with others; he went beyond mild acceptance of the concurrent observances to ask if Kamin-Tolagh, in view of the shortage of firewood hereabouts, would accept the gift of some charcoal from the cargo they were carrying, his understanding being the burning of a fire was part of the rites to Zhôl. Only with that offer made and accepted did the Hrin ever-so-casually raise the question of *dao* spice.

Kamin-Tolagh's company spent night in the shelter of the one building of which any substantial part was standing, thick-walled, near where the east-west axis had crossed the main way up from what had been the harbor. Months ago, the first patrol Kamin-Tolagh had sent this way had found an impoverished nomad clan occupying the place, living, so it appeared, mainly on seaweed and mussels. The soldiers had driven them out, and the place was now habitually used by the patrols, the men having decided it had been palace of the great Larghai after whom the port was named. In fact, Iruvakh said, Larghai could never have lived here, a little fishing-village with a different name in his lifetime, and the central building was certain to have been a cavalry-barracks; two miles northward along the course of the stream were faintest remains of what had probably been a Great House for the governor over this region, surrounded by walled gardens, all-but swallowed in the shifting earth. The same process made it hard to estimate the original extent of Larghamit; though the ground all about was hard, it was nothing but packed sand, which seemed still to be coming in slow, silent waves, especially against the northern and western sides, where scattered snaggles of cut stone were evidence of buried ruins.

Next day, midday observances, improvised in the absence of a practising *atarlai*, were cut short by arrival of a message, relayed from the Abu, but coming from Nizhadh, on duty in tribal country. He wrote of a new outbreak of raiding by surviving Hill Froghul, the Gudi-la having both suffered and inflicted loss. Nizhadh had dispatched a message to Freighanai, who had two regular cavalry squadrons to the east of the hills, and he had sent help to the Gudi-la, some of his Kargul', together with as many tribal levies as he could rapidly collect and were ready for fighting. He was worried, at the same time, over the dangers of concentrating all the available forces too much to the south, and begged for early reinforcements. In the terse phrases of Nizhadh's dispatch could be detected the underlying strain of an effective follower, suddenly with tactical decisions to make; the man had been a half-squadron leader when he rode to the Jinzai War.

With night at its shortest, there were hours left of daylight, and Kamin-Tolagh quickly decided he would leave unfinished the business with the Hrin, and return to the Abu at once. Reliable troops, as from the start, were too few; he had to guard against the chance his father, or the *rabhsai*, or the two in improbable alliance, would suddenly strike, and he could not leave the Abu, his essential base, unguarded. He was haunted, as often, by the feeling his empire was a kind of precarious trick, one of the illusions produced by a Pledging-time conjurer, which the slightest change of viewpoint could instantly expose as a nothing; counting the long empty spaces between, where supplies and communications had to be protected, he had laid claim to wider territory than the whole of the largest province, his own Kargul, and had fewer real troops to guard it than the *Mankh'* used merely to protect the Patriarch. He had been fretful that with the end of raids by the Hill Froghul, the valley tribes might feel safe enough to resume warring among themselves, or one or several, ignoring gratitude, could revolt against his rule; with the Hill Froghul back on the roster of dangers, any two challenges coming at once would leave him unable to respond.

Another old fear had returned: passing through the Abu, the dispatch from Nizhadh had been endorsed by Kambanal, in temporary command, who appended a note to say he had put the remaining two squadrons there on alert, and the men would be ready to ride at an hour's notice. To this he added: `*a* jinzai *child was born last week in Man-mani country. The woman was employed as servant by some men of the squadron Antighal now leads.*' In accordance with Kamin-Tolagh's instructions, the baby had been killed as soon as its *jinzai* traits were unmistakable, and the mother had been confined at the warehouse used by the cavalry.

Inevitable, as foreseen; not all potential *jinzai*-mothers, women of the Man-mani with a mixture of Owani blood, could have been identified by the former masters of the Lunu. Yet it filled Kamin-Tolagh with a peculiar horror, and had, ever since learning the seed of *jinzayum* lurked in the purest of Owani blood, blood he had been taught was his most precious heirloom. That repugnance mastered, there remained a practical side: in his long letter to Dolvid he had not mentioned *jinzal*, a subject he knew could not be far from forefront of the *rabhsai*'s mind. His draft had included an assurance about his intentions, but in the end he had to agree with Lavsila, that what was unlikely to be believed was better omitted. He had no doubt the realm would act swiftly and with crushing force if convinced he meant to raise and deploy a new *jinzai* army, but they had only to interrogate the men of Kargul who had returned home to learn how from the first his policy had been to prevent conception of new *jinzal*. *Jinzal* babies were two to three weeks less time in the womb than a normal child, and counting back, the one just born must have been conceived very soon after his arrival at the Man-mani village, perhaps at the feast for his first victory over the Hill Froghul.

In the saddle, with most of his troops, leaving behind Lavsila, and a half-file to escort him back when he came, Kamin-Tolagh pondered what else he could have done to prevent that mating, or, rather, what must be done to prevent further such births. He had been lax about enforcing his intended ban on the use of Man-mani women as servants, a rule which would be unpopular both ways; the Man-mani were approaching what for them was prosperity, with money and goods their service had brought into circulation, and of all tribes they were easily first choice for servants, their long association with Owanil people having made them far easier than others to train.

Servants were a large part of life at the Abu, all the more important to those of lowlier birth, those wives in particular, who, their whole lives back in Kargul, would have expected to do their own cleaning, washing, mending, the tedious household drudgery that took up most of the waking day. Recognizing money he distributed in pay for the troops would bring no benefit if simply hoarded, Kamin-Tolagh had decreed workers must be paid, no matter how absurdly low the rate, and a group of ordinary troopers, quartered when they were at the Abu in what had formerly been the so-called Hatchery, pooled resources to share the labors of half a dozen Man-mani women. Until recently, he had allowed his men great latitude in the treatment of servants, but with the coming of the women, loud complaints about the laziness and ignorance of tribal girls had been matched, in a number of cases, by cruel maltreatment, and Kamin-Tolagh had to lay down some rules forbidding excessive punishments. According to an amused Lavsila, precisely those women who, without a husband in the cavalry, would themselves have been of the servant class, were most determined to get value for their money, drove their girls the hardest, and were readiest to use rod and lash.

In other ways, arrival of the families had changed life at the Abu for the better, and Lavsila entertained himself again with the paradox that soldiers' wives, some of whom could outcurse their men and drink whole half-squadrons into oblivion could, by their presence, bring about a marked reduction in profanity and drunkenness, a tribute, he maintained, to the mysterious power of hypocrisy.

In these increasingly settled conditions, Kamin-Tolagh had discovered skills among his men that would not have appeared during a campaign, nor in the makeshift life of a camp. Some soldiers had followed trades before enlisting, and even those who had joined the provincial cavalry at seventeen, when not the sons of soldiers, had knowledge of the family craft, or were from farm folk, with a smattering of many. There were several serviceable carpenters, one the son of a sawyer, who knew how to get the most usable planks out of rough logs. Two of the best smiths had put the Abu's forge back in order, and, using the inexhaustible supply of charcoal from tribal country, found enough metal-working skill not only to forge weapons, repair body-armor and harness-fittings, but to make parts for Lavsila's wind-driven pump, according to his drawings. Less successful than he had hoped, due to the swirling air-currents in the great depression of the Abu, it provided a trickle of water to irrigate a few vegetable-patches. Another cavalry-man, the nephew of a master-mason, had enough of the craft to direct conversion of what had been the long, gloomy barracks for the *jinzal* into living-quarters for Tau-Suaka's Hill Froghul, knocking out additional and larger windows, and constructing dividing walls inside.

Other less useful but equally interesting talents emerged: a few played stringed or blown instruments, and Kambanal, finding earths to use for pigments, painted fine pictures on walls or on stretched cloth. Some women were weavers or dyers as well as good brewers and breadmakers, and most knew how to preserve foods in various traditional ways. Kamin-Tolagh, who in all his years had never had a reason to question how the comforts he expected came into being, now marvelled at how many accomplishments went towards making a tolerable life, and what fantastically various creatures humans were; the simplest tribes had spinners and weavers, potters and builders; the uncouth Hwenala made hats and baskets, mats and hangings of plaited reeds, with subtle patterns finely worked, and K'daab's People, in their ramshackle fenced village, carved iron-hard roots of a particular thorn-bush into doorposts, lintels and staffs with the form of animals or the faces of men, women and children, all perfectly finished and hauntingly lifelike, even where most fantastic. Examples of these native crafts had made their way to the Abu, and were, probably for the first time in any quantity, being traded, tribe to tribe; Kamin-Tolagh did not see how the conditions for peaceful trading and introduction of a miniscule amount of money could point towards a general increase in prosperity, and unlike Iruvakh, who made farfetched comparisons with the agricultural technique of transplanting, or Lavsila, who talked about the power of wakened greed, made no pretence at understanding. Plainly, however, neither the Hrin, nor Rodlakh's realm, would pay large sums of gold for tribal manufactures, and unless gold could be found, with or without war and revolt, the Empire of Kargusai would founder; not in half a century could Kamin-Tolagh maintain himself with tribal forces alone; he had to have real troops, and soldiers had to be rewarded.

In deepening dusk, he reached the Abu, where unexcitable Kambanal reminded Kamin-Tolagh there had at the time of the fire been rumors a body of the Hill Froghul had escaped by fleeing southward, where was said to be desert country. How they had survived there was anybody's guess, but no doubt to feed themselves they had returned to raiding. "Acting-*kimukan* Nizhadh may have a lesser problem than he believes, *Asai*. How could there be above a few dozen raiders?"

"He is right to show concern," a mild reprimand to the younger officer. "We had hoped to end this plague for good."

Modestly enough, Kambanal observed it was not reasonable to suppose the Hill Froghul could ever regain their power to strike anywhere at will; the dense cover that had been their ally had hardly begun to come back, and there were wide areas where it would be slow to return; the tender green shoots that had poked through on the charred hillsides were, in the most accessible places, excellent grazing for goats, a double and treble benefit, since it also meant a portion of lowland pasture could next spring be put to the plow.

"The way they use cover, it may be, *Asai* they can never be completely stamped out, only kept down, like rats in a barn. But you have claimed the best fighting rats — when the raiders see how much better their tamed kinsmen live, most likely they will want to join them instead of fight them." In the months since the great fire, scattered small bands of Hill Froghul had surrendered themselves.

Kamin-Tolagh examined Kambanal with new eyes; the young man, who retained his love of idealizing, was developing a sense of long-term strategy unique among Kargul' officers. At the start of the Jinzai War, his rank had been below Nizhadh's, as it still was, but he had been with Kamin-Tolagh's personal squadron, where a half-file considered himself minimally the equal of any other squadron-leader. He was, besides, of better lineage, though not a true man of Kargul; his father, a merchant who had settled in Inilun, came from Ninkufu in the south, and was distantly related to Doleni, Saidhan's lady, hence, with numberless others, could claim a remote connection with the House Gabh'Owan, the former ruling family.

Though he had been given a great deal of unsought advice by Lavsila, and constantly instructed by Iruvakh, not once since coming to the West had Kamin-Tolagh voluntarily submitted a decision for debate, till now. "What would you say, then, about sending Tau-Suaka with the best of his men to reinforce Nizhadh? Are they ready to fight — as soldiers, I mean, to take orders and stick to them?" He had in fact already decided to see what Tau-Suaka said, but wanted to hear how his best disciple dealt with the question.

Kambanal thought it through out loud: "They came from their cradles fighting, and they have made themselves into mounted bows as good, man for man, as those we saw fight at Kamsilat, if not as disciplined. Tau-Suaka drives them hard, and is not slow to use the lash — they all go in fear of that kinsman of his, Hunghi, who is a master of the whip, as Dorrmas with a sword. The question, *Asai*, is whether they are ready to fight for *us* — for you, and against their own kind."

"Your opinion?"

"As I see it, they have less idea of kinship than any of the tribes — maybe because they are not truly a people, taking their women, as they always have, where they find them. Their loyalties are kept narrow, and if Tau-Suaka says, fight hill men, they will."

"And his loyalties?"

"He has only one, *Asai*. To you. He would obey if you told him, go and fight the hills themselves."

Whether true, the sentiment was certainly echoed by the man, when summoned. Given news of the raiding, his fleshy face showed a contemptuous anger. "Thieves," he said, and then, oddly, struck the same simile as Kambanal: "They will not stand and fight as men should; they're just rats, who steal and run to hide."

"They are of your blood."

He thought Tau-Suaka would spit. "Not now, Lord. They have no helms." Plain helmets from the large stock left here were accepted by Hill Froghul as a proud emblem of their new standing, as they moved from ditch-digging and clearing of brush to training with horses and weapons.

Two hundred of Tau-Suaka's men were judged ready to ride, with men of Kargul furnishing squadron officers; Kamin-Tolagh meant to show his confidence by putting Kambanal in overall charge, but realized for the valley tribes this would be first sight of their ancient enemies rearmed, and decided he had better ride with them, at least as far as the Man-mani village. There, he left the troops at the barracks by the river, at midsummer a sluggish trickle feeding a shrinking reservoir, before riding, with only regular cavalrymen for escort, to the village, where he was given a rapturous reception, as when they had first hailed him as a god. Chamya, in the saddle with a dozen of his youthful followers to greet Kamin-Tolagh, explained the news from the Gudi-la country had made everyone edgy, fearful about recurrence of their old plague, and return of Noh-Sra-Lal-Hin brought new hope.

A little later, sharing cold melon at the head-man's hut, he learned what troops were chosen to send south, and came as near as he dared to a quarrel. He took in stride conversion of Tau-Suaka's men to allies, but had been eager to go himself, leading the best of the Man-mani auxiliaries, the more so because among the raiders killed in recent fighting were men said to be not Hill Froghul at all, but of Chamya's own tribe. "What is left of Sranadatta's brood," with a loathing face. "Who else would ally themselves with thieves?" This was a guess, but if the dead were Man-mani, they must be of that family, who, whatever their shortcomings as a ruling clan, had the knack of ingratiating themselves with former enemies.

It made sense, then, to give Chamya his wish, since Man-mani would be useful in identifying their own among the enemy, and if they rode south, Kamin-Tolagh's presence would be needed to prevent bickering in the mixed force. He disliked removing himself so far from the Abu, but enjoyed the company of Chamya, with his admiration, his curiosity and eagerness to learn all he could about war and the ways of Kamin-Tolagh's powerful realm. Tau-Suaka was devoted, fierce and able, and every tribe and clan produced natural leaders, gifted men and (though they had to be hunted for) women who could get outside the narrow vision of their surrounds and imagine a better life, but

Chamya's qualities would have made him stand out, with proper training, even at Kadon Dinul.

The mixed riding had made a timely arrival at the main settlement of the Gudi-la, which had successfully beaten off a determined raid, while Nizhadh, with most of the available cavalry, was putting himself between the raiders and their retreat. Though hemmed in, the Hill Froghul were far from beaten, having withdrawn into wooded lands, where they had taken and slaughtered a number of pigs, enjoying a meat-feast as if to taunt their adversaries. Nizhadh was unwilling to risk cavalry among the trees, where the Hill Froghul' bows had already shown themselves to be deadly; he had been trying to persuade the Gudi-la to take the offensive, and drive the raiders out into open country, formerly dense brushland, which his force commanded.

Tau-Suaka barely waited for permission to begin the attack, and here bows were matched by bows, the old ferocity made more effective by discipline; Kamin-Tolagh's Hill Froghul, in contrast to their untamed kinsman, had learned how to cover and support one another, and utterly outfought the raiders. Exulting in slaughter, Tau-Suaka's only regret was that a last demoralized remnant of their adversaries, flushed from cover and soon pursued, were surrounded by Nizhadh's horse, and so able to surrender; there were otherwise no prisoners. Tau-Suaka had many wounded, and lost eleven killed, the only losses to Kamin-Tolagh's combined forces in this action. Among enemy dead was a young man Chamya identified as a nephew to Sranya-Dalhitta, but the last leader of the remnant Sranadattanil, Sra-Min-Talla-Tyu, unless his body was unrecovered, was not with the slain, and neither were the counsellor, Nifra, Siv'loi's despicable father, nor the woman, Myanachë.

In this one engagement, as prisoners unanimously confirmed, the enemy strength had been shattered, and what Nizhadh shrugged off as tidying-up, the hunt for any remnant bands of would-be raiders, could easily have been left to him with his Gudi-la auxiliaries. But Kamin-Tolagh did not want to ride back north to the tame life of the Abu; notwithstanding dust and parching heat, the difficulty of keeping clean where every drop of drinking-water was precious, he was enjoying himself in the field, exulting in action and in comradeship, the company of other stubbled, grimed and, at day's end, weary men who stank as he stank. Tau-Suaka was like a hound, ferocious and faithful, proudly bringing trophies to lay at Kamin-Tolagh's feet. Chamya too, though with a quicker and more independent intelligence, constantly sought praise for his actions, but the unassuming Nizhadh restored Kamin-Tolagh to comfortable humanity, treating him as a fellow-officer. A superior officer, certainly, one whose tactical choices were not questioned, but still a soldier, not a different order of being. Cracking pork-bones by the campfire in the evening, he made bawdy jokes, and reminisced about `his' country, the sparsely-populated coastal strip beyond Peframi in westernmost Kargul. Astonishingly, on the evening after the major battle, when Kamin-Tolagh insisted the Gudi-la show their gratitude by broaching jealously-guarded reserves of their tribal drink, a kind of shrub beer without much taste but inducing light-headedness in even experienced drinkers, Nizhadh, with a leathery, terse sentimentality, ventured a remark or two about the great love of his youth, an ethereal girl he had somehow failed to capture; clearly she was not the solid, workaday wife he had spoken of before, mother of his near-grown children.

"Foolery," Nizhadh summarized the other, clearly meaning it must seem so to Kamin-Tolagh of the thousand bed-friends, but Kamin-Tolagh assured him many men could tell such tales.

"Even the *rabhsai*, I do not doubt," curious substitution for his counter-confiding urge, induced by the subversive Gudi-la beer. This mood of fellowship was good to know, but authority demanded an illusion of immunity to human weaknesses.

Ten days directing, with scant success, the search for enemy survivors, and a sojourn, on the northward return, in the Man-mani village, where he renewed his sport with the enthusiastic Imyë, and taught Chamya some of the more straightforward sequences of dismounted sword-fighting, lengthened his absence from the Abu to six weeks. When, on a warm mid-morning, he returned to the Great House, as he had renamed the former residence of the True *Rabhsai*, Kamin-Tolagh discovered Lavsila and Iruvakh in passionate disagreement.

Lavsila, at least, was passionate, as he protested something was out of the question, while Iruvakh, seated, was in his irritating mode of bland imperviousness. Freighanai, auditing from a short distance, lower lip pinched between thumb and forefinger, appeared bemused by the quarrel.

If there was one, Kamin-Tolagh's arrival placed it in a state of suspension. Here were three men, he recognized, whose ranks and functions were going to have to be defined more exactly. Freighanai, with none of the learning of a Kambanal, nor the filial respect the men gave old Yaënsilat, was acting as military chief-of-staff, not asking whether he was to have the captaincy and pay commensurate with those responsibilities; Lavsila and Iruvakh both performed ministerially to Kamin-Tolagh as sovereign, but with no definition of either their own authority, nor their standing relative to each other.

Not a question that troubled Iruvakh. Lavsila, for want of an abler *bôdhrai*, was aboard Kamin-Tolagh's boat, riding with it downstream; Iruvakh was on his own path that happened to run along the same riverbank, reserving the right to strike off in another direction. Exasperating, but it had to be tolerated, so long as the man showed no interest in money, or rank, or authority beyond what could be borrowed for his work with the tribes. From the first he had been impervious to threat, and like his former would-be masters, Kamin-Tolagh found him too useful to dismiss.

"What is out of the question?"

Lavsila, going instantly from dogmatism to reticence, allowed Iruvakh to explain. After carrying a supply of *dao* to their home country, the Hrin traders had quickly returned; Huolafidn and his fawning companion had visited the Abu. Dvasslo, indeed, was still here. They had brought with them on pack-ponies articles of Hrin manufacture, and done good business, largely with soldiers' wives, selling both lengths and made garments of fine linen cloth, and taking orders for a rich, glazed pottery, of which they had samples to show.

Kamin-Tolagh shrugged. "Hardly the wealth here to pay for their journey."

His two advisors agreed, and remained in accord on the proposition the Hrin had some other purpose in mind, but while Lavsila, predictably, held the Hrin were spying out Kamin-Tolagh's military strength, trying to ascertain numbers and quality of the tribal levies, Iruvakh, conceding that, as an incidental purpose, such a course would be only prudent, believed the Hrin were mainly following Hrin nature, pursuing trade, the friendship it fostered and was fostered by, as a bee went to blossoms or a blossom leant to the sun. Taking at face value the promise these domains would soon have foodstuffs to sell, they wished to establish in advance an offsetting market for their goods.

That they were seeking friendship, Iruvakh expanded, was impossible to doubt. "Of all things, they do not toy with religious questions. I myself was away, *Asai*, when the man

Huolafidn was here, but this Dvasslo gave me his message when I came. Huolafidn seeks permission to erect a shrine to Noh-Sra-Lal-Hin."

"Why?" The notion amused Kamin-Tolagh, but Lavsila was frowning.

"Two shrines, that would be," Iruvakh amended. "One at Kafai Zhaëli, by Larghamit, and another on the Hill of Shrines in their country."

"Three, then," Freighanai unexpectedly put in. "Well, stands to reason," as everyone stared. "If they're that careful to do their shrines twice, they'd have another secret place no one knows about."

Emboldened by this stroke, he took up the tale. "Young Kambanal, I fancy, put the idea in this H'olafidn's head. First time the Hrin were here, he told them the whole story about Noh-Sra-Lal-Hin, and how the Siv'loi banner came about." Just the ghost of a smile hovered with Freighanai, and Kamin-Tolagh could guess the high-flown manner of Kambanal's recounting.

"Huolafidn, I gather," Iruvakh resumed, "learnt the Man-mani legend of Noh-Sra-Lal-Hin from one of the servants here — the first time he had heard either tale in full, old or new. Now he regards Noh-Sra-Lal-Hin as one who has touched the gods, and conformable to the doctrine of *dveyust-ranga-hrindan*, to which Iolfrant's people subscribe. Therefore — "

"My view," Lavsila interrupted, "is, as a true Son of Yoëlladhu, *Asai*, you cannot permit your name to be lent to a shrine belonging to an alien cult."

"Noh-Sra-Lal-Hin is not the name of any Son of Yoëlladhu."

"Exactly," Iruvakh agreed. "In the days of the First Empire, some of the Shâls permitted western peoples to worship them as gods."

"In their own lands, yes," Lavsila argued. "This shrine will be within borders claimed by Kargusai. My contention — "

"I understand your contention quite well," cutting him off. Momentarily odd that Iruvakh, child of the *Mankh'*, had no scruples about the shrine, while the religious sensibilities of the worldling, Lavsila, were genuinely offended. But Iruvakh's tolerance was that of a man who has ceased to believe anything for himself, and found all religion equally valid or equally meaningless, while Lavsila's habitual contempt took in all faiths except the one he had imperfectly acquired as a child.

"What is your opinion?" Kamin-Tolagh asked the former *atarlai*. "Would this be helpful in our dealings with the Hrin?"

"At worst, as far as I can see, it can do no harm. True, there are deeper purposes behind Huolafidn's request, but there is no reason why they should affect you."

"What deeper purposes?"

Iruvakh sighed slightly, exactly as Kamin-Tolagh could recall doing, at a dinner-party, when the wife of a winemaker, for instance, insisted on a detailed explanation of some military technicality — the sigh of an authority who knew his listeners would soon be out of their depth, and bored. "It is a complex matter, *Asai*. But it must be made clear to Hrin of all persuasions that by permitting the shrine you are not proclaiming yourself an advocate of the *dveyust-ranga-hrindan*."

"Explain," Kamin-Tolagh said unwillingly; he would be bored. Freighanai, hoping it would not be noticed, was very slowly sidling for the door.

"Well, *Asai*, there are in all six *Hrithuod* — the proper plural form for *Hrithust* — and each of their territories is called an *onhritha*. Four of the present *Hrithuod*, all, in fact except for Iolfrant and his ally, Svedion, are of the *tveyusto-hrid-minyist*. I cannot understand all that doctrine implies, but have been able to learn its central tenet is that time, the gods, and the world all came into being at the same time, so when time ends and the world ends the gods also will die, and there can be no new time thereafter, unless, as one faction holds, the gods can be reborn."

"And this is what grown men spend their time disputing? They are worse than the *Mankh'*."

"Much the same, I would say, *Asai*," he assented cheerfully. "Except, of course, the Island exegetes are not at the same time attempting to govern a province, or foster trade. But, yes, these are matters for endless debate. All I have met are clear the *tveyusto-hrid-minyist* is absolutely irreconcilable with the *dveyust-ranga-hrindan*, which holds that before time, gods were, and a god who seems to die is only sleeping. You will readily see, *Asai*, how to Huolafidn's mind, the older legend of Noh-Sra-Lal-Hin would agree with the *dveyust-ranga-hrindan*."

Kamin-Tolagh had heard at least four different endings for the tale of Noh-Sra-Lal-Hin. In one, he tried to embrace and lift a great rock, not seeing it was the world itself; the strength went from him, and women beat him with cornstalks and drove him away. The wonder was that a single Man-mani teller could give two completely different endings, unbothered by inconsistency.

"I doubt Kambanal would have recounted that version," Iruvakh, drily, but could not get the confirmation he sought; Freighanai, at a slight nod from Kamin-Tolagh, had at last escaped to more soldierly duties.

"The ending he told must have been where Noh-Sra-Lal-Hin is borne away by the great hawk he defeated and then tamed, and rests on the summit of the Mountain of All Mountains, till his time comes again. For Huolafidn, who, according to his man Dvasslo, besides trader, is also a goldsmith, and therefore an *atarlai*, the echo of the *dveyust-ranga-hrindan* would be plain. Even by Hrin standards, he is a passionate advocate for his faith. For this reason he desires this shrine."

For Kamin-Tolagh, the explanation did not quite work. "Who, then, is Huolafidn hoping to persuade? Does his master, Iolfrant, have ambitions? What would he gain if he converted all other *Hrithuod* to his belief?"

Iruvakh was doubtful. "I do not know such a thing could be accomplished. Certainly Iolfrant, so Dvasslo boasts, is richest and most important of the six *Hrithuod*, said to control more than half all the gold of the Hrin. He might, I suppose, hope to impress the other *Hrithuod* with his influence by erecting the new shrine. But, *Asai*, this is nothing strange for the Hrin, who have a way of, as it were, collecting their demigods. Well, the original shrine to Zhôl, after which we call Kafai Zhaëli, was erected not by Owanil, but by Hrin, who at Thenimala had learnt the reputed sway Zhôl held over gale-winds, as also against becalming."

"*Reputed* sway!" Lavsila's right thumb piously folded down. "What honor can there be there, *Asai*, in a shrine alongside the dozen other shrines of a people who regard Zhôl Himself as one among a collection of who-knows-what?"

Kamin-Tolagh was growing tired of the issue. "Let me remind you, you are the one who has been making plans for the anniversary observance at the tomb of Siv'loi." Bent on keeping that legend fresh, Lavsila had devised a touching ceremony, which included a bareheaded Kamin-Tolagh casting dried *dao* flowers on the hilltop grave. It would please, he insisted, both soldiers and their wives, and Kamin-Tolagh, to whom Siv'loi was no longer anything but a name, could see that was true when, straight-faced, he outlined the details of the proposed ritual to a rapt Kambanal. Lavsila knew these things, not out of wisdom, but because beneath his Heartland graces he had a narrow mind that understood narrow minds; his real objection to the new shrine had nothing to do with its effect on others; he simply thought it blasphemous to share a place devoted, however unworthily, to Zhôl, for Kamin-Tolagh, a chance not to be missed of extending his influence into the Hrin lands.

"Let us tell this Dvasslo," instructing Iruvakh, "there can be a shrine, but it must be to Noh-Sra-Lal-Hin and Siv'loi together. For the Hrin, it can be the Noh-Sra-Lal-Hin who has been with the gods, but does not choose one doctrine over another. For our people — " turning with a beam to Lavsila —

"it should be a memorial to the love of Siv'loi for Noh-Sra-Lal-Hin, honored by travellers from distant lands."

"But," Lavsila started, and lapsed into silence.

"What can it mean," after Iruvakh had taken his leave, "the *Hrithust* Iolfrant controls the greater part of Hrin gold? Over and again we have been told the Hrin have little or no gold of their own." From his earliest boyhood, when he first heard of the Hrin, the one certainty was that at long intervals, one or another of their traders who came to Thenimala would offer an intricately worked golden brooch, or necklace, or vessel for drinking or serving, for which extremely high prices were asked; almost every aristocratic or merely moneyed family of the realm boasted at least one treasure of Hrin craft — and these, it was understood, were pieces the Hrin considered less than perfect, which is why they were sent abroad. Though there were travellers' tales that put roofs of solid gold on the Hrin temples. their traders always made out that very tiny quantities of gold, all obtained from overseas, passed through Hrin hands, and had to be accumulated over months or years to make the admired artifacts, but a goldsmith of Kargul once remarked to Kamin-Tolagh's father, those skills needed constant practice.

"Iolfrant's ships, perhaps, import most gold," Lavsila offered.

"Why?"

"A traditional monopoly, like the Patriarch with *raminat* or fine glass."

"Or the use of force," Kamin-Tolagh said, though unable to imagine it of the Hrin. "This man Dvasslo — he seems inclined to bragging. There is more to this affair of the shrine than we have been told. When we first met his master, Huolafidn, he demanded we deal only with Hrin who advocate his doctrine. Dvasslo, in the proper mood, might tell us the truth."

"Wine," succinctly. "Ours is stronger than the Hrin are used to." Lavsila had evidently already drunk with the man.

"Where is he staying?"

"With Freighanai, but I have suggested he would be more comfortable with me. Freighanai, I mean, is absent a great deal." Lavsila had taken for his own a moderate-sized but well-furnished house, near the eastern end of the Traëvu.

"That will do very well — " reluctantly deciding they would treat Dvasslo, whom he disliked, as an honored guest.

Huolafidn returned to Larghamit and erected the new shrine, a ceremony Kamin-Tolagh observed only from a distance appropriate to its dedicatee, but when the master departed Dvasslo stayed on, and became a fixture at the Abu. He was permitted to use a small former storehouse as a shop or trading-post, selling or bartering not only Hrin goods, but household items exchanged by soldiers or their wives, and various things of tribal make, such as the wide-brimmed rush hats of the Hwenala, excellent in the sun, and the wood-carvings of K'daab's People. Apparently all Hrin who were not farm-laborers or common seamen had knowledge of metalworking, and Dvasslo also made himself useful at the forge, advising on alloys and the use of fluxes, though there were processes for which the materials were lacking, and others he said he was not permitted to reveal.

For Lavsila, apparently Dvasslo's self-definition as a shopkeeper created a gap of class far less gratifying to bridge than any difference of race, belief and language, but outward signs of friendship persisted longer than might have been predicted; in the end they had too much in common, but before Dvasslo's insistence on cultivating a circle of cronies caused coolness between them, Lavsila was able to learn much about the mysteries behind Huolafidn's actions.

His relationship to his *Hrithust* was only through Iolfrant's marriage to a cousin, and in Dvasslo's judgment Huolafidn's lineage was the superior. By this he seemed to mean only that Huolafidn's family or clan had been adherents through generations of the *dveyust-ranga-hrindan*, whereas the *Hrithust* not only had many forebears lost in falsities of the *tveyusto-hrid-minyist*, but had himself been brought up in that unfortunate error, having been fostered by Frasti, a kinsman, most powerful of the four *Hrithuod* who were its champions. As third son to a younger brother of the then-*Hrithust* in Huolafidn's *onhritha*, Iolfrant's chances of figuring in the succession had appeared remote, but a series of misfortunes, in which chance, it was darkly hinted, had sometimes been lent a helping hand, left Iolfrant, on the death of the *Hrithust*, among three possible claimants.

Precedence, apparently, could not be determined either in law or tradition, and while Iolfrant had the support of a former foster-brother, Nestos, now the neighboring *Hrithust*, he was opposed by leading families of his own *onhritha*, including that of Huolafidn, on account of his beliefs. Abruptly, Iolfrant had declared himself a devout convert to the *dveyust-ranga-hrindan*, and his candidacy was promptly endorsed by one Svedion, feeblest and poorest of all *Hrithuod*, but a man of great influence in Huolafidn's circles, on account of his deep religious learning, and unswerving devotion to the true doctrine. Aided by the timely death of the most likely opposing candidate, and with the grudging assent of *atarlai*-goldsmiths such as Huolafidn, Iolfrant had become their *Hrithust*.

That was fourteen years ago; his rule had been strong, his reign, if that was the word, a prosperous one. Himself a master-mariner and successful trader, he had financed and encouraged ships of his *onhritha* to visit distant lands, not only eastward into a history Kamin-Tolagh recognized, but south and west to lands hitherto unknown. "Lands," Lavsila quoted, adding his own rote skepticism, "where the only season is summer everlasting, and there are snakes ten paces long that can swallow a man whole, pitch-black people who would give equal weight of gold for an iron pot or a common hatchet, trees taller than the Abu here is deep, giant lizards with sharks' teeth, and I forget what else. Dvasslo believes anything he hears himself saying. For the largest of places where his people gather to chant and worship, Iolfrant has given a new roof entirely of gold."

"By this account — " wishing he could believe in that golden roof — "Iolfrant should be loved by all."

"Ah, but you see, it is suspected he wants to become lord over all the Hrin, a thing they have never had, and for that he would either have to change a lot of religious belief somewhere, or else find a twisty way to embrace both doctrines. His chief advisor, who is his mother's uncle or some such, has openly declared the two rival beliefs are not beyond all reconciling. Oy — Oy, something, his name is, and Huolafidn and those hate him. He is learned with herbs and such, maybe poisons, and they believe he did more than pray to help Iolfrant become *Hrithust*. On top of that, there is Hridveyuth."

"Is it important?" wearily.

"To the Hrin — and so to anyone who wants to know the mind of the Hrin," Lavsila echoed Iruvakh, and came very near taking offence. He had labored to acquire and master this information, suppressing his own contempt.

Hridveyuth was the name of a holy man, or perhaps a designation short of an actual name. His style, anyway; every so often, for countless generations, men of special gifts had been given the name, in full, *Hrid-Hryinda-Hridveyuth*, meaning, so Dvasslo said, Speaker of Words of Gold (or, of True, Holy Thoughts) to People in All Lands. The present Hridveyuth, who wandered from place to place addressing large gatherings, was, like Iolfrant, talking about making the Hrin into one people. Despite the absurdity of some of his pronouncements — Dvasslo had been particularly scornful over the notion that in a perfected realm, women might be counted of priestly rank — Hridveyuth was heard with respect, even awe, by the lowly. He had been allowed to conduct a meeting at the allegedly golden-roofed place — "Their *Mankh'*, Dvasslo called it, as if these crude superstitions — "

"He spoke there," Kamin-Tolagh insisted.

"And ended, as always, with an invocation, in which his perfected realm shall be so *to the end of time*."

Kamin-Tolagh failed to detect special significance in the commonplace phrase, but the point for Huolafidn and his allies was that in the *dveyust-ranga-hrindan*, time had no end. By lending Hridveyuth the sanction of their chief temple, Iolfrant had given wings to the rumor he would use the holy man to help unify the Hrin, but under the despicable *tveyusto-hrid-minyist*. That was why Huolafidn had tried to get Kamin-Tolagh's undertaking to trade only with those of his doctrine, and was reason, also, behind the shrine to Noh-Sra-Lal-Hin, which Iolfrant would be obliged to acknowledge. The goldsmith-priests were trying to make it impossible for their *Hrithust* ever to renounce the *dveyust-ranga-hrindan*.

Kamin-Tolagh shook his head despondently; all lunacy to him, and there was nothing here he could use; even the gold was the remote and fabled gold of stories, not yellow metal he could see and handle. Evening now hinted that summer's heat was relenting, and he was restless to be in the field again, seeking new ways to extend and consolidate his rule — and to pay his troops.

"To me," with his oblique face of conspiracy, "it seems there might be a key in this holy Hridveyuth, if we could make him our ally, with a promise of armed assistance. He affects indifference to wealth or power, but that is only his way of gaining the support of those who have neither."

"How is this conference to take place? Shall we have Huolafidn deliver an invitation?"

"No, Dvasslo. He serves Huolafidn, but would embrace the *tveyusto-hrid-minyist* tomorrow, or swear he was a true Son of Yoëlladhu, if he saw profit in it."

"And what have we to offer Hridveyuth that he cannot obtain quite easily from Iolfrant? If Dvasslo wishes to profit by double-dealing, let him tell us where the Hrin mine their gold."

"They do not mine it," Lavsila, triumphantly. "They trade for it."

Moderation in weather renewed fears of an assault by the realm, and Kamin-Tolagh redoubled watch on the principal approaches, sending daily patrols as far as the place where the *jinzai* road made its descent from Landegh. A year to the day since his first entry into what was then the Lunu, the massacre at the Hatchery, first meeting with Iruvakh; Kamin-Tolagh was preparing to leave for Man-mani country and the fatuous anniversary rites at the tomb of Siv'loi, when word came a patrol had encountered, parleyed with, and escorted to the Abu a half-squadron contingent from the Army of the West, under command of the *Kímukan* Idmas, He was carrying a message from the *Bôdhrai*.

13.

"This makes no real difference," Kamin-Tolagh repeated.

"It is in Dolvid's own hand." By bad candlelight, Lavsila had been studying the sheets for what must be an hour, in order to produce his comment.

"I don't care if his saddle-horse wrote it," but unable to stifle curiosity, "How would you know Dolvid's hand?"

"He often writes his own official letters," airily. "Even with a scribe sitting by. His father, after all, was not much above a common scribe, and about Iruvakh's height. *His* father was a chandler."

"Iruvakh's?"

"Iruvakh is of excellent family — " Kamin-Tolagh could remember him, in this same place, with equal assurance, condemning the man as one who pretended to good breeding — "Dolvid's grandfather made cheap candles for his living."

"We should have him here." Kamin-Tolagh improved the light a little by touching a new candle to the guttering other, taking longer than he should; like Lavsila, he must be a little drunk.

"Whoever the scribe, more than one hand went into making this. I have not seen such delicacy since the Investing, when Rhunilat made deference to the space between Orbanak and me, so as to avoid giving any offense."

This, he was aware, was a lie by implication; there was nothing equivocal about the letter, which reiterated Rodlakh desired no expansion of his rule, that he, Kamin-Tolagh, had been confirmed in Council as Captain of Rodlakh's Household whose place was at Kadon Dinul, that the assertion in his letter, therefore, that he remained a loyal subject and soldier was not tenable. All the caution had been lavished on the expression of these principles, the language evidently striving not to slam any doors, without offering smallest hope of a compromise from Kadon Dinul; in effect a hint at clemency if he came home and said he was sorry, and it would not happen again. Not an offer, but in what posed as and might actually be a postscript added after the *rabhsai* had endorsed the letter, Dolvid wrote, `*You will understand,* Asai, *recollection of your shared experience, especially in the battle at Kamsilat, now only deepens the* rabhsai*'s disappointment and anger over the course you have chosen. My belief, however, is that those same memories would prove decisive in effecting a reconciliation, even at this late date, if you will only place yourself once more under his undoubted authority.'*

The same care had gone into choice of courier, Idmas, his rank of *kimukan* now permanent, a conscientious officer who had served with unspectacular courage in the War, competently again in the expedition that brought Kamin-Tolagh here; his patrol had been the one to find the mass grave of poisoned *jinzal*, and he had contributed usefully to their conferences; his standing, then, was adequate to avoid any suggestion of insult, while at the same time proclaiming he was not empowered to negotiate; the letter was the whole message.

Still, Idmas had surely been instructed to keep his eyes open, and after ascertaining the letter had nothing to demand urgent attention, Kamin-Tolagh had taken him on a tour to see the changes a year had brought the former Lunu, the new and more extensive growing-plots, the old *jinzai* barracks altered for human habitation. At a guess, Idmas had been told to watch in particular for any sign the breeding of *jinzal* had begun again, and Kamin-Tolagh wished he could show the officer the small corpse of the *jinzai* infant killed in early summer; he could not initiate the subject without seeming over-anxious to reassure.

On the quartering of himself and his escort, Idmas had behaved with what could easily be construed as discourtesy, declining to be separated from his men as Kamin-Tolagh's guest, proffering no thanks when allotted one of the roomier houses. From the man's stiff manner it could be deduced he had, absurdly, been told to omit any acknowledgment of Kamin-Tolagh's right to offer hospitality here.

Whereupon he set out to shame him, sending him and his men a quantity of cool and delicious melons, and going personally to be sure he was comfortably installed. Later, after the still-fierce sun dipped below the far rim of the great depression, Idmas could hardly refuse an invitation to dinner at the Great House, the best meal that could be assembled at short notice, served with plenty of wine. Though his cup was kept full, Idmas drank in moderation, and had very little to say, talking mainly about minor Colony events. Not late, excusing himself on grounds of fatigue; while he had delayed his journey so as to avoid the worst of the heat, on Landegh there was not much sign of autumn, and the crossing had been wearisome. After seeing him to his bed, Kamin-Tolagh and Lavsila came to the former Captain's house against the eastern cliff, where the store of wine would soon be in need of replenishment.

"There is mention here of Kargul — " still poring over the letter. "`Your recent dealings with your own province — `"

"Have angered my father," Kamin-Tolagh supplied. "Dealings!" A private joke here; Tovakh could complain, no doubt had complained to the *rabhsai*, about his son's suborning the loyalty of provincial cavalry, and might not have minded making himself ridiculous accusing the Heir in Kargul of an unauthorized visit to his home province, but about what must be sharpest spur to anger he could never say anything at Kadon Dinul, concerning as it did the theft of something he could not admit having.

In past centuries, the province had been horsebreeders for the realm, suppliers, in particular, of *pefral*, the great, fierce cavalry mounts. Long ago, the *Atarlum* had discovered a way of treating *pefral* colts to render them sterile, without, as in the case of gelding, losing any of the animal's fighting qualities. This had given the *rabhsai* a means of limiting the numbers of first-class cavalry each province could possess, the only untreated stallions being kept for breeding-stock. About eighty years ago, charging the province with unlawful practices, especially supplying itself with mounts for far more than its legal allotment of cavalry, the *rabhsayum* had demanded surrender of the breeding stock. Kargul's refusal had led to civil war, the War of the Royal Stud, but although defeated the province had managed to hide some untreated stallions in a remote mountain-valley, and to this day continued to breed its illicit *pefral*, and to mount iilicit squadrons.

Kargul, nevertheless, remained careful to treat its colts, in part because a virile stallion was often impossible to break to the saddle, or might be subject to sudden outbursts of ungovernable wildness, but also, as Tovakh had explained to a youthful Kamin-Tolagh, because it would be an embarrassment to Kargul if, while on escort duty in Kadon Dinul, one of their supposedly sterile *pefral* covered a mare and sired a foal.

Now, so as to breed fighting-horses for himself, Kamin-Tolagh, on his brief visit to the province, had raided the stud, leading away a dozen stallions. Breeding of true *pefral* required *pefrayul*, tall, big-boned mares of their own kind, but it would have been impracticable to steal enough mares for his purposes, and mated with ordinary mares, the *pefral* would sire splendid, strong colts, in some ways preferable; Vinilat of Dramal, famous for his hunting, habitually used a half-*pefrai* in the chase, praising its stamina and manageability. Kamin-Tolagh was amused that while their visitor, Idmas, had been keeping his eyes open for evidence of *jinzal*, he had been conducted right past the start of the breeding of warhorses, in newly-irrigated grassland at the far end of the Abu.

In the letter, the reference to his father's anger came in a passage where Dolvid was evidently trying to warn him Tovakh was putting pressure on the *rabhsai*, to have him, Kamin-Tolagh, declared an outlaw. In effect to say, time for him to make his peace with the *rabhsai* was not unlimited, leading to the proposal for a meeting with Dolvid at Drin Navuna with a date designated. *Or as soon thereafter as can be arranged*, Dolvid had judiciously added, realizing his message would be delayed by the Landegh summer; his originally proposed date was now only ten days away.

"This so-called meeting at the Frontier may be nothing but a ruse to take you prisoner."

"Nonsense," though the thought had occurred to him. "If Rodlakh does give safe-conduct, he would die sooner than see it violated."

"You think the *rabhsai* will come to Drin Navuna to meet with you?" He sounded skeptical. "He has a new baby; the *rabhsayu* has borne him a son."

"That news is stale. I heard it from Huolafidn, who got it from his *Hrithust*, who heard it at Thenimala. The boy must be a half-year old by now."

"Then you think the *rabhsai* will come?" swift to mask his pique at not having been told.

"No," Kamin-Tolagh decided. "Dolvid."

"Well, then," as if a point had been clearly demonstrated. "What would there be to stop him having you captured — killed, even — and then telling the *rabhsai* any story he cared to invent? If you knew this man as the Heartland Families do — "

Kamin-Tolagh yawned, an involuntary, not a deliberate yawn, but it could not have been better timed to express his boredom with Lavsila's obsessions. "My not being there would stop it," he muttered, but would not confirm that as his intention when Lavsila tried to press him. He was not sure he had any intentions.

Despite the wine, despite earlier enjoyment in baiting Idmas, he felt flat, feebly challenged by an artificial dilemma. In reality, as against wild imaginings, he would never have expected approval at Kadon Dinul for his scheme to make a new province out of half-accidental conquests here in the Farther West, and yet he was not prepared for a choice so complete and final; he was being asked to choose between halves of himself. Absorbed by unendingly various problems in trying to make a self-sustaining and eventually prosperous though not necessarily peaceable state out of a fragile coalition of impoverished tribes, intrigued by a story whose end could not be foreseen, his fascination was still that of a Karguli, an Owani, a man of Rodlakh's realm.   He could no more contemplate final renunciation of his birthplace than he could imagine turning his back on the accomplishments and preoccupations of the past year.

Careful still, Dolvid, or the circle that helped construct the letter signed by the *Bôdhrai*, had taken that reluctance into account, suggesting the *rabhsai*, not wishing to cause the tribes of Froghushei any undue hardship, might for a time make available supplies of food and other needed materials so as to ease any difficulties caused by withdrawal of `*the undoubted benefits your presence among them has conferred*,' surely a faintly mocking reference to the claims made in his letter to Dolvid. But the offer stopped short of an actual promise; careful, careful, careful. Kamin-Tolagh had fought a war in alliance with risk-takers, apparently to make the realm safe for the prudent, not least the prudent men and women all the other gamblers had turned into, Dolvid, Shumat, Rodlakh, even Âna, once most daring of all.

14.

In the outer room to the Personal Suite, Dolvid came near bumping into Âna, who had just emerged from the royal apartments. "Your pardon. I was looking for Faëdhal."

She was skeptical. "Is something troubling you?"

"I have not yet thanked him for his birthday gift to Sedukh. He found a bell-ball, such as has not been made since Plakhsila's time."

She smiled a little at the evasion. "Faëdhal was with Orbanak."

"So I was told. I seldom can make time to see him nowadays."

"But Orbanak hurried off to sword-lessons with Dorrmas, and Faëdhal went away muttering about degenerate times."

They both laughed. The Master of Tongues, Dolvid's old friend and colleague, saw distressing implications in the taste of his chief pupil, Rodlakh's younger brother, for swords and lances as against Old Owanilú or the Script of Shâl — not an unpredictable preference in a healthy boy of fourteen.

She continued to gaze at Dolvid. "Your meeting with Rodlakh and Shumat? I had meant to be there, but I was detained." In an unconscious gesture, her hand made sure her bodice was fastened.

"I thought you had a wet-nurse."

"So I have. But once a day, at least, it pleases me — " she paused, and made a loose-wristed, circling gesture. "To be a mother, as well as all the rest of it."

"Aëlu, too."

"Sedukh has been such a model child," abstractedly. "At times I think Lambakh must be half mad, or half-witted. Not really," she hurriedly corrected. "Only — Just now I almost said, once a day it pleases me to play at being mother. Often, it seems like that, all of it; I play at *rabhsayu*, at mother, at — magistrate."

The rather lame conclusion was, on the whole, a relief for Dolvid, whose vanity guessed at and preferred what she had nearly said. Most of the time he managed not to be alone with Âna — without a word between them on the subject, they seemed to have agreed to avoid such encounters.

"I don't know that anyone ever does more than play. What we play at long enough and earnestly enough, we may come near becoming. Only near."

"Same Dolvid," with a swift smile.   Lightly, affectionately, still an accusation against his habit of using portentous generalities as a defensive wall about his feelings.

"Even as a play-*Bôdhrai*, I am failing."

She heard rancor. "Are you angry with Rodlakh?"

"No," and then, because only truth did for Âna, "Not half as much as I am with myself. You heard about Kamin-Tolagh's reply to my letter?"

"I heard the *Kímukan* Idmas returned with no written answer."

"That was his reply." Belatedly, from his informant in Kargul, Dolvid had also heard about Kamin-Tolagh's theft of the blood-stock, another sign of intended defiance.

"Rodlakh," she added, "said hardly anything."

"At our meeting, also. He *noted* the report of Idmas, and listened to a single comment, then asked Shumat about keeping men available for road-clearing." With winter imminent, it would not have been an unreasonable subject as part of a routine general discussion; in the past heavy snows had interrupted food supplies for the capital.

"You know why. Let us talk where we shall not be interrupted — " one hand on his arm, other reaching for the side-door to her own apartments.

"I think we shall do very well here, *Asayu*," lightly pointing the honorific.

"Well," turning to seat herself on one of two long couches. "You must realize Rodlakh has to address the question of Kamin-Tolagh in his own way and his own time. He is like a man trying to come to terms with death of a brother."

"Unfortunately, it may not be his own time to spend. But I told you, I am far unhappier with myself."

He went on to recount, or recall for her, he was not sure which, the other information that had come back with Idmas, the settled nature of life at Abu Ninusai, its estimated garrison, not above three squadrons of regulars, three or so of mounted bows, and indeterminate, probably fluctuating, numbers of tribal auxiliaries, poorly mounted, whose fighting potential had not impressed Idmas. Nor could the growing-plots he had seen be adequate to supply the needs of the Abu, assuredly not to stock it against a siege.

"The obvious conclusion is that we should strike now, before he has more and better-trained squadrons, better-mounted."

"Assail Kamin-Tolagh?"

"Say, attempt to arrest him. Shumat has said how easily the Abu could become a trap for its occupants. If Kamin-Tolagh is there, we have him. If not we can occupy the place; at best he can then be waylaid when he returns, or we have deprived him of his capital. He could not hope to keep his Kargul' troops and their families with him if they are forced to live like the tribes. This could be accomplished using twenty or two dozen squadrons, entirely from the Army of the West."

"You mean, now, at once?"

"It would require some preparation, but a month into the new year would be ideal, both for the cool weather on Landegh, and the rains; if there is no immediate capitulation at the Abu we shall need water that does not have to be carried a six-day journey."

"What is Shumat's opinion?" puzzled by the disparity between the force of the arguments and lack of any in his presenting them.

"Shumat no longer needs to prove anything as to his skill or bravery; he is a soldier who would much rather make peace, but nothing I say goes against anything he has said in the past."

"Meaning, you have not spoken with him about this."

"Only in the most general terms," not very different, in these circumstances, to saying, not at all; as he himself had defined it, the current state of affairs called for questions about where to find enough feed for the horses, and who Shumat would choose as his field officers, not bland theoretical agreement on Kamin-Tolagh's relative weakness.

"But you do believe this is the right course?"

"I am not fit to be *Bôdhrai*," as if making an historical assessment. "I don't *know* we can capture Kamin-Tolagh so easily; only Kamin-Tolagh *knows* the strength and effectiveness of his new troops; he just might be able to break a siege of the Abu with a relief force, and that would mean our total defeat; no one could manage a successful retreat across the entire width of Landegh."

"War has its uncertainties. A *bôdhrai* is not expected to be a seer."

Dolvid, without joy, laughed. "On the way to Dônshei, when Rodlakh's accession was still in doubt, Dorrmas began telling me all the things that could go wrong. I told him, there comes a time when all *ifs* must be put aside. But if we had not fought and won at Dônshei, no help could have come to Rodlakh; we would have lost the Jinzai War."

She contemplated for a moment, palms pressed flat together under her chin. "What will happen if we fail to stop him? Some might say. these indications he intends a long stay are all to the good; he means to make his life there in the West."

"Do you imagine he is finished with the realm?"

"I don't understand you. You think if we do not act now — "

"We shall have a graver danger to face in years to come. A year from now, we could fail, using twice the troops and losing five times as many lives." He touched only lightly on the additional point, discussed recently with Shumat, that the increase in Kamin-Tolagh's strength would coincide with an inevitable decline in the Army of the West. That force had suffered heavy casualties in the Jinzai War, and was still below full numeric strength. It had been between the years 2920 and 2930 that Saidhan had strained relations with Kadon Dinul by expanding the Army, skirting the edges of legality in raising and training his Frontier Cavalry, and young men recruited at that time had become the veterans who fought the Short Retreat and the Long Retreat, defended Vonni's Jaws and Kamsilat. Most of those who survived would, over the next few years, be reaching their full term of service, claiming the farms that were their reward — *kímukan*, squadron and half-squadron leader, field officers, the spine of the Army. At need, they could be called back to the colors, and would willingly return if there were a new enemy knocking at the gates of Drin Navuna, but after woundings and loss of comrades in the war, many must long now for peaceful retirement. Nor was it reasonable to suppose Saidhan at ninety could play much part in rebuilding his army; loss of his soldier-son, Sebhal, was without easy remedy. Again, time was working for Kamin-Tolagh, if he meant to defy the realm.

"But you are unwilling to tell this to Rodlakh? Are you asking me to urge him to this action?"

"No, no," though for a moment it was a tempting way of avoiding direct responsibility. "I really did come here looking for Faëdhal."

"Then I'm sorry to disappoint you." She made a feint at standing to leave.

Shockingly, he had to fight off a dart of anger; as lovers they had not had time for these coquetries; to begin them now would be altogether wasteful. "You know that was not what I meant."

"No," perhaps with a hint of contrition.

Making a fresh start, he did his best to explain the dilemma. At some point, the realm would have Kamin-Tolagh to deal with; he did not tell Âna his recurrent waking dream of Rodlakh and Kamin-Tolagh as destined rivals, but without that there was plenty in logic to suggest eventual confrontation. Unless Kamin-Tolagh met with serious reverses — revolts, say, among his subject tribes, or war with an unexpectedly powerful enemy — to delay a reckoning with him was only to make it costlier in blood and treasure, the resources of the realm.

"And that is why I am not fit to be *Bôdhrai*. I am convinced I have done the sums right, but see it will require strong and sustained advocacy to get Rodlakh to agree to act. The Jinzai War was a question of outright survival — "

She stood, and was very close. "You are not willing to send men to die for anything less," a curious mixture of emotions in her voice, contempt decidedly not one of them.

Deliberately disrupting a dangerous pattern, he wheeled to pace, making vigorous, somewhat artificial gestures. "The questions become obscene, but they are what it comes down to: would you let ten men be killed today, to save the lives of a hundred next year, or a thousand five years from now? Never happily, but I or anyone would, if the hundred or the thousand deaths were a certainty."

"As you describe it, this action will not call for any levying of fresh troops; the men we would send would all be soldiers by choice, men who have knowingly chosen a profession with danger and death in it."

He had already tried that argument on himself. "I'm a fool."

"No you are not."

"No, I am not, but as *Bôdhrai* I am a cripple. I should resign the post, and go back to writing my histories."

"Yes," she mock-agreed, and a remembered humor was in her eyes. "Except the others would soon bring us all to ruin. What does Elamirr think?"

She had at last hit on the source of resentment detected from the first. "The *rabhsai*," he said, "asked him; Elamirr only — " reaching a hand to touch a bare arm, to forestall her response. "Yes, it is the *rabhsai*'s way to seek advice in all quarters, an engaging trait, except in such a case, with me standing by, where it is an affront. Elamirr is my assistant; he attends these meetings to listen, to gain experience. In any event, we all know Elamirr from the start was hanging Kamin-Tolagh as a traitor."

"Do not look for tenderness towards Kargul in southern Paowan — " but she herself came from well to the south of Burantal, Elamirr's home. "Don't you think Rodlakh knew what he would hear from that quarter?"

"Of course." At the time Dolvid had seen it as a clumsy ruse, of which Rodlakh himself might be unconscious; Elamirr's uncomplicated and unchanged opinion gave him a thin excuse for dropping the subject.

"But at least — " Âna was interrupted by an incurious servant, reminding the *rabhsayu* she was due to meet with the elders of several cities, to discuss unemployment.

Peace, increased general prosperity, and lifting of the fog of fears that had typified the last years of Ban-Sila's reign, had brought some unforeseen and distressing consequences; despite the increased number of smallholders, improved methods requiring fewer hands had done nothing to slow the drift away from the land, and those leaving came to the cities in hopes of finding work; Kadon Dinul had added numbers without real occupation, too many without proper dwellings. Scores were now housed at what had been the barracks of the Special Cavalry, just outside East Gate. Though they might require new taxes, works to the general benefit could employ numbers; for centuries there had been agreement it would be good to have a bridge across the great Paowan River much nearer Kadon Dinul than the present one north of Kred Bakali, and there were also roads in poor repair; Dolvid concurred with Âna's brother Konir that, given the money, they could readily give work to a couple of hundred, planting trees.

Partial relief was coming from an undesired source, with the great landowners taking the opportunity to expand their armed followings. These retainers, many of whom spent a portion of their time as farm laborers, were nothing like a match for regular cavalry, either in training or equipment, and no private citizen was permitted to own *pefral*. Nevertheless, there was unease in the simple existence of so many armed men. Their employers maintained the forces were needed to deal with the increase in crime, and undeniably other workless men were keeping themselves alive through robbery. Far to the northeast, the long, lonely road from Yuvakh Din to Narn was again dangerous for an unescorted riding, but even in the Heartland travellers had been waylaid and isolated houses ransacked; Shumat was reinforcing cavalry posts long understrength.

None of these problems as yet approached a crisis; as Âna said after a sigh and a grimace, the servant having departed, "Yet this would have appeared as a new Blossoming Age when we were ruled by fear under Ban-Sila, or when there were *jinzal* in the streets of Kamsilat."

Yes, but it was troubling that where there were exaggerated and opposing views on any of these subjects, as when some tried to explain away the most brutal crimes, gratuitous rapes added to robbery, or the killing of an unarmed man for his purse or his shoes, as the inevitable result of inequities, or when others called for deaths, mutilations or two-hundred lash public floggings as penalty for the theft of a loaf by a starving man, or a woman with hungry children, all too often the opinions could be divided by race. That was not to say there were not many Owanil who sought to remedy the need for crime at its root, or that most Others did not condemn vicious criminals of any origin, but of the minority who held either of the extreme opinions, the race was always perfectly predictable.

"Another reason why it would be good to tidy away the Kamin-Tolagh affair as soon as we can. You know some of the young Heartland brats have begun trying to turn him into a folk-hero, the proud Owani defying a despotic rule. Then, too, one of their kin is with him, not a hair less foolish than they. But if and when we do capture Kamin-Tolagh, Rodlakh must be careful not to make a martyr. Of either."

"Kamin-Tolagh could be killed in the field. He will not be tame to accept either defeat or captivity. Oh, Dolvid — " seizing both his hands. "Your distaste for dealing death does not make you any the less as *Bôdhrai*. I — " She struggled for a verb, and had to begin again. "I honor you for your scruples, but you have to take the lead here. If you and Shumat together press for a swift campaign, then I can use what influence I have."

Gently, he took back his hands. "I truly was looking for Faëdhal," moved by her sympathy, but suddenly embarrassed to find himself drawn into backstairs policy-making.

Her eyes at their largest held him. "It is not disloyal," firmly, "to open your heart to an old friend — nor to bring a *rabhsai* advice he would as soon not hear. He will learn that; he is younger than we are." Âna in fact was just weeks older than Rodlakh, and fifteen years younger than Dolvid, who still felt mysteriously flattered.

"And he loves you," she added. "You must not forget that."

"I'm not very good at forgetting."

Suddenly she made a sound like a suppressed sneeze, start of a giggle, quickly stifled. "He asked me whether, if we had another son, we might not name him after you." Now her frank gaze held a sort of challenge, and all at once she was deeply blushing.

"I think not." The tone was wry, but his mouth was parched.

15.

Forearms crossed, hands cupping elbows, Kamin-Tolagh tried to bring his shivering under control. A persistent wind nagged its way up the shallow declivity where they had made camp, a wind of no substance, with the unnatural power of piercing all shields, it reached the small of his back through sleeping-bag, outshirt, tunic and body-linen; for sleep, he had removed nothing except his boots. Fuel was scarce, watchfires small and guttering, and from time to time the wind would gather itself for a gust in which tiny pellets of snow came stinging.

Nothing had prepared them for such cold anywhere in this sun-parched West, surely not here, by estimate of the map-maker, Dubovai, farther south than any part of the distant realm, except perhaps the port of Thenimala, white and green under unfailing sun by its sapphire bay, a place where lemons grew, oranges, sweet early peaches and fat figs.

Kamin-Tolagh envied the Hill Froghul under Tau-Suaka's command, or at least those on the inside of the compact masses into which they huddled, like colonies of bees in winter. Where there is no remedy, cold, he grimly decided, beyond even hunger or pain of a wound, could become the whole universe, a consuming obsession.

Which he must not allow, not with this expedition going wrong in unpredictable ways. He had begun with a rather vague but not senseless plan, and enormous confidence in his luck, which for the past two years had seemed inexhaustible. In the cold, a twinge in the scar along his chin reminded him of another time when he had come very near overspending good fortune.

But his luck was still there when *Hrithust* Iolfrant, or Huolafidn, acting on his own and blaming his master, had provided him with an excuse or vague precedent for his intended action. At Lavsila's suggestion, Kamin-Tolagh had imposed a landing-fee for the ships of the Hrin when they came to Larghamit. A token amount, the proceeds could not have paid a single trooper, much less defrayed the expense of keeping a half-squadron at the port, but with incomprehensible parsimony Huolafidn and his colleagues began beaching their vessels on the foreshore just to the west of where Kamin-Tolagh had set his frontier. A new fee for crossing that border could have been set, but although irritated he let it rest; when there was enough business to make it worthwhile, he would levy a tax on transactions, but in the meantime he could use the example the Hrin had set.

By this time he knew the Hrin maintained, somewhere on the long westward shore of Flamûrai, a station where they traded for gold, mostly in dust form, brought from an unexplored interior by men of the wild. Wheat, apparently, either as grain or ground into meal, was a chief trading commodity, which helped explain Huolafidn's premature eagerness to obtain it from Kamin-Tolagh, as also the long journeys the Hrin made to Thenimala to bring back grain. But simple tools and weapons were also traded, if not, as in Dvasslo's tales, for their weight in gold. From his unguarded utterances Lavsila learned the Hrin, with their timid ways, laid claim to no territory beyond the limits of their small trading-station, and Kamin-Tolagh concluded if he could find the place, described as the mouth of a considerable river, nothing could stop him from establishing his own post to landward of Iolfrant's; there were picks, spades, hoes and plowshares at the Abu for trading, and more could be forged; also a quantity of coarse, bright cloth the *jinzai*-breeders had used in dealings with the tribes, which Iruvakh assured him would be coveted by any primitive folk. Later, when he had an idea how the land lay, Kamin-Tolagh might seize the source of the gold, or subdue the wild men who had it to trade, incorporate them into his empire.

Iruvakh, with his ear for languages and quickness in adapting to unfamiliar customs, would have been useful on the expedition, but with brief rainy season and the planting coming on, critical time for establishment of improved growing practices, he would be needed in the Froghushei. Kamin-Tolagh had not wanted to delay, for fear of excessive heat when summer came, but had not foreseen a journey into high, chilled mountain country where deep snow could be found.

His selection of troops was more complicated; Freighanai and the personal squadron had always been with him when he rode to new lands, but it was dispersed now, most of its file and half-file leaders acting as squadron officers with tribal levies. He had also to leave behind some trustworthy leaders of good sense and unquestioned loyalty, in case Kadon Dinul took advantage of the cooler months to launch an assault — an event which seemed likelier with every mile Kamin-Tolagh distanced himself from its probable target.

Shivering on his mountainside, he wondered what was happening now at the Abu, what even Kambanal and Freighanai might do, if Shumat came, at the head of a mass of cavalry. In Kamin-Tolagh's absence, for what should the men of Kargul fight, knowing the *rabhsai*'s quarrel was with him and no one else? Seriously doubting his hardiness for a long and difficult journey, Kamin-Tolagh had also left Lavsila behind, as he plainly preferred, and he was quite capable of opening negotiations with the *rabhsai*'s captain, more, of using his eloquence to persuade the men of Kargul to decline a fight they were going to lose. None of this could be helped; leadership of this expedition could not be entrusted to anyone else, nor his empire in any case endure without a new source of wealth.

It had appeared simple: the trading-station of Iolfrant was where a big river opened on Flamûrai, a place which must eventually be encountered if, crossing at the head of the gulf, he turned southward and followed the coast, keeping the water at his left hand.

Nizhadh, tonight's duty officer, who had been kneeling next to one of the small fires, came to where Kamin-Tolagh half-sat, carrying something heavy. A sudden smell of scorching linen, a lunatic reminder of the washroom in the Great House at Inilun Barabhi, women taking irons from on top of the stove, making spit bounce on them to test their heat, before attacking wrinkles in half-dried shirts. "Take this, *Asai*," the weathered little man said. "Careful, now; keep it covered." It was a roundish stone, warmed through, and wrapped in a spare outshirt. Gratefully, Kamin-Tolagh pushed it down his sleeping-bag till its warmth was at his icy feet.

"Tomorrow, we'll sleep warmer." Nizhadh's face was too shadowed to see whether he was joking.

After Yaënsilat, he was senior among only nine men of Kargul included in the expedition, most acting as squadron and half-squadron leaders for the one hundred and fifty Hill Froghul bowmen, though Dubovai, always busy making notes and sketches for his maps, had no other duties, except to take his turn with the watch. Days ago, when they passed through the ruins of Larghamit, he had conjectured the faint westward continuation of the trail must follow the line of the ancient Imperial road, and miles ahead swing to the southward into the heart of lands once called the Kufshei. A long journey to the south, that road had ended at the farthest of all frontiers of Owan, Gronu Kizh'klaëdhiyu, a mountain pass where the great Larghai had fought a famous defensive battle, and slaughtered, songs said, the manhood of five confederated tribes.

Momentarily tempted at the chance of a well-defined way south, Kamin-Tolagh had decided it ran too far inland for his purpose; there was a chance, however slight, that the Hrin trading station lay to the northward of the old frontier, in which case they could easily miss it entirely. Yet his determination to

remain within sight of Flamûrai was quickly thwarted by the
ground; foreshore becoming a maze and torment of rocky pillars,
mounting to cliffs and soon impassable. Finding no way by
which their mounts and pack-train could scale the cliffs, they had
to backtrack, but passage to landward had been frustrated by
clefts, ravines, and then a dangerous swathe of stinking salt-
marsh. Again forced inland, they had been barred from sight of
the gulf by a line of coastal hills, steadily rising, which on the
eighth day after leaving Larghamit swung sharply westward to
bar any further progress to the south.

For four days beyond that now they had struggled along
rocky skirts of what became a wall of mountains with no gate;
clambering high in their search for a pass they had reached the
fringes of snow, and there had been too much retracing of steps,
many places where they had to dismount and lead their stumbling
horses. Even when they rode, the Hill Froghul' rode silent, no
longer breaking into song or swapping jokes and lighthearted
insults, as they had at the outset. This night, having climbed
higher than before into what they hoped was a pass and turned
into another dead end, they were camped far above the foothills,
but with jagged and snowy peaks towering over them.

Not yet too late to turn back. Northward, beyond and
beneath the rocky land where there were blind gullies and sudden
drops, tumbles of loose scree where no horse could be risked,
glimpses of a less savage country where a way could surely be
made; without retracing their westward route, it should be
possible to pick a way back, with loss only to prestige, to the
legend of Kamin-Tolagh's invariable success. Yet if he returned
without gold, very soon he would be unable to keep the promises
made to the men who had chosen to stay with him, some
bringing their wives and children here.

Nearby, Yaënsilat was sleeping, untroubled. Tough as old
cheese — so Kambanal had once affectionately described him —
and his temperament was ideal; after a lifetime of soldiering
extending well beyond the term which would have earned him

honorable retirement, nothing upset the wry set of mind that turned complaint into a humor to invite sharing; in the wetlands he had told an uncharacteristically bad-tempered Luzhan, if roads could be paved with curses, stonecutters would starve — a side-reference to the near-proverbial foul-mouthedness of roadmakers, a thing most boys of decent family heard about from their mothers, often between blows, at some point in their growing up. Because of their relative ages, Kamin-Tolagh had almost brought Kambanal instead, but Yaënsilat had borne the hardships of this journey physically as well as any younger man, helping to haul the pack-train up rocky, shifting slopes the animals had declined to cross, accepting heat and cold, fatigue and thirst with the same imperturbable practicality. Prospect of having to admit failure made Kamin-Tolagh all the gladder of his choice. Kambanal's streak of sentimentality was no handicap to performance, but he seemed genuinely to live in a realm of legends, where the purpose of difficulties was to test and prove a man's ability to overcome them, and he would never have understood a decision to turn back; told their supplies had dwindled near the point where return was no longer feasible, Kambanal would have wished to press on, and make a new epic out of heroic futility. His passionate belief in Kamin-Tolagh could be a heavy burden for its object, who did not think his chances of undying fame would be lessened by staying alive. Yaënsilat, told they were giving up, would make a glum face, shrug, and say they would do better next time.

Beyond the question of immediate personal survival, however, Kambanal's romantic view might paradoxically represent hard-headed reality; if Kamin-Tolagh failed here, he could not see how empire could go on. Without the prospect of wealth, he was not sure why he should want it to.

A succession of days followed, the same for their tedium and exasperating tale of checks and reverses. The column remained high on the mountain-flanks, and any southward progress was because the line of the range bent slightly in that direction. There was no reachable gap, and at times he had a vision of leading a nomad band, wandering forever in these unrewarding uplands. In provisioning the expedition, he had counted on reaching some sort of inhabited parts, where food could be obtained, if necessary by force. Here, where melting snows fed icy streams, there was no danger from thirst, but feed for the animals was becoming very short, and no sign of human habitation had been since leaving the shores of Flamûrai, where, second day beyond Larghamit, they had encountered a knot of small, impoverished huts belonging to a dark, stunted folk, too preoccupied with their search for shellfish to do much but glance up with minimal interest as the column of horsemen rode by. Here, on the bare bones of a bleak world, there was small chance of replenishing supplies; there was no game, and the only birds apart from a small, flitting swift or martin were eagles seen circling well off to the northward, or returning to inaccessible eyries on their economical wings.

　　　Near evening of the day he had decided must be their last before attempting to find a better way home, they came to the pass. First inkling of its existence was a distant rush deepening to a roar, too incessant for wind, the sound of falling water. The fall was larger and farther than they first assumed; several times, sound growing, they were certain the next negotiation of a turn, breasting of the next rise, must bring them in sight of the water, and were disappointed. At last, the fairly level rocky shelf on which the column had been marching came to an abrupt, precipitous end, at a deep cleft where the roar of water, still invisible, echoed sonorously. In the bottom of the cleft, hundreds of near-vertical feet below, ran what could only be a well-worn trail.

　　　Necessary once again to backtrack, pick a meandering and tedious way down to where at last stands of brush grew among rocky outcrops, and they could descend to the trail, which wound up from the north, and climbed to vanish into the curving cleft. All the men were glad to be back where going was comparatively straightforward, and Nizhadh, as if this signalled end of their difficulties, was unexpectedly exultant, but Kamin-Tolagh exchanged a grimly rueful glance with Dubovai, knowing what his thoughts must be.

The hoarse rush of water grew yet louder as they climbed the narrow corridor, and at a sharp turn past jut of a knife-edged cliff, they were looking up from deepening shadow to a slender ribbon of waterfall, struck by the setting sun. From a high, worn ledge, it dropped with only one glancing deflection from a projecting knob, a distance Dubovai estimated at six hundred feet, shattering into boiling clouds of mist, and a descending fan of lesser falls soon lost to sight among rocks, shadows and spurts of green growth.

By Kamin-Tolagh's elbow, Luzhan, youngest of the men of Kargul here, exclaimed, "A pillar of gold! Some would call that an omen, *Asai*." But it must be solely at sunset the falls were golden; this could only be Gronu Kizh'klaëdhiyu, Pass of the Silver Spear.

He turned to Dubovai. "In the days of the Empire, do you recall how many dayrides Larghamit to this last frontier?"

"Not exactly, *Asai*," a little nervously. "I know there was a garrison-town, Iska-something, in central Kufshei, and that was three full dayrides beyond Larghamit, so it must have been about as far again to this place."

Kamin-Tolagh nodded. Those dayrides were for cavalry or messengers on good mounts, and the road, still showing signs of use, would have been kept in excellent repair in those early days, but with every allowance for deterioration of the route and the slower pace of their pack-train, they could not be above nine to twelve days beyond Larghamit, a point it had taken them nineteen to reach: no getting back those wearisome and taxing days.

At the head of the pass was a widening, and the level there was a small patch of luxuriant forest under a constant drizzle of spray. Above, high on the north-facing wall, they had been at the edge of winter; here, open suddenly to warm air pressing from the south, the evening was of spring, or early summer. Pleasant to be under dripping trees, and the horses bowed gratefully to the rank grasses; near the water Kamin-Tolagh with a shock recognized the gross under-foliage of trees as nothing but linden-leaves, grown to gigantic size, some as large as the serving-platter for a whole piglet at a feast. On that side, below the falls, there was a dark, polished pool fed by many trickles and spurts of cold water, and nearby was a favorite camping-place, to judge by the ashes and scorch of many past fires, a sandy stretch kept dry by the overhang of massive grey-brown rock face, which also oddly muted the roar of the falls.

To the question of Yaënsilat, Kamin-Tolagh nodded, they would spend the night here. With Dubovai and Nizhadh he walked down to where the ground fell away more steeply on the southern side, and foam-flecked water glid smoothly over a broad rim, start of a stream that meandered away, somewhat west of due south. Though light was failing, the river's course for miles could be traced by denser growth along its banks, standing out in a landscape otherwise only stippled with bushes and low-spreading trees. Far off to the southwest like the most ominous of thunderclouds, the dark mass of other high mountains rose.

"The trail," Dubovai, pointing, "runs beside the river. It must lead somewhere, *Asai*."

Kamin-Tolagh grunted, but his gaze was scanning leftward, where any distant prospect was prevented by a line of low hills, rounded but with their tops flattened as if they had been planed off. He must be miles now from the gulf, and while the trail would obviously make for easier going, the old objection was stronger than before; by following a course so far inland they risked missing their objective altogether.

As the three returned up the slope to where Yaënsilat had disposition of the campsite capably in hand, they passed near scattered remains of some structure of cut stone, inscription on the stump of a pillar too weathered to be read. Dubovai turned for another look at the country southward. "Somewhere there, *Asai*, Larghai had his only defeat."

"So said the envious," Kamin-Tolagh corrected, memories of ancient lessons stirring into life. "Others doubt the forces he led were ever meant as a serious army of invasion. From the first, his intention was to spy out the country and then withdraw." Withdraw *here*, a dreamlike thought; at these rocks, beneath this same waterfall, Larghai's army, undeniably harried by vastly more numerous enemies, had turned like a cornered beast and bared its claws, and enemy dead were piled six deep in heaps, *here*.

"I have heard that also, *Asai*," Dubovai said, absorption in notes for his maps making it sound satirical.

A new point of desperation was reached when, with hesitation and extreme repugnance, Kamin-Tolagh gave permission for the Hill Froghul to kill a couple of now-unburdened pack-animals for meat. An Owani, not merely an Owani but a Karguli, not any Karguli but a highborn *péfrapravádai* of western Kargul, he was unsure he could eat horse-flesh if it came to a choice between that and starvation, but while still well short of Iruvakh's exaggerated refusal to condemn, he had learned to tolerate or to ignore many ways that would never be his, and the despised meat-feast of Tau-Suaka's men left more of the kiln-bread and jerked beef to be doled out to his officers. Those men, sharing much of his upbringing, he did not expect to condone devouring of horsemeat, but with the stench of scorching flesh blanketing the camp, he was still startled by their anger and disgust; even old Yaënsilat muttered against the greed and uncouthness of their allies. No doubt patience had worn away in the frustrations of their journey, and

no doubt an unbidden envy fed their bad temper; Kamin-Tolagh
himself felt hunger as well as revulsion when he saw and smelled
the roasting joints.

All these unpleasant feelings were made worse by
knowledge they had once again wasted days on a useless
meander, and in doing so turned aside from where food would
certainly have been found. In the first day beyond the pass,
marching now under warm skies, it became obvious any
settlements of people would not be far from the river; before
encountering their first huddle of huts, the soldiers glimpsed fish-
traps and places where trees had been recently felled. Though
evidently primitive, the river-folk knew enough to keep watch,
and to be warned in time to abandon their rickety dwellings
before the column arrived; not till the third or fourth such
waterside hamlet did Kamin-Tolagh have a sight of the small,
drably-clad men, or attempt communication with them. No
tongue spoken by any of the expedition was understood;
knowing the traditional history of his Man-mani, Kamin-Tolagh
supposed the language here would be akin to theirs, but was
without Iruvakh — or young Chamya — to test that theory.

Nevertheless, offer of some squares of the bright cloth the
expedition was carrying for trade obtained fresh fish and an
unfamiliar stalk-vegetable, which looked like celery or unripe
rhubarb, but had the taste of bitter cabbage. The encouragement
this small purchase of food gave was more than balanced by
Kamin-Tolagh's concern over the continued slow westward curve
of the river's general course, and when, late in the day, they came
to a branching of ways, a smaller but well-defined track heading
southeast, evidently making for a gap in the endless brown ridge,
he decided they must leave the river in hopes of getting back to
the coast, and whatever chance remained of finding the Hrin
trading-station.

The trail led them into a bare, tumbled country, and
eventually to a small fishing village on low cliffs, which, to
crushing disappointment, faced southward on the water; they had

returned to the coast of Flamûrai where it ran back to the west in a vast bay. An entire day was used to reach where the coast resumed a mainly southerly direction, and there the march was again forced inland by impassable terrain. Only first of several glimpses of the shore, as again and again they interrupted the southward march to take ways that led promisingly eastward, each time reaching only small settlements of coastal people too wretched to replenish their supplies, unable to comprehend questions asked in sign-language about gold, or visitors from the other side of the water.

Now they were struggling on only because they could no longer save themselves by turning back. Dubovai, though he grumbled about all the changes of direction which made distances hard to calculate, continued assiduously to collect sightings for his maps; Yaënsilat with his one lapse over the horse-flesh, remained calm and workmanlike and the other men of Kargul took their tone from him. Tau-Suaka glanced darkly over at Kamin-Tolagh more and more often, but was too proud of his time with the Army of the West to do other than soldier on, and under his eye and that of his whip-wielding kinsman, Hunghi, the Hill Froghul stayed the course, though Kamin-Tolagh suspected that given their choice they would have headed back for the river-country, and reverted to the old raiding ways.

Endurance was near its limit when, struggling over high, domed hills, they came to a kinder part. In stunted woods, they could only follow a trodden path which led to headwaters of a small stream, trail continuing on its left side. Choice no longer played a part; fording tributary rills, they marched down beside the swift-running stream as it grew, at last spilling into a substantial river, path a tunnel through what were thornlands rather than woodlands, still holding to the muddy bank. Unvaried, it stretched on for miles, and in this dark unwholesome place they were at last obliged to make overnight camp. They woke in clammy fog, and the morning march was sweaty and despondent, river-mists reluctant to lift, though a hot sun behind ignited them into a white glare.

Then the brambles began to thin and part, and the stream, curving more southerly from its south-easterly course, widened and merged into the brown, unclear waters of a far greater river, larger, pewrhaps, than the Navu at Kamsilat. Not a mile eastward, it opened into the unbounded, glistening waters of what could only be Flamûrai, if not the Southern Ocean itself. The place was so much what he had imagined that again it was as if his dream had created reality. Crowning what must be a man-made mound just to landward of the estuary's brown sands was a small village, not unlike that of the Man-mani, except this was fenced with dense thorn. Beyond, the curve of a slight, pale-grassed headland was neatly walled with upright palings, enclosing, under a small cluster of shade trees, three low, white structures of painted stone or masonry, plainly not of tribal construction, though their roofs were of broad-leafed thatch. To dispel any doubt this was the trading-station, at least two twin-hulled Hrin vessels were drawn up where the compound embraced its section of beach.

"Where do they think they are," Yaënsilat murmured, as the column in fours rounded the flats to ride between village and water, "the Avenue of Treaties? — " an allusion to the lack of vigilance. "Or does this vanga-banga-ranga business guard them?"

At just that moment a dozen helmed heads and the tips of bows became visible behind the palings of the stockade. The guards were darker-faced than Hrin, and without their chinless appearance, probably, like Kamin-Tolagh's main force, tribal auxiliaries.

Tau-Suaka's eyes gleamed as he gestured for his men to ready their own small, powerful bows. "Shall we kill them, Lord?" hopefully.

"Not unless they first shoot at us." With his bowmen, he was confident of winning any duel. But when the tide was out, as now, a frontal challenge was absurd; compound fence, ending well above the water, could be bypassed on the firm, brown estuary sands.

Assigning a squadron under Nizhadh to stay with the pack-train, Kamin-Tolagh issued careful instructions, keeping an admonitory eye on the war-hungry Tau-Suaka. What was required here was not a bloody victory, but swift, concerted action to overawe. From what he knew of their character, he doubted any Hrin that were here would fight, even if some of their hired soldiers were killed, being men who most likely subscribed to neither *dveyust-ranga-hrindan* nor the other one. In any event, Hrin were not to be killed unless it became unavoidable; Kamin-Tolagh would preserve as long as he could the fiction of friendly intent.

The unfurled Siv'loi Banner flapping in the van, weary mounts urged to a canter, the column passed between end of the stockade and edge of the water. As they did, the guards stepped down from the fence, one man trying to loose an arrow on the run, while two others dropped to one knee to bend their bows. All the shots were very wide, and the running man crashed down with at least two arrows in him. The other guards fled for cover, one with a shaft through his shoulder.

Two of the white buildings looked like storehouses, walls with few windows. The third and largest, more habitable, was made imposing by broad, shallow steps up to a central double door, and had guards on its entrance, once again not Hrin, armed with swords, which were drawn. Hardly knowing he was doing it, Kamin-Tolagh made an instant professional assessment; dark sheen of the blades meant good steel, unquestionably Upper Dakbân. Excellence of weapons was not enough to inspire suicidal courage; as they saw the numbers they faced the guards began letting their swords droop, then drop, clattering, to the ground.

Before Kamin-Tolagh could dismount, the double-doors swung outward, and four men, all Hrin, emerged. Most important among them, hand up to shade his eyes from bright sun rippling through trees not yet fully in leaf, was about fifty, solidly build, proud bearing to make the best of his moderate height. He must have just put on the brocaded, high-collared tunic; the day was too warm to wear such a garment except ceremonially. Unlike his guards or the three men flanking him, he declined to show any fear of bows ranged in an arc about him. Abruptly, Kamin-Tolagh recognized one of the subsidiary figures as the trader Huolafidn, and that told him this leader must be the *Hrithust* Iolfrant.

Kamin-Tolagh gestured to Tau-Suaka to have his men lower their weapons, and at once took the moral offensive. "Why?" he shouted, "Who has instructed your guards to shoot their arrows at friendly forces?" Astonishingly, he found his anger becoming real.

Freighanai said, "We were not certain it was you, at first, *Asai*. You are very thin," he explained apologetically. By chance, he was at Larghamit when Huolafidn's boat beached, and a broad smile had come to the normally mournful face when, riding down to the foreshore at head of a half-squadron, he recognized Kamin-Tolagh.

"We were obliged to miss a dinner or two." For the reticent Freighanai to comment on his appearance meant he must be gaunt indeed. "How is it you are leading a patrol in person? Is there trouble at the Abu?"

"Not trouble, *Asai*, to say, *trouble* — " sideways slewing of his glance indicated he would have further to say about this. "Truth is, I took this patrol out of boredom, and to give my *pefrai* exercise. I didn't understand my orders were to stay all the time at the Abu, *Asai*."

"It is well," Kamin-Tolagh assured him, relieved of his worst fears. For an instant he had imagined an attack by Rodlakh's forces, and that these two dozen were all the troops left to him here.

Newly mounted, leading his travel-worn and perhaps seasick *pefrai*, he made the short ride to the cavalry post where he spent the night, and heard added news from Freighanai. Kambanal had been down in Man-mani country or south of there, training levies; Iruvakh had rarely been seen at the Abu, but had found time for some minor quarrels with various officers of Kargul over his claimed priority in use of men during the important planting season.

"And Lavsila?"

"Lavsila is Lavsila, as always, *Asai*," cautiously.

Pressed, he got up courage to offer the opinion it would be better in Kamin-Tolagh's absence if the army men had a clearer idea of Lavsila's authority.

"If I made him my *Bôdhrai*?"

"He seems to think he's that already, *Asai*. Well, but other times — "

"Would he have the confidence of the army?"

"Of the army?" Invited to speak as a captain, Freighanai evasively took refuge in a long-familiar style. "Some in the army give him too much confidence, it seems to me, *Asai*. Wine-talk as it all may be."

"You can tell me your thoughts."

"Thing is, he's a man of authority, *Asai*, so what he says carries that much more weight."

"What that he says?"

"A file-leader, Nuvakh, *Asai* — "

"I know the man." Tall, long-necked, rather countrified.

"Nuvakh told me Lavsila told him — well, it's all marshfire, *Asai*, and there was nobody to say for sure when or whether we would see you again, being well past the four weeks you said you would be, *Asai* — "

This was reminiscent of trying to pick up a bead of quicksilver between finger and thumb. Kamin-Tolagh guessed, "If Shumat and his armies came, it would be foolish for men who had no quarrel with the *rabhsai* to get themselves killed, not even knowing whether I was still alive."

Freighanai gaped as if he had second sight, but for Kamin-Tolagh the coming-true of so obvious a prophecy had him struggling to hide fury.

"They had been drinking, *Asai*. But the acting-squadron, Antighal, says Lavsila said, if you, pardon me, were to be declared an outlaw, the oaths we all took when we joined the cavalry would make us your enemy, otherwise we would all be outlaws, too. Strange thoughts come, *Asai*, when... " This thought was completed with an awkward shrug, and Kamin-Tolagh read *when men doubt whether their master is alive or dead.*

"Only one step beyond that," with heroic serenity, "is that others could earn forgiveness, maybe, by changing allegiance." With effort, he made a small laugh. "When the malcontents were still with us, Talfoyan and the rest, Lavsila and I spoke about how some hero might think he could earn Rodlakh's favor, or my father's, by attempting to take me hostage. Not much more than a joke."

"Well, as you know, I can enjoy a joke, too, *Asai*," he said, a dubious proposition. "In their cups, *Asai*, men boast about how they're going to win a bout at swords with Dorrmas, or bed with some great lady. Only that, being Lavsila and what he is, soldiers, when they have no war to fight, are worse than any weekwife for gossip, and things said lightly are taken wrong, *Asai*."

Freighanai's task was impossible; he was doing his best to reassure, while not backing away from his dislike and distrust of Lavsila.

"But he is right, all the same. No one can be bound by conflicting oaths. I intend to devise a new oath of loyalty to me, explicitly renouncing any prior allegiance. Anyone unable to pledge himself wholly to me will be permitted, as before, to return." He watched Freighanai sidelong. "But they will not see any gold."

"Gold, *Asai*?" No one was immune.

"The *Hrithust* Iolfrant is sharing his gold with us."

"Then he is your prisoner," Freighanai concluded, and as a refinement or second guess, "your hostage."

"Not at all; my partner, our ally. Iolfrant is a man in whom sense outweighs courage; facing three squadrons of mounted bows, he soon agreed we had as much right as he to trade for gold. I came back north in the ship of his subject, Huolafidn."

On returning here to the Abu and to the Great House, not wanting to wait while food was prepared, he had made a substantial evening meal of cold meat and fresh bread, with some of the sweet fruits that had come with him from the south.

"What was Iolfrant doing there? He does not conduct his own trading?"

A cogent question, and Kamin-Tolagh had soon judged Iolfrant's presence was no less a surprise to most of the Hrin; notwithstanding extreme agitation caused by Kamin-Tolagh's unexpected arrival, there remained an edgy tension between Huolafidn and his *Hrithust*, and at last, in private talk, Iolfrant, who had excellent command of ordinary language, admitted he had been disappointed lately with the amounts of gold coming in, and had arrived here without prior announcement, to see if he could discover what was wrong.

"Or, who was cheating him."

For once, Lavsila's habit of suspecting the worst was justified. By this time Iolfrant had reconciled to the inevitability of Kamin-Tolagh sharing in the gold, and his admission was to serve a shrewd purpose; he was warning there were limits, both to profits Kamin-Tolagh could expect, and to his own acceptance of diminished receipts. But perhaps he hoped Kamin-Tolagh would help stop the leak for him, so in the end he would not lose much by the enforced partnership.

"If there has been cheating, the same people are going to steal from us, from you. You could have driven out the Hrin altogether, and taken it all for yourself."

As so many times before, Kamin-Tolagh was more than irritated, was exasperated to the point of disgust, that a man so vain about his acumen could be so simple-minded. "All what? Can you tell me how you would go about trading for gold? Would you recognize gold if you saw it?"

He got up, and went to where he had hung his saddlebags over the back of a chair. Pulling out a small drawstring bag of goatskin, remarkably heavy for its size, he tipped part of the contents out on a piece of parchment in front of Lavsila.

"Sand?" Lavsila gratifyingly said, just as Kamin-Tolagh had at first sight of the dull, coarse yellow grains.

"Feel the weight. It is gold." But that was a thing he had to take on trust; at the trading-station, the Hrin had a man who with scales and bottled fluids was able to test what was brought in trade, and at once calculate its value.

Not the only consideration. The estuary was only a few days' sail from Iolfrant's lands, and ships, moreover, carried their supplies; the Hrin were reluctant to fight, but if ejected entirely from their foothold on the westward shore of Flamûrai, would predictably return in greater force to take it back. Not a stupid man, the *Hrithust* Iolfrant must see that without ships of his own, Kamin-Tolagh had no means to carry on large-scale warfare in so distant a place — just as the Hrin could not hope to fight him here. It was the tale of *The Bold Fish and the Brave Hare*; in that story, the two creatures with much bragging taunted and defied each other, both knowing it meant nothing.

He did not need telling it was a precarious arrangement, of its nature unstable, but two years was the soonest he could expect tribal armies worthy of his confidence. With sixty squadrons under arms, he would risk provoking the Hrin to war — part of the Hrin, so long as they remained divided by their absurd beliefs — but for now he hoped Iolfrant, left with over half the gold, would continue to shirk open conflict.

"To me, this alliance is similar to some Heartland marriages, held together by property, not esteem."

"If a man is useful to us," pointedly, "we do not need to look too closely at what might be in his heart. There are precautions we can take against treachery." Clear from certain glances Lavsila was trying to outlast Freighanai here, so as to be alone with Kamin-Tolagh, no doubt hoping to give a carefully tailored version of his behavior in Kamin-Tolagh's absence. Typically, at a guess, he would have been *keeping watch on the soldiers' loyalty*, going so far as to bait them with near-seditious words, to see how they responded. But he would have wanted his account to come first, and that Kamin-Tolagh must have already heard something made it much more difficult for Lavsila, not knowing exactly what.

"True, true," lamely.

Freighanai said, "Are we to keep a garrison there, where the gold is, *Asai*?"

"I persuaded Iolfrant with the demonstrated inadequacy of his tribal auxiliaries, it would be better if we took over defense of Zelu Bablakhi."

"Zelu — ?"

"Bablakhi, so Dubovai named it." It meant, Estuary of Gold, and sounded a little like the tribal name the Hrin used and had tried without success to teach Kamin-Tolagh.

Command there, he had decided, would be a rotating duty for officers of Kargul. "Yaënsilat remains there now, with a single squadron from Tau-Suaka's men, under Hunghi. Later, we may use local levies, but train them better than the Hrin did."

"One squadron?" Ever since Kamin-Tolagh disembarked with a dozen Hill Froghul under Tau-Suaka, and only two men of Kargul, Freighanai had been trying to nerve himself to ask where the others were.

Kamin-Tolagh grinned. "No, we had no losses. The rest, with Nizhadh and Dubovai, are making their way back overland." Dubovai was carefully mapping the route, but based on his best estimates of directions and distances, believed the tributary river they struck the day before the estuary would prove to be the one whose source was the falls at Gronu Kizh'klaëdhiyu, and that northward of the pass the route of the ancient imperial road would still afford a clear trail; he was confident without the side-excursions, checks and backtrackings of the outward journey, not less than half its thirty days could be saved. In Huolafidn's vessel, with not especially favorable winds, it had been six days' sailing to head of the gulf.

"But the gold is not there, at Bablakhi," belatedly correcting Freighanai. "The native people on that coast are something between Man-mani and the Hwenala, they fish and they herd goats, and have prospered somewhat, serving the Hrin. The gold is brought from far upriver, by little brown men in crude little boats. The river flows eastward into Flamûrai, but it makes a great bend, and is said to come down from uplands to the southwest, or due south. Hrin say the river is the only road; it is densely wooded country, with many wild beasts and snakes."

"So the Hrin would say," Lavsila sneered. "Being so timid themselves, they are afraid you will go seeking the source of the gold. An expedition up the river might not be so hard."

"You, perhaps, would wish to lead it."

"I mean, it is a venture to be kept in mind."

"The boat-men, *Asai*, are they warriors?" Freighanai asked.

Kamin-Tolagh, in his short time there, had seen only a few, lean, muscled, nearly naked, though they loved adornment, and the Hrin profited enormously exchanging for a gold a bright, trinket jewelry as sold on the Avenue at Pledging time. "That is of their own make," he said. "But much of what they trade there is brought from Thenimala, including wheat. Yaënsilat's former half-squadron, Niburai, whose father is a factor at Zelkova, he judges what the Hrin get in gold for wheat gives them at least a fivefold profit."

"No wonder they were eager to buy wheat from us."

"They will sell Dakbân blades to the wild men, but the simpler tools for trade, shovels, hoes, hatchets, can be made here at the Abu."

"Till our stock of iron runs out."

"By that time," tartly, "we shall have wheat of our own to sell." He'd had ample leisure on the tedious boat-journey to consider both the earning and spending of gold; they would be able to trade some of the tribal manufactures, and there might be a market for *dao* spice. His empire would continue to need the Hrin, for their skills as well as their goods, and it amused him to think traders such as Huolafidn would eagerly make the journey north to earn back the gold he was taking from them. Their fruits and wines would help vary the diet for the Abu, but he hoped, also, to be able to hire Hrin masons and other skilled craftsmen; he envisaged a rebuilt city of Larghamit, and fresh construction at the Abu, as well as defensive walls, and stone bridges over ravines to help straighten the tortuous roads of his domains. If the gold could be kept coming, this was a second and more plausible birth for empire. The agreement with Iolfrant he described so airily had in fact taken a whole series of meetings, alternating blandishment with threat, against a wily adversary who tried to take back with one hand what the other gave, and whose veiled but immeasurable pride had to be kept constantly in mind, so as not to goad him into the belligerence his caution tried to avoid.

Lavsila also possessed a self-serving shrewdness, and recognized he was beginning to irritate with his cynicism. "You have won a great bloodless victory," standing, "Which should be celebrated in wine."

16.

To underline his resolve, when he rode for the Man-mani country it was with Tau-Suaka and a half-squadron of his Hill Froghul, no Owani but himself. Two days earlier the overland force had returned from Zelu Bablakhi, under a cheerful Nizhadh and a faintly smug Dubovai, both proud of having covered the distance to Larghamit in thirteen days. Without, Nizhadh maintained, undue haste, though the mounts looked hard-ridden, and Nizhadh had evidently been out to impress.

While a considerable improvement over a month, it did not cure the precariousness of the toehold at Zelu Bablakhi, nor lessen his dependence on Hrin seamanship — as on bluff — for maintaining it. Nizhadh warned the overland route would not be safe for any riding less than a full squadron, unless Kamin-Tolagh decided first to subdue the country north of Gronu Kizh'klaëdhiyu, the plain of central Kufshei, which he had inadvertently three-quarters skirted with the expedition. This Nizhadh and Dubovai described as relatively habitable but potentially dangerous country, with wooded hills and shallow valleys where there was grazing for animals, amid patches of inferior cultivation. Tribes encountered had been warily hostile; Nizhadh believed there were several sporadic wars in progress, but like the valley tribes of northern Froghushei before the Great Fire, the settled peoples of the Kufshei lived in fear of raiders, in their case fierce hunting-folk coming from farther west to pillage and vanish. Such weapons as he had seen among tribes or clans encountered had been poor, and Nizhadh succinctly dismissed their capacity for fighting as an even match for the Hwenala when first met, but they were numerous enough to be a threat to unescorted or under-escorted messengers.

Kamin-Tolagh began a sober assessment of how, when he had his sixty squadrons of tribal troops, he might indeed set about incorporating the northeastern Kufshei in his empire. Establishment of a secure military post at Gronu Kizh'klaëdhiyu would give him the ability to reinforce, relatively swiftly, his garrison at the trading-station against any attempt by Iolfrant to expel him, and to judge by descriptions, the new lands were less inhospitable than most over which he now ruled. Nizhadh and Dubovai had actually ridden through two days of steady, soaking rain, of which only traces had fallen east of Flamûrai, suggesting a more promising region for Iruvakh's agricultural schemes.

He was dizzied by the thought that further conquests westward might be needed to make the new ones secure, and after that, yet again more. He would like a chance to propound to Dolvid, historian rather than *Bôdhrai*, the idea the First Empire had grown so vast, not entirely out of the greed of the Shâls, but in just such a cumulative process of trying to win safety for lands already conquered.

Imagined expansion of empire with continual enlargement of his armies put him in mind of heroic childhood dreaming, and abruptly he laughed at himself; unsure whether imposed partnership with the Hrin would hold, still baffled why the *rabhsai* had not reached out to crush him, vulnerable everywhere, he was soothing himself with grandiose visions of a world at his feet. The laugh was something only Kamin-Tarú could share: there was never a time when he did not wish his sister could be with him here, but this was one of the vivid moments when in feeling she was; he felt himself meeting her amused eyes, joining him in recalling, revisiting the river at Inilun Barabhi where all waking dreams began.

He had wondered if Chamya would have a grudge over flogging of his men by Nuvakh, but could detect no difference in the enthusiasm of his greeting; at the head-man's hut, his hut, he was full of how, on a practice course improvised by Kambanal on the hillside by the *dao* valley, his own intimate group of youths had outperformed not only all other would-be lancers of the Man-mani, but the best of Hwenala, Gudi-la and Chon'la levies as well. The boy's Owanilú was more rapid and fluent than it had been, but, under influence of the *Hwanió* used by the troops and their trainers, much less correct.

He was openly reproachful of Kamin-Tolagh's failure to include his best men in the expedition to the south. In that and the disapproving face of his mother, Osré-dnë, Kamin-Tolagh could read an undared comment about the presence here of his new personal guard, the Hill Froghul, certainly the first time any of that feared people had been peaceably within the village.

She, the mother, still with the same bland, elusive mockery, made herself his servant, bringing drinks and cold food. Half a morning had passed before Kamin-Tolagh asked, "Where is Imyë?" Leading to an absurd ceremony, where Chamya, who must know the answer for himself, translated the question for his mother, who, even if she understood no more than she pretended, could hardly have failed to hear the name and guess what was asked.

She spoke, and Chamya said, "Your man Kambanal took her and the, the *birth*. He has her in the stone house across the river." The warehouse now used only as barracks, that was.

Kamin-Tolagh felt relief. He had no rational desire to see the *jinzai* infant, his undoubted son, but would have found it hard not to, if mother and child had been here, or at the Visitors' Hut.

Outside, Tau-Suaka, with the file Kamin-Tolagh had kept with him, was alertly on guard, an unblinking hound.

Handing him a written authority he had scribbled, Kamin-Tolagh instructed the man to go down to the barracks, where squadron-leader Niburai was keeping a *jinzai* child and its mother. Using only a couple of his men, Tau-Suaka was to take both to some lonely place out of sight of Man-mani dwellings, where they were to be killed, and the bodies buried.

Seeing an unpleasant appetite in the man's eyes, he added, "The girl has committed no crime. She is to be killed swiftly, without suffering."

A hard decision, but he saw no alternative; he could not have Imyë alive to be pointed out as the woman who bore a *jinzai* child to Noh-Sra-Lal-Hin, a grotesque counter-legend to set against, perhaps blend with, the tale of the Siv'loi Banner. That would be so even if he brought her back to the Abu, which was in any case out of the question; he could not bear the thought of looking at her, and to keep a *jinz'onoyu* where she could mate with other Owanil was nothing but folly. Death, if repellent, was by far the simplest answer. Though Imyë had not been so identified, each known *jinz'onoyu* still wore the silver ring in her ear, but he would not descend to the savage logic of Dorrmas, and have them all killed. In future, however, he was going to put to death any woman who actually gave birth to a *jinzai* child, not with any crazy idea of punishment, but to emphasize to all — to Kadon Dinul, too — his determined policy against breeding the creatures. Since he had no hope of preventing the death of Imyë from being guessed and rumored, it would also make plain her execution was a part of that policy, without personal animus.

At last, he saw Iruvakh again; the little man returned to the Man-mani village while Kamin-Tolagh was down in the *dao* country with Niburai, inspecting Kambanal's practice-course for lancers, and making sure his men understood the new importance of cultivating the spice, and of keeping loss through theft to a minimum. Though limits of the growing region were ill-defined, he made the suggestion of a long fence to enclose the area where the flower grew in abundance. The failed battle-dogs of the

Hwenala could be put to a more plausible use helping the night-watch over the valley.

Riding back, he encountered Iruvakh by the stockade gate, setting out again, leading shabby mount and pack-pony loaded with supplies. Kamin-Tolagh's intent was to reprimand him for assuming authority to excuse men from military duties, but dismounted, before as much as a greeting was exchanged, was under unexpected attack.

"Look at this, *Asai* — " gesturing to the hillside beyond and above the village, where a wide segment had been newly cut back into terraces like giant steps. "We have crops planted there; I took time and hands away from established plots on the prospect of water, and now if anything is to be saved we will need men and women to labor all day carrying water to the head of the slope when summer comes."

His annoyance was in reality with Lavsila, who, with the hills now free from their chief danger, had come back to his idea of diverting new sources of water for use of the valley tribes. Questioning some of the Hill Froghul' captives not yet advanced from laborer to soldier, Iruvakh had found a man whose former haunt had been to the northern end of the hills, and knew a "wet place" only a few miles away, directly above the Man-mani settlement.

Lavsila, after several delays Iruvakh called dilly-dallying, had been persuaded to come down to the village, and with no great enthusiasm join an expedition into the hills, from which he returned with news of a high bog, clearly fed from a central spring, where evidence of vegetation tended to confirm their Hill Froghul guide's assertion it flowed year-round. To one side, the former inhabitants of these hills had dug into the containing banks to produce a usable streamlet, but Lavsila, having surveyed the lie of the hillsides, was certain a larger flow could, with moderate labor, be made to descend on this western side. No great torrent, but ample, he was confident, to irrigate the terraces proposed on the slope most readily reachable. On this assurance, Iruvakh had set men to work digging out the terraces, so arranged that water introduced at three or four points at the top would gradually seep and spill down through the whole length of half a dozen steps.

By now it was rainy season, and Lavsila, according to Iruvakh, after remaining some days in the Visitors' Hut without once emerging, for the first time remarked there were two places where water would have to be carried over low spots in artificial channels, one only a few feet, the other longer. Though eventually he would prefer a more durable construction, he believed they could for the time being be made of wood. Further days of toiling at the terraces passed, and then Lavsila, *mumbling*, Iruvakh said, there was no suitable wood here, left for the Abu. He had not returned.

For the hundredth time Kamin-Tolagh decided to be rid of Lavsila, send him back to the indolent Heartland, though not till he had finished the watercourse here, an enterprise not mentioned while Kamin-Tolagh was at the Abu. "I shall find out what the delay is," he conceded.

A curt nod implied skepticism, and brought a swift change in the direction of Kamin-Tolagh's irritation. "Meanwhile, you will not issue orders, in my name or otherwise, pretending to excuse men from their military duties."

Obviously prepared for this, Iruvakh was waspish. "As I told you a year ago, there are no second chances in this country; if we miss the brief time when we can plant, there will be no crops. *Asai*, you had better instruct all your would-be Larghais that knowing how to carry a lance is not going to save men from starvation. If there is nothing to eat, you will not have any tribal armies. I am going now to the eastern tribes."

He prepared to mount, but Kamin-Tolagh caught at his shoulder. "You will go when you have my leave, you will follow my orders, or else no longer be permitted to go anywhere."

"Kamin-Tolagh Tovakhati baKargul *Asai*," wearily, but for the first time actually addressing him, man to man. "Do you not recognize a good bargain when you see one? Have I asked for rank or wealth or any other reward?"

He had not, and that was what made him such an annoyance, but over and again Kamin-Tolagh had been able to browbeat him, protesting, into aiding policies of which he disapproved; who could guess what had suddenly stiffened his spine? "You want only power to do as you please."

"Which for you is all gain. You have the use of my languages, my knowledge of the tribes, my powers to persuade, my skills. *Asai*, or Lord, if that is what you are to be called now, haven't I been through this before, with the *jinzai*-breeders? They would suspend me from my duties, send me back to Irbat, or if those threats failed to intimidate me, I was to be flogged, tortured, put to death for insubordination — "

"You will be lucky to escape punishment," menacingly.

"Not lucky, useful. What sense is there in trying to make me into a slave? I see what needs to be done, and I do it, it is the life I have made. As distinct from some who are near you, I do not at one moment claim to speak with your authority, and the next encourage others to think in terms of conditional loyalty. Nothing I can say or do lessens your power."

"You must obey my orders," but in a reasonable tone which took himself by surprise. He guessed now the dispute with Lavsila, and Iruvakh's reflection on their respective positions, was behind this renewal of the fearlessness he had displayed at their first meeting. "An empire is building here, and there can be only one master."

"Granted," as if the point had been resolved.

"You are useful to me, yes, but not indispensable."

"Nothing is indispensable," equably. "Nothing is necessary."

True or not, unanswerable, touching on the rim of nightmare, the ultimate futility of will. So as to command, he had to have obedience, and without his command there could be no empire; only if he set a point at which to stop asking *and then, what?* could he be free of the question whether it would matter if he had never been born. That terror suppressed, there was still a struggle with the idea he should be working himself up into a fury with what he ought to see as Iruvakh's defiance, before he could admit his unexpected relief, to have one man who was not intimidated.

"But I have freed them from their worst fears," gesturing at the valley, the river, the near-full reservoir. The village was as if melting, and sliding down the hill; beginning to recognize the end of raiding meant they no longer needed to keep to a huddle of dwellings behind a stockade on high ground, some of the Man-mani had used the wet season and its mud to put up new huts, a long straggle of them, drying now, soon to be inhabited, next to the river. An older, larger structure, a storehouse left empty when safer ones were built within the compound, had been put in repair and was functioning as a drink-shop, while beside it, according to Iruvakh, the new hut would be a general store selling hats, pottery, the goatskin outshirts of the Gudi-la, anything worth trading for.

"And from a tyranny — " glancing to where, too distant to hear any of their talk, Tau-Suaka sat, forearm on saddlebow, trying to judge whether this meeting would call for any action on his part.

Other discussion followed, and not till he was starting the ride back to the Abu, wondering if they were passing anywhere near where poor Imyë and her child were buried, did Kamin-Tolagh hear in Iruvakh's rejoinder a possible irony, though too nebulous to accuse him with. He, Noh-Sra-Lal-Hin, had freed the Man-mani from the tyranny of a head-man who needed a foreign bodyguard to keep him safe, and to carry out his killing of a defenseless girl. Iruvakh, with his habit of making any foolish tribal superstition stand beside the Tale of Yoëlladhu, and any clan-chieftain's childish cunning into the statesmanship of a

Plakhat Gabh'Owan, if he had made and intended the comment, could never be brought to admit the difference between vindictive pride of a Sranadatta, and Kamin-Tolagh's regretful surrender to hard necessity, an act without rancor or joy. She had been very pretty, and a joyously greedy bed-partner.

Lavsila, partly through astute choice of drinking-companions, kept himself extraordinarily well-informed about distant events, but Kamin-Tolagh did not see how any report of that meeting with Iruvakh could have preceded his return. It must be the general probability he would hear about the languishing irrigation-plan that had Lavsila ostentatiously overseeing the loading of a pony-train with many sections of square channel, each of which, stood on end, would be about chin-high for the average man, built from the stock of well-seasoned wood at the Abu, joints caulked like a ship's seams, with pitch. And Lavsila earnestly implored Kamin-Tolagh to allow him to take the two men of Kargul who had done the building, best near-carpenters the Abu possessed; supports for his conduit, he was confident, could be made from materials available in Man-mani country, such as the same stout, tough cane, bound in bundles, which the tribe used as corner-posts for its huts, and for its stockade.

He had too many reasons for sudden urgency after apparent sloth; now, he said, with the rains evidently done with, was exactly the right time, ground still somewhat softened, but slopes no longer coated with the slippery mud that made going hard for both men and pack-animals. The area near the bog which was source of his water was likely to be particularly soggy during the rains, and it would be too easy to misjudge its normal extent and begin his new watercourse above what would be the dry-season water-level.

"It would have been wise to have kept Iruvakh informed as to your intentions."

"As he keeps me informed of his?" The challenge had some justice. "No one can tell you from one day to the next whether he is planting beans with the Gudi-la, or showing the Ntara-golal how to graft a turnip-tree."

"I have spoken with Iruvakh. He sees the need for being more forthcoming about his plans." The accord they had reached was in fact a curious one, very near an agreement Kamin-Tolagh would not interfere with Iruvakh if he would only keep up an appearance of abject obedience for other eyes.

"Not now, but when you return here, we must discuss your future with the Empire. When summer is over, there is going to be a new general oath-taking, and before that a last opportunity for those who are unable to bind themselves fully and finally to me. To leave."

Lavsila, troubled, "Friendship, I would suppose — " but Kamin-Tolagh cut him short.

"Later, when there is time," turning away.

For the oath-taking he would have a great ceremony here under the flagstaff at the Abu, with tribal head-men and elders also included, and formations of tribal troops as well as his own. It would be near Autumn Halving-Day, near, but not on, since he wanted no association with any ceremony of Rodlakh's realm, or of the *Atarlum*. Five days later, the twenty-first birthday of his sister, Kamin-Tarú, and if his plans went well, she would be here with him.

How this was to be accomplished connected with the shadow that had fallen across Freighanai's pleasure at his captaincy; after initial gratitude, he said pensively, "*Asai*, my wife and the girls... "

No need for a finish. The wives and families Kamin-Tolagh had been able to bring back with him from his raid on

Kargul a year ago had all come from western parts of the province; Freighanai's home was a dayride beyond Inilun Barabhi, farther than Kamin-Tolagh had dared to ride. Freighanai was doubtful, too, whether his wife would have been willing to pack up and leave on such short notice.

The new alliance with Iolfrant, however, meant the possibility of sending messages to the realm, with no need for a crossing of Landegh, and little risk of interception. He had spoken about it with the *Hrithust*; ships of his *onhritha*, coming to Larghamit, could take any letters, which would make their way to the realm in those ships or others sailing to Thenimala in Ninkufu. From there, they could be carried privately to any part of Rodlakh's realm.

"It will take time, *Asai*, for a letter to get where it's going. A month?"

"Six weeks may be a better guess, longer if the Hrin have no ships going to Thenimala. But they have also undertaken to carry passengers back by the same route, at no great cost. Nothing can stop it; no law of the realm exists to prevent a woman or a family of Kargul from visiting Ninkufu, nor forbid her boarding a ship, once there." True for the wife and children of Freighanai, but not for Kamin-Tarú, who would be closely watched.

Freighanai gave his dry, mirthless chuckle. "*Asai*, you could not get my wife aboard ship, not with a law of the realm to say she must, not if it was to cross that pond by the Man-mani village."

"Some," now very much with his sister in mind, "if they can be forewarned in time to be ready, can be brought back as before, by the mountain way, which I mean to use again."

"Soon, *Asai*?"

It would have to be while summer was here. On the first raid, he had been hampered by snow in the high passes, and Iruvakh had afterwards informed him he had been lucky, so early in spring, to get through at all; the *jinzai*-breeders of the Lunu had considered it a safe passage only from near midsummer to a little past Autumn Halving, and in cooler, wetter years snow had occasionally made it impassable at high summer. It would be best, Kamin-Tolagh had decided, to make his new journey as near as he dared to end of the safest season, so by time a pursuit could be organized, snow might block the way behind him. For Freighanai, he dismissed the thought of any provincial cavalry being effectively deployed against him, saying lightly that, as before, he might win some new recruits. Privately he knew his father would by now have worked hard to have the way guarded by men he could rely on, perhaps under officers who had demonstrated allegiance by leaving Kamin-Tolagh; the sour Talfoyan, for example, would have no questions about assailing his former commander. He, too, would recognize that in the region where it crossed the undefined border into Kargul, high forest with little undergrowth, the way itself could not be defended against one who knew the province as Kamin-Tolagh did; correct military choice was to maintain only a watch, with garrisons in villages of the region, ready to ride to places an incursion might threaten. Or else to set up a defended barrier out beyond the notional frontier, in one of the several places where the mountain-road, sheer wall to one side, sheer drop to the other, could easily be held. That was less likely, because its purpose would be to turn away an invader, and Tovakh would wish his son trapped and captured. Kamin-Tolagh tried to believe he still had a good chance of reentering his province unopposed, even undetected.

When Lavsila heard of the Hrin offer to carry letters, his first thought was of the Heartland, and of news coming in the other direction; some of his kin among the Families, his cousin Ghuradh, for instance, could keep them informed about happenings at Kadon Dinul, what could be known of the *rabhsai*'s intentions. At the same time, he added, support for Kamin-Tolagh could be encouraged in the Heartland. But

Kamin-Tolagh's thoughts, for the present, were in southwestern Kargul, the wild but peaceful lands between the upper gorges of the two rivers, Peframi and Inilu, where he owned a country house. A so-called hunting lodge, though the only hunting he had done from there was in surrounding farms and hamlets for promising bedpartners. Kamin-Tarú knew the place well, and if she could come there at the end of summer, unguarded, or with a sympathetic escort, nothing could prevent their celebrating her birthday together, here at the Abu.

In a curious way, Iruvakh's unexpectedly forthright and uncowed response to reprimand had sharpened the need for Kamin-Tarú, by reminding him how seldom he could be fully himself. Most of ruling and military command was a series of faces he wore, stern, heroic, displeased, generous, judicious, threatening, but without someone to confide in, late at night, when all posturing was over, it became harder and harder to know what was real. With Kamin-Tarú, he had always been able to speak his thoughts, try out half-formed notions that nowadays died for lack of light and air.

Came the old wrench of anger against his mother, nothing to do with newer knowledge about her actions and aims. Largely through Petakoi's teaching he and his sister had grown up in the belief they were virtually a race apart, their blood a mingling of two purities, Island and Kargul. Even among other Owanil, they had learnt, there were hardly any others good enough to drink *raminat* with; why, then, should Petakoi be so astonished, so outraged, to find her son and daughter sharing a bed? the natural outcome of her teachings.

He was older by four years, and Tú was not his first partner, as he hers, but with her there had been a boundlessness to sharing which remained unique. Since their being pulled apart, she had bedded as many men as he had women, or nearly, but still he was sure of her, confident she would come to him if she could, here in a place where no one could criticize, much less prevent, any life they chose. Yes. she would come, if his message could reach her.

Freighanai was again present when Kambanal, newly back from tribal country, came to give his report. The young officer was the one man in whose joy at the expedition's success there was no trace of personal greed, and if he too tended to dismiss any troubles there had been in Kamin-Tolagh's absence his was a different perspective; whereas Freighanai's reassurances were only to reassure, Kambanal's came out of unquestioned loyalties, which could not imagine serious disaffection.

He enlarged on Freighanai's hint of disputes about the use of men. "Youths of the Man-mani due for their lance-training, *Asai*, but I would have excused them for the planting if I had been asked, except I was away to the south. But Nuvakh who was duty-officer had the lads brought in and flogged. Young Chamya had told them not to report, and when I got it all unravelled, it turned out the mother, Osré-dnë, had advised her son, and she had word from Iruvakh, who informed her the will of Noh-Sra-Lal-Hin desired the planting be done. I told young Chamya, when his men carry lances, they are under army discipline along with all of us, and his lads were lucky not to have been treated as deserters — if I had been there, I would have found out the story before having them whipped, but I had to stand behind Nuvakh with the Man-mani." He had, nevertheless, brought Nuvakh back to the Abu, and replaced him with Niburai.

"You did well." concluding he had not had the youths executed for obeying their head-man. He was not pleased by interference with the head-man of his creation, nor by Iruvakh invoking the name of Noh-Sra-Lal-Hin, but unless he defined the powers of his various deputies such disputes were inevitable; at present, in his absence, no one had authority where military, civil and tribal questions converged. He wished Freighanai, not lacking in loyalty or plain sense, had better lineage and greater experience outside army matters, or Kambanal, with his broader mind, had a few more years behind him.

He was recounting now how one of the "new men," as veterans of the initial expedition and the Great Fire called those who had returned from the incursion into Kargul, had given him, given Kambanal, namer of Banner and chooser of tomb, the *true* story of Siv'loi. Kamin-Tolagh, as now related, had first found her during the Jinzai War, and meant to bring her back to Kadon Dinul to be his bride, she being a princess of her own people. But she had vanished back into the West, whereupon Kamin-Tolagh had come here seeking her —

"That is the tale of Plakhan's Bride-Quest." Kamin-Tolagh had heard Dolvid talk lengthily about how existent tales 'attached themselves' to later figures, but never thought he would be part of so plain an example.

For Freighanai, an admirable illustration of the earlier thesis with which he had minimized rumblings of potential mutiny. "Aye, the Odi Kukkuk tales are nothing to what hardheaded soldiers will tell you with a straight face. The less true, the better; they would sooner believe any marshfire about Siv'loi than the real tale of the *rabhsayu*."

Something here of a knowing nudge, but Kamin-Tolagh was in no mood for comradely reminiscences. "What tale about the *rabhsayu*?" coldly.

"Before she was *rabhsayu*, I mean, *Asai*, when — "

"There is no such tale. None — "

"As you say, *Asai*," stiffly complying.

Kambanal had no comment, though he should have sour memories of the day on the Tan Lughsai road when Kamin-Tolagh's squadron encountered Âna, and he, junior file-leader, had been obliged to lend her his mount, and walk a good part of the way back to Kadon Dinul. Odd; without the Jinzai War to prove his quality, Kambanal might still be simply the personal squadron's youngest and most vulnerably earnest officer, a natural butt of jokes.

Opening the subject of reorganization, Kamin-Tolagh began with what would be the least popular element. "Tau-Suaka and his men performed superbly on the expedition. I am considering drawing my personal guard from among the hundred best of the Hill Froghul, with Tau-Suaka as their commander." In fact, the decision was already made, and waiting only for the main body of the mounted archers to return. Tau-Suaka had been ecstatic, told the guard would wear a distinctive tunic with brocade facings, and its members would be, except in war, exempted from all other duties, and enjoy other perquisites, special accommodations and a selection of tribal women for their pleasure.

Freighanai jutted his lower lip, and Kambanal ventured, "Your men of Kargul would be disappointed, *Asai*; they consider it their special privilege to be your guard."

"A privilege the empire can no longer afford. It wastes too many good men, to use them as ordinary soldiers, when we need squadron and half-squadron officers for new tribal formations." Besides, he did not add, none of the Hill Froghul could buy safety for themselves by selling him to his father, or to the *rabhsai*. Ferociously loyal now, Tau-Suaka would be even more so in the pride of his new responsibilities and prerogatives.

"You and Yaënsilat, after the new oath-taking, will receive rank and pay of captain, as will Freighanai, who is Senior Captain. In future, Iruvakh and Lavsila will be instructed, any plans they have requiring use of regular troops or men of the tribes must be approved by me, or one of the captains." He was still unwilling to define, even for himself, the precise position of Lavsila.

Self-conscious, Freighanai stammered his gratification. For Kambanal, the promotion was a leap over the heads of men hitherto his superiors, but he showed no concern, accepting his new rank with calm trust in Kamin-Tolagh's wisdom. He had, besides, a piece of news from Man-mani country to report, one

which was giving him a struggle. "*Asai*, you should know —
another *jinzai* child has been born, three weeks ago."

"And was killed." Hardly a question.

"Not so, *Asai*. The mother is Imyë."

"That cannot be." Yet long ago he had thought the
features too defined for the ordinary Man-mani girl; that she
could be, unidentified, a potential *jinzai*-mother had never come
into his mind. For his part, he had taken all precautions as
established by the *Atarlum*, but doing his best to reject the idea
he could have impregnated Imyë, Kamin-Tolagh knew for certain
no other man of Kargul would have dared bed the girl, just as no
one had been brave enough to kill the *jinzai* child, because it was
his. *His*, the idea was revolting; *I have fathered a son*, he
thought, and then with an additional, sardonic wrench, *just like
Rodlakh*.

17.

"Farming here, Lord," Tau-Suaka, wiping water from his eyes, "must be play for children." His voice was almost awestruck, and all the Hill Froghul had ridden in wonder or perhaps unease on the forest path amid dripping trees greater and in greater numbers than any they had ever seen or imagined.

Near forgetting for himself till now what it was to ride most of a day under cool, soaking rain, hands cold, reins at the same time slimy and clinging, Kamin-Tolagh understood how it must seem to a man of Froghushei, whose previous standard of moister lands had been formed by his years in the Colony. But rain itself was not what provoked Tau-Suaka's remark; descending from pines and fir, the column was passing through a belt of mixed oaks, beeches, smaller hornbeams and maples, still in the green of high summer, and from the ferny forest floor rich humous smells coincided with a glimpse between trunks of lush pastureland below. For the first time, Kamin-Tolagh felt the muddled emotions of homecoming; *Kargul!* — and with that, a surge of anticipation, though he had no knowledge of whether Kamin-Tarú had received his careful instructions, nor, if so, whether she would be able to comply.

Having slipped across the border yesterday evening high above the site he now knew to have been invented for the tomb of Owan-Alladh *Kirova-Kindhri*, Kamin-Tolagh and the entire riding had spent the night in the tumbledown sheds of a long-abandoned summer shieling, its pastures soon to be reclaimed by forest. In the morning Freighanai with a dozen men of Kargul had set out north and east on their two-day ride to where, just off the road between Peframi and Yuvat, they hoped various wives and children would be waiting. Kamin-Tolagh, with an equal number of Hill Froghul, stayed higher on the flanks of the main mountain-mass, leaving behind a third dozen, those who had accepted this final chance to leave Kamin-Tolagh's service, including two of the wives who had joined their men last year, and failed to the unfamiliarities of the West. He had kept the parting amicable, and the group had solemnly sworn to spend another night at the shieling before heading for their various homes, and not to speak of Kamin-Tolagh's presence here in Kargul till at least five days had elapsed. On balance, he would have been glad to see Lavsila among them, which he was not; of all who had chosen Kamin-Tolagh's empire, not counting the special case of Iruvakh, he was the only one whose undivided loyalty was an open question.

Rain had all-but stopped, and the chilly evening showed signs of clearing, when Kamin-Tolagh reached the rough, gravelly country southward of his rural retreat. Ordering his men to dismount, he led his *pefrai* quietly down a dim path through younger woods, black birch, maple and dogwood, and came within sight of the steep-roofed lodge. At the edge of the clearing, he decided to go on alone, murmuring to Tau-Suaka he would come back for him if needed. Unwillingly, the man stayed behind.

Lights showed from more than one window of the house, single-storied and modest by Great Family standards, set on a slight knoll, which Kamin-Tolagh approached from the gently-sloping rear, coming first to the connected stables. A dog barked, and from shadows a short, broad-shouldered man emerged, ready to challenge till he recognized him. "*Asai*," low-voiced, evidently not entirely surprised.

He was Neliukh, who had been both his stablemaster and in charge of the house-guard here, retaining half-squadron rank in the provincial cavalry. He was also half-brother to Nizhadh.

"There are soldiers here, *Asai*. Provincials."

"So I see." They had stepped back into the dim of the stable, and Kamin-Tolagh could discern the great mounts for about a file of cavalry, and some pack-animals. "Who is the officer?"

"Squadron Pivrekhan."

Kamin-Tolagh exulted. His sister would never be permitted to ride here without escort, but he had trusted her to influence its composition. It was news that Pivrekhan had returned to service, but certainly the young man could not have recovered completely from the near-killing wounds suffered in the Jinzai War, not enough, surely, to lead a squadron in battle. Of good family, with a childlike freshness of face, he had been a great favorite of his sister's, and equally a devoted admirer of Kamin-Tolagh; his presence was virtual confirmation Kamin-Tarú must be here.

"Fretasi told me you would try to come, *Asai*."

"She is here?" The unmarried woman had ably managed his estates, with a special skill for finances; Kamin-Tolagh had written her a separate letter making no mention of his sister.

Neliukh went in search of her, and with dusk deepening Kamin-Tolagh waited impatiently under the eaves of the harness-shed, till the scullery-door opened, and a woman appeared, an *ôthu*-lantern in her hand.

With only a deferential word of murmured greeting, Fretasi led him swiftly and quietly past the kitchen where, inexplicably, there was clatter of pans, up three steps, and along a passageway to his well-appointed private quarters. There, by added light, he saw she was unchanged, tall, angular, with her plain, bony face, and the drab style of dressing which had earned her Kamin-Tarú's description, `dowdiest woman alive or dead.'

She was nervous now. "*Asai*, we are glad to see you again. She is here, *Asai*."

"My sister?" With a leap of the heart like being wakened by a dream of falling.

Bewilderment: "Your mother, your lady mother, *Asai*. She arrived this afternoon."

Petakoi. She must have intercepted his letter to Kamin-Tarú. His instructions to the carrier were meant to make that impossible, but Petakoi's arrival on the exact day he had set could hardly be fortuitous.

"Where is she now?"

"*Asai*, in your small dining-chamber."

"Alone?"

Fretasi nodded silently, wondering what he intended.

"Are there servants?"

"Those she brought, *Asai*."

"Have two places set," he instructed. His mother had never been one of the many women who had dined with him in that pleasant little room. "I shall change," indicating his mud-spattered breeches. "I trust some of my clothes are still here."

"*Asai*, I brushed out your brown-and-gold suitings, and laid them out for you myself." Certainly not among her duties.

"You will be returning with me to the West?"

"I have a few necessaries packed, *Asai*." Her lack of fuss was typical and admirable.

"We shall leave, I think, at first light." He began to wonder where Tau-Suaka and his men would spent the night, with cavalry already billeted here. "Do you know where the officer, Pivrekhan, is?"

"In the kitchen with some of his men, *Asai*."

At his desk he found small squares of parchment, and wrote a note for her to give Pivrekhan. She went off filled with purpose, and Kamin-Tolagh, going into his bed-chamber, found the promised clothes laid on his bed, which, under coverlet of yellow brocade, was stripped. He had washed hands and face, and was swiftly dressing when Pivrekhan appeared.   After tapping at the half-open door, he sidled slowly in, but that, rather than furtiveness, was the result of his wounds.   The round-cheeked face was unchanged, but he could not straighten his upper body, and the right leg dragged stiffly; a wonder to Kamin-Tolagh the man could mount his *pefrai*, as he must have to be here.

He had half-thought the note was someone's bad joke, and his joy at seeing Kamin-Tolagh was a stammering that had to be cut short.   Time later for tales, Kamin-Tolagh told him; for now he wanted only to be sure Pivrekhan had the men of the escort firmly under his control.   Understanding, the young man dismissed all idea they would make any attempt to take him prisoner, citing familiar names among the soldiers.

Saying again they would speak at greater length after dinner, Kamin-Tolagh left him still sputtering his pleasure.   But there was a puzzle in this; if Petakoi had known Kamin-Tolagh would be here, why had she not provided herself with a stronger escort, men she could trust to obey her orders rather than his?

Coming through the inner door which connected directly with his rooms, he was not at first in his mother's view, though he could not mistake her, with the always upright posture, as she sat at the small table of polished golden oak, where a serving-girl was at that moment laying a second place.   Someone had made a cheerful wood fire in the flagged hearth.

"What is this?" Petakoi demanded of the servant.

"If you would rather eat alone," Kamin-Tolagh said, "I can have food in the kitchen with Pivrekhan and his men."

If astonished, his mother did well, missing only a half-second before rising to extend a hand.   Despite what must have been a damp and comfortless ride, she looked ready for any company, quietly but richly dressed in dark, soft fabrics, hair glossily in place.

"Mother," taking the hand, and stooping to kiss her forehead.

As he stepped back, she said, "Is this how you come to table, now you are a wild man of the West? — " a reference to the sword he had belted back on over his fresh clothes.

"I am a soldier. And the table, after all, is mine. However, as you say, there is no danger here." Disarming, he placed sheathed sword on the sideboard.

"The table, I fear, will not be what I might wish," he said. "Regrettably, we could not make any preparations for your visit."

"I brought with me both food and a cook. There is to be pheasant, at least, and a drinkable wine. Do you mean to sit?"

He did so, after her, and they exchanged distant, courteous enquiries as to each other's health, as chance-met princes.

"And my father?"

"Is at Kadon Dinul, from where he will go north for the hunting." As if suddenly reminded, "The table, in point of fact, is not yours. All your lands and possessions in Kargul are forfeit now to the *Nim'*, who has petitioned the *rabhsai* to make the same true for the entire realm, where forfeiture will include, in effect, your life." She displayed no emotion, and he could not tell if she approved his father's effort to have him outlawed.

It would be normal to ask next about Kamin-Tarú, but as he hesitated two women, one scarcely beyond a girl, and pretty enough to think of for sport, brought a first course of smoked eel and smoked fish with pickled fruits.

When they had left, he said, "And my sister?" It would be unnatural not to ask, more suspicious than to avoid it, on the slender chance his mother's presence here merely coincidental, nothing to do with attempted reunion. If his plan had failed, he would have to try again, but forewarned his mother would keep even closer watch over Kamin-Tarú. That she was a woman now, and should be able to go where she pleased, meant nothing at Inilun Barabhi.

"She is well," mouth giving a slight twist of disapproval normal when speaking of her daughter. "We sent her to spend summer with your uncle. I shall be going there, after Halving, and she will come back to Inilun with me."

Back from the Island, from Pedhival, a tedious man who knew nothing but genealogy and the extent of his wide estates. No clue here as to whether Petakoi's forestalling of Kamin-Tolagh's plans had been sheer accident, or deliberate, after intercepting his letter.

"She is past twenty, You cannot keep her in chains forever."

"In chains!" She drank wine, and wiped her mouth with a commenting flourish. "Well, it is true she argued against the journey. She must find a husband soon, or be found one."

Again, to show anger would concede too much. "Kamin-Tarú may have her own thoughts."

"She must face her responsibilities. I am not likely to bear another son to Tovakh." She meant, Kamin-Tarú would be Heir in Kargul, if Tovakh succeeded with his son's outlawry.

"What would you expect, after two years of rebellion?"

Coming from this woman, a stupid question. The last time he had seen her, she was trying to persuade him not to go to the West, giving every dredged-up reason but the true one. "What would I expect? If such a sentence were to fall on any of our house, I would expect it to be on the one who spent twenty years conspiring with the worst of the *Atarlum*, to breed and train *jinzal*, for marching against the realm." His smile was a hard one. "If my father knew about that crime, he would not trouble to petition the *rabhsai* for a remedy."

She scarcely blinked. "It would serve no purpose for him to learn about it. After twenty-seven years, he has come to depend on my counsel. Where is the crime?" going on the offensive. "If we are shown a weapon by Raëdhi, we use it gratefully to further His Will, not asking whether it is a noble or a base weapon; a true Child does not question the Way. The *jinzal* were to have been discarded when they had served their purpose — like Ban-Sila, if you wish."

"Like Tovakh, too," grimly. "Through your counsel he came near being killed at Dônshei, believing he was fighting to settle the affairs of the realm, not guessing if he had won he was still to be ruled over by those the *jinzal* armies brought to power. Twenty-seven years of your counsel, and for most of it he was, unawares, nothing but a hunting-dog for your *Atarlum*, and your Island dreams of Owani nonsense."

"You men of Kargul! You have all the subtlety of battering-rams. You go clanking about with your *pefral*, your lances, and think cavalry-tactics make you great. The Word of Raëdh, not the sword of Larghai, made the Empire, the same word that kept Owan alive through the Island centuries, when swords had failed. The Promise of Yoëlladhu never failed, Tam."

He could not prevent a laugh; it was like pages from a romance he was no longer moved by, the more absurd for having once been thrilling, a voice of the past, nothing to do with his rope-walker's alliance with *Hrithust* Iolfrant, his race to train tribal troops to make him strong enough to defy Rodlakh, with the scarcity of water. His mother, in her more formidable way, was as ridiculous as Lavsila. "The Promise — " he began, and the main course arrived.

The pheasant, a tame one of course, at this time of year, was well-fatted, and had been carved in the kitchen. After it had been served, together with chestnuts and some green stuff, a cold yellow Peframi Gorge wine poured, the women were dismissed, by which time Kamin-Tolagh's amusement and his mother's incipient outrage had dwindled away.

"The Promise of Yoëlladhu," he said mildly, "was left behind with the rest of my childhood toys."

"But you are there in the West, at Lunu Jinzalladhiyu." This, with a familiar tilt of her head, was the beginning of an elaborately casual attempt to find out whether any of the expert breeders and trainers of *jinzal* had survived, how many of the women who gave birth to *jinzal* remained, what Kamin-Tolagh would do if he had well-trained *jinzal* under his control — clearly, she could not imagine why else he or any Owani would remain there in the West. At first he gave minimal answers, at the same time wondering crazily what she would have thought about her short-lived *jinzai* grandson, but recognized from the gleam of conspiracy in her eye that his dismissiveness was being heard as canny evasion.

"My policy and my strict orders are, any *jinzal* conceived accidentally — and none are by design — is to be killed at birth. Now the tribes are at peace, we expect intermarriage to become common, so Man-mani blood will become mingled, and there cannot be *jinzal* again. With the Owani dream you tried to further using the creatures, they belong now to the past."

"Yet the men who have joined your adventure are of Owani blood. Some, not here, so much as the Heartland, see your quarrel with our mongrel *rabhsai* as a question of race and its privileges. You could be leader of a new purification."

That, put another way, was Lavsila's vision, when he had one, so that the making of an empire was shrunk down to added luxury and leisure for fools of the Residence Quarter; it amazed and exasperated Kamin-Tolagh that these racial obsessions could bring even his mother to the same stupidity. He wished he had Tau-Suaka waiting just outside, and could bring him in and introduce the commander of his personal guard.

Instead, "Why should I want what even the *Mankh'* has abandoned? His Enlightenment says we are all Children of Yoëlladhu now, Gabhanil farmers and Froghul' herders as much as the best blood of the Island, Shumat and the *rabhsayu* equally with Finú or Saidhan." Just before leaving on this expedition, a Hrin trader had brought Lavsila a reply from one of his cronies or cousins, or both, filled with news of the Heartland, and bitter complaint about innovations of ga-Dozhusai-Arbhali.

"His Enlightenment!" she sneered, and exactly echoed that assessment: "A puppet Patriarch, made and worked by Rodlakh and his *Bôdhrai*."

There was an elegant and eventually irrefutable argument against this view, cast in what would be Petakoi's own terms; a faithful Child was required to accept the Patriarch's elevation as the Will of Raëdh, and there was nothing to say that Will could not express itself through Rodlakh's actions; the *Mankh'* taught Raëdhi might at times turn the unbelieving, the foolish, the wicked, the apparently powerless to His purpose. Equally necessary, then, to hold the Patriarch's utterances were guided by *aën'modha*, even when in contradiction to his predecessor, or to every previous occupant of the Golden Seat; Petakoi and the Heartland friends of Lavsila were not permitted to decide one Patriarch was right, another wrong, and when they did, they, not He, strayed from true faith.

This Kamin-Tolagh left unspoken, bored by the subject. He said, "What brings you here?"

"I could ask the same of you." She was surprised but not altogether displeased at the abrupt change. "I came to see what of your furnishings here can serve a turn at Inilun, now you no longer use them. Those hangings in your large dining-hall, in particular, excellent Heartland weave. We need something of the sort for the entrance hall at the Great House."

No hint of guile here. Was it conceivable, after all, her presence on the day for meeting his sister was pure coincidence?

"Take them," waving airily. "Take anything you fancy — but as you tell me, they are no longer mine to give back." That *back* was an adroit jab; the tapestries had been a present from Petakoi herself, some birthdays ago.

She finished her meal, and now wiped her hands slowly and carefully, before looking up into his eyes. "Tam," letting a note like tenderness come into her voice. "Do you think it pleases me to have your father renounce you, to see my only son as a declared outlaw? Have I been your enemy? If I wanted you captured, I could call the guard and have you arrested here, but you see I do not."

"My guard is also here, and they would free me — " deliberately concealing truth about Pivrekhan's sympathies; an ally near the Great House, trusted by Tovakh and Petakoi, could be useful to him in future. "But no, I do not think you want me captured and brought to Inilun Barabhi, where I would recount to my father the whole history of how I began my empire in the West. That would mean telling him all I discovered at Lunu Jinzalladhiyu. All." He was completely unmoved by his mother's recourse to sentiment, doubting she had ever been capable of affection. People, a husband, children for her had no real existence except as assets or liabilities in her incurable, and by now fatuous scheming; her life had been devoted only to power, and she ended powerless.

"I have my Island allies." That, too, was pitiable, meaning only she had a last place of refuge, but it gave an answer before asking to a question Kamin-Tolagh had begun to consider; whether threat of exposure could be used to force her to help him. Perhaps, to smuggle him weapons or books or *raminat*, but not in the one place where he would want her covert assistance; rather than help Kamin-Tarú escape to be with him, she would go to earth on the Island and defy his tale-telling.

"The home of worn-out ideas. Meanwhile, clanking about with my lance, I have won more in two years than you in twenty of your subtleties." Too late, he saw the need for this boast conceded too much about his mother's influence with him.

"We have heard you had some luck, overawing some of the wild men."

"Tribes. Every one with a different tale of how the world began, and what must be done to please their gods. I do not care what they believe, so long as they know they have one lord, and I am that one."

"For this," shaking her head, "dominion over the uncouth, an empire in the dust, you gave up all you won in your mad alliance with Rodlakh? I admit," quickly, before he could mock her, "your cause was other than mine, and I was wrong not to trust you with my secrets. But you fought as you did, and having done so and survived, you accept your rewards, only to throw them away? Captain of the Household, a seat in Council, the admiration of Kadon Dinul — "

"Those," evenly, "were less my rewards for success than your consolations for failure. I never failed. But you were never wrong not to confide in me, if by that you dream I would ever have helped you deceive my father, or plotted with you to bring terror to the realm."

The door opened, and women came in, one to clear away the meal, the other carrying a dish of sweetmeats, warm *raminat* in a silver pot, and small, ornate glazed cups, Kamin-Tolagh's own, a gift from Kamin-Tarú.

The *raminat*, blended with honey and lightly spiced, was particularly good for a cool, damp evening. "What you are doing," when they were alone again, "is without purpose."

"Without your purpose, certainly."

"There is only one purpose."

"For you." He could approach but not quite feel pity for that.

"For you, also." She had taken on a well-remembered bearing, lofty authority, face a carving in stone. "You cannot escape it; you are my son and a Son of Yoëlladhu. No one has the power to deny what made him."

"No one, nothing made me," equalling her pride. "I have the face my mother gave — " fingering the scar along his jaw to point the added meaning. "But I was born in the Jinzai War, and came of age at Lunu Jinzalladhiyu, when I discovered what my mother was."

The mountain road, the secret way, had been made not only with unimagined craft, but considerable foresight. Its slopes and turns could be negotiated by any moderately-skilled rider, so long as panic and dizziness were resisted in those places where it clung to the steeps with nothing but space beyond its rim; while long stretches were safe only for single file, at intervals it reached broader places where camp could be made; at five of these there were small stone-built cabins with iron stoves for heating and for making hot drinks. Not surprising, when the former Patriarch, not a young man, had used this road a number of times.

The column riding westward had grown in both numbers and burden, pack-horses loaded with all kinds of household goods, and there were added animals, pack and saddle. Among them a peculiar treasure acquired by Freighanai to the pedantically strict instructions of Iruvakh, a large sack of seed-wheat. Kamin-Tolagh considered it more than adequate for one of his rank to be able to distinguish on sight between wheat and barley, and that it was necessary to know there was something not only wheat, but hard, white and winter wheat, was akin to the religious hair-splitting of the Hrin. Iruvakh solemnly assured him that if for the first time there was water for a late-autumn planting, this and only this wheat could have a magical transforming effect on the valley tribes.

Fretasi rode silent, sober and very upright, asking questions, whenever he was near, about the keeping of accounts. Neliukh was here, and would take charge of the horsebreeding, in which he had experience, and Fretasi's cousin, Marsilakh, a stonemason, had also come. On his part of the incursion, Freighanai had been intercepted by provincial cavalry, but men from the squadron that two years ago had immediately followed Kamin-Tolagh's at the storming of the gate at Kamsilat; they greeted Freighanai and his men like brothers, and from the meeting Kamin-Tolagh gained three new followers, eager young troopers willing to go west with nothing but their arms, their *pefral*, and the uniforms they wore. Freighanai's wife, Avedhoi, might be shy of boats, but she was a woman of Kargul, and managed a saddle-horse with easy skill; she was a short, thick woman with a surprisingly pretty face, in which the girl still lingered; their two daughters, the elder twelve, straddled pack-ponies and had no difficulty keeping up with the reduced pace of the company.

Maddeningly slow to Kamin-Tolagh. From the summit of the first long climb under a cold but clearing sky he had been able to look back on the green valleys of Kargul as they ebbed towards Arnan, but already his mind was running ahead to the brown hills and grudging streams of his domain, and chiefly to the dangers, north and distant south: had Iolfrant continued to honor the imposed alliance, or had he come in force to drive Kamin-Tolagh's token garrison from Zelu Bablakhi? Had the Army of the West assailed the Abu?

In the same letter to Lavsila with the grievances against the new Patriarch now echoed by his mother, there was news, confirmed and enlarged-on in talk with Pivrekhan, which might explain why, if it had ever been intended, there had been no spring campaign against him led by Shumat. In forests far to the north of Kamsilat in the Colony, eastward of the great bend of the Navu, there had been a sudden fresh outbreak of attacks by *jinzal* on outlying farms and a small village.

This was where, in the war, *jinzal* armies, having made their long march to circumvent the defended road, gathered to descend on Kamsilat, and with this memory, a large part of the Army of the West was withdrawn from the Frontier when the news came, and hurried eastward, some to join the hunt, others to take up defensive positions around the port.

Immediately, at least at Kadon Dinul, between a conjecture and an assumption was that Kamin-Tolagh was in some way behind this new threat, having after all discovered and cunningly concealed a remnant of the *jinzal* armies. But after ten days in which a dozen *jinzal* were flushed and killed, most singly, three weeks of fruitless hunting made clear they were only an isolated hunting-pack, most likely survivors of the War, reverting to their normal behavior. For an age, people had perversely enjoyed making a mystery of how *jinzal* lived in periods between their attacks on men, but the creatures would eat anything that moved, and Kamin-Tolagh assumed these had been drawn out of deep cover by their hunger, having spent two years killing and eating everything nearby.

Not reassuring. While the random nature of the incident seemed now generally accepted, that he had been blamed at all showed how much he was in the thoughts of Kadon Dinul. He had been toiling in the mountains of the Kufshei searching for Zelu Bablakhi when the Army of the West was hastening back to the defense of Kamsilat, and Shumat, who had gone to the Colony at first news of the *jinzal*, would have been slow to return troops to the Frontier, till he was sure the threat was dealt with. The affair, then, occupied what would have been a critical time if there had been plans for an early spring campaign against the Abu, and could be sole reason no attack had come. In which case, the imminent moderation of summer heat on Landegh was full of menace. Still, he hoped, too early, but he was glad he'd had the foresight to have his treasury smuggled down to the Man-mani country disguised as a fresh supply of wine for the Visitors' Hut, which Kambanal had the responsibility of guarding. Chiefly his money, but swelled somewhat by new gold from the south, smelted, with helpful advice from Huolafidn, into small ingots. To return and find the Abu in Shumat's hands would be a blow, but loss of his gold a catastrophe beyond recovery.

In places the road was in poor repair, edges crumbling, and where stone slabs palpably shifted or rocked under their burden it was judged safer for riders to lead their mounts. As much a mystery as how — and by whom — this road had first been built was by what means, in these places where it clung to the face of sheer and lofty cliffs, it could ever be mended or restored. Soon after passing the icy summit where a light powdering of early snow was lifted and swirled by a whipping wind, they came to one such place, a straight stretch across a steep slope of stone falling two hundred feet to where a stream boiled white in a grim ravine, while eighty feet overhead great boulders at the clifftop menaced.

Here, he broke the road. The stonemason, Marsilakh, led efforts to further weaken stone buttresses already attacked by time, weather and ferreting weeds, while where the road at last made its turn, younger and more agile soldiers could clamber to the parapet above. The first boulder they manhandled over the rim missed the road entirely, bounding off a projection and arching into space before striking halfway down the slope with splintering force. The next, even larger and harder to launch, lumbered down to meet the road just where Marsilakh's efforts had been concentrated. For a half-second it seemed even now the ancient masonry would hold, and then with a crack and roaring rattle a long section of road gave way and went bouncing and sliding down the slope.

He had hoped to have Kamin-Tarú with him when he carried out this plan to make already improbable pursuit impossible, giving his domain one fewer approach to be watched and guarded. Now she would have to come, as she surely would, by another way, and he recognized the meaning of this severance went deeper than practical military concerns; he was cutting a lifeline to his first home, the link to his origins. An answer to his mother's assertions of an inescapable past: he was his own man, still Kamin-Tolagh, no longer of Kargul.

End of the Second Part

Genealogy
Rabhsayum: Owen Navu

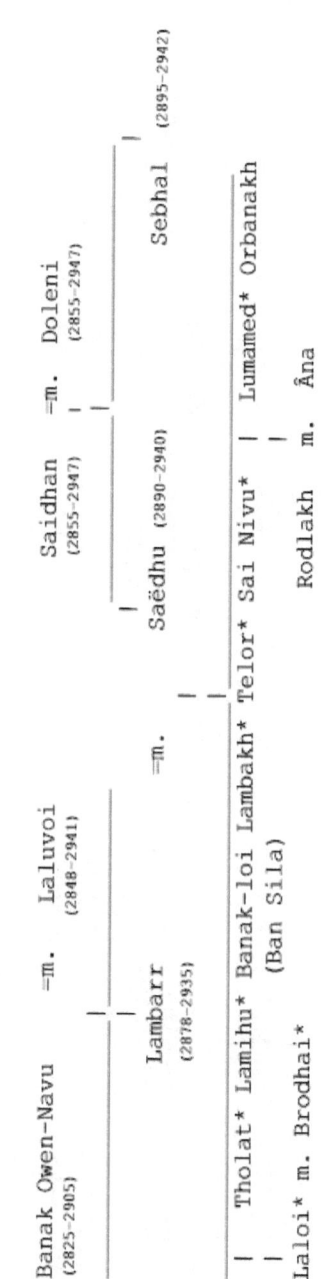

Banak Owen-Navu =m. Laluvoi
(2825-2905)   (2848-2941)

Saidhan =m. Doleni
(2855-2947)   (2855-2947)

Sebhal (2895-2942)

Lambarr =m.
(2878-2935)

Saëdhu (2890-2940)

Tholat* Lamihu* Banak-loi Lambakh* Telor* Sai Nivu* Lumamed* Orbanakh
(Ban Sila)

Laloi* m. Brodhai*   Rodlakh m. Âna

Kargúl

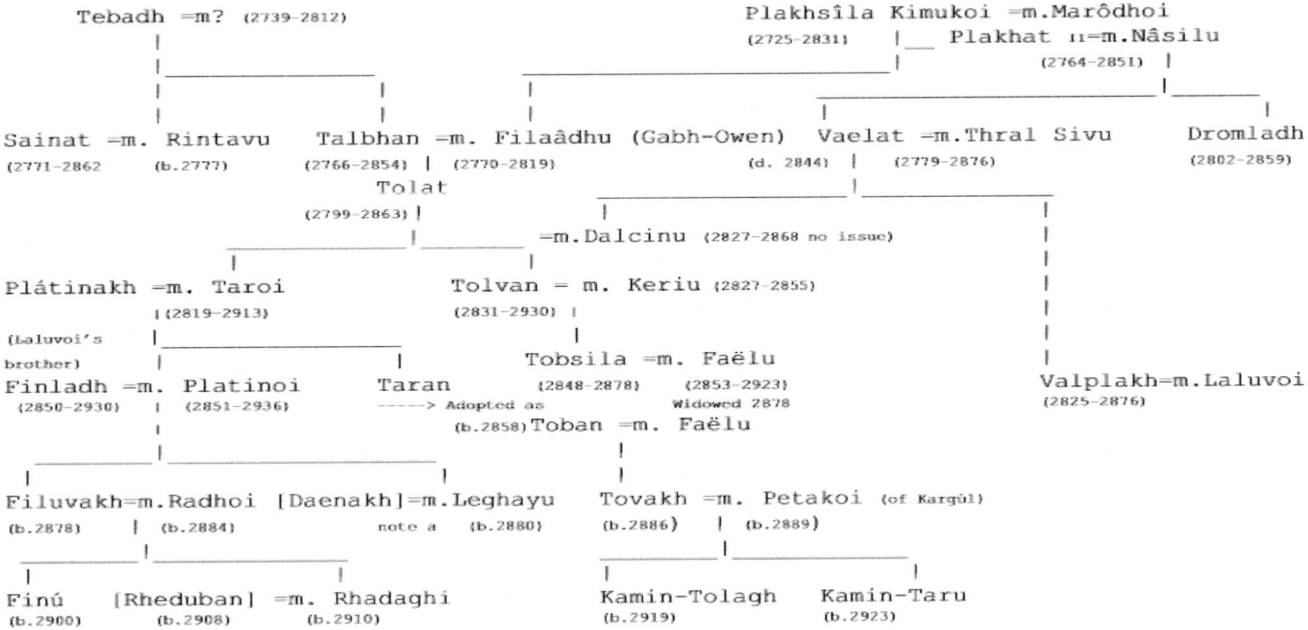

Plakhsíla Kimukoi =m.Marôdhoi (2725-2811)
Plakhat ıı=m.Nâsilu (2764-2851)

Tebadh =m? (2739-2812)

Dromladh (2802-2859)

Sainat =m. Rintavu (2771-2862) (b.2777)

Talbhan =m. Filaâdhu (Gabh-Owen) (2766-2854) (2770-2819)

Tolat (2799-2863)

Vaelat =m.Thral Sivu (d. 2844) (2779-2876)

=m.Dalcinu (2827-2868 no issue)

Valplakh=m.Laluvoi (2825-2876)

Plátinakh =m. Taroi (2819-2913)

Tolvan = m. Keriu (2831-2930) (2827-2855)

Tobsila =m. Faëlu (2853-2923) widowed 2878

Tovakh =m. Petakoi (of Kargúl) (b.2886) (b.2889)

Kamin-Taru (b.2923)

(Laluvoi's brother)

Finladh =m. Platinoi (2850-2930) (2851-2936)

Taran (2848-2878) Adopted as ----> (b.2858) Toban =m. Faëlu

Kamin-Tolagh (b.2919)

Filuvakh=m.Radhoi |Daenakh|=m.Leghayu (b.2878) (b.2884) note a (b.2880)

Finú |Rheduban| =m. Rhadaghi (b.2900) (b.2908) (b.2910)

(a) Brodhaí, son of Leghayu and Daenakh m. Laloi bi Athhi-Navu, 2932; both killed at Tan Lagsaí in 2935. Brahdíaí, their second son (b. 2910), led the Cavalry of Ân under the command of Rolan Bakir, Yovakh Din 2928.

Telnauv ("The Colony")

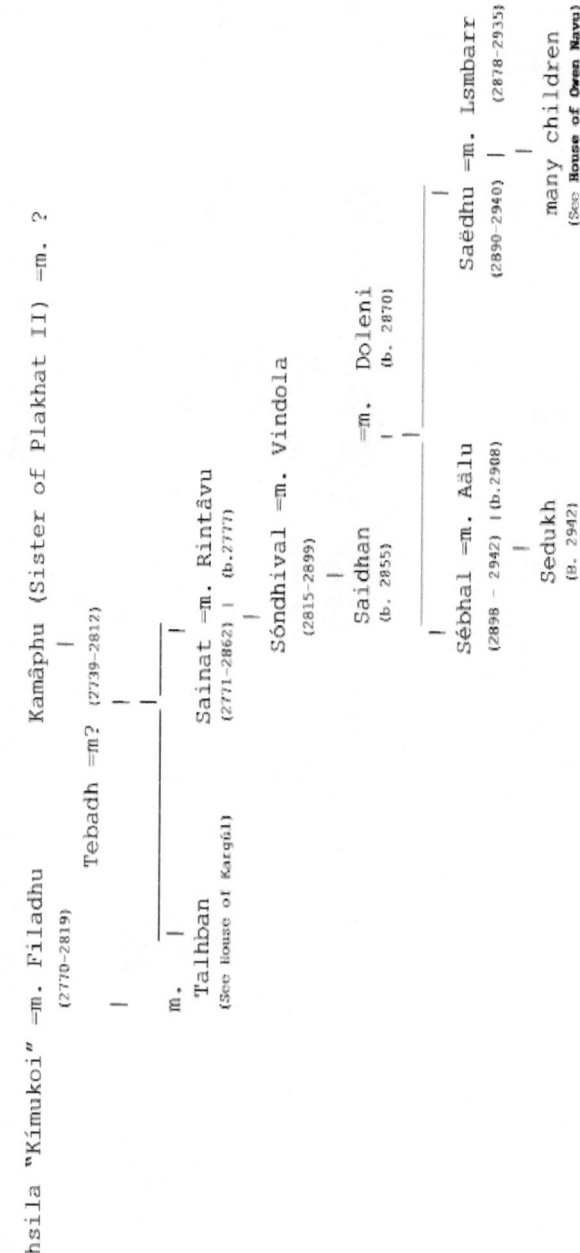

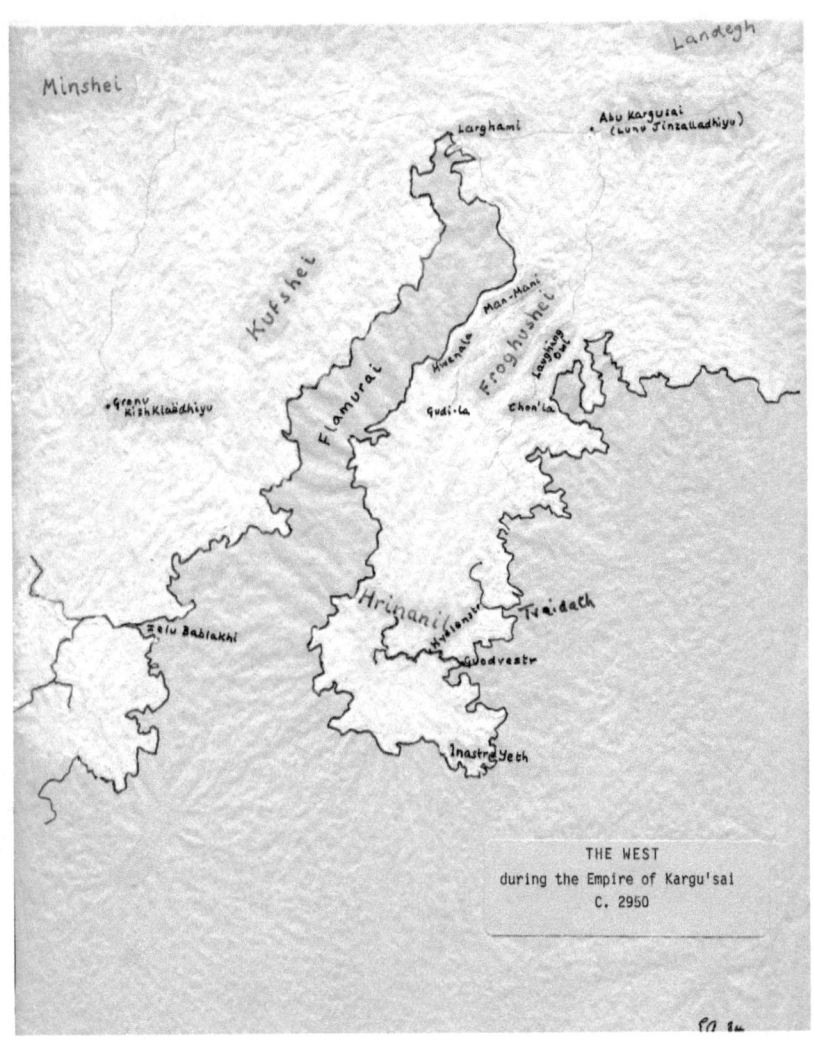

THE WEST
during the Empire of Kargu'sai
C. 2950

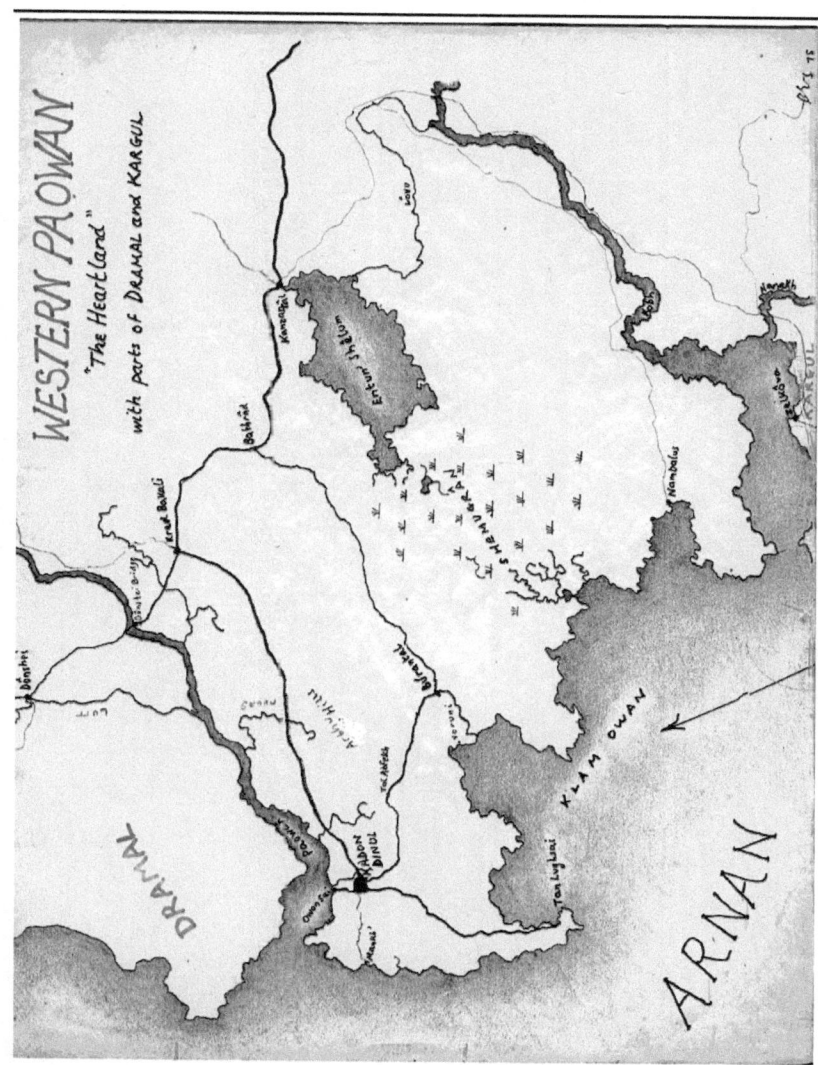

www.ingramcontent.com/pod-product-compliance
Lightning Source LLC
Chambersburg PA
CBHW020324180626
46812CB00001B/42